STEPHANIE DOWRICK

Tasting Salt

a novel

The author wishes to thank the authors and Bloomsbury publishing for permission to quote from Krishna Dutta and Andrew Robinson, *Rabindranath Tagore: The Myriad-Man*, London, 1995. 'The flower says . . .' is translated by John Boulton; 'Whoever wishes to . . .' is translated by the authors.

Published in Great Britain by The Women's Press Ltd, 1998
A member of the Namara Group
34 Great Sutton Street, London EC1V 0DX

First published in Australia by Penguin Books Australia Ltd, 1997

British Library Cataloguing-in-Publication Data
A catalogue record for this book is available from the British Library.

ISBN 0 7043 4554 4

Printed and bound in Finland by WSOY

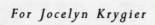

For Jocelyn Krygier

This is a novel about friendship.
To all those people I am honoured to call friend,
my deepest thanks.
I want most of all to acknowledge
Barbara Manning Ward, 1920–1997,
whose collected presence and dazzling smile
first inspired Cordelia's story,
and Pam Benton, 1942–1997,
who shared so abundantly the priceless gifts
of support and love.

Just as the great oceans have but one taste,

the taste of salt,

so too there is but one taste

fundamental to all true teachings of the Way,

and this is the taste of freedom.

BUDDHA

$\overline{\text{I}}$

Our true life lies at great depth within us.

RABINDRANATH TAGORE

1

I pick up a penguin. Six inches tall, it is chiselled from a piece of solid crystal. It is heavy, cool, kitsch, and yet succeeds well enough in its likeness to its feathered, real-life model to make me smile.

I put it down, briefly missing its weight in my hand. I realise, with a start, that I don't quite know how many moments have passed while I stood, outside time, a penguin in the palm of my hand.

Time. My thoughts concentrate. I am tempted to sigh. I feel entitled to sigh. For years there was not enough of it. Now, as with so many things, I am returned again to childhood. Time feels pulled into awkward, unaccommodating shapes that need bullying with plans, schedules, routines.

Unlike childhood though, it is up to me. Mixed blessing, but I am certain that I prefer it. Even now my body can stiffen with the same hopeless rage the child felt when pushed to tasks others thought more worthy of attention than her own dreamy choices.

In these late days I can dream or read or gaze all day should I want. No one would comment.

I am, I notice, beginning to adjust to this idea of no one commenting. It hasn't been long and I don't suppose I will ever get entirely used to it. George's flow of commentary on all that went on around him, and I was latterly central to that, was sometimes irritating when he was alive. There were many moments when I longed for rather more silence than I was getting. But then, out from among the steady flow of words, would jump comments that were guaranteed to make me smile or wince, or look at him – which was what he wanted of course. My attention, fixed on him, with him laughing almost through his nose, immensely amused by whatever had at that moment taken his fancy. And amused by his own cleverness. That cleverness lasted him too, right up to the end. Thank God for that. As for much else.

George was, beneath his confidence and easy warmth, occasionally a little fearful. It's what leavened him of course; made him human like the rest of us. Too much talk was one measure of it. An urbane, always successful man who was also glossy-magazine handsome, George never experienced himself as anything less than fortunate. But fears were there through all the many years I knew him. Most of them hidden, even from himself. A few only too well known. Fear of helplessness was one of those. I rarely saw him less than patient, but when friends were lowered by strokes or other plagues of age, it was only with determination that kind George could bring himself to visit.

So his own lightning fast death was a final bit of luck in that largely lucky life. At least for him. And in the way of marriage, or long marriages anyway, what was lucky for him was probably lucky for me also. But for all that, I could have done with a hint to warn me of what was coming. Then those final days might have passed differently.

I would so very much have liked to know them for what they were: final days in nearly five decades of marriage. I would like to have slowed them down, observed them in all their most minute particulars. I would like to have savoured them to the last.

Or am I simply kidding myself after the event? Would I have acted differently? *How* would I have acted differently? In the face of imminent loss, could I have done anything wiser or braver than panic and clutch?

Kidding myself. I have probably had as much practice at that as George: same cause, different effects.

I was planning a party.

Seventy-three is a mixed blessing of a birthday whichever way you look at it. Without much difficulty, I decided to look at it optimistically. George and I used to give and go to parties often, years ago. Not just work functions either. Parties to please ourselves and our many friends. Big, extravagant parties with catered food and lots to drink and wonderful talk, or so it usually seemed. We slowed down, though, or grew lazier, then lost the habit. In more recent years, we had also lost some of the most essential friends: Larry, Alison, Dick, Maurice, Jean, Maeve. Even their names are hard to speak in the face of such permanent absence.

There have always been old friends and newcomers in and out of our house. George drew people into his orbit and welcomed them when they came. Unashamedly curious and knowledgeable about a whole range of topics, predictable only in his pleasure in seeing people, George was a social magnet throughout his life. But, perhaps cautious of intruding on the habits of old age, in recent years they came less often, and fewer at a time.

For all that, with the force of an ancient and too-long repressed habit, the necessary organisation for a successful larger party came swiftly back to me. Lists arose like troops from long-dug shelters to occupy my mind. Names of still-living friends tripped over the names of canapes and recipes for cocktails I had neither shaken nor drunk for years.

Cocktails it was to be. The glasses I had saved from obscurity in the back of a cupboard were Art Nouveau pieces in a particularly sickly shade of lime. They never failed to make drinkers giggle. Even without the glasses though, it was impossible to think 'cocktails' and not also to think 'pep'. And surely 'pep' is exactly what a seventy-third birthday party should be about?

I broke the news of my plans to George with diffidence. Convivial George had been deafish for some time. He wore a hearing aid, sensibly, but it tended in crowds to exaggerate the wrong sounds and not help much at all with those he actually wanted to hear. The tête-à-tête has always been George's preferred form of human communication. His hooded, nuggetty eyes making steady, *meaningful* contact beneath rather alarming eyebrows, his head bent – for George was tall as well as lean – his body arching towards the favoured one, though never infringing. It's quite an art, the tête-à-tête, and time and again I saw that George was quite an artist.

His increasing inability to enjoy that kind of exchange when other noises were swirling about, and his totally unprecedented anxiety that perhaps he wasn't getting it, when 'getting it' had once been to George as breathing is to most of us, had turned him off larger gatherings. Even before I had become steadily more mournful about those upon whom cocktails could no longer be pressed.

But, seduced by my plans, or maybe tickled by the ludicrous notion that he was a man whose wife was about to turn seventy-three, George immediately took up the mood of the lists. He surprised me and, yes, he pleased me, yet again.

We have been married for almost five decades. I am repeating myself, forgivably I think, for the sheer tenaciousness of it causes me some pride, and it is really only in old age that I could say – and would if anyone dared to ask me – that I have come fully to appreciate George in ways that I had once imagined would be the fabric of my married life.

Thinking back, and increasingly I do that, I could fairly say I have consistently admired him. Everyone admired George. It wasn't anything especially personal to me, nor sometimes especially intimate. Though it has been a useful bolster to my own wavering confidence to be married to someone as fully alive and as eventful as George invariably was. I felt flattered, plainly, to be married to someone as coveted as he. It also mattered to me that he was out in the wide world, making a difference, rather than staying closer to home and only making money. That is not the same as a sustained intimate unfolding between two souls, however.

When we were engaged to be married, as cheerfully arrogant as most other self-absorbed, inexperienced young couples I guess, I assumed that everything would be possible. By 'everything' I would probably then have meant an intertwining of minds and ambitions and feelings; a coming together through ideals, as well as bodies. Or perhaps I would have thought of it as a quality of sharing between us that would be essentially and satisfyingly different from the sharing we might do with anyone else.

Or maybe 'everything' would also have implied no barriers between us, never mind upholding them. But I learned: *everything* is rarely possible. It may not even be desirable. That, however, is the reflection of an old woman. The dreams and desires of the young Cordelia, setting out in marriage, were different.

Passion brought us together. George's passion for me first. His passion and his fascination. Both were unexpected, inexplicable and almost unbearably welcome. And then, on my side, nervous longings that redistributed the moisture oddly around my body so that my mouth was always dry and my palms were always wet.

But passion failed us, taking years to revive and then only unreliably.

Passion! The word itself makes me feel odd. I want to push it away to conjure up a distant image of handsome, talented George and the bold, wry bride, Cordelia. George and Cordelia. Names that could have been pulled from a trashy romance. Yet, in the end, just linked names out of which we had to make something fresh.

Now, all these years later, it is impossible quite to track it back, those definite slips between young Cordelia's idea of everything, and what was. It's made harder still, perhaps, because in many things and ways we were indisputably blessed.

'To the gift of you,' was George's favourite toast in private, even in our leanest years. 'To the gift of you,' he would say, and would raise his glass, even his cup or mug if that was all he had to hand. He would take time to look at me, and smile. It was hard sometimes to hear, harder still to respond with the graciousness the words called for, but his toast, his wish may possibly have been adhesive.

For there were griefs, too, tucked in there. Some of which I could name.

Too many pregnancies. That was part of it. Worse, far worse, we had no children. Their constant absence lay behind but could not be part of George's animated chatter. Along with that and inseparable from it was too much unfulfilled ambition on my side. Bitter remarks, even now, occasionally attest to it. And, on George's side, ambition was almost too richly fulfilled, over-inflating that side of his life, making mine look even thinner.

There were times, maybe years on end, when the image of the seesaw was never far from my mind. I saw George on the high end, of course, the end that allowed for magnificent long-distance views; for exposure at first hand to thrilling shifts and changes in perspective – and for ready sightings by anyone approaching. I saw myself weighting down the lower end: heavy as lard, close to the ground, viewless and unviewed.

Recalling the persistence of that image it seems a little mysterious to me now. I am tempted to admonish myself: things were good far more often than they were bad. Things went up as well as down. You exaggerate, Cordelia, I feel pushed by shame to say. And indeed, seesaw-like is not as others would have seen us. People have always envied George and me, called ours an ideal marriage, even an ideal partnership, and began to do that in the days when marriage could be taken for granted in ways it simply cannot now and comments of such a personal kind were rarely offered.

No one else can see inside a marriage, however. And for all that I might then or now exaggerate, it is the remembered persistence of that image that niggles away at me. I am confident enough to say that heavy as lard is never a good way to feel, and to add that it is perhaps harder still to feel it when to speak of it, or hint at it, would have seemed churlish and ungrateful, even to myself.

Retirement is, however, a great leveller.

Retirement and old age: the seesaw certainly faded as an image, and if I search now for one that might replace it I am smiling as I see George and myself on large, encompassing swings, side by side, or even taking turns to push each other round and round on the kind of rocky, multi-seated wooden roundabout that I don't believe I have actually seen in a park for years.

That latter image may simply arise from widow-talk. I'd not be the first or last to do it: tidying away old resentments and pains; polishing up a little wishful thinking until, unchallenged by reality, that becomes what was. Yet as guarded and as cautious as I know myself to be, I believe that I was able to perceive and even to be thankful for the times when George and I were in harmony, more or less. I'm not ungrateful either for the harder moments. At least not now. More often than not I've had the sense to know it was a life. And a life we shared, for the most part.

To mark that time of George's retirement, we planned to travel. As with party-giving, this involved a good many lists: George's in neat lines on yellow legal pads; mine sprawled across the back of envelopes or around the edge of pages I'd saved for casual notetaking. We adored our separate foraging for what we brought to those lists. Piles of books and magazines grew taller on both sides of our big carved bed. But George's increasing deafness, and perhaps an awareness of how much involuntary travel he had already clocked up during his working years, then a worrying increase in my usual quota of headaches, and my timidity – much greater than I had ever expected – kept us making lists rather than taking off. After a while we admitted to each other that we didn't really care. Those books and magazines disappeared and others – on quite different subjects – took their place. We spent all the money we would have spent on travel, and then some more. And although we spent the money together, I felt as though it was entirely spent on me.

For some years I had been working professionally as a potter. It started as a hobby, chosen damn near at random. In those early days I was no better at it nor any keener than half a dozen others in the class. What distinguished me was that I kept at it, doubling the number of my classes and the effort I put into them, fuelled by increasing relief that finally I, too, had an activity in which I could lose myself.

Later I became good, and then really quite good. In my late middle age I could stand in front of my wheel or bend to empty the contents of my kiln and feel fully stimulated, and, at quite the same time, at peace.

I will never lose my gratitude for this finding of work. Not only having it, but even losing myself in it while finding myself through it; feeling refreshed and recreated by it much as George had done all through those protracted, tricky years when I had stood alongside and envied and fretted.

Love and work, Freud said, are essential for men's wellbeing. Did he mean women too? Who knows. What I do know is that when work was joined to love in my life it changed my entire existence.

Even my posture changed. I don't mean any sentimental nonsense about standing taller. I am quite sure that I was standing wider. I was bending deep and freely from my hips when that was called for; using the muscles of my legs, arms and back when that was called for; squatting without discomfort when I needed to; standing and even sitting with feet sturdily apart whenever that increased my sense of readiness and balance. For the first time in my life I possessed my body's vigour. That elated me.

Now that I am much older, I am anyway stiffer and also have a minor hump on my back, which I try largely to ignore. But I set those difficulties, and a few others besides, in context. I have not forgotten how way past my youth, past my so-called prime too probably, my body revealed itself as a source of strength for me. Even its decline is less dramatic and certainly less saddening than it would have been had I continued to fear my body and live outside it, as many women did and probably do.

With all that focus on the work, and on the near-blissful release from self-consciousness and restlessness that the work brought with it, I never minded nor even thought to complain about the second-hand wheel and kiln that George and I had bought together and erected in the shell of what was once a roomy wash-house.

I had access to other more elaborately equipped studios when I needed them and had anyway never been convinced of any correlation between the quality of facilities and the work produced. In fact, I was rather smugly fond of citing the work done by local potters in Africa, under the worst possible conditions, work that was graceful and strong and useful as pots should be.

Then, as our plans to travel fizzled and faded, George had a proper studio designed and built for me on the sunny side of our long stretch of back garden.

He gave up a substantial chunk of his beloved garden to set this plan in motion, and never once hinted at any kind of loss. That precise mixture of decisiveness, action and restraint typifies George. I could wonder at my good fortune.

I stopped going on about Africa. Even as it arose from drawings on the page, the studio was my place, my haven in which to work without worries about time or weather. The old wash-house, impossible to heat and sometimes difficult to keep dry, was never pleasant for mid-winter or late evening work.

Long before the new studio was ready I felt sure that I would pot there in quite new ways. And I did. From elegant, functional thrown pieces, my style slowly but absolutely unhesitatingly moved to embrace hand-moulded, flattish pieces that exist just for their own sake. Now they are sometimes barely ornamental: big near-clumsy pieces, which only on close attention reveal themselves as complex, teasing, even delicate. I find them most satisfactory.

It was also clear to both George and me that the space should be large enough to have working parties there with potters of my own choosing. That increasingly matters: being companionable when I want it; staying alone when that seems to be my need. Being companionable as one works seems almost the perfect way for me – the work making the connection, rather than talk.

That was yet another insight that I seem to have made rather late. But not too late. I am still learning.

George, characteristically and enthusiastically tête-à-tête over several months with the architect of my choice, created a perfect studio for me. Purposeful, mellow in its shapes and forms, it is also exceptionally light. Long, tall windows open the studio to the garden, and the garden to the studio. A glass roof gives glimpses by day of the trees that sweep it from above; by night it allows the night sky to enter the room as a welcome friend.

Such walls as there are we had painted in off-centre reds, blues and yellows, in part inspired by the books and brochures we had studied so closely when planning our trips. Those colours add playfulness and depth to whatever or whoever stands before them. People sense this and rise to the occasion as they unselfconsciously allow the room and its deep, matt colours to work as their backdrop.

The wheel and kiln, the drawing board and even the storage shelves and cupboards chosen for the studio are each a marvel, serving the work, serving me in my work, for George is a perfectionist as well as generous, and has always loved my pots, even latterly in my much less pleasing phase. I believe he loved it too that, finally, there was work in my life that would keep me in the studio way past the time when I had said that I would be home.

That gave him a chance to tease me about neglected husbands hovering over dinners congealed or grown cold. He was not mocking me, for in my stubbornness, or perhaps out of sheer inadequacy, I had long ago refused to be that kind of wife. He was mocking himself, mocking the fastidiousness with which he undertook his myriad household routines as well as the pleasure he was taking in having our house to himself for hours on end, there to mix time in his study with large and small domestic tasks, always exquisitely completed.

Preparing for the birthday party I willingly neglected my work, and largely put off my usual crew of fellow potters. The lists grew, gripped onto the fridge with colourful magnets – presents from friends, relieved to know there is something cheap and tacky they can bring into our house with every prospect of giving lasting pleasure. The old high-minded can be hard to give to.

Lists of people. More people. More food. Cocktails. More cocktails. Like retirement, cocktails are a great leveller. I wonder sometimes why so few people make them these days. I have concluded it is that ubiquitous problem: time. Cocktails do not get made well in a rush. That's part of the fun of course.

Some of my fellow potters – the women mostly, and Laurie most of all – took on the tough ends of the project, coming around to clean the best silver and vacuum behind the larger furniture and even to get the woollier corners of George's garden into newly spruced shape. They seemed to be having fun, especially when I decided that some of my wilder cocktails could benefit from a dress rehearsal.

We were hanging curtains. In a mad obeisance towards perfection we had taken down the heavy Thai silk grey and yellow drapes that had graced the upstairs sitting room for years. They had most obligingly hidden whatever dust they had collected, but suddenly we knew dust was there and that it would have to go. I sent them off to the most expensive cleaners I could locate with copious instructions and excessive misgivings. I worried unduly. Back they came, smiling. And I was smiling too as Gudrun stood high on one step-ladder and George high on another, looking down in triumph at Laurie, Angela and me, dwarfed below.

'Hey, man,' crowed Angela, 'check out that shine!'

She was right. They were indeed shining, those magnificent old bits of cloth.

'Want to climb up and see the view from here?' Gudrun asked. 'It's not only the curtains that are shining. The room itself looks wonderful. And you all look extremely cute with your dinky upturned faces! I feel quite like the Giant Mother looking down on her sweet little charges gathered around her skirts. This is certainly not a perspective I often get to enjoy. Maybe big old George here gets plenty of chances to look down on the rest of us folks, but those of us doomed to shortness see rather too much of the hairs on the undersides of tall persons' chins!'

Gudrun's combination of German accent with a heavy layer of mock-Southern made us laugh, as she knew it would. But no one took up her offer and Gudrun and George stayed where they were, Gudrun standing on her extra pair of tall steel legs, George making a neat seat on the top of his and then leaning forward easily, trusting his balance, to accept the tiny roll-up Angela was handing him. He only smoked a few times in any year, and only at a moment of conviviality like this one. Then he would draw in on the tobacco with the pleasure of a thirsty man reaching cool water.

'What do you think about the UN's latest cop-out in Botswana, George?' Angela asked, serious suddenly.

George turned to her. Angela's striking, beautiful Jewish face was cloudy and intense. George knew, I guess, almost exactly what frustration fuelled her question, and how little that frustration could be met by any answer he could give her. His own frustrations about political justice in Africa, and perhaps also about the predictability of her question, he would be able entirely to set aside. He would respond, I knew, as though hearing this question, or some version of it, for the first and not the forty-thousandth time.

'Have you kept up with things? Do you know more than the papers are telling us?' Angela's voice was harsher than she probably intended. She liked George and I know how skilfully she made the most of any opportunity she had to talk with him.

'Kept up with things? As much as one can. Special information? I'm afraid not,' George began, cautiously, easing his way into what he actually wanted to say. 'But in any case, decisions, as you know, must inevitably open and close with considerations about resources.'

'Or who gets access to them,' Angela rushed in.

'You're right, of course.' George's tone was even and entirely without any note of impatience. 'There's no fairness there, any more than there is fairness about where rain falls or doesn't fall. But Africa is not without its voices in the corridors of power. The problems may even be less there, where resources are allocated and decisions made, than within the countries themselves, where rather too many geographical and psychological versions of the word "drought" have drained reserves of goodwill and fairness. Some countries, and I am not talking only about Africa here by any means, are burdened with a level of corruption that one can only call *impacted*, so that the necessary steps between decision-making and enactment cannot unfold at even the most minimal level. For some countries the request to carry out decisions that the world has decided are what their citizens need is too much. They can bear neither the weight of what is asked of them, nor the consequences of not doing what they are told they "must". This is more burden, not less. More tension, not less. Though this is not a happy thought as the people who suffer most are in no way relieved by any understanding of ours of what this depth of paralysis breeds – or disallows.'

George had kept his gaze on Angela, speaking so moderately neither she nor Laurie nor Gudrun would probably ever guess how often his rage at bureaucratic incompetence and corruption and individual greed has matched her own.

I am not nearly as patient, and in less than a minute had heard enough. That seemed as good a time as any to go downstairs to the kitchen and to return, a little later, with the United Nations and now the United States and Haiti also hanging in the air but almost at once forgotten – perhaps shamefully – at the sight of me with my big tray weighted with the lime green glasses and several icy cold-beaded steel cocktail shakers circled in heavy napkins to hold in the frost.

'Bravo, Cordelia!' said George, moving from ladder to floor in a single easy movement that belied both age and gravity. 'Let me help you, darling. You sit down and I'll be Jeeves.'

George took the laden tray from me and rested it on a small but sturdy table, picked up a shaker, shook it while he grinned and danced a lively step or two, and then began to pour the freezing, delicious combination of potent flavours.

'Wickedness to launch the day!' George said, handing me the first shining glass. 'How can we possibly resist? What about you, Laurie? Are you corruptible?'

'Yes to that, and no I'm not corruptible at all, George,' Laurie laughed. 'More's the pity. Hey, why don't you sit down too, and let me take over. I've always wanted the opportunity to say "Shaken or *shaken*?" This may be my only chance!'

George handed her the tray at once, with great good grace, and then sat down on the yellow sofa, by my side, holding his lime green glass in his long, bumpy fingers that echoed in their own way his long, bumpy nose beaking out above his laughing mouth.

'Shaken or *shaken*?' said Laurie to Gudrun, and then again, though barely able to speak now for laughter, to Angela.

And when they and Laurie too each had a glass, they looked to me. Colour rose to my face. 'To friends,' I said, raising my glass, and oddly moved.

'To birthdays – and to parties!' Gudrun toasted.

'To many more birthdays, to many more parties. And to you all!' said George, leaning back now, taking in each one of us, and exuding what was surely a feeling of near-complete satisfaction for the sometimes perfect moments of joy that life, and friendship, can bring.

The day before the party there was nothing left to do. George found me irritably banging around with a pile of trays in a pristine kitchen. He embraced me from behind, nuzzling down into my neck as he hadn't done for ages. His nose felt bony and slightly damp. I elbowed him away, still with the trays in my hand. He moved to stand in front of me, taking the trays from me as he did so and placing them on the red formica bench.

Then I looked at him, perhaps for the first time that day. If he looked tired or faded or in any way like a man about to leave life for good, then I missed it. What I saw was my elegant husband George flirting gently with his ancient wife; my charming, attentive husband George laughing, probably at my compulsive fussing when there was no need to fuss and virtually nothing left to fuss about.

He nuzzled again, this time embracing me from the front. He even kissed me, affectionately, on the lips. And then told me he had booked Peking in the Park for lunch. Was he sheepish when he said that, or do I imagine it now? 'Cordelia, my busy Cordelia,' he cajoled. That kind of initiative – impromptu lunching – had more usually become mine. It could be that he wondered, worried even, whether I would have the grace or even the sense to accept.

I remember, quite clearly, that his hand remained resting on my arm. The picture of that detail stands out in my mind with the most curious sharpness. I picked up his hand and turned it over, kissing it on the palm. Then I held his hand for a moment against my cheek. I told George I would love to lunch with him.

'Do I even have a choice?' I teased. 'Not when I am offered the prospect of prawn toast and velvet chicken. And my darling to eat them with.'

I laughed, too, when I said that I thought a little dressing up would be in order, but that first there was a small job I had promised myself to get done in my studio.

George made a joke, mixing metaphors about slavedrivers and sweatshops, forgiving me I expect for my customary stalling, but by then my mind had leaped ahead to what I wanted to get done, and I took almost no notice of what he was saying, interrupting him, I now feel sure, to ask him to call out to me if I wasn't back in the house within the hour. As I hurried from our kitchen towards the back door, my mind had left him.

Distracted as I was by my drawings for a new large piece, birdbath in size although not in intent, it took me some time to notice that George hadn't given me the call he had promised. I went on for a few minutes longer, but without much concentration or pleasure. Then I took the keys from where they usually hung, looked around my studio to wish it well, covered my drawings carefully with large sheets of dark tissue, locked the door and walked back to the house.

I was not anticipating that George would be annoyed by my tardiness, but I was somewhat anxious about how to make up for time while still managing to turn myself out reasonably well. Going about with George, not wishing to be the too-dowdy creature at his elegant side, had pushed my standards of appearance up rather higher than they might naturally be. Slinging something smart over something comfortable was my speciality; but for this occasion I thought I would take a little extra care with all the layers.

As I entered the house I called out, as I always did, 'Back home, George. It's me.' A fatuous announcement, but a habit and cherished for that.

The day's post was sitting on a small polished table at the kitchen end of the light-filled, long hallway. I paused to see if there was anything of immediate interest.

There wasn't, and my mind turned again to what I might wear, and onwards to our lunch. To the treat of it: some leisurely hours in public together, eating, talking. Maybe walking a little afterwards. Just the two of us, dressed up and enjoying each other.

Going up the stairs, I called again to George, 'Are you there, darling? It's me.' As I did so, and even in my state of relative self-absorption, it became impossible to ignore that the silence of the house was not the occupied silence of someone reading or writing or thinking or listening to music with headphones. It was an empty silence. No one was there.

Standing at the door of the sitting room, I saw at once that George's body was there. On his old maroon velvet chaise-longue, there was his dear body stretched out. But George himself had gone.

I felt, first, utter incredulity, and then, on the out breath, such sorrow that he'd had to go alone. That thought came into my mind and has stayed with me almost obsessively. George was a man of rituals, of careful, stylised goodbyes on departure, of loving, exuberant greetings on his inevitable return.

Now he had gone. No one saying goodbye. No one to see him off. While I had fiddled about and drawn sketches in my studio, unable perhaps, unwilling certainly, to set my work entirely aside. Was I, I was later to wonder, making a point of some petty kind while George was dying, or was he, for some reason I will never be free to understand, dying in the way he needed to?

In those first dreadful, unreal, time-stilled moments, I knelt at his side. Not wanting to believe it. Not believing anything else. I was lonelier than I have ever felt in all my life. Or ever will again until my own time comes. Lonely for George, wretchedly lonely for myself. *Lonely* isn't the word. There is no word. Desolate and beyond desolate. That doesn't describe it. I open my mouth now for the word and nothing comes. My mouth is empty. I feel only an arching sensation, grasping for what isn't there.

From one second to the next, George had moved from life into death. He had been here. Now he was gone. As abruptly, what was most familiar about my life also ended. Kneeling, crouching, hunched into myself to resist new waves of pain, I reached out for what I knew. I picked up the hand that I had kissed not much more than an hour before. George's long, bony hand: clean, smelling of soap; familiar, loved, extremely beautiful. Again I kissed it, and held it to my cheek.

Some time later I roused myself and rang people. Close, kind people to whom I needed to say almost nothing at all. They arrived. In due course George's body left. People stayed. A few days later, those days a painful blur now, there was a funeral: packed, resplendent with flowers, kind words, witty words, a shower of compliments to rival Danae's gold; ravishing music that was hardest of all to bear. Every speaker, every flower giver, every attender meant well. I would have preferred silence, and envied George the neat trick he had of slipping his hearing aid into his pocket when the level of aural pleasure dropped too low.

People stood, afterwards, on the gravel outside the church. The crunching, unsteady noise this fresh gravel made as their shod feet moved across it grated on my ear and also comforted. Then those who could, or felt they should, came to our house.

The preparations for the party came in handy. Not more cocktails. George would certainly have liked to have been seen off through the bottom of lime green, Art Nouveau glasses awash with potent mixes. But for me that was too much.

I felt barely able to focus, or even to stand easily erect. Had I a choice I might have curled up into a ball in the corner of the room and stayed there until I turned gradually and appropriately to dust. As it was, I resorted to what was easy: putting canapes and sandwiches onto side tables, along with bottles from which people could top up their own hefty glasses of brandy, gin or whisky.

Later there was coffee and tea, then more movement still of cups, glasses, plates, napkins, hands, mouths, eyes.

How strange that death, too, should involve so many catering decisions.

Late in the afternoon of the after-funeral gathering, George's sister Sarah came up to me. She is tall, lean, attractive, and only a few years younger than George. Old enough, anyway, to know better. We have never been more than superficial friends. Maybe once upon a time in the dim dark ages of our youth I might have tried to be close to her. It's hard to remember ever thinking it would have been worthwhile, but it is certainly possible that for George's sake I did try. Or maybe for my own sake. I wanted George's friends and family to like me and admire George's choice. I wanted them to see that no one else could possibly have done. It seems ridiculous now. They probably never thought about our match with a particle of the intensity of enquiry I brought to it. They would have been far too concerned with their own questions and insecurities. But I didn't know that then. So Sarah's sibling relationship with George had been more than enough reason for me to think that she should be wooed, and that her opinions must matter. Though surely it wasn't long before I learned to be wary, and then increasingly disinterested as years and then decades passed. And we all grew older.

Sarah was a social worker for a number of those years, a professional busybody of the worst possible kind who in retirement has taken to meddling in her unhappy adult children's lives with remarkable ruthlessness. So unlike George. Knowing all that, I nevertheless found it extremely difficult to hold onto the remnants of my composure when Sarah sat rather too close to me on our big yellow sofa, stared at me rather too hard, and asked me what my plans were.

'Now that George is *dead*,' she emphasised. As though that could possibly be news.

Before I could begin to compose even an inadequate answer to that impossible, appalling question, the very question I wished most to avoid, Sarah went on to say that she had always wanted me to know that she herself had seen that marriage had not entirely suited me. Her voice at this point was softly caressing. She smiled then, before finishing off by saying that for women for whom marriage did not seem entirely . . . inevitable . . . widowhood could be a kind of liberation. With that said, and in the face of my perhaps too obvious distress, she patted my shoulder and added that she wouldn't wish to hurt me for the world.

'Indeed,' she finished off, her voice intimate and nauseating, 'I am simply reminding you, Cordelia, that even in the darkest of situations there can be, and indeed, my dear, there always is, *hope.*'

Did she smile again then? In the wake of her outrageous platitudes did she actually smile or have I only imagined that she stood, gleaming; that she stroked the dark silk of her expensive tailored dress in a gesture of self-satisfied affection before turning to face the crowded room resilient in her belief that there is no problem that she, Sarah, could not willingly attend to?

My own sisters could not save me. Elsie is painfully vague these days but not so vague she wouldn't notice a blow to her sister when she saw it. One of them sensed the bewilderment that stuck me to my seat, as I certainly do recall a warm arm around my shoulders, a hug that gripped me, a filled glass put in my hand and a promise whispered in my ear that, really, I was bearing up most wonderfully. With what loving goodwill the pure of heart among us sometimes deny the evidence that is right before their eyes.

I was not bearing up. I was barely standing up.

The worst of it was George could have turned my relaying of that claustrophobic, invasive exchange into a wicked, relieving joke. George could out-Sarah Sarah to the most delicious extent, so perhaps she was getting back at him for the lack of adoration from an older brother that possibly she once craved. But in the unyielding night that followed the hard day of George's funeral he wasn't there to laugh with me about Sarah, and I was left alone with my guilt: that there had been no inevitability about my capacity to be a wife, and that perhaps for George, as well as for me, there had sometimes been too little grace.

3

Hours later, Cordelia sleeps. She lies, as George has often watched her, with his bedtime drink in his hand, leaning against the doorframe soaking up the very sight of her, she lies at the far outside edge of the large bed she and George shared. She lies as though poised for flight, as though the slightest call will have her up and out the door at a speed reserved for disaster. Her long arm hangs out from the bedclothes, towards the floor. She is encased in a white nightgown. Lace grips her wrist. On cold nights, seeing her arm exposed, George would lift it, tuck it in, enjoying when he thought about it the contrast of fine lace and roughened potter's hand, knowing, even in the dark, that under her carefully filed nails clay lingers, beyond the reach of diligent scrubbing.

The large room gleams in the dark. White bed cover. White walls. Heavy white linen curtains. In a house filled with colour, only this room is white. The smells of various pot pourri mix pleasurably in his nostrils. One night, a thousand nights: George draws into himself the sight of his wife, Cordelia, taking her in, having her, as she sleeps, in a way she would inevitably resist when awake.

Sometimes George stays there for an hour or more. Sometimes he pulls up a low upholstered easy chair and stretches out, a pillow tucked behind the small of his bony back. His attention is not always with Cordelia or on her, but he is conscious of rejoicing that, when his attention returns, she is still there, a silent figure alongside whom he will shortly sleep.

Tonight, sleeping, knowing even in her sleep that George is dead, Cordelia turns restlessly. She is running, in her dream, towards a castle. It is there. She knows it is there. She cannot see it. She is running across twigs, small sharp stones, around bracken and between looming dark green trees, running fast, needing to get there quickly, she is not sure why, but is compelled forward. She has someone to save. Someone to warn. But of what? Never mind what; she must get there. Race. Hurry. Run. Faster. The confusion is horrible. Her feet protest, cut up by rough terrain. She hears laughter somewhere. The sound is unpleasant.

Cordelia, slow of movement, quick of thought in her waking life, is racing now, keeping her eyes fixed on the castle wall, then the castle gate, now crashing through the gate to find, on the other side, propped against decaying stony walls, only the dead and the dreaming.

In her own dream she cries for help. Cries aloud, although tonight there is no one to hear her. A bird swoops. As though to pick at bones. She is frightened. Her hands fly up to protect her head. The bird whispers in her ear, 'Let me help you, let me help you. Cordelia, let me help you.'

'Someone to save,' she pants. 'Someone to warn.'

'Someone to save,' she pants, again, more quietly this time. 'Someone to warn.' And again, 'Someone to save . . . someone to warn . . .'

The bird has gone. The stone walls fade. Who were the dead and dreaming, dreaming against the castle wall, passing so quickly now from her mind as she reaches to turn on her bedside lamp, passing so quickly she could wonder: were they ever there?

4

Towards the tail-end of a silent, empty afternoon, Cordelia walks awkwardly up the uncarpeted wooden stairs and into the big light bathroom
at the back of the first floor of her house. The house will soon be dark.
It is already a little too cold. Cut flowers have sat in her laundry sink
since early morning. Guilt has driven her late in the day to get them
out of the sink and into vases.

She pushes the door open with her elbow. The vases she is holding
are full and she takes care not to disturb the flowers nor spill the water.
Once she has put them down she pays them no more attention. Heavily,
she lowers herself into a cane chair and gazes into space. Her sculptured,
clear-featured face is tired. The lines around her deepest eyes and full,
curving mouth have deepened with grief and anxiety and lack of sleep.
Her thick, straight white hair, usually cut in a weighty bob to just below
her ears, could do with a trim. Her fringe is ready to meet her eyes.
Her shoulders droop. Her hands sit numbly in her lap. After a few
moments her eyes flicker to the vases and driven by habit she gets up
to move a couple of flowers from one vase to the other, restoring
balance and not caring about the few drops of water that form a tiny
trail. She sits down again and with relief closes her eyes, hunching her
body forward as she does so, protecting her belly and the pain that's
lodged there.

Cordelia and George's larger bathroom was once a fourth bedroom
in a house that was home to only two people. It is spacious, welcoming

and is usually brightened by large, bold arrangements of flowers like those Cordelia has just put down. The walls are painted a dusky turquoise that looks as though it's many layers thick. The door and window frames are sharp Granny Smith green and the tall, shapely skirting boards are rich yellow. Draped, full-length curtains in navy and white narrow stripes hang beside two long windows. The blinds on the windows are rusty red.

'It's overdone, isn't it,' Cordelia had said to George when the painting had been completed, blinds and curtains hung, and the workmen had gone home. 'Doing a whole room at once is fatal, clearly. It looks as though I've lifted it from *Vogue Interiors* or, worse, tried too hard.' They had been standing together at the doorway at the time. George had poured and brought them each a drink that sat untouched in the glass each held in their hands while they both gazed and Cordelia fretted.

George could only guess how many sketches Cordelia had drawn and punctiliously coloured to come up with a colour plan she thought they would both enjoy. The room had previously been a bedroom wallpapered in sober stripes, giving it a much more formal effect than most of the rooms in their house. Despite a view over the garden, it had rarely been used except when all other space for guests was filled. He looked around, attempting to see the bathroom as if for the first time.

'Overdone? Only by the most *cramped* standards. What it reminds me of is life inside a lolly jar. The kind of jar one gazed at as a small, pocket-money-less scruff of a boy, through two layers of glass, shop window and glass jar, with one's nose pressed against the former in order to get closer to the latter. I think I shall have serious difficulties in restraining myself from creeping in here to lick the walls. Have you had them flavoured, Cordie? Surely those skirting boards taste especially good. I can see myself idling away many a happy hour lying on the floor right next to that juncture of yellow and turquoise, believing I am resting in the land of striped lollies forever.'

'George!' Cordelia was laughing. How could she not? 'It is too much, isn't it? I could change something. The skirting boards maybe.'

'Don't.' George's voice was decisive. 'Not because it would be a nuisance. But because this room is fun, darling. It's the skirting boards that are most fun of all. Every time we come in here, flavoured paint or not, it will lift our spirits. You'll see; it will become one of your favourite rooms in this house, and it's already one of mine. Let me bet on your imminent conversion to life inside the lolly jar. Your talc against my shaving cream? What do you say?'

'We'll try it out for a month, shall we?' is what Cordelia said, reassuring herself now, not George. 'If it seems too embarrassingly garish at the end of that time I'll repaint it myself.' Cordelia was still fretting, and ignoring her drink.

'Only if I agree! I love it. Already, Signora mia, I *adore* it!' With a flourish George signalled his total approval of the room, his wife, and the drink he emptied in a single, satisfying gulp. Cordelia nodded, as much to herself as George. A month would do it.

The bath was old when they bought it. Long and deep, it still smells faintly of iron. When George or Cordelia noticed this smell it reminded them of childhood baths and bathrooms. They liked that. A new bath, they agreed, would never have yielded up such a treat.

Next to the bath now, years later, is a recently acquired heated towel rail. It holds thick, white, warmed towels at the ready.

On a Victorian bath stand sits a row of ivory brushes, neatly placed in line. Each brush bears on its back a tiny silver shield on which is engraved: G.D.A.F. They were given to George David Alexander Fraser by his mother for his thirtieth birthday when his hair was still thick and dark. The brushes were made to last. Next to them, and in line with them, lies a bone comb, old and extremely clean.

Two toothbrushes hang side by side. One red, one yellow. Cordelia uses the yellow one and skilfully avoids the sight of the red one when she bends over the big, oval basin, twice a day, to brush her teeth.

A large mirrored cupboard hangs on a wall, housing a small collection of bottles of aftershave and expensive men's cologne. There are also disposable razors in that cupboard. One of them was used once and put back to be used again. It still carries a few dried hairs. This cupboard is easy for Cordelia to avoid. Her own toiletries are cluttered on shelves next to the bath.

Less easy to avoid is George's heavy white towelling bathrobe hanging from a brass hook on the back of the bathroom door. In its large square pockets are two saved rubber bands and a crumpled handkerchief needing to be washed. It has not yet occurred to Cordelia to empty the pockets or to move the bathrobe out of sight.

Opening her eyes, getting up from the chair to face whatever's left of the day, Cordelia walks towards the door that had swung closed behind her. Then she sees the bathrobe, hanging loose and empty. She buries her head in its most immediately accessible mid-section. She wraps it right around her head, and tightly squashes her face. She binds herself to its textures. She smells her way into the memories it exudes. Binding her head tightly, but body wilting and glad to wilt, she is leaning against the door for support, not thinking, not feeling, barely breathing. As long as she can lean there, time and grief are stilled.

5

Hearing the phone ring, turning down the music that has become almost essential to me during waking hours, running to the phone as though it could possibly matter, I recognise the voice of one of my fellow potters. Laurie. Could she, she was asking, come back occasionally to work in the studio? If it isn't too soon? If I wouldn't feel intruded upon?

I tell her there's someone at the door and put the phone down.

After what I hope is a convincing interval, I pick it up again to say that her coming would be no problem at all. She should feel free, and should perhaps even suggest to one or two of the others that they might like to come along as well.

'Really? Are you sure?'

'Really. I am sure.' Maybe I am.

Laurie is obviously grateful and relieved, and keen to bring the call to an end. 'Bye!' she says, vigorously. 'See you soon, Cordelia.' I guess the call was hard for her to make. It will be good to see her.

Various thoughts jostle for attention in the wake of Laurie's call, most of them clichéd. I have been cross to notice how frequently in my grief clichés land on me with a grip that is sometimes hard to shake off: it will do you good to have people around. Time you got on with living. Moping only makes things worse.

This is not the way I like to think, and I am grumpy as well as helpless in the face of it.

When Laurie arrives, coming first not to the studio but to the house where she stands, shy but concerned, at my opened back door, I give her tea but otherwise let her get on. Yet, when I think about it, I am genuinely glad she is in the studio and that the studio is again being used and can come alive with someone's work. No special need for that work to be mine.

I am glad, too, when a day or two later Laurie comes again and a couple of other potters join her and I go out to the studio with a tray piled with cups and a pot of decent coffee and packets of expensive Dutch biscuits and they stop work and we talk pots and potters, and economics and elections, quite in the old way. And when the coffee is drunk and the cups are neatly stacked on the tray by those good young women I find my way to my own usual bench and corner and pick up my drawings while the others, too, get back to work.

George. I am littering his name over pages, just as I once did when I mooned over impossibly unattainable boys in my adolescent years. I want to carve his initials into the trunk of a huge tree, fill a billboard with a list of his virtues, take out a permanent lease on a small plane that could drag his name around the sky. Urgently and hopelessly I wish that I were a sculptor instead of a potter, or that I were a painter. I want to recreate him, give him new form. I want to bring him back to life.

To say that I miss him is to say nothing at all. I roam our house mourning him, but how inadequately! Gestures I can't make tingle at the ends of my fingers: tearing out my hair, ripping at my clothes, beating at my breast. Howls I can't cry form themselves impotently in my mouth. I do cry sometimes, but I long for that constipated, meagre trickle to become hot torrents of tears that will shake me and cleanse me and change me.

Not for the first or last time, I curse lessons of refinement and containment learned too well. Sex and grief: inevitably shaped in their individual expression by larger collective forces of time and place. And my time and my place have not served me well. What I have been most admired for – my poise, my calm – is a lie. A bitterly confining lie. They are what I only partially became. Now in new widowhood I am a dam that frets to break loose, that wants to be the rushing river of clear, cleansing feeling that I surely was as a child, but won't be again in this corseted lifetime.

And, mourning my husband, however inadequately, I am almost horrified to find that far less predictably, and perhaps entirely unforgivably, I am also mourning the loss of my party.

It is wretched to admit this. Indeed, even thinking about it seems almost obscene when linked with the death of a beloved companion and spouse. Yet linked those two events certainly are. Perhaps I am fishing for excuses now, but it was, after all, almost certainly the last party we would have had together, the last time we would have come together at the end, no matter how separate we had been for the duration, to hear happy farewells: Goodbye George, Goodbye Cordelia. George-and-Cordelia. Shrunk now. Just Cordelia.

It seems vilely petty, mourning the loss of a party, but spurred by this recent loss my mind has returned me to the long-ago birthday when I turned nine. I had been promised a party that year, my first party ever, by my hard-pressed, distracted mother. Then she had gone into labour early, had a difficult birth, a distressed, screaming infant, and of course my party was off. It does my battered self-esteem no good at all to acknowledge how petty my disappointment was on both occasions. What could a party matter in the face of birth, and of death? And I worry about the persistence of that early memory when so much else in my childhood is surely worth remembering, but feels irretrievably forgotten.

As though that unwieldy mix of grief and shame were not enough, I found myself looking out from my bedroom window down onto the garden and seeing under one especially large, greening, spreading tree, not only a sweep of early bulbs and the first, welcome sight of blue, pink and white forget-me-nots, but also a frightening mirage: my own body lying among the flowers, flattening some of them, obscuring others, like a discarded, wasted scarecrow thrown to the ground and left to rot.

Perhaps this sight would have seemed less shocking if it were George's body that I was seeing. He has died. I remain alive. Yet, looking out of that window or, for a few days, any window that faced towards the garden, it was decidedly my own body I saw: perfectly still, lying quite tidily and gracefully in a frock I haven't worn for years, but with absolutely no sign of life as birds landed then flew away, as leaves fell, as some flowering plants grew and others choked beneath the weight of the woman who was once Cordelia Fraser.

It is too hard not to feel sorry for myself. There seems no other way to feel. I am trapped in self-pity and for some especially wretched days I have felt caught up in a spiral which oddly enough is peopled less by George than Sarah at her sweet-smiling worst and my mother at her most unavailable. I go to bed hearing the voice of one, and wake up trying vainly to reach the other.

George could laugh at Sarah but was uneasy with my mother. She must have been one of a handful of people in his lifetime with whom he could not easily talk and joke and connect. I have no doubt that my mother regarded George as an admirable husband. Certainly, she was tremendously relieved that he was mildly rich as well as good-looking, intelligent and kind. But she never allowed him to charm her. She may even have chosen to resist him. I suspect George felt restless and thrown off balance by the unfamiliarity of that.

After her death we rarely spoke of her. There were almost no shared anecdotes that were easy to recall and whatever thinking I have done about my mother, I have done alone; whatever talking about her I have fitfully managed, I have done with my three sisters. Not much of that though. Just hesitantly and occasionally. The feelings are too strong and too uncomfortable. They are not relieved by talking. We tip-toe around our memories, nothing more than that. We are too afraid, I would guess, to stir the pain any more than we must. Feelings of pain. Hers and ours. Feelings of frustration. Hers and ours.

In memory, my mother stands. I long to speak to her and, more urgently, to hear her speak to me, but her head remains turned away, her shoulders drooping in the frightful, all-enveloping, dark-print frocks she took to wearing long before middle age. My once-beautiful, raven-haired mother: monochromed. My once-clever, opinionated mother: avoiding contact. My mother who could sing as though at one with angels: silenced. My mother with insight and poetry enough to name the eldest of her daughters Cordelia: lost. My mother: hidden in the attitudes, then even in the form of a drudge. Why? Why?

The memory shifts. She is scraping away at pots, or peeling mounds of vegetables, or setting eight places at a long linen-draped table, or ironing my father's and two brothers' boiled, starched white shirts with grim patience. So many tasks. *Someone has to do them*, she would say. But would never allow herself to add: *Why should it be me?* Refusing our help, frustrating our efforts to obliterate or even disrupt the terrifying sight of our mother acting as our slave. *I can manage*, she would say. Again, and again: *I can manage.*

Even after each one of her six children had long ago crept away from home, she continued to *manage*, to fill her day with busy tasks, just done more slowly. There was by then no possible rational need. My father's patented inventions had borne abundant fruit and there was plenty of money to buy help and leisure for her. Dad would have done it, too, glad to ease her unfathomable pain; glad to ease the loss of the woman he had married. She couldn't see that, and it had long ago become impossible for any one of us to press too hard.

I remember as a woman in my mid-forties leaving my own home for a day and going to hers, then watching her through almost that entire day while she measured sheets of thick white paper and cut them up, slowly and exactly, to line her old, cream-painted wooden kitchen cupboards. It was not only the paper that demanded from her a ludicrous sense of exactness. Each item that was removed from a cupboard, no matter how recently washed, was scrupulously re-washed and slowly dried again. One cupboard emptied, washed; its contents washed and dried; the cupboard lined immaculately, and then onto the next one and the next. My mother's back was bent throughout the day. I saw her back but not her face. Occasionally her hand would go up to push back a stray hair or two. Otherwise her focus remained entirely on her task.

I made cups of strong, sweetened tea that she drank without really shifting her position. I prepared cucumber and cress sandwiches for her lunch that she barely ate, and I tried to dry the washed dishes for her until I saw that she longed to dry them again herself in case I had missed a millimetre and the china might not shine. Intermittently throughout that day I tried to chat, sharing stories of George's latest travels, of my own attempts to establish a pattern of colour in the garden, of my impressions of how well my sisters' children were taking on the challenges of young adulthood.

My voice, even to my own ears, sounded false and strained. Did she listen? Did she want me there, at her side? Occasionally she would comment, but not always about the topic I was raising. Only once did she respond directly. Speaking of George she said, in a flat soft voice, 'It's a full rich life he has, Cordelia. It's a useful life. One can't ask for more than that.'

It's horrible to recall how much I wanted to hit her then. I wanted to strike her across her head and back, so deeply and with such pain did I feel that she was commenting not on George and his good deeds but on her own wasted life as my mother, and on mine as George's wife – and not a mother.

But my hand would never have moved. No amount of will could have lifted it from its limp place in my lap. A moment passed, not more. The wound in me and perhaps the matching wound in her had no sooner opened than it closed again. Anyone observing us would have seen nothing more remarkable than two women, one well past middle age, side by side in peaceful silence.

Is it now my own cycle of self-pity that is linking me to my mother? Certainly I've been hating the way Sarah's cruel, piercing words have trapped me and rubbed me raw. So many kind words were said to me on the day of George's funeral. Those words are largely forgotten in their details, though I am grateful for them. But I worry that Sarah's poisonous arrow stays with me only because it hit a bull's-eye. Only because it carries an unpalatable truth. I hate that.

I am hating too the slowness of my own days and nights. And the sight of my own body abandoned, not even buried, beneath the great, greening tree in our garden.

Not inevitably a wife, I hear. Droning like a March fly. And, from much longer ago: *I can manage. I can manage.*

What should a wife do? Simply framing the question, I feel ashamed. I should know. I should *know*. Fifty years a wife, and still I am asking, what should a wife do?

Not even a wife, a widow.

But hopeless. On some days, simply hopeless.

I have tried to take myself in hand. I have tried to *manage*.

Finding more physical strength than I knew I had – and some satisfaction in that – I have moved things around the house to give them fresh life: paintings, objects, books, rugs, even the larger pieces of furniture. I have taken down and shaken and cleaned curtains and blinds. I have cleaned, aired and rearranged cupboards. My clothes and household linen have never sat in such distinguished piles. In one ghastly, excessive day I scoured the oven and then without pausing defrosted and cleaned the fridge. I have spoken willingly to friends and gratefully to neighbours. I have sent large cheques to all the many causes that have George or me on their mailing lists. I have read pamphlets and articles about those who are much worse off than I. I have listened to uplifting radio programmes and to music that made me weep with frustration and rage as well as loss. I have opened and soon closed books that promised relief, insight or inspiration. I have tried and failed to pray. I have made lists.

I have stayed in the house.

I notice, wryly, that with every reason to leave the house, now I cannot. Even the half-minute's walk to the studio seems quite impossible.

Believing I must, I planned to clear George's drawers and cupboards, to give away those clothes that had life in them still. But I feel sour and bitterly resentful: that his clothes should have life when George does not.

Believing I must, I planned to tackle the daunting task of clearing out of his study those papers and books that should before my own dotage and death be donated or destroyed. But picking up this book, turning that page or two, seemed to exhaust me as pushing and shoving the bulky furniture had not.

Around the walls of George's study are photographs of Rabindranath Tagore, the Bengali poet George long admired, taught and wrote about. How often had I heard him quote lines that seemed to both of us almost divinely inspired in their aptness. George loved what he knew of the man; loved the effect his words had on others. I have known for decades now that Tagore's wisdom did much to sustain George's inner life and that kind man's eyes seemed most readily to understand when one day I shouted out loud, 'I can't do this. *I can't manage.* I am simply not ready yet!' And put down what I was doing and left the study to go to my bed and cry.

6

Pull yourself together, Cordelia. Pull yourself together.

When I seek to follow this order I find I am quite without instructions. Someone should produce a pattern or a recipe which the newly grieving could follow. Take one cup of fortitude, add a spoonful of oblivion, stir in a pinch of optimism, and so on.

I have tried. I have planned and have even half-written notes inviting long-distance friends to stay. And have toyed with the idea of entirely new interests, dallying with the alluring promise of a Fresh Start, of evening classes that would reveal to me at last the mysteries of musical composition, papermaking, or comparative religions. I went so far as to send for brochures, and when they came I sat down in the hall and read them with genuine excitement. Then I thought of coming home from those classes. I imagined re-entering the house with lots to say and no one to tell. My courage – such as it ever was – sputtered before it had really ignited, and then died. In its absence, I felt dreary and ashamed.

But, still pushed by demons, I continued to make lists: people to see; pots to plan; exhibitions, plays, films, concerts I should not miss.

Some of those lists, too, I put up on my fridge until one particularly bleak morning when I began to imagine that they were looking at me, rather than I at them. Those lists, those plans, had become a rebuke – as lists and plans quickly can. I tore them to shreds and burned them. I have made no such lists since. I am sticking to what I already know.

Indeed, I fear I am retreating ever more anxiously into just those routines which George loved and which, when he was alive, too often irritated me. Without George, I need them. Without George, I remain stuck in the house.

What a queer business marriage is.

Rather shyly, I've taken to wearing the once-shiny, dark brown plastic pinny that George usually wore when cooking. *Man at Work*, it declares in faded yellow letters. Then, in smaller letters, now cracked and hard to read: *Disturb only with liquid refreshments*.

This doesn't mean I am cooking or coping as George could, but in the tying of the strings behind my waist, and the patting of that shiny surface, there is at least some thread of continuity. I have become grateful for what I can get.

Graham Duncan has been to see me. He was George's friend and is our solicitor. Graham is at least a generation younger than George and I, but born old and sensible in ways which George and I were not.

Graham was, in difficult circumstances, impressively kind, telling me in a matter of fact voice how well George has provided for me, how little I will need to worry. 'You of all people know how thoroughly organised George invariably was,' said Graham. 'In every possible way he anticipated your needs and comfort.'

My hands met each other in my lap, like hesitant strangers needing solace.

George. Thinking not only of my needs, but of my comfort. Yet the comfort I most want he cannot give me. To avoid Graham's kindly gaze, I twisted my rings. I wanted to look at Graham, to thank him. I could not. Misunderstanding my awkwardness, Graham went on to say that he himself is willing to take over any decision-making until such time as I feel ready.

Hearing Graham's slow, cultivated voice, listening with the greatest possible interest to that word *ready*, I tried extremely hard to imagine such a time. It is as difficult, perhaps more difficult, than projecting myself into Central American villages or Bhutanese monasteries as George had wanted me to do when we still believed we would travel.

I long for that place *ready*, and can scarcely believe in its existence.

The potters continue to come.

I have not, after that first time, felt much like joining them. The urge to pot, even to draw and plan, continues to be something I can remember, but no longer seem capable of feeling in the present tense. I am not *ready*. Instead I have taken to propping open the back door in a way that is unmistakably welcoming and, one by one, and with admirable delicacy, the potters trail from the studio, through George's sprawling, abundant garden, into the house.

If I am in our roomy kitchen at the back I might sit down and join them at the long wooden kitchen table for mugs of tea or coffee or just some talk. If I'm not there, they don't come to find me, but sometimes I have woken up from a snooze, or have come downstairs into the kitchen from trying to read or simply listening to music in the sitting room, to find a plate of biscuits or sometimes a stew or vegetable mix of some sort in a small casserole dish, left by Laurie I suspect, ready to heat up.

When Laurie comes along the path past the house from the studio, for on some days she does work longer hours than the others, I try quite shamelessly to catch her or even to persuade her to eat with me. Most unexpectedly, I am hating to eat alone. After years of relishing whatever solitary meals I could muster, of enjoying losing myself in a book while also eating, I have had to face it that sitting down to my evening meal alone is one of the hardest moments of my day.

George made such a ceremony of food. My cooking was never worth a fuss, the careful setting of the table with good silver, flowers and often candles, the choosing and pouring of wine. But George's cooking was worth all that, and during his years of retirement we ate better than at any time during our married life.

Now I am thrown back on my own meagre resources and feel I can raise the will to do no more than a bare omelette, cheese on toast or a pot of vegetable soup and some fresh fruit. And even something as simple as that can be too much to contemplate. There are still grim days when I go to bed hungry or biscuit-filled, out of sheer inertia.

Eating with Laurie, finding colourful napkins and plates, lighting candles, pouring out some decent wine for her, I find myself quite animated, and curious too to know more about Laurie's life and her irregular routines.

A modern story, Laurie calls it, laughing as she does so. A husband who lives near her own small house with another man. Both the men librarians, that new clever breed who have never stamped the back of a large-print Winston Graham novel but who speak the language of computers, of information retrieval and of microfiches. Two men who look superficially alike: neat, trim, modestly muscled, bearded, sincere. *All good friends*, claims Laurie. I believe her, in a qualified kind of way, and want to know more.

Two quite big children, Gregory and Rhea, spend a couple of days each week with their father and it is when they are with him that Laurie can work longer hours in my studio. Her work sells well, she tells me proudly. They've lived from her sales and some irregular teaching for years. I am not surprised. Laurie herself is almost sombre in appearance, rugged, dark-haired and steady-eyed with broad shoulders and wide, strong hands. She often stands with those hands worming their way awkwardly into her jeans pockets as though she doesn't quite know what to do with them when pausing between practical tasks.

Until you know her, Laurie could easily be overlooked. Her clothes make almost no statement at all, or anyway the clothes she wears for work say very little. But what she creates with clay, glaze and a fine imagination demands all the attention she avoids turning on herself: highly glazed, brilliantly coloured and blatantly stylish teapots, huge jugs, basins, plates, and lately even fountains, all of which are saved from cliché and certainly from self-satisfaction by the skill of Laurie's craft. And by her wit. I'd like to own some of her pieces myself, and tell her that.

She has an adequate studio at home, much like the one I first had in my wash-house, I gather. But the pleasures of getting away from her domestic scene are as great for her as the charm or even the facilities my studio can offer. She likes the company of the other potters she says, unknowingly echoing my own pleasure in working alone, alongside others. Then, looking at me, she says she likes to see me, too.

'Sharing all this with me, Cordelia, I do appreciate it.' Laurie is gesturing with an eloquent shrug that probably encompasses the studio as well as the kitchen table.

She herself has provided most of what we have just eaten. Moreover, it is her company that has saved my evening. Nevertheless, I accept what she says. I smile. Then get up, as George might have done, to select and offer a half-bottle of splendid dessert wine to accompany tinned quince jelly and some near-perfect dense, moist ricotta cheese.

After Laurie has gone, refusing the taxi I offer and insisting on the speed and even the safety of her pushbike, I leave the clearing up and go to stand, as though led there by some compelling inner force, in the middle of George's study.

Such a familiar room, as long and as wide as the most generous sitting room. Each detail so well known to me I have to concentrate to bring it into focus. The Tagore photographs, one by one: from Christ-like young man to a white-bearded version of age that looks not old, but ancient and lit like a lamp from within. Chairs – a couple of large easy chairs that were re-upholstered some years ago in deep green slub linen; one hard wooden swivel chair for thinking and writing and latterly for typing at George's computer; hundreds of books carefully shelved according to subject; the best-loved books in two sleek, glass-fronted cabinets into which a particle of dust would attempt to enter at its peril; magazines stacked into orderly, appropriately sized boxes; two grey steel filing cabinets burdened to the limit with papers; paintings – some of them good with at least two of the Expressionists each worth more than our house; framed photographs of a much younger Cordelia than the woman looking around now; handsome shots of George and Cordelia the couple, of George's childhood home and family and one or two of wartime friends, forever uniformed and young; an especially palatial desk which George relished less for its size than for its many tiny drawers and a hidden cupboard; William Morris Persian-patterned curtains clumsily drawn across the front of a cumbersome standard lamp.

The rather too acid yellow of the walls had been my choice, not George's. He had wanted something subdued, an absent colour that would seek no attention. Why, I now ask myself, had he given in? Why, when this was his room? Why, when this was the room in which I spent almost no intimate time at all?

Giving in. For years I railed against it, feeling sure that only a sustained effort of will was saving me from total submersion in the quicksand of George's highly articulated, impressive, convincing opinions. Not realising how little need there was to struggle. Not allowing myself to recognise that it cost George almost nothing to give in himself, and that he was not the enemy lined up against me.

Not seeing what was in front of my nose: that *not giving in* was for me as *managing* was to my mother. A noose of my own making.

Had I grown old before I had grown wise? It seems entirely possible.

I sit down, tentatively, shyly, on the wooden swivel chair, finding it difficult not to feel like a trespasser. With even greater hesitation I turn on George's computer although after it has chimed and smiled at me I don't know what else to do and turn it off again, worrying that this rapid dismissal might result in some permanent malfunction. Perhaps

Laurie will know? Perhaps Laurie or her children would like to have the thing?

With some surprise I notice that there are notes lying on George's desk, tucked neatly into the edge of a redundant blotter. I hadn't seen them during my previous timid forays into this room. Lists. I can't get away from them. 'Book table for lunch' I read, in George's tiny hand. *Book table for lunch.* Then, floating on its own, not necessarily connected to the lunch thought, I see his familiar version of my own name: Cordie. Next to that, a tiny sketched fish. My face burns like a young girl's.

I run my finger over those six letters, eliciting from them almost as much tenderness as if I were being touched by George. I feel brighter than I've done for ages. Ahead of me is the possibility of new discoveries. I look around the room, tentative still but excited, too, by what it might reveal to me. Is it ever possible to know enough about a beloved other person?

George spent hours in this room, long after his voluntary retreat from full-time development and aid work. In retirement, he continued to work hard on many committees. Maybe too many; he was often tired, though rarely less than cheerful, even in the face of those repeated acts of greed, stupidity, short-sightedness and cruelty of the most base kinds his committees were intended to relieve.

Like a tide coming in and going out again, dumping what it had to bring, then returning for more, the same words, phrases, problems and partially evoked solutions swirled around our house that always had: Third World debts, First World greed; too many people, too few resources; polluted oceans and shrinking rivers; loss of topsoil and deforestation; indigenous peoples' rights; soybeans not tobacco; soil replenishment not exhaustion; more literacy projects, fewer arms; more birth control, less corruption. Those phrases – and all that lay behind them – were as familiar as our own names and sometimes more defining.

George's last years of activity sought to expose and perhaps even contain the tentacles of multinational agribusiness, a fight he likened to grappling with the Hydra: strike off one head and several more arise. Amnesty International was a more personalised effort. Named prisoners with faces, pasts, families, who could be spoken of, written to, agitated for. And by no means at the end of his list of interests were the scholarly papers that he wrote carefully, modestly, on Hindu and Buddhist mystical poetry and the values they express – and create – for various obscure journals whose survival he valued highly.

Those were George's passions and a good part of his reason for living. Funded in no small part by his equally exceptional talent for buying, selling and investing, those were the causes this successful capitalist from a privileged, conservative family had fought for with animation, skill and even optimism for almost half a century from this graceful, well-ordered room.

My loss is their loss also. I do not doubt that.

8

George is his mother's favourite. Though he is only a young man, still to make his way in the world, she receives all his news and all news about him as good if not actually great news, and projects towards him an air of excitement and confidence that only rarely he finds daunting.

The whole family knows that George is Mother's favourite. No one minds. It would be churlish to mind. In this family, they can afford to be good-humoured. The only daughter, Sarah, has a widely admired complexion, is quite clever enough, and always smoothly pleasant to her parents' friends. Each of the four boys has survived the war, life and limbs and optimism intact. They can never cease to be grateful for that. Each boy is already doing well, just as he has always done. Each played for the top cricket and rugby teams, or rowed for his school and university; each won, in his day, chess competitions, or archery, or debating; each graduated at the time he should; each now has a con-stantly renewed clutch of elegant printed invitation cards on his mantelpiece. Each is confident that, when the time comes, he will marry wisely.

George is fond of many girls. And girls seem very fond of him. Sometimes an individual girl will frighten him a little, when she seems to want too much too soon, or anyway more than he cares to give. He likes the clever girls who know how to banter, who can flirt with words and spiky arguments as well as with their eyes and occasional kisses. Perhaps he trusts the girls who know the value of a little distance, although he could not yet articulate that thought quite as clearly.

George is not a virgin. During the war and since he has had a number of intense, rushed sexual encounters that left him feeling guilty and unsettled. He blames himself. He knows that those were not the girls he liked enough. He laughs at his own romanticism but believes in it, too; believes that sex will be quite different, even ecstatic, when it is accompanied by love and commitment.

His own parents are still in love. He can see that in the way his mother brightens when she hears his father's key in the door each evening. George watches the way she pampers her husband; how she tolerates and smooths away his occasional moodiness; how proudly and generously she describes his achievements while rarely mentioning her own. He is equally aware how courteous his father invariably is to his mother; how carefully he moves her chair out for her at their own dining table; how he helps her into and out of their large car; with what ease he notices and comments if she is wearing something new or especially pretty.

In later years George will come to see just how rare a man his father is. Rich and clever, George's father is also wise enough to know that he can use his wealth to express or enhance his happiness but the source of that happiness is not his investments, his businesses or his houses. Without ever having to put his conviction into words, George's father knows, as all his family knows, that his happiness derives from the constancy of love he gives and gets from his wife and children.

George meets Cordelia at a friend's house. It is a tennis party, the end of a hot afternoon. He is bored, and about to leave. He has played three games of mixed doubles and has lost them all. He doesn't mind losing but as the games have continued he has become uncomfortably aware that his partner, whom he scarcely knows, is becoming increasingly giggly and possessive. He wants to escape her giggles and the party, and would have done so even sooner had he not been cornered by a man who is about to go to India for the first time, and who has been told that George speaks Bengali and Hindi and has been to Calcutta twice already.

This man is going to Madras. If he is to stay there, he will need to learn Tamil. George has told him this, and has twice said that he knows nothing at all, really, about that language or this man's destination. 'It's an immensely complex, diverse country,' he has said, more than once already surely. He is fretting to get away.

Over this man's shoulder George sees a tall, striking girl. *How cool she looks*, he says to himself, wondering how she manages it on a day as hot as this one. She is thin, with unexpectedly heavy low-slung breasts. She is wearing a cream knitted cotton sweater with short sleeves and some kind of roll collar softening a V-neck. Her arms are unusually long. Her elbows turn out, making corners. Her slightly baggy slacks are also cream. On her head she is wearing something that is more turban than hat. It is bright red, almost scarlet. On anyone else, on a woman whose face revealed the slightest hint of rosiness or sweat, it would look appalling.

This girl can obviously trust that her creamy skin will stay pale and fresh. She is laughing. Her dark eyebrows move as actively as her mouth. Perhaps her hair is dark too? Perhaps it is long and dark and straight.

The girl's forehead is unusually high and marble smooth. George's mother takes pride in her own high forehead, and once told George that the only compliment her own mother ever paid her was to tell her that her high brow indicated high intelligence. His mother's cheeks flushed as she told him this, and she had laughed at the need she'd had to savour that rare praise and share it with her son.

The man who wants to go to India but not to understand it is still talking. George's eyes shift to the cool girl's mouth. When she smiles her teeth are white and straight. She puts her hands in her pockets and seems to ease her back while doing so. It is a gesture that George often makes himself. His own lean back is just a tad too long, a risk for lower back pain.

He strains to hear her voice, to hear her laugh. He wants to hear a certain something in her voice and an absence of something else. He can't hear anything except this boring man continuing to go on about his cousin's adventures in Bangalore. The cousin sounds ignorant and boorish. *Who cares?* George thinks. Nevertheless, he smiles and says, 'Do excuse me for a moment. I'll be right back.' He is approaching the girl and as he does so he meets his host and can ask, 'Who is she?'

Jack, his host, does not need to ask who George means. He places his own plump body squarely between George and the girl. 'Not for you, ducky. She's a bluestocking that one. Was an anti-Spanish War zealot even before her unmentionable peace activities during our most recent war to end all wars. She might even be a Quaker for all I know. Though they're all dowdy, aren't they? And the one thing you can say about Cordelia with any certainty is that she isn't dowdy. I've seen her turn up at the most unlikely boring events and always looking smashing. I expect that if I were another woman I should hate her. So sincere, so clever and so pretty.'

Clever, George registers, with relief. Pretty, he can already see. Better than pretty. *Serene*. It's a quality he's observed and admired far more often in Indian women than here at home. 'Her name's Cordelia?' George smiles, somewhat inanely. His tongue feels a little large in his mouth.

'Yes. Not quite a princess I believe. Beware of Daddy's daughter, though.' Jack's tone changes. 'I suppose you'd better meet her then.' Now Jack is managing to look both slyly pleased and theatrically defeated.

If Cordelia has noticed George, his interest, or his move towards her, she betrays nothing other than graceful surprise when Jack says, archly, 'George is eager to meet a fellow idealist, Cordelia. He complains there are too few of us about! God alone knows whether this is wise, but Cordelia Williamson, do meet George *Hindi* Fraser. With caution, I am compelled to add.'

Cordelia turns from Jack, looks directly at George, smiles, then looks away. He wonders, for the first time in his life, if who he is, or who he appears to be, could possibly fall short of what's acceptable.

'I was leaving,' he says, 'but am on my way to a carillon recital. I don't suppose there's the faintest chance that such an arcane choice might appeal to you?'

'Why not?' Her voice is amused, not defensive. He sees her smile and white teeth up close for the first time. He sees her eyes. They are pale, flat green. He has seen green algae cover a river in India; the colour would have matched Cordelia's eyes. Those eyes are much more wary than her smile. He looks away first this time, though recovers quickly. Jack is watching George. His is the greedy eagerness of a fisherman about to see a salmon caught. George says to Jack, and to Cordelia, too, 'I'll say goodbye then, and off we'll go.'

'I heard the Hindi bit, but that was all. What did Jack say your name is?' Cordelia asks as they walk together but at some distance from each other down broad, well-kept steps towards the path. Her tan pumps make no sound.

'Tom, Dick, Harry, *George*,' George laughs. 'But you, you're blessed with a name that no one could forget.'

'Blessed? Yes.' She seems surprised at his choice of word. For a moment it hangs between them: a weighty thing. Then she relaxes. Her nostrils move when her mouth does. 'I like it. I like George, too.' Now she does redden beneath the scarlet turban, just a little. 'The name I mean. We'll have to see about the rest.'

9

Cordelia, Norah, Elsie, Peg. Was my mother writing her autobiography through the choosing of our names? In between came Allen and Frank: the clues are less obvious there.

The young mother of Cordelia adored her clever husband, believed in his genius and fostered it. The young mother of Cordelia was still the daughter of her own father, a country doctor who relished the role accorded to him in that place, at that time. The young mother of Cordelia was also the daughter of her own mother, almost certainly a manic depressive who shamed her doctor husband by her protracted inability to get well because he wished it.

The still-young mother who gave birth to a second daughter, Norah, had to struggle a little to make ends meet. No real shortages, but she had reason enough for anxiety in the face of a steady trickle of letters which in one way or another expressed reluctance to respond appropriately to the genius inventions of her husband.

A lifetime's worth of hours spent in his laboratory, building tiny models, making intricate mathematical calculations, pursuing perfection, painstakingly moulding metals and envisaging how fine machinery could work ever more efficiently. And too often as many, though far less happy hours, spent in conversation with cautious manufacturing men upon whose investment courage he had necessarily to depend.

Is that how my mother saw it? Did her increasing exclusion from his life wear her down? Or too many births? Though they seem not to be at the heart of the problem.

Could it be that the wearying woman who gave birth to Cordelia, Norah, Allen, Elsie, Frank and Peg (not blessed with Margaret but actually christened *Peg*) looked around her and saw mouths stretched wide open, like so many baby birds wanting to be fed? Could it be that she heard her husband's legitimate complaints, and attempted to fill up his bucket of confidence from the empty pail of her own? Could it be that when her own mother grew ill and quickly died she listened to the woes of her father and cried with him for the loss of the girl he had married, and his grief for the distraught wife she had become, but did not make time to grieve herself, for the mother she had long before lost?

And where was God in that? Once prayed to regularly, sung to in rousing low-church hymns, invoked readily in conversation with faith and love. But then not there? Like a disgraced family member of whom suddenly no one should speak. As though silence could do anything but intensify the absence. An absence of God in the soul of a believer. I feel pity for my mother. I want to reach across the decades to say how sad I am for her. No more hymns. No more Bible stories or heroic tales of Christian fortitude told to her children. No more confident reminders that in times of confusion or insufficiency we could trustingly turn to God. No more heated, emphatic reassurances that she knew that God knew what was best.

I guess it is fair to speculate that as her own children grew in size as well as in number their needs must have seemed more complicated and, perhaps quite suddenly, impossible for her to meet. Especially without God's help.

A devastating loss occurred for my mother. I am sure of it. But it is the particularity of the loss that I am haunted by and can't locate.

Finding response and meaning in the then-blue eyes of her first infant daughter she surely believed that this welcome child would have a charmed life. Named – or was I? – for poor foolish Lear's discarded, misunderstood daughter. What unconscious prophecy did she wield in that?

Or named, perhaps, only for the music of the name, a joyful tumble of letters that assured Nell how magnificent she would be in her maternity; that she would be generous with her time and interest; that she could, as easily as she breathed, be rich in love as her own intermittently mad mother had never been; that she would in all her modesty as well as in her skill be inspiring to behold.

That her husband would, looking at her, see in her not only the perfect wife but the perfect mother to his children also.

Yet neither his search for perfection in his workroom, nor her mirroring search for perfection in the home, could ever have been acknowledged between them, much less articulated. Even to have given shape to it in thought would have seemed immodest in the extreme: a threat to the gods – hubris for which they could only be punished. As, in many ways, they were.

Reconstructing in my own mind something to resemble that passionate idealism, I can more readily understand her gradual but persistently increasing sense of emptiness as her impossible vision slipped away in the face of real-life fatigue and conflict, disappointment and a gargantuan capacity for self-blame. Unable to look at the reflection of her imagined inadequacy in her children's eyes, or what she dreaded to read into her husband's worried concern, Nell turned to the safety of work that unfailingly needed to be done, of routines from which she could not be cast adrift.

The head turned away. The constancy of tasks unfolding. That is what I am forced by repetition to remember when I think back to find my mother. Yet it was not a drudge whose gaze met mine on my first day of life, who held me with pride in her arms, who offered me to her husband like a prize: 'Look at *our* invention!', then took me back to shelter against her body and to suck what I needed from her breasts.

It was certainly not a drudge who had captivated my clever, desirable father and who had sung as she walked back down the aisle with him on her own wedding day.

The bride: high-coloured, smooth-haired and girl-slim, expensively and stylishly dressed in billowing satin and lace. The groom: his look more dappled, reddish browns in hair, skin, glowing with good health and pride. His moustache and beard neatly tailored, his borrowed clothes immaculately pressed.

The couple have turned, are walking back down the long church filled on either side with relatives and friends, all just as it should be and then, suddenly, her voice, elevated almost unnaturally and carrying right around the church. So much breath available in the slight body, despite corsets, despite her own excitement and nerves, and eventually her laughter at her own glorious audacity. Singing, at her own wedding!

I couldn't resist it, she said, when pressed to expand the story. *I heard the organ and this had, after all, been promised to me as the happiest day of my life. I loved to sing and it felt impossible not to do so. I had to join in. And perhaps I had even anticipated it. I sang the 'Ode to Joy'! Imagine that! I sang it! I had insisted that the organist should play the 'Ode to Joy' as we were leaving the church, and then there I was, singing aloud as he played and as your father and I walked together down the aisle, your father beside me, I leaning on his arm, and on the guests' faces such undisguised shock and only after several moments were any of them smiling.*

Remembering this story, I want to share it with Laurie.

Laurie. From being one among a small group of potters I like to work alongside, Laurie has become, quite unexpectedly, that most precious being: a friend.

It seems to have happened almost without my noticing it. Certainly without the hesitations and formalities and circlings I've become more used to as I've got older. Whatever magic has been put to use, I'm grateful for it. With Laurie, I am no longer alone. It's not merely her physical presence that gives me that cherished comfort. My aloneness is worse, if anything, with most people who are not and never will be George. Inexplicably, but wonderfully, this isn't the case with Laurie.

I told her about seeing myself strewn beneath the spreading branches of the tree. I hadn't meant to tell her. The story came tumbling out and I felt ashamed and startled as much by that impetuous lack of containment as by the awkward tale that I was telling. Laurie didn't say much. What a relief that was. She nodded a bit, clucked a bit, then got up from where we sat and made some tea. Welcome tea. But I felt sure she had heard what I was saying. What I hadn't said, too. What I had been too afraid and too ashamed to say: she heard that, I'm pretty sure of it.

Laurie is company. I am, when I am with her, befriended.

Laurie is interested in mothers. She has had two of her own. A birth mother and an adoptive one who is the person she refers to when she says — though she rarely does — 'Mother'.

Not only her own children but her sense of herself as a mother quite obviously dominates her thinking. It's through her maternity that she seems to experience the world. I have quickly learned that unlike many of her contemporaries she talks about her life reluctantly, though with most ease and animation when she talks about herself as a mother.

Drawing her out, I have been listening with increasing interest to her well-told stories of motherhood. Many of these tales are amusing or even, in Laurie's dry telling of them, hilarious. But sometimes between the lines I hear a different note: of fatigue or uncertainty. Where should she draw the boundaries between herself and her children? Between her children and her work? Between her needs and theirs? As key players in her fractured modern tale, when should they be asked to recognise limits, or needs in other people's lives and to consider and respond to them?

Their father, Guy, and his lover, Wynston, favour long discussions out of which consensus will, they believe, eventually arise.

It sounds convincing, and reasonable. Laurie is less sure. Directions continue to be appropriate, she believes, even orders, sometimes. 'Not just appropriate, necessary,' I say rather pompously, and am warmed when she looks at me gratefully.

Then I realise that I must in all honesty add, 'Not that I would know. Too old. Times have changed. And no children of my own.'

She hasn't ever asked about that. She doesn't now. Good girl.

We are eating as we talk, a delicious Greek salad laden with olives and sharp cheese, along with tiny pungent slices of Italian sun-dried tomatoes and generous slices of prosciutto on great chunks of French bread. Bits of Europe lie on the table ready to be gorged. Laurie puts down her bread, and tidies a pile of olives onto a corner of her plate. The plate is from Spain I notice, not entirely inconsequentially.

'You are not that old,' she begins, untruthfully. Clearly wanting to say something quite else.

I wait, curious, but not too curious to fail to notice how much I am enjoying the salty taste of the ham mixing with the squash of unsalted butter against the hard crust of bread. Perhaps I am, indeed, not yet that old! At least, I observe with considerable gratitude, I am squashing and chewing with my own faithful teeth.

'Could you stand a few days with them? I wanted to ask you.' She hesitates and, uncharacteristically, avoids my eyes. Laurie is keen on eye contact that is rather more intense than even George would have chosen. It is one of several things about her that reminds me that her social customs are different from mine. She was not, after all, even born until about the time I was beginning to wither and turn brown at my edges.

My mother's ideas of what was possible; my own; Laurie's: how different each would be, and yet it is not only the differences that intrigue me. It is what also remains the same. Hesitation, reserve, prickliness. A sense of waiting. But for what? There is not time to speculate about this now, for Laurie is still speaking.

'I want to ask you if you'd like to come to stay for a couple of days in the little beach cottage I jointly own. To be honest – if I must! – I only own it for a few weeks a year. It's not at all glamorous but the beds don't squeak or smell and the landscape on that stretch of coast is spectacular. Do you know it? Wild seas. Rocks the size of elephants. Rock pools. Old trees that tickle the sky. All kinds of birds. And quiet. Lots of kinds of quiet, too. Quiet with ocean sounds; quiet laced with wind in the trees, and quiet-enough-to-hear-the-mouse. Well, it's that quiet when the children are asleep! I'd planned to go during the holidays when I usually try to take the children away. Then I thought . . . well, I hate to think of you alone.'

I wonder about that. She knows perfectly well that being alone is not what haunts me. She is also aware that I am less and less often leaving the house for any reason at all. I have taken to having deliveries of most of what I need which I had thought was a thing of the past but which I now discover is still possible – if only for spendthrifts.

Unsure where I am going, or being led, I respond, rather aimlessly. 'Yes, or rather, no. You must not worry about my being alone. I rather like it,' I lie. 'And am even thinking of getting on a little more vigor-ously with the heap of tasks that champ at the bit for me in George's study.' Which is true enough. 'You must not regard me quite yet as a delicate old crock.'

Laurie flushes. 'Cordelia, there you go again. You are still calling yourself an old crock and I am beating about the proverbial bush. Of course I know only too well you can look after yourself. That isn't the point. The point is me. Or, rather, that I would like to have the pleasure of your company somewhere other than six inches from your kitchen sink, charming though your kitchen sink, and indeed your kitchen, is. Are. Whatever!'

As she speaks, Laurie is leaning towards me. Her usual composure is momentarily absent. She is staring at me intensely. Her eyes are bright.

How dense people can be, even old people. Perhaps especially old people. With a rather sinking feeling of familiar failure, I realise, reluc-tantly, that Laurie is not merely offering me her warmth and company that I have been greedily willing to accept. She is also asking me for something. Lost in my memories and feeling perhaps overly needy of recovering memories, I have failed to recognise this or see it coming.

The sense of *disappointing* floods me. It's an old, old enemy; I know its every face.

And I know the war that immediately ensues: my own needs ranged up against another's. My needs now are to reflect, to walk not in a new, unknown place, but through the familiar territory of my own thoughts. My mind tips forward, then rocks back.

George.

Nell, my mother. Griffin, my father.

My sisters: Norah, Elsie and Peg. Elsie not well, vague before she should be. Norah's and Peg's children, their husbands. Their grandchildren.

My brothers' families; my brothers themselves: tall thin Frank, the judge; tall round Allen, the businessman.

Still-living friends who ring or write or call around. Still-living friends who simply beam the odd message of awareness through the airwaves.

Dead friends, not forgotten. Treasured sometimes in quick flashes and mourned in other slower moments.

Books to be read or re-read. Poems. An infinite number of poems still to be discovered or read anew. The concentrated intensity of poetry suits my stage of life. No time and energy to waste on what doesn't matter in content or in form. George's poet Tagore to be taken up – not where George left off, but wherever I find myself meeting him, taken on somewhere or somehow further than my current second-hand acquaintance.

The Bhagavad Gita. Tao Teh Ching. The Dhammapada. *Memories, Dreams, Reflections*: surely it would help me to re-read that? Christ's own teaching in whichever gospel might turn out to be most palatable. Then on to Julian of Norwich? I could do with some of her robust certainty and sublime joy.

Handel's *Messiah*. Bach's *St Matthew Passion*. God-in-music. Hildegarde of Bingen. That talented girl, Emma Kirkby, singing centuries-old music like an angel, bringing ecstasy into my body through the heart.

Brahms' and Beethoven's violin concertos. For heaven's sake, Mozart's first violin concerto! Strauss's *Four Last Songs*. *Figaro*. *Cosi*. Bits of Mahler, effortlessly reached with the editing tools of modern technology whisking from one highlight track of a CD to another. If only one could do that with one's own internal meanderings: skip the boring bits and go straight on to the next refreshing thought.

Graham Duncan, the solicitor. George's will. *Thy will be done* — while I am still on earth.

The causes. The charities. Without George they surely need even more flamboyant cheques than usual. I can do that much at least. I have also been toying with the idea of accepting one or two of the kind invitations to replace George on his favourite committees. Should I ever again feel easy about leaving this house.

The garden. Petra has worked there for years, her hours changing with the demands of the seasons, freed from a sheltered workshop and blossoming as George's right-hand garden woman. Slow, at one with nature as some so-called retarded people can be, she will stay on here to weed and sow and water and sing and chatter to the plants as long as I am alive, but I will also need a decision-making gardener. And why not? In these awful times of decreasing employment some regular well-paid hours in George's garden could be a delight for the right person. Working alongside Petra.

Which takes me to my own work.

My pots. For several nights now I have been seeing pots in my dreams.

Back to talk of Africa in these dreams, oddly enough. Some much plainer shapes again, graceful and steadfast in their simplicity. Or so they seem with my eyes shut. George's loyalty to the less-pleasing period was impeccable, but there's no denying he would find these sturdy objects easier to admire. My hands are beginning to itch. Thoughts and drawings can take me so far, then I have literally to feel my way through the next stages, allowing my hands and the clay itself to guide me.

And God? Whatever or whoever. I still want to know. Is that what I am asking Tagore to do? To help me to know God? Or if not to know, then at least to experience whatever I can of something I don't know what else to call but divine love. I have glimpsed it, like a blink, a few times; or at least, I think I have. But that, perhaps more than anything, needs quiet time, solo spaces. Not coming at the end of a list either. Imbuing everything. *The world is charged with the grandeur of God.* Hopkins, not Tagore. *The world is charged with the grandeur of God.* Look around, Cordelia. Just in your own garden would do: look around.

I have drawn the walls of my world right in since George died. I have been huddling. Enough! The very word *grandeur* sets my spine a little straighter. Which takes me to karma yoga. Meditation through doing one's dishes; meditation through throwing one's pots. It feels more real to me than sitting. Bringing awareness of God into the every-day. Breathing God in and breathing God out. That kind of practice seems possible, though less possible to talk about. Even to Laurie. Even in the leisure of long walks by the sea, out of earshot of her two charming, vital, rowdy children.

This seems quite the wrong time to leave this kitchen for several days on end, or even one or two. Yet when I turn my attention outwards from this long litany of thoughts, when I actually turn from myself to look at Laurie and hold her hands in both of mine, and attempt to explain this, I am horrified to see Laurie's face fall, almost as a child's might at the refusal of a treat, and I feel sorry, sorry, sorry that it is not in me to give this generous woman whatever she believes she is needing.

Cordelia seems to have such difficulty taking herself seriously.

I could swear that in the days when George was alive she would sometimes stand there, an astonishingly strong, dramatic presence, *behind him*. Whether she was actually physically behind him it would be hard for me to say now with certainty. It seems unlikely. Yet there was, and to some extent still is, some odd way in which she tried to crawl under the carpet of her husband's enormous personality, apparently unaware of that enormous personality or presence she has of her own. It mystified me at first and then later made me quite angry. I guess it also confused me. It seemed obvious that if anyone could afford to take centre stage it would be Cordelia, yet there she was, peeping around the metaphorical edge of George's glowing moments with his admiring public.

As long as I've known about Cordelia Fraser I have admired her.

It's been an odd experience. I'm not especially given to hero worship from afar. Generally I like pleasures I can trust and which are absolutely close to hand. That's the Taurus in me: charging at things, head down, but determined to have them right now and here on Earth. It's definitely not my style to wait for the hereafter.

Yet from the first time that I heard about Cordelia I knew I wanted to meet her, even though now, several years later, I'm still not quite sure what set that off. I am usually reserved with strangers and in the presence of rich, old, relatively famous strangers I would normally rather disappear than in any way push myself forward.

It wasn't like that with Cordelia.

Did I see her pots even before I heard about Cordelia herself? That may well have been it. Those weird, wild, anarchic pots she produces ensnared me. I couldn't believe my eyes when I first saw them. They were part of a group exhibition put on by three or four people. The others were probably better known at that time than Cordelia herself. It was a smart gallery; all the work was elegantly displayed, but I couldn't take my eyes away from Cordelia's array. Looking at those pieces you'd have to believe they'd been *carved* out of clay rather than potted, and probably by a self-promoting male *artist*, obnoxious to his last pore on the personal front but bursting with confidence and talent on the art front and able to get away with murder.

Then you find out that they've been made by this reserved, grand old woman whose very posture reminds you that you haven't straightened your shoulders for years. Who does straighten their shoulders these days, for heaven's sake!

There is no sense to it. That's what's intriguing. Wild, challenging work. Elegant, stately woman. And a good deal older than I am. That got me in, too. I was utterly bowled over by the freshness of that work, the youthfulness of that work: I guess that gives me hope. It doesn't all have to be now, or before I'm forty, or sixty, or seventy.

Who was she, this woman? Who were they, this couple?

Cordelia. The wife standing *behind* George. The better I know her, the less I can believe that memory. Yet it persists and rankles, even now.

George. Always unfailingly charming and lively so that it was impossible not to adore him and to feel stirred and flattered by his attention even when you knew that was truly ridiculous. But sometimes when I'd had my few minutes with them both, I would go home mad. Mad that somehow or other and yet again I hadn't got a word in to Cordelia and perhaps hadn't heard a word from her either beyond the murmurings of her unfailing politeness. She did and does, however, specialise in piercing *looks*. Her oddly flat green eyes are the colour of lichen.

Her pupils stand out against that green and it is almost possible to see them expand and contract. As though that wasn't enough, they really do seem to *connect* with yours and she holds your gaze much longer than most people could ever manage. I'm not sure if she realises how disconcerting it is, or is for me anyway. She certainly betrays no obvious awareness that the effect is delicious. 'I'm deeply suspicious of charm,' I've heard her say. 'It's a kind of untruth.' She's said that not once, but in several versions several times. Each time I found the statement shocking. My generation is really rather short on charm, and I regret that. What's even more confusing is that Cordelia is so charming herself: at least in my reading of her. And George was super-charming. But I guess they are, or he was, charming through and through. Who they *are* is charming, therefore they do not need to charm.

Or is that true? Whatever Cordelia truly feels about her charm, and about her piercing looks, I know they hit me like an electric bolt to my stomach. Or worse, straight between the legs; though I'd die rather than have her know.

Electric bolts can be addictive. Especially when they're in short supply. I have always made absolutely sure that I hover well within eyeshot. I've had my share of looks, and more than my share probably.

And I've got my share of smiles. When Cordelia smiles it really is possible to see the girl she once was. Her smile is absolutely dazzling and absolutely fresh. I find the sense of continuity that smile displays extraordinarily affecting.

Sometimes I look at my own daughter Rhea when she smiles and I think, 'You could still have that same smile when you're old, when nothing much else is the same but that lovely way your lips move and light up your whole face and whoever is watching you.' The promise that thought offers is immensely reassuring. Like the idea that you can go on working and not grow repetitive or stale.

Cordelia's smiles move across a face that is softened and crumpled by age. Her skin is like tissue paper, like the softest, most delicate tissue paper that's almost more gorgeous when crumpled and re-used than when new. But the smile leaps out from a different time zone entirely.

Guy says, with rather an unpleasantly hectoring edge to his voice, 'Laurie, *surely* you must see that you idealise Cordelia? Certainly she's an interesting and probably quite remarkable older woman but *surely* she's not the marvel you proclaim her to be?'

I'm not sure why he's saying that. Why should he be so bloody *sure*? Why the hell shouldn't she be a marvel? God knows we need a few real live marvels. And why, come to think of it, with such implicit criticism in his manner, does he rant on that she is the ideal older woman I want to become myself? I don't even think that's true. I could never be a Cordelia and don't believe I'd want to be, which doesn't in any way detract from my fascination with her. Maybe Guy's saying it because he's prickly about his own mother who is almost exactly Cordelia's age but is as different from her as it would be possible to be: amusing and generous when she chooses, but also invasive, unreflective and sometimes hideously sentimental. And not an artist. Not a feminist. And definitely not *sexy*.

Maybe it's that. In some dim way – because certainly it would be impossible for him to admit it – maybe Guy's jealous that I can idealise someone else considerably more successfully than I ever idealised him? Could he care?

He's been with Wynston for five years, maybe longer. They are undoubtedly a much tighter and more devoted couple than Guy and I ever managed to be. Yet Guy is a sponge when it comes to admiration. Soaks it up and there's always room for more. It's one of the many things I found exhausting and eventually repulsive when he and I were together, but Wynston apparently doesn't. Wynston adores admiring Guy, and Guy adores Wynston for admiring him so lavishly. Clearly it's a marriage made in admiration heaven, and they're welcome to it.

Perhaps Guy's irritated by the sheer preciousness of my admiration for Cordelia. It is fun of course. Worshipping from afar offers its own peculiar delights. I can hang on Cordelia's every word, and treasure those words at a time of my own choosing. I can read what I want into any snippet of interest she shows in me or my work. Then, while I clean or shop or peel the potatoes or endlessly run round after the kids, I can sneakily and safely juggle my thoughts about Cordelia.

Even when I'm sketching out my ideas, I can fantasise about what Cordelia will think of what I'm doing. It feels good. I haven't wanted that kind of input before. I have worked well as my own judge and jury, but I like the idea of some sharing with her. I respect her own work so much. And, unlike Guy, I know that Cordelia would never attack me or undermine me for the bitchy pleasure of it. It wouldn't even occur to her. She'd probably be shocked that two people could have lived together and one was not able to turn to the other for some respect and support.

She has said she'll buy some pieces from me. I'd like to give her some. Although in that wonderful house . . . but perhaps she will enjoy their acidic flavour even more in that house. After all, her own pieces in no obvious way derive from that tall, elegant house, which is very much like Cordelia in shape. She fits that house and that house fits her. They have been together for a long time and it shows.

She got all the support she needed from George. I am confident about that. It is impossible not to think of Cordelia's work without also remembering how eloquently and at what length George went on about her pieces, about their shape and range of colour, about their contrasts and neat tricks of technical this and that.

While he spoke, she would stand there. She would stand there and smile and seem to be totally present and at exactly the same time there would also be an odd absence that made you wonder if she wasn't a million miles away. Then, occasionally, she would become completely animated. She would move out of that stillness and begin talking on and on in that deep, posh voice of hers that sends shivers of pleasure up and down my spine, that delicious melodious deep-pitched voice that I could never, ever hear often enough. But only about George, or George's work! Never was a man more aptly named: St George to the rescue. There, in front of him, she would suddenly stir to life and give this illuminating rap about whatever horror here or there in the world George was currently instrumental in relieving. How *important* it is that we under-stand it. How *crucial* it is that we all act. How vital that we know what is *really* going on and not accept the scraps the media choose to throw us. We must write letters, she would tell us. We must push for this reform or that one. We must know exactly who to write our letters to, and she was the one who would tell us.

It was just so quirky: such passionate, immediate rhetoric coming from a reserved, privileged woman. But that contradiction is Cordelia all over. It fascinates me. *She* fascinates me. On and on she'd go, and I would be lost in the pleasure of the sound of that malt-whisky voice and the mere fact of Cordelia talking in such a stream and would have to pinch and push myself into awareness so that if anyone else failed to do it I could give her the kind of response that might encourage her to continue. Or which might encourage her to talk about herself, which is what I really wanted.

And why wouldn't she? Sewn-up, says Guy. But he doesn't know her. He's met her for any decent length of time only once or twice and like most people, or certainly most people our age, I guess he mistakes her reserve for aloofness or even arrogance. He's twitchy about what she thinks of him, too, I'm sure, although he'd never admit that. Maybe he even wonders what I have told her about him. May he sweat!

I thought she was utterly charming with him, and with Wynston. Leading them both around the garden with glasses of champagne in their hands, introducing them to the plants, shrubs and trees she likes best while I walked lamely behind trying to keep the children in some sem-blance of order. Then watching, moved almost to tears when she was pressing early lily of the valley and a great bunch of parsley on them to take home.

It's hard bringing parts of your life together and, for all my reser-vations about Guy, I had wanted her to like them. I had wanted them to think well of her, too. The children do like her. Gregory calls her

Fruit Cordial, perhaps inevitably, and Rhea has taken up the name as well, but they sense she is someone special for me and I am sure they really do like her.

Wynston has been careful, too. Asking me enough questions to express his awareness that he knows it is delightful and frightening to feel something special about someone, but not so much as to trivialise my feelings or his interest. There've been no remarks or innuendos about her age either, or mine. Wynston's a good man.

Guy can be damned stupid sometimes, and lacking in generosity. His paternal grandmother was Chinese and Guy inherited a noticeably Eastern look. With that comes an illusory aura of calm and knowingness. Buddha gone hip. Guy is well aware of it, I'm quite sure of that. It sucked me in: the steady gaze from densely brown, almond-shaped eyes; the soft skin and voice to match; the grace of a slim, finely balanced body. Almost feminine, but at the deciding point, quite definitely masculine.

I can still admire all that, but over the years it has become much harder to admire the man inside.

In those first unsettled days and weeks after George died I was afraid that Cordelia might stop potting. I was afraid of this not so much for her but, God forgive me – as Guy's Mum is given to saying – because I would then be without an excuse to see her. I knew how marginal I was to whatever really sustained her. One of half a dozen potters welcome to use her first-rate facilities. One of what seemed like a host of fascinating friends of all ages and types who would certainly have far greater claim on her than I would dare make. My skills as a potter are exceptionally good and she knows that; and I can be warm and amusing and careful and caring. But how was I to judge if she needed that, or had even noticed me as someone with any particular qualities she is looking for among our potting crowd?

Who indeed knows what goes on in the private recesses of Cordelia's life? The social floors of their tall, narrow house are the two lower ones. These are largely occupied by their gorgeous big kitchen and a rarely used formal dining room on the ground floor and a sitting room on the first floor that manages to be spacious and intimate at the same time. Spacious because it is a big, traditionally shaped room with long, formal windows at either end. Intimate because it is so colourfully decorated: walls, curtains, cushions complementing – but in no formal way *matching* – furniture, paintings, lamps, *objets* – including big and little statues from the East, India I suppose, though maybe Indonesia and Thailand too – that are invariably stunning and personal, even sometimes quite quirky. They could only have been chosen with love. There are a couple of bathrooms, too. One big, one little. Also colourful, light, dashing. It's intrigued me to notice that Cordelia decorates them with lavish vases of fresh flowers that are often more copious than those used in the more obvious rooms for flower arrangements.

Despite all that space and detail, there are still two more floors above those 'public' floors and they have come to seem to me to represent in some unfathomable way what you simply cannot know or pry into with Cordelia. Parts of her mind are like that too: shut off from public viewing. One can almost see a little gold rope marking the boundary, and a discreet notice warning off the hoi polloi.

Maybe I shouldn't be too pessimistic, though. In recent weeks the situation has changed for the better.

After those first few times when I came around after George's death, then later with Tom or Angie or Gudrun, and when it slowly became clear that although she wasn't herself working, it was fine if we worked here, it was then I began to feel safe.

I also realised that I was moving like a wild kitten wanting to be tamed, into her house. *Her* house. The garden had been my patch before, and the studio of course that is almost part of the garden, as open and light as it is. And separate. Then, as though for a kitten, bowls of milk in the shape of cups of tea, or simply a prominent kettle, were left out and I went lapping, licking, following their trail, allowing myself to rest, briefly, on one of many brightly coloured cushions lying on wooden chairs, or to lean, gingerly, against the sweep of red formica benches, or to hover, cautiously, until such moment as the mistress of the house might emerge and favour me with a word so I could relax and purr.

Shamelessly, I even left offerings to lure her kitchenwards. I'm such a boring cook but Wynston is brilliant and I would carefully divide some of the casseroles he regularly cooks for us all into a dish to tempt Cordelia.

She enjoyed them, too, and I've found myself unable to admit yet that Wynston is the talented cook, not me. 'Laurie,' she praised, 'you clever kind girl. It looks wonderful. How did you manage it? The colour of the food perfectly complements the colour of the dish! Should I eat up the dish also, do you think? You are spoiling me!'

I really do want her to think well of me. I want to hear her say again, 'Laurie, you clever kind girl . . .'

No one in my world ever calls grown-up women girls. But Cordelia isn't patronising me. I don't feel that for a minute. Or if she is, I like it! I like being 'her girl' and, absolutely at the same time, my own woman. Then, to my complete amazement, I realised that the kitten was being asked in, was being asked to stay to eat; that the kitten's company was being sought and was regarded as something not kittenish for patting, but grown-up, supportive, even desirable. Well, maybe *desirable* is going a little too far, but desired certainly. Wine was being poured for me. Delicacies were being offered to me with style and tenderness. With a care too long absent in my independent, coping life, I might add. I was, with my strong, stubby, craftswoman fingers, picking up and unfolding an ironed linen napkin, lifting to my lips heavy Prague crystal, tasting wines that owed much to George's wily cellaring. My nostrils were assailed by the delicate smell of scented candles, of excellent coffee, and occasionally of Cordelia herself as she bent to serve or take away.

All this. For me?

And, so close I could reach out to her, sits Cordelia. She is laughing at my stories. She wants to know more about my children. When I tell her, briefly, about two dead adopting parents and one briefly traced then lost birth mother, grief and pain *on my behalf* rearrange her face. Expanding my repertoire of Guy and Wynston stories, I find she remembers details from other times and asks me questions. *She wants to know.* My children grow more singular than ever as she laughs at stories I share about their lives. I boast and she laughs, encouraging my boasting, understanding better now why I am boasting about those two untamed, precious monsters I love more than life itself. Who are life itself. Cordelia cares. Cares! My ordinary life is suddenly perky, novel, cause for lively conversation.

Cycling home, I sing. *Who are the witches? Where do they come from? Maybe your great-great grandmother was one!* It's Rhea's favourite – which I cherish as a good sign that I am raising a feminist daughter. I whistle tunelessly and very loud. I take my hands off the handlebars and race, foolishly fast, down through the tunnel of night between her home and my own.

And then I almost blew it.

Taking my time, using words I had carefully chosen and rehearsed, shedding all off-putting intensity, or so I thought, I asked Cordelia if she would like to come away for a few days. Away with the kids and me. I hoped the children would be a bonus. Making it easy for her to be both companionable and private in the hurly-burly of their presence. I guessed that on my own I might seem a little much, or the situation might seem a little too intense.

'I could drive us all, Cordelia.' Was I pleading? Shit. 'We could keep the children more or less quiet with some new tapes and bribes of McDonald's on the way. You could rest as we drive and I can guarantee that the land around the house really is remarkable. Those big trees that surround the place I think of as stately guardians. They're not at all put out though when we sling up our hammocks and sink into them with a gin and tonic and a sigh.'

Hardly had I got my lightweight words out than Cordelia went into her numb mode. Even as I watched, she was disappearing from where we had just sat together. She was absent like she often used to be when she stood behind George. But George wasn't here to cover up the space or add heat or whatever vital ingredient was suddenly missing. There was only an awful silence and a big loud voice shouting in my head telling me that I had overstepped the mark, and had presumed where I should not have. Pushed when I should have waited to be led forward, if at all, if ever, by Cordelia herself.

At last, but quite slowly, she focused back on me. She turned her famous look on me, but not quite the version of it I had seen before. She looked sad, and motionless. She looked ancient like a crone and as young as a new child. It was weird. I have never seen a look like it. It was completely mesmerising. I stared back at her. There wasn't any choice. Anyway, it was what I wanted to do. I was drawn into her eyes. There wasn't any need to shift my gaze, and even when she took my hands into her own, I just sat, staring at her and soaking her up.

She did say something, but afterwards I had no idea what it was exactly. I know she isn't coming away with us. I know I mustn't push for more than I'm already getting. I also feel sure for the first time since I have known her that she won't disappear. At that strange moment of saying no she was also saying yes to having me somewhere in her life, and not just for five minutes either.

I tried to talk about this to Gudrun. It all seemed a bit much to keep to myself. Beneath her cynic's rhetoric Gudrun's a real romantic – and a mid-life crisis veteran – so I felt sure that she would hear what I was describing through all my nervous hesitations. Yet she didn't. Or I could say so little, when it came to it, that the event made almost no sense at all.

Halfway through I turned it into a funny story, inviting Gudrun to laugh as she imagined how absurd it would have been to plant best-posture Cordelia in the just-habitable shack that we nobly call a cottage.

Gudrun did laugh, good friend that she is. Then, when she most obligingly opened a bottle of decent wine, I drank a glass or two quickly, sprawled out lavishly in my chair, helped myself to a generous handful of nuts and began without effort to talk of other things.

11

How hollow a house can feel when it is empty of people, or when its people are lost to sleep. Even the shape of rooms may change: some shrink, almost cower in the darkness; others expand with silent night-time secrets. In the darkness the shapes of the furniture become ambiguous as they slip away from duty. A tiny, dropped silver ornament lies buried in a thick rug. Sharp, rigid: it is a trap for the unwary. Cut flowers stand warily in vases; their next move is not a pleasant one. Clocks go steadily forward, choiceless, and tick, unobserved and unheard. Wisps of dust unite in corners.

Behind Cordelia's tall house, the long, narrow garden resembles an elongated shadow to the building and stretches considerably further than the eye can see, although by day the high brick back wall is only a glance away. The glass roof of the studio, and its tall plain windows, catch whatever light the clouds allow and the moon can give.

Petra has left her tools lying on the ground outside. They are damp, and at risk of rust.

Petra and George were in the habit of putting their tools away together. At the end of an afternoon's chores if George was home he would always come to admire what Petra had done, if he hadn't already worked alongside her. Among Petra's many gifts is a capacity to delight in the ordinary: to see the ordinary and extraordinary as one. 'Look, George, look at the size of these pumpkin plant flowers! Big as plates, eh George? And the leaves, too,' Petra would say. Or, 'Manure and mulch spread everywhere today, George. Compost too. Smells good, eh? Better than perfume!' Or, 'No more green bugs on the roses, George! All squashed on my jeans now! Good and squashed.' Or, 'Parsley and beans and carrots for you today, George. All fresh for you and Cordelia, all taste fresh for you.'

'Splendid, Petra,' George would reply, beaming. 'You must take home some flowers and veg for your household too. You'll enjoy them just as much as we will. You've done a magnificent job, as always. As always, Petra. This garden is a slice of heaven in your care.'

'In my care, eh George! It's Petra's garden as well as George's garden, eh?'

'Certainly, it's Petra's garden. Now what about Petra's cup of tea, and Petra's several biscuits? I know I'm starving, and parched for my tea. I could drink a potful in a single gulp! First, however, we must put our tools away. What do you say? Dry them off, and put them away. First things first, and next things next.'

'First first, then next next!' Petra would echo, striding towards the shed alongside George.

Their routines, in the garden, in their conversations, and in their tea-time afterwards, rarely changed. Each played their part and treasured the part the other played. Petra misses George. She misses him every day she comes here even though she still loves the garden and loves the care she gives it.

Cordelia tries to make up for George's absence. She also frequently and lavishly admires Petra's work, and after Petra has finished her day she often makes her tea and puts out a generous array of biscuits, just as George did. But she doesn't always say the same things that Petra became used to hearing. Sometimes she says new things, or asks too many questions. Petra misses her cues, and misses the joy of knowing exactly what it is her turn to say and when she should say it.

She has talked about George a lot to her friend Carol who runs the group home where Petra lives. Petra knows that George has gone to heaven. Their garden was a kind of heaven. 'A slice of heaven,' as Petra explained to Carol, but there's another heaven too, a heaven that is always light and always early summer, and that real heaven is a good place to be, but Petra often wishes George hadn't gone there. If she could have her way George would be in the slice of heaven of their own garden with her.

She can't say any of this to Cordelia. She can't even speak about it to Carol as she would like to. In her own way she has told the plants and trees; that will have to do.

Next to the tools which Petra abandoned, meaning to go back for them and then almost at once forgetting, lie a pair of worn thick leather gardening gloves. They are stained and rather stiff from having dried too often in the sun. They used to be George's gloves. These days Petra wears them.

Back inside the house, in the kitchen, a small pile of rinsed, unwashed dishes is neatly stacked in the sink. The dishwasher seems too large to use when there's been only one for dinner. A couple of books lie opened, text-side down, on the kitchen table, next to a crumpled napkin and a pot of tomato relish. During extended solitary mealtimes, Cordelia is currently moving between V.S. Naipaul's *India* and Sibylle Bedford's *A Favourite of the Gods*. She has read the Bedford several times. With luck, she will live long enough to come to it reasonably fresh at least once more.

Naipaul's version of India bears little resemblance to her own; a man from another place and another race, it's necessarily different from George's version also. It is for that difference that she reads, even while she acknowledges, smiling wryly, that one of the great pleasures of travel writing – of any writing if it comes to that – is that you need be with your chosen companion for not one moment longer than you wish.

Light begins its move into the house. From the unencompassable sky outside a ribbon of light descends, edging its way slyly between curtains that have been carelessly drawn, coming in more boldly where a window is bare to receive it. Light comes in transformed through the stained glass of the front door, spilling little pools of faint green, red and yellow onto the polished boards of the long hall. In Cordelia's bedroom the off-white linen curtains create almost no distance between outside and in. Light falls like a ribbon across Cordelia's bed, pulling her away from sleep, though not yet waking her.

The house gets ready for a new day. Rooms assume their more conventional proportions. Furniture settles down to match shape with function. Birds sit and shit in black and white on the glass roof of the studio and then, freer, swoop down to the green untidy grass beneath the spreading trees to catch their early worms.

1 2

The dreams are making me frightened to sleep.

I have always loved to sleep and have often been reluctant to wake. George rarely seemed to mind that I frequently went to bed an hour or two before he did and got up an hour or two later.

Perhaps even more than sleeping I have loved the delicious moment of getting into our big wooden bed carved with fruit and flowers at either end, stretching out the full length of my body, enjoying the feel of the extravagant white damask bed linen that is among my least curbed indulgences, knowing that there is nothing else to claim my attention until morning, then reaching out to pick up any one of the several books I always have on the go, reading before drifting off on the journey towards morning.

These dreams are markedly different from any I had before George died. At first I wasn't worried. I didn't like them but I know that grief is an intense stress – who doesn't? – and that with stress often comes either a dampening down or a winding up of one's dream life. These particular dreams suggested to me that the latter was happening and I sensed there was little point in resisting.

But now, months later, the dreams seem to be growing in intensity and power, and not diminishing as I hoped they would. If only I could bring some daytime control to this night-time anarchy. If only I could slow them down, or even finish one because the lack of any apparent conclusion leaves me feeling needy and dreadfully unsettled.

If only I could rise up to the surface of my dreaming and shift into wakefulness with a single dream held in my mind intact and ready to be examined and then understood and perhaps, in that way, over with and neatly buried. Yet that is about as useful as wishing that one could quicken the dead. It just ain't on.

Night after night, back I go.

George and I are in our tail-end thirties. It is the beginning of what was to be the worst period of our marriage. George is drinking too much. I am probably drinking too little. I have become twitchy: pursed lips, tight, prickly to touch, certain of my opinions, sharp with my responses, easily offended.

I was minding getting older; I can understand that now. I am sure, too, that I am remembering it as clearly as I am in part because getting older is Laurie's current obsession, as I'm beginning to discover. The dear, beautiful girl looks freshly young to me, but not to herself it seems. 'I catch glimpses of myself in public windows or mirrors,' she confessed, as though to some singularly nasty habit, 'or I see photographs of myself taken when I haven't had a chance to arrange myself, and I think: is that squat, dumpy, middle-aged woman *me?*'

She did have the grace to blush when she told me this, and began to giggle when I spread my wrinkled, sun-spotted and richly veined hands on the table and insisted that she lie her own hands out flat next to mine. Her nails are neat but are cut painfully short. Her fingers are broad and strong. I thought to myself, 'I love your hands. I could trust those hands with my life.' The skin still wraps them tightly and smoothly. There's so much flap and excess once you begin to get seriously old, even on the bits that are scrawny.

Laurie could see what I was showing her and laughed again, and then, backtracking to save face, protested, 'It's different for you, Cordelia! You are so graceful or stylish or smart, or something that makes the ordinary rules that apply to the rest of us seem irrelevant in your case. Yes, of course by any conventional measure you are old, but it's a word that becomes intensely complimentary in your case. You transform it. Old. Older. Oldest. As in, good, better, best. Whereas with me . . . I feel that whatever fraction of beauty or even attractiveness I once had came from my liveliness, and that my liveliness was a reflection of my youthful zip and zap, and that without that the whole castle of blocks I call my life is shifting about or even tumbling.'

That was more than she had meant to say. And less amusing than she had intended to be. The giggling had stopped and there were tears in her voice. Her life isn't tumbling. We both know that. We have come to be able to speak often of how well she copes – and does better than cope. How well she keeps in balance the tugs and pulls and pushes and conflicts of parenting and housekeeping and pottery and some teaching; that's much more than merely 'coping'. None the less, something inside her hurts a lot and one doesn't need to be terribly wise in these matters to guess that perhaps it is her carefully maintained internal defences that are, just a little, 'tumbling'.

Maybe for too long she's been without admirers. Without someone touching her with wonder at the marvellous privilege of such proximity, or someone holding her with love. Someone who's not her own child. Or 'just' a friend, precious as friends always are. I haven't asked. I could be quite wrong. Maybe there is a lover tucked away somewhere. Yet somehow I doubt that, and not because she is in any way unlovable. On the contrary.

These speculations made me, too, momentarily teary, but it was not the time for that.

I stood to make tea, but before turning to that welcome task I stopped behind Laurie's chair, touched her shoulders, lightly, and then leaned forward to hold her head in my hands and to plant a kiss, right on the top of her head, leaving my lips there for a moment and enjoying the clean smell of her straight, shiny dark hair. As I began to edge away ever so slightly her hands came up and grasped mine, gently, and she held her head lightly and briefly against my belly. Laurie. She has the cleanest, sweetest smell always. It does me good to breathe her in.

Then, as all moments do, this precious moment passed and I straightened up slowly and moved away from her in the silence Laurie effortlessly allows. Moving away, I remembered, quite unexpectedly, one of the images that has been recurring in my troublesome dreams.

I am sitting here, in this space that wasn't then the kitchen. It was a rather clumsy sun-room affair attached to the back of the house. I am in a large white-painted cane easy chair that squeaked if one wriggled. My head is bowed. Perhaps it is even buried in my hands. I am alone in the house and am crying gracelessly, loudly, and I suspect with a mild degree of satisfaction. George has just left, spinning out through the long hall to the front door, leaving behind a trailing, pervasive vapour of exasperation and self-righteousness. I am assuming he will not be back. I whined at him when he came home an hour or so earlier, tired. I whined because I am bored or restless or I fear, with every reason to do so, that my life is wasting away on trivia and I am doing nothing to halt that erosion. George has tried to be patient. For five minutes anyway. But he is tired. Patience is in short supply. He is tired because he has spent much of this day and every day meeting other people's legitimate demands: being important, decisive and gracious.

Surely, it is easy to be gracious when you are, in your very being, in your status, your job, in other important people's minds and expectations of you, *impressive*?

And surely, surely, it is markedly more difficult to be gracious when you are not impressive at all, when you have no significant role to play, no view that others automatically want to hear, no experience to bring that is other than second-hand, or so I thought that bleak day as I wept and contemplated my immediate future as a husbandless-wife.

I should probably have contemplated my future as a professionless-woman, yet despite wide and reasonably intelligent reading, such thoughts then had little shape or force in my mind. 'Not part of the discourse,' is how Laurie would put it. 'Not part of what people generally talked about,' is how I'd more prosaically say it.

Of course some women friends of my own age and much older did have careers that could stand up against any man's. My best friend from school became a successful general surgeon. Evangeline, one of George's early girlfriends who became a friend to us both, eventually got the Chair she had long deserved in classics. Not insignificantly, however, both those women remained unmarried. Some married friends did work, but generally in 'jobs' rather than 'careers'.

Before my marriage, I had been a reasonably happy research assistant to a minor academic ambitious enough for both of us. He never questioned my apparent absorption in his goals, and I was rather short-sightedly delighted that my work was flexible enough to leave time for politics and absorbing enough that sometimes I would forget politics as I fastidiously leafed my way through one pile of papers and books in search of a tiny fact or reference, and then the next. Leaving that work had not felt like a loss. Once it was gone, I barely thought about it again. I missed the morning tea trolley more than the work, especially the array of sticky buns like rouged breasts. I never liked such buns before or since, but I liked them then, and the thick white mugs of strong tea twice daily.

Half a lifetime later, sitting down at my great sweep of a kitchen table, the kettle on but the tea not yet made, I am captured anew by the persistent dream image of that bleak afternoon: my younger self seeped in fear and self-pity.

For all its unattractive pathos, I wanted to share that image with Laurie.

'It wasn't only that I had no work to speak of,' I explained, as if talking of a time utterly remote and gone for ever, 'it was rather that I felt completely dispensable. Neither at home nor anywhere else was I remotely useful in any kind of singular way. I was busy all the time. I believed I had no time. But that activity was synthetic. What I was doing as George's wife could as well have been done by any sensible woman. It was as though whatever individuality I might once have had was utterly and irrevocably gone. On top of that, and feeding that, I knew that my youth was over, that the years of *becoming* had passed.

I was not becoming, I had arrived. And I didn't like my point of arrival. I didn't like what I saw on the outside and I didn't like the way that I felt on the inside. No more miscarriages was part of it. Too late even to risk those.'

I stopped speaking. My anecdote had left me feeling oddly upset.

In my recent dreaming, there is a great deal of reaching out with empty arms. Not just towards a baby who is not and will never be there. Some other more metaphysical goal is also remaining out of sight and out of reach. I can't find the words for it, or the shape of it, or even the sense of it. Yet I can almost taste the longing, and that taste is harsh and bitter in my mouth.

Grateful as I often am for a practical task, I picked among the Twinings royals and made Queen Mary tea, Laurie's favourite, put out some crumbly shortbread biscuits, piled all the necessaries onto the tray and put the tray on the table. Laurie, bless her, set out the mugs, lifted the gilded teapot and began to pour.

'My face had begun to crumple inwards,' I said, warming to my theme. 'Lines were taking up their positions across my forehead and down beside my mouth with all the glee of marching girls on parade. Even my once-firm arms had begun to sag . . . and as for my belly . . . the word can only be *slump*.'

I stopped to sip from the mug Laurie had put in front of me, and then went on, laughing now as Laurie was lapping up all this gruesome body detail, I could see. 'Packed pockets of flesh were beginning to be all-too visible. I had been eating too much and my stomach was plain fat. My thighs too. And across my back was a layer of fleshy softness, flab really, which was most repugnant of all to me. I had liked my bony back, and despised the lard that now covered it. I wasn't especially vain, I think it's true to say, but it had become impossible to lay the most tenuous claim to being svelte! Of course there weren't any fitness classes in those days. Not that I would have gone if there had been. What a notion! Some women – some of my friends – played tennis or swam, but that didn't appeal to me. I could neither hit a ball nor put my head under the water so those were yet two more areas to avoid if I was not to feel entirely useless. Other friends occasionally went somewhere off into the country and played golf but that seemed even worse somehow, an admission perhaps that one had run out of useful activities or had grown tired of reading or thinking or gardening or whatever it was I prided myself on doing in those days.'

Unexpectedly, I thought of my mother, Nell, almost always on her feet, and even when seated, still working, head lowered, hands moving. 'Golf and idleness were linked for me. Fitness wasn't a justification I could have swallowed. I feared idleness. Perhaps I still do.'

'Did George come back quickly? Did you make up at once?'

Laurie's question was perfectly reasonable of course, but lost less in drifts from my dreams than in only too vivid memories of my own female flesh plumping and slumping, I had forgotten George and his exasperated charge through the front door to freedom.

In fact I was startled altogether by the real-life anecdote that had provoked this discussion. I wanted to be alone to reach out, reach towards . . . I badly need to know what the dreams have not yet told me.

Avoiding Laurie's gaze, looking instead at the rather pleasing mixed-blue mug she held in her hands, one of my own earliest pieces, I said, truthfully, 'I can't remember exactly how things went. Obviously he did come back. We both know that. But was he angry? Was I forgiving, or forgiven? Gracious, or dependent on his grace? I'm afraid that I'm not at all sure now. It seemed to matter hugely at the time but have you also noticed how unpleasant times merge? How they bleed into each other, feed off each other and then either blow up or disappear so that their particularities are hard to recall?'

Laurie was disappointed. A generality wasn't going to do. I had omitted the punch line and clearly would have to try harder.

Eager to please, I moved back a step, looking inwards for a larger picture.

'Those were the seesaw years, I do know that, with some very bad lows and only rather mediocre highs, at least in our private times together.'

Our private times: I paused for thought. They had been required by me to justify almost my entire existence. But in those same years our private times were, for George, only erratically fulfilling pauses to recoup between jousts with what Really Mattered.

In our own circles, I was not the only wife who fretted and envied while I admired and supported what my husband did. But we wives didn't speak about this paradox except through jokes and codes, and even then we always returned to the lines we'd learned best: 'We mustn't complain. It's not too bad. So many others are much worse off.' As, indeed, they were.

While I rolled my thoughts forward over thirty years, Laurie was waiting, a tiny line of sweat glistening on her upper lip. She has such pretty lips, has Laurie. I wanted to make sense of things for her, and for myself, too.

'The public world of George's work – and especially his earliest work in India – was marked by more optimism than anyone could summon up now. As the end of this century beckons we can see only too plainly that all aid work is a task of Sisyphus ... which doesn't mean it should not be done. The urgency is greater than ever. In the early post-war years, however, more could be hoped for, and was. Ends were believed to be in sight. Perfectibility in this life rather than in the next was what we sought!

'George brought to that work, as he brought to everything he touched, his own particular brand of enthusiasm and effectiveness. Not that he would have pretended to solutions; he was too much the realist for that. But before lateral thinking was named as such, that's exactly what George practised. The more horrifyingly closed-off or impossible some situation might seem, the more enthusiastically *lateral* George would become. With good reason, I was proud of what he could achieve then, and later, too – right to the end of our life together. Yet at that time in our marriage, in that room at the back of our house, I suspect his heroic public life contrasted all too painfully with my private world which felt unreliable or even stagnant.'

The larger picture faded. I abandoned George and India and the needy and hungry and was again returned to myself. How relentless are the demands of memory!

'It seems embarrassingly trivial now but standing out as an exceptionally vivid memory I see myself squeezing that flab on my arms and pinching and holding with absurd distaste the flesh on my stomach and thighs.

'I was ashamed of my petty concern about a little excess fat when George's work was attempting to relieve the anguish of the starving. Sometimes though it is beyond hard to leave oneself completely behind, and I think that was such a moment for me.

'I felt old then, older than I ever have since. I think in part it was the sheer shock of being, for the first time, not-young. This was true even for someone of my generation which didn't have the fixation on youth that you grew up with, Laurie. In my time we expected to age, and were expected to accept it. Yet even that difference in social perception didn't make it easy for me, individually, during those hard months or couple of years. But that passed. It passed almost totally.'

Seeing Laurie's scepticism, I had to press the point, enjoying, not for the first time, the advantages of extended hindsight.

'After a while, as with everything else, you grow used to your changed body. Perhaps you even grow to like it. Not in the phase of discovery, of novelty, however. You, Laurie, seem to me to be in that novelty phase, or the incredulity phase: *This couldn't be happening to me. I'm the one who'll never grow old. I'm the one who'll live forever.* It's not an easy time. I'd give the body a miss for a while, if I were you, and let it take its own course. You've a great deal else on your plate. On your wheel. Look to your pots. Thank God for your work: work is women's true salvation.'

'Work is women's only salvation! Ain't that the truth, Cordelia? Work – and maybe children.'

'And friends?'

'Yes. Definitely, yes. And friends.'

She laughed then, lovely Laurie, and looked every inch a girl, although I refrained from saying so. As I get to know her better I understand she is perhaps more restless and certainly more touchy than I first thought. I don't mind that one bit; I understand those feelings from the inside out, but it does make me a little more guarded than I might otherwise be. Cautious too not to overstep my mark.

There are some unmapped areas lying between us. I think we both know that.

Like homing pigeons we left our emptied mugs and wandered out to the garden. The air was fresh, for all the city life that swirls around us. The black cat from next door looked down on us with considerable disdain from the high brick wall that separates me from my neighbour.

We gathered a few herbs and some leafy greens, stuffing them into a plastic bag and the bag into her bicycle basket, and then, hugging and waving and saying, 'See you soon,' and, 'Take care. Take care,' like a safety mantra bestowing blessings, we exchanged a final kiss and a wave before she was a precious dot on the road and, then, but just for a while, completely out of sight.

1 3

Alone, my smile fades and my energy drops. It was fun – and consolingly safe – to do some recalling with Laurie, but now, crossly, I find myself kicking at my memories and even more at my dreams, resenting them for ruining my pleasure in going to bed, and unable to find even a clue why my dreams are erupting from that particularly unsettled time.

It wasn't only my flabby arms and belly that caused me pain. Face facts, Cordelia, I tell myself. You were then most distanced from George and most unhappy with yourself.

George was, for all his professional demands, engaged with what I presumed to be an affair, though maybe it was not quite that. It was impossible for me to ask and George would never have dreamed of spelling it out. Thank heaven.

The woman's name was Iris Purse. It's an ugly name but this really rather exceptional woman made a virtue of it. 'It's *Irispurse*,' she would announce when phoning, supremely confident of her welcome. She was clever and wore that, too, with pride, as she did her fame as a Dorothy Parkerish journalist on a big daily paper: picture, byline, polished, confident opinions. The women's page of course. There was nothing else in those days. But she made of it something truly sparkling. In the face of my own shameful decline, her public vitality seemed rather a lot to take.

She was at least ten years older than George. That didn't seem to put him off. On the contrary, in the hands of *Irispurse*, it became another virtue. I think George liked her roguish, almost mannish ways that she managed quite unconsciously to transform into a thoroughly female coquetry. What a fascinating woman she is, when contemplated from the safety of almost thirty years' distance.

Irispurse could not have been more different from me. I sensed that and it frightened me. Her choices had not been mine but might have been. My choices had not been hers but might have been. In the heady, attractively demanding excitement of Irispurse, George might have left, as I believed he would on that night I sat crumpled and damp on the squeaking cane chair. Yet he didn't. Faithful George. And I'm glad he didn't, because when we eventually pulled ourselves out of that awful period, or drifted out of it not even knowing we were doing that until months or even years later, we really began to hit our stride together which allowed me, I think, further down the track, the luxury of discovering my own work.

After that, everything changed.

Iris Purse was not the only thorn piercing the side of our ailing marriage. And George was not alone in seeking a more enticing reflection of himself than the one he could see in his spouse's gaze.

I haven't forgotten George's friend and brief, brief rival, Cam Hutchence. A constant visitor to our table for three or four years who had surprisingly quickly stepped over the border that divided dutiful, good-works-associated dinners from those dinners and parties we gave only for pleasure. Cam: a charming, inexplicably unattached man with the most disturbing body and eyes. A big, athletic fellow whose muscled body was covered with impossibly fine golden hair that gleamed like spun silk. It was hair fine enough to soften a baby but it covered a man who was almost blatantly masculine in size and strength. A Norse god he seems, looking back. Laurie's Gregory would know which one. Maybe Loki, god of mischief.

I found myself willingly transfixed through any number of evenings by the sight of this golden coat that seemed almost to hover over his hands, rather than growing out of them. Cam. A complex, ambiguous man, astute and perhaps even calculating in George's description of him, who nevertheless declared his love or maybe only his passion one afternoon when he and I both knew George was far from town.

It was tempting. Whatever Cam was offering, it was tempting. Bored, unfocused, needy: I was profoundly tempted. I had thought often about my hand pressing down to flatten that net of gold, and about reaching through it to the man beneath. In fantasy I had reached towards him, even possessed him, but had not thought about his hands on me. I baulked at the thought of my own self being reached towards. It was no part of my desire to be in any way held down. Neither figuratively nor emotionally. Even thinking of it made me feel trapped and smothered. Short of breath. I wanted to taste Cam. I really don't think I could bear to be tasted.

There was also the limitless, perplexing question of how I saw myself. This seems always to have troubled me. Taking myself for granted is not a luxury I ever learned to enjoy. Perhaps being an unsuccessful daughter got me off on the wrong foot, though really I do not blame either of my parents for that, and especially not my mother. I simply regret the awkward fit that left both of us feeling uneasy.

Thinking of myself with Cam, I could not, even momentarily, see myself as a successful adulteress, much less a *femme fatale*. More painfully, thinking of George and me, I could not convince myself that I fitted the part of Wife well enough to risk putting it on the line.

When my courage failed, when I found that, needy as I was, I could not bring myself to accept anything more than some fairly furtive and disturbing kisses, our shared friendship with Cam wilted and rather quickly died. And that became something else to regret. Cam's beauty – and his seductive, mysterious availability – had added a good deal to our most successful evenings.

Perhaps that was the theme tune of that difficult personal time: regret. They should have been years of such plenty. Post-war, into the heady years of the welfare state and full employment, of free milk and university education for the less well-off, of fresh respect for formerly colonised nations; with our notions of human perfectibility fully fired, our desires for social justice seemingly achievable, we had a great deal of what we had once dreamed of and planned for, and had, in George's case, fought a war for.

Yet our capacity to stretch out and to know or really much care what each other was feeling was then at its most stunted.

In these awful nightly dreams, it is the act of stretching out that needs to be interminably repeated. My arms are raised. I am trying to haul myself up. I am reaching towards . . . and then I lose it.

Sometimes George is there. Those dreams are worst. He is not my companion nor my champion in these dreams as, later, I increasingly felt him to be in my life. He appears as a tall, shadowy but fully dressed figure beside my night-dressed self in the bed, a figure that seems to be leaning over me in a manner that could be proprietorial, or it could be menacing.

Why don't I know? Why can't I judge?

With a fierce act of will, I am struggling, pushing upwards both from sleep and from the pull of heavy bedding laid too thickly over me. I am trying to get clear of what has just been, but I am stuck in the moment. Over and again: the weight of the covers and my own inertia; wanting to reach out; failing. Failing, falling, fallen.

Why am I haunted by this now? Why am I without the peace I badly need?

Laurie has said, smiling as she speaks, 'I feel refreshed just being with you, Cordelia. It's a madhouse, my house, and coming here feels like a visit to a health farm. An hour with you and I'm set for anything!'

Generous Laurie. But her words, kind and distracting as they are, don't help me.

Music, tidying, writing thin letters and fat cheques: none of it is helping me. I have a series of piles spread across the floor of George's study which more or less contain the key papers I believe should go to public collections, but the next stage, of reading them in detail and deciding, defeats me.

Back in George's study, looking at the photographs of Tagore for guidance, I believe Tagore to be saying, in the mellifluous sing-song Indian voice I am sure must have been his, 'Leave these here a while, Cordelia. Look elsewhere for what you need to find. Go back to work.'

Well, I may have imagined this instruction, or not. Either way, it has the ring of conviction to it.

Back to work, Cordelia. Back to work.

African simplicity is not easy to achieve.

The wonderful thing about my wilder years was that in the name of art and experiment I could get away with just about anything. Now I am relying almost totally on shape, on smoothing shapes to such perfection that all one would notice when looking at them is a sense of inevitability as shape serves function.

This is much harder to achieve than I'd remembered.

I want to persist. Such extreme simplicity is absolutely what I am crying out for but in making this latest effort, I realise how deeply it goes against my grain. Sleights of hand come readily to me: a gorgeous silk jacket allowing me to get away with baggy comfortable clothes beneath – and me baggier still beneath those clothes. Fine wine with a thrown-together meal. My gilded teapot drawing attention away from solid, capacious mugs on the same tray. Egyptian damask allowing me a nightly toss in luxury. A house glowing with paintings – and some wonderful paintings among them – lets me get away with a minimum of dusting and tidying, or so I reassure myself.

Nor am I bored with the lifting of the heart that beautiful or amusing objects can allow. Laurie found me a wonderful tea cosy that has had me smiling for days. It was knitted with scraps of different colours and weights of wools that became magical in their combination as they grew together. She pulled it out of her backpack with the flourish of confidence that comes from having found just the right thing. I put it first onto my head, modelling it around the garden where we had been standing, where she had found me picking masses of tiny white roses that would only last for a day but are no less gorgeous for that, and only then taking her by the hand and taking the cosy inside to try it on its rightful owner, the gilded teapot.

It is safe to predict that I shall go to my grave with things of beauty and, I suspect, far too many of them. But in my work my focus is suddenly quite different. Big jugs, mostly without any outer glaze, with only the merest lines of sober decoration driven into the clay when it is leather-hard. For that scheme to work, the shape, the size, the modelling and the firing must all be perfect. Nothing else will do. There will be bowls, too. I want these to be plainly glazed in muted blues with only the merest shading of difference from top to bottom, as though green or brown had been added with a fairy's touch, no more than a glancing wing. They must rely for their effect on an irresistible message of usefulness. Sturdy and hardy yet still aesthetically pleasing; I am challenged by the shaping. To get something down to that is certainly much harder than one would think.

The perfection of what I am seeking lures and eludes me. In my worst moments of frustration I envy Laurie. She is in a completely different phase of her work. At just the moment when I am discovering how difficult it is to do next to nothing satisfactorily, Laurie is bursting into a kind of extravaganza of colour and allure.

And not Laurie only. Gudrun's work is also, in its different way, bursting with colour and boldness of contrast more usually associated with cultures much brighter than our own. It's the new breadth to Laurie's work I am most intrigued by, however.

For some years she has been selling some of her more highly detailed and larger pieces to a fairly serious and apparently quite wealthy collector, Luciana O'Reilly. Now in her fifties and the veteran of several financially advantageous marriages, Luciana is well known for the rococo hats in which she is photographed for whatever passes for the weekend social pages these days. She does more, however, than catch the eye.

Small, thin, fast-moving, with blackcurrant eyes and a raspberry mouth, she is obviously shrewd and perhaps kind, as well as relentlessly social. Certainly she seems not to take herself or anyone else too seriously, which is endearing, and now she has through some contact or other landed herself the delightful task of setting up some exhibitions in a small but chic and extremely well-located gallery.

Her idea is to expand as extravagantly as she can the repertoire of her small group of artists. In Laurie's case she has inspired her to create an entire room that will mirror, exaggerate and enhance the challenging style of Laurie's large decorative pieces, especially the magnificent, flattish platters for which she's best known. There will be some fountains, too. I am curious about those.

Gallery visitors will step from the cool, expensively understated hall and reception area into a wall-to-wall blaze of colour, gathering up their excitement and desire to spend as they go, one hopes.

Laurie's plan is to set up a room-within-a-room inside the gallery. She will paint the floors, walls and ceilings in her pottery style. There will also be huge cushions, birds in flight and even papier mâché standing figures all echoing the odd proportions and startling colour combinations of the central ceramic work.

The general idea is not new. What can be these days? Vanessa Bell painted far beyond the edges of her conventional canvases, and so did other painting Bloomsberries. Bell had large woollen carpets woven to her designs; she painted over chairs and chests, up walls, around and across doors, onto canvas and off again. But this is not a looking-back. There is a deliberate hard, shiny brilliance to Laurie's work that makes the overkill effect truly dashing and quite her own.

As she has been setting this work in train, I have observed that her clothes have gone from muted to dull. She seems to be wearing only clothes that have long since surrendered their colour up to drying breezes. I offered her some of my silk jackets and shirts, not so much because she admires them, although she does, but because clearly whatever spare money she has she spends on Gregory and Rhea, leaving little for herself. She seemed cautiously pleased, but I couldn't come up with anything that would fit her. She is even broader, and I suspect stronger, than she looks. Perhaps some of George's more flamboyant jackets or his wonderful linen or fine cotton shirts would fit her as well as suit her.

But I am not ready yet.

Her children wear the bright clothes that are closer to Laurie's work. They are cleverly gathered at white elephant stalls and in second-hand shops with only underwear, school clothes and shoes needing to be bought new.

Each child has a trace of Eastern beauty from their father's side, and exquisite skin, but each is also delightfully and unfashionably plump. Laurie tells me that Gregory minds and Rhea claims not to mind. Either way, it doesn't stop them being wonderfully greedy guests. Heaven to buy cakes for.

I am not unaware that increasingly I have been seeing the children here rather than at their home, and then only fairly briefly. Does Laurie worry they will overwhelm me, or burst the fragile bonds of reasonable behaviour should they stay too long? But I like those children a great deal, and despite my current reluctance to go out after dark, I was more than willing to accept an invitation to dinner at Laurie's.

I hadn't had time to think about it. She phoned, not knowing that I'd had an old friend staying here and was feeling somewhat empty and restless after Franny's warmth and familiarity had disappeared homewards.

Franny is also fairly recently widowed and we enjoyed good, easy talks together and some companionable silence, too, sitting side by side in the garden like a couple of old ducks stranded in our deck chairs, soaking up late afternoon sunshine, and drinking more tea and certainly more icy calvados than we probably should have. Franny is not someone I can talk to about my work but in the face of my continuing unsteady grappling with the demands of simplicity, it was something of a relief to set thoughts of that aside and to reminisce, gently and then more honestly, about our married lives, and about our husbands.

Franny told me for the first time that Jacob, throughout their marriage, had suffered from periodic bouts of severe depression but had never allowed her to speak of this to anyone, and would not seek any help for himself. He saw it as a weakness, of course, as a lack of spine. Unmanly: Franny didn't say that word, but I felt it hovering. What she did say was that Jacob saw his collapses as a shameful failure of mind over emotions. Especially galling and mysterious to him as his war had personally been less frightening than for many others. He survived and so did most of his immediate family. Why, he tormented himself, wasn't that enough to keep the wolves of unwanted feeling from his door?

Franny, even now, had difficulty in meeting my eyes as she told me, 'I sometimes feared for his sanity or even for his life. Several times suicide was a real possibility. A terrifying possibility. But I was even more afraid that were I to turn to anyone, friend or doctor, or even to our own girls, Jacob would see this as an unforgivable betrayal.

'I shall never know if I did the right thing, though. How can one know? I go over and over it: should I have acted differently? Could I have found the means to be less afraid and more responsible? I just don't have an answer. All I can say is that Jacob valued loyalty above all other virtues. No fervent explanation of good intentions could have made up for breaching that.'

Now Jacob is dead and she is able to speak of all this to me without fear of disloyalty, and probably to others, too. But although I was able to reach over, take her hand, sit with her, silently comforting, I also felt regret that somehow the secrecy if not the illness could not have been different.

In both our minds we were, I think, seeing Jacob. He played the piano exceptionally well and sang, too. His was the kind of high tenor that one can hear in almost any pub in Ireland, a voice that can turn a listener's heart full circle and he was, many years ago, tremendously keen on amateur musicals, Gilbert and Sullivan, *Merry Widow*, that kind of thing. Well-off, successful in his legal practice, he was always willing to help with money when George convinced him about some cause or other. He shared George's love of poetry, though differed on favoured poets. He was a Yeats man who could also keep us enthralled with great chunks of memorised Dylan Thomas.

Later still that same afternoon Franny said, abruptly, 'The worst thing about depressed people, well about Jacob anyway, is that they attack when they feel low. It's like passing the hot potato: "If I feel dreadful, why shouldn't you?" '

With difficulty I restrained from asking questions. Not because I didn't want to know. What Franny had just said was startling, and quite discordant with my knowledge of Jacob and with the memories Franny had easily and willingly shared earlier in the day.

Yet I didn't want to examine that shock. Instead, involuntarily, I thought of my mother. My depressed mother. She didn't attack; she never attacked. Nevertheless, the miasma of her unhappiness had been intensely pervasive at almost every moment of our young lives. I thought of my own dark moods, my own monstrous capacity to attack my own self, to gnaw at my self-esteem, to see myself as grossly imperfect and then to scorn and occasionally even punish George for loving me. I sighed, and looked at the flowers flowing over the edge of the bed nearest to where I sat. Columbines looked back at me in an array of gentle colours. There was no strain there, no self-hatred nor any of the dark ills that flow from that wretched emotion. We have a lot to learn: *teach us, oh flowers!*

Franny went on, still needing to talk, 'I know it's hard to believe, but in that mood he would pick at me, criticise and undermine me in ways that were quite foreign to his usual nature. It could go on for days or weeks or months on end. Even when I made excuses to myself for what he was doing, it hurt my feelings dreadfully. I knew and he knew how much he depended on me. I didn't mind that dependence, not at all, but I did mind that he would pretend it wasn't so and would try sometimes to take me down with him.'

Her voice was astonishingly calm. I guessed that she'd had years of practice keeping her feelings in check. Her hands were shaking though, and she put down her cup, resting it on the stubby grass against the side of her deck chair. When she straightened up she went on, still in the same even tone. 'He had an eye for my weak points too, which gave him an almost uncanny ability to strike where the blow would hurt most, and be least easy to defend. In a voice that was almost kind and certainly was tinged with unctuousness, he would say things that were not at all kind like, "You *know*, Franny, that your memory isn't very reliable these days . . ." or, "You *know*, Franny, that you sometimes *bother* the girls by calling them as often as you do . . ." or when I'd finally explode and blurt out how much he was hurting me, "Must you always worry about *yourself*, Franny." It really wasn't nice. It was horrible.'

'God help us,' I said, all restraint gone.

Franny laughed. 'God didn't help us. Not about that, anyway. And the worst thing is, being unkind would sometimes give Jacob a burst of energy when nothing else did. I could never understand that. It's a variation on the vampire theme. Not a pretty variation either. Once he'd brought me down, he could sometimes go up. Not pretty at all.'

I knew what she meant. I wish I didn't. I knew what she meant not because that had been any part of the way that George behaved with me, nor I with him, but because when they were younger my sister Peg's husband too had worshipped at the altar of rationality, while liberally projecting his dark feelings outwards and letting them run amok. When Peg would, rarely, confront him with what he was doing and how he was hurting her or their children with the differences between his generous rhetoric and his punitive behaviour, he would cleverly twist what she was saying so that it always, always became *her* problem, *her* over-active imagination, even her hysteria. 'And in the face of such denial,' Peg confided more than once, 'who wouldn't feel hysterical or even crazy?'

Yet, to the world at large, Peg and Sebastian, and Franny and

Jacob – like most couples of their time and class – presented a united, even a contented front.

'A twist on Dr Jekyll and Mr Hyde, too,' I said, turning back to Franny and thinking again about Jacob's erudition, talents and charm. 'Which one is the real self?'

The image that arose of Jacob was of a slim, bright-eyed, attractive man, obviously clever, a bearded man who did not look unlike a more approachable Freud, sitting on the arm of a big chair, ready at any moment to stand, waving an unlit cigar in the air with one hand, holding a pin and lighter in the other, and declaiming with great energy about some theory or other which currently engaged him. To all intents and purposes, this was a man pleased with himself and the life that he had created. Was that on the surface only?

What a waste, I thought. What a damned shame that a man so full of feeling, and willing to respond so openly to the worlds of emotion conveyed through music and poetry, could not claim his own complexity.

For all that, I couldn't like him less. I have lived too long and know my own weaknesses too well to pick up a stone, never mind cast one. How sorry I am though that Franny lived with contradictions that were quite that stark and painful. And how sorry I am that she couldn't speak of it, even to her oldest friends.

Jacob and Franny lived for most of their married life in a large, flower-filled house, a house that could have seemed grand but was saved from that off-putting fate by their abundant friendliness and skilful hospitality. They drove expensive, late model cars that I occasionally hankered after for their ostentatious comfort. A lucky life, seen from the outside, that had its secret sadness.

I'm glad that Franny could tell me. Perhaps it helped. Certainly we parted warmly and with emphatic resolve to see each other soon. My impression is that we can now move to a different level of friendship, something more nourishing and long-lasting than mutual concern and entertainment. I hope so.

In a day of fresh discoveries I also learned that it is Wynston and not Laurie who has been feeding me for months! That made it virtually impossible to resist when Laurie urged me to join the two households for a birthday dinner for Wynston which he himself was preparing. How kind they are to bring me into their family circle.

Needing to offer a special gift that would begin to thank him for his cooking, as well as being adequate for a thirty-fifth birthday, I found on our own shelves a 1935 first edition of Isherwood's *Mr Norris Changes Trains*. I was rather pleased with that. Then I picked out two stylish ties that I don't believe George ever had an occasion to wear. One of them was especially pretty, like a Kandinsky painting on silk.

Wrapping the gifts in abundant sheets of white tissue paper, tying each parcel with dark green curling ribbon, then attaching a small card, I felt unusually cheerful. If I manage to step up my party acceptances I shall have less reason to worry about the necessary shedding of our possessions.

We gather around a charmingly set table, squeezed together but no one minding. The children, the couple, Laurie and me.

Having cooked, Wynston is sitting back to allow Laurie and Guy to do the serving. We eat greedily, noisily: raw fish marinated in lemon juice, coconut milk and a touch more chilli than I would have dared; a highly spiced chick pea stew with a cool, crunchy salad; lavishly garlic-buttered French bread. There is much leaning over the table; much passing of snippets from one plate to another; from one person's fork to another's mouth. Gregory and Rhea are tucking into chicken sausages as well as selections of the adults' food, and their voices and views soar with the rest. I am still getting used to that. Or, at least, I notice once again that it is not what I am used to, but I like it.

Rhea is an exceptionally clever mimic and manages by the end of the evening to do an excellent impersonation of everyone at the table, as well as long speeches in the personae of Mrs Lemon-Face, clearly her unfortunate teacher, and Mr Orange Peel, fussy, harassed caretaker of the school grounds, as well as Guy's mother whom she calls Gwandma Wosy. Her repertoire is apparently limitless, with fine back-up of guffaws and repetitions of all her best lines provided by Gregory.

However, and to my eventual relief, Laurie offers them the choice of a little more listening and less talking, or a video. Their decision is entirely predictable and when we have cleared the table of the dinner debris we adults sit back to more wine, then coffee, brandies and tiny petit fours that seem too much, but prove irresistible.

I want to speak about Africa to these three, or about that mythical self-created place I name as Africa that is inspiring my pots. I want to talk to them about this astonishing volte face that has me seeking simplicity when so recently I was mixing clays, colours and multiple firings in ever more elaborate combinations.

Yet I hesitate. Not because I mistrust their interest, or my own interest in how any one of them might respond, but because I don't know how to talk about what I am doing without seeming to elaborate a theory. Doing so would set up a paradox that makes me uneasy even before the words are spoken. How can I speak about simplicity simply?

Only simple and quiet words will ripen of themselves.

In the end, Laurie speaks for me. I am pulled away from my own thoughts to hear her telling the two men that they might be interested to see what I am doing, now that I have started to work again.

'Cordelia calls it her African quest,' Laurie is saying, shyly but with some pride, looking at me for permission to say this perhaps, as well as at them. 'But there's a stillness that's coming through in this work that seems to me to have its source in some more universal place than Africa. It's there in all early ceramic work whether it's from China, the near and Middle East, Africa – wherever. Pots thousands of years old that hum down to us in an utterly satisfying tune that we can recognise at once.'

Wynston listens, laughs aloud his pleasure and appreciation of what Laurie is expressing, then turns to me to say, 'Now I want you to listen to my Africa, Cordelia. This may not be the simplicity you're talking about and maybe not the serenity either, but there is a beat to this, too. This beat reaches straight in to meet up with my beat. I just love it. No matter how down I might feel, this music lifts me up. Listen and tell me what you think.'

He moves over to Laurie's hi-fi player, clearly familiar with her collection of CDs and quick to find and put on what he tells me is mbalax dance music from Senegambia.

I have little idea what to expect. The music fills the room and silences us. Listening, and not only through my ears, I can indeed feel at least something of what Wynston describes: that my blood hears the music and runs faster in my veins; that the pulse of my body leaps with relief; that my cheeks are getting pink; that my usually still shoulders are swaying.

Closing my eyes, apparently giving myself over to what I am hearing, I am nevertheless struck by a thought, a bolt of familiar, unsatisfied curiosity as to why it is 'Africa' that speaks to one person; 'India' to another; 'China' to a third? The objective external reality of each country is obviously part of the explanation, but it certainly does not provide a full picture. Some of what I am worrying at when I think 'Africa' is so entirely subjective and self-created that it must bear little or even no resemblance to any part of that diverse continent that also exists far outside my own mind.

George, my dear love, was to the end of his life nominally a Christian. His funeral was a conventional and conventionally beautiful Anglican service. As he had wanted it. And I have never had reason to doubt that he got something more than aesthetic pleasure from his intermittent Christian practices and from his very genuine feelings about Christ. Yet what fuelled and inspired him, and kept him going in the face of work that would have torn most people to cynical shreds years earlier, came from fifty years of reading, poring over, pulling apart and putting together and simply relishing the work of Eastern mystical writers, and especially Rabindranath Tagore. Why Tagore?

At the rational level, one could say: because Tagore reflected and inspired George's own need to combine practical work in the outer world with an equally passionate honouring of the more subtle, internal life of the spirit.

Whoever wishes to,
May sit in meditation
With eyes closed
To know if the world be true or false.
I, meanwhile,
Shall sit with hungry eyes,
To see the world
While the light lasts.

Like George, Tagore also became more and not less radical as he aged; George relished that. But there's more to this fascination than any rational explanation could tell us. Just as my own Africa does and does not exist, so too George's Tagore does and does not exist. Tagore is and is not poetry, prose, plays, paintings, polemics, letters. Like any writer he can exist as inspiration only when he — or something that emerges from who he was — falls on the fertile ground of someone else's interest. So, too, more generally, George's India, and George's visions of India, must inevitably shift between the deepest possible experience of subjectivity and something more obviously shared — or shareable.

That first aspect, that self-created 'reality', is as much a haven and inspiration as it is fantasy and autobiographical statement! George's internal India is what tuned up his pulse, and sometimes even gave him reason to go on when the external India threatened to be too much, just as this pulse-jumping, triumphant music is creating 'Africa' for Wynston, and giving him what he needs.

Opening my eyes, I am struck by the dark, bearded beauty of Wynston, the pleasing shape of his exceptionally well-sculptured lips as he listens, smiling, eyes shut, occasionally moving to the beat while keeping his head resting lightly on Guy's shoulder. They are touching hands, easily.

Wynston and Guy are more relaxed this evening than they have been so far with me, yet I am aware of an occasional feeling of sadness that Guy's teasing and soft looks and considerable grace are entirely directed to Wynston and never to Laurie. He is invariably pleasant to her, and appropriately respectful of her views, but what she gets from him is certainly neither passionate nor devoted. It is not even especially attentive.

There are striking traces of each of them in the children. Nevertheless it is hard to imagine they were once the couple, and not that long ago. I find myself wondering if Laurie minds witnessing Guy and Wynston's passionate devotion. Is there any longing in her still to have such devotion from this man, or from any man?

We are able to talk frankly, Laurie and I. Or what I experience as frank, at any rate. But with all friendships, as the revelations from Franny showed me only too pointedly, there is always more to discover. *More reaching out.* My own entrenched reserve may make it hard for Laurie to think it entirely easy or safe to be frank with me, and my diffidence might prevent me from convincing her otherwise. But the words 'reaching out' do strike me with some conviction as I think of Laurie, and whatever risks there are in this, they seem easier to confront than the painful, fruitless reaching out that still persists in my troubled dreams.

Twice lately I have got up, hauled my quilt off the bed and bundled down in the spare room, hoping desperately that a change of location will produce a shift in point of view in my dreams. But the dreams come with me.

Waking in the spare room, last time, I caught sight of myself in a wardrobe mirror left ajar. A little too thin and certainly rather too wrinkled, somewhat unkempt, but eyes bright. I was not totally displeased and having made tea I brought it back to bed remembering that it was in this room and not in our own shared room that George and I last made passionate love about a year before he died. It had caught us unawares. Not that sexual love between us had ceased, though quite understandably it had diminished, but passionate love has for us always been like dust motes that are transformed into magical things only when by some miracle the sun catches them at just the right angle.

Was I dreaming unhappily then, too? Or sleeping badly? Perhaps George had chosen to sleep in the spare room rather than in the carved bed? We had just had early morning tea then, too, I remember, and had lingered, lying back on a pile of pillows to talk, and then George had quoted some lines to me from the Bhagavad Gita – I wish I could remember what they were – and the sun hit us at just the right angle and we were young again or anyway momentarily transformed so that youthful vigour could be ours along with a depth of union that had never been ours when we were actually young.

There were no words that could have been spoken afterwards. We lay together, arms around each other, only very slowly coming back into the present, back into consciousness of our aged bodies that never-theless felt if not younger, then certainly renewed. I think I must have slept, perhaps for an hour or more. I woke alone. George had risen, dressed and got on with his day. But there was a tenderness and sweet-ness that stayed with us and warmed our hearts and filled the house for days.

Now, remembering George, the bony feel of him, the weight of him, the sweet-sour smell of him, he is so near and that memory is so real it is impossible quite to believe that such an experience as George and I shared on that stray morning won't ever be mine again.

Dear God, I miss him.

16

A small, dark-haired woman sits at a long polished dining-room table.

Each chair, other than the one on which she is seated, is placed neatly at the table's edge. The chairs are evenly spaced, uninviting in their determined order. On a deeply mellowed mahogany sideboard, highly polished, plain silver candle holders stand, gleaming, on a long linen runner embroidered with spring flowers in cross-stitch by this woman herself. The heavy, brown, lined chenille curtains that hang in this room were also made by the woman. So, too, were the intricately woven silk cords that tie back the curtains. And the elaborate green and grey tapestry covers fitting tightly on the seat of each chair are also her own carefully perfected work.

She is, for once, resting, but poised to get up at the slightest sound. Her children are in bed. They are not all asleep, but they are quiet.

The woman has six children and when they are awake the house is never anything but bedlam to her ears, although when they withdraw to their shared bedrooms at night she can know that there will be no more than an occasional burst of laughter or argument, quickly stilled. Her oldest daughter, Cordelia, can almost always see to the younger ones. Frank and Elsie are no trouble at all. It would be a rare day when Cordelia had to appeal to her mother for support.

The woman's crossed arms nurse her belly. Her legs ache. She has painfully swollen varicose veins that she hesitates to mention to the doctor. What could he do? The thickly prominent veins not only ache, they also look extremely ugly. They look as though they want to burst away from her body to begin a life of their own. She hates them for their ugliness. She hates all ugliness, hates it. Her legs have become another part of her body that she cannot look at, and must also keep covered from her husband. Not for his sake only, but her own.

She believes he fell in love with her beauty. She could never see it, but whatever it was that he saw, he regarded as a cause for wonderment and delighted comment that both embarrassed and bewitched her. She believed her beauty, such as it was, was less than skin deep; it was a mask put there by his love. Now that her beauty is gone, she fears who he sees. She feels embarrassed still. She does not feel bewitched.

He continues to be tender to her. She wonders why. He is scrupulously considerate. At night in their shared bed she often cries. Her children don't know she cries, but although she is as silent in this as she is in almost everything else, her husband knows what she is doing. He is careful not to ask her why she is crying. Long ago she told him that when he probed for reasons she believed she had to justify herself, and that only made it worse. She cannot justify her crying. He respects that. It is her greatest source of shame that she has no reason for her crying. Her husband is a wonderful man. She can still feel her breath coming much more easily in and out of her body when he is in the house.

He is lovable. Good. Handsome still. Perhaps he is even more handsome now than ever, and increasingly well-off as businessmen learn that his inventions really can increase productivity and safety. Good men like her husband don't leave their wives. But she knows that he deserves much more than she is giving him; he deserves someone very much better than she is.

She can't help being afraid. She fears losing him: to a woman who is still beautiful, to a woman who doesn't cry; to a woman who still has something to say when she herself might as well be dumb despite all the thoughts that tumble through her mind by day and also in her dreams.

There's no reason for her to cry over her children. This woman has children who are healthy, intelligent and obedient. Strong-willed certainly, but that's no bad thing, and they have learned to be unusually considerate. It's true that her own mother cried herself to death. Not silently but hysterically, deafeningly, defying anyone to miss her wails and shrieks. Though she was ill — mad, indeed — and this woman is neither ill nor mad. There is no rhyme nor reason at all for her misery and she would give almost anything in the world to regain the high spirits she is quite sure she had as a girl.

In fact, as a girl she knows she was often in trouble, not for crying but for being loud, thoughtless, wild, a tomboy, a hoyden, daring in ways her own children have never been. She was vital then. She could call out and shriek and laugh every bit as loudly as her mother could howl. Now she believes whatever is left of her vitality drips away with her desperate tears. If only, she thinks, she could find a container to catch and hold those tears, and some way to bring them back, cleansed of grief and thus transformed, inside herself.

She cannot speak of this to her husband. None of it makes the slightest bit of sense. Wordless, she cries. Wordless, he rubs the small of her back, just to the edge of her buttocks. Gentle, patient strokes. Round and round and round his hand moves, until he grows too tired and is asleep.

17

Today is my mother's birthday.

I have remembered this only with the day partly gone although I have been thinking about her increasingly often and had consciously been looking forward to this anniversary of her beginning. She would not yet be one hundred years old so could conceivably still be alive. I sound aloud her name: 'Nell'. I never called her by that name, not once.

In my imagination, I bring her into the present, a very old lady, gentled by time, living in a comfortable, tastefully decorated nursing home perhaps, with a cashmere shawl around her shoulders, her grey eyes bright, and in them a look of easy gratitude when I come to bring her home to sit together through a long, peaceful afternoon, here, in this heavenly garden, helping her with her tea, her slice of cake, her rug . . .

That scenario is impossibly hard to believe. Not just that stereotyped portrait of ancient mother in expensive nursing home. Nor the ease between us that picture suggests. The woman herself feels 'long ago' and I suspect that in part it is because she began to die many years before she did in fact succumb to a short, horrid bout of cancer.

That erosion of self, that turning away from relationships, that diminishing of her life force until it was little more than candle-strength: it all bothers me deeply and I remain restless and unsatisfied by any explanation I can give myself.

Laurie is never short of solutions, shared with the best of intentions.

I had scarcely hinted at this worrying elusiveness of my mother before she had told me I should conjure up an image of my mother, look at it and ask the image some direct questions. 'What went wrong for you? In what way were you hurt? What held you back from loving your husband and your children? Are you at peace now?'

With enviable faith, Laurie assures me that such an encounter can bring forth results. I doubt it. My nature is to doubt. I *am* doubtful. How can I ask an image of my mother what I could never have dared even to broach in real life?

'That's the point,' Laurie says, not willing to give up. 'You *can* ask what you could not in real life. Try it, Cordelia, what do you have to lose?'

What do I have to lose? I could give her no convincing answer but I couldn't either even begin to satisfy her urge that I should make contact in this way with my own dead mother. Kind Laurie is doing all she can to expand my horizons and mostly I am glad enough of it, but perhaps inevitably, her pace and style are sometimes not mine.

So much that is unexpected has brought Laurie and me together. Her vitality when mine is drained and thinned by grief. Her innocence — not least, of what old age brings and takes away. My 'steadiness' which she refuses to see is mere illusion. The peace of my house and studio: I accept that.

Yet that peace is working for me now much less well than it did while I could take for granted that George was alive. Can it be true that only months ago I sometimes thought of George himself as a distraction, breaking in on the peace of my thoughts?

I am filled with shame and regret at my own unkindness and appalled at my own stupidity, for it is in George's permanent absence that I am painfully distracted, not least by thoughts of him.

It is impossible to think of George and not also to think of death, and the questions that gnaw away at me about life after death.

Where is George now? *What* is he now? *Is* he now? Is whoever or whatever he is at peace? Can he be at peace when I am not? Is he, or the essence of him (dare I even shape this question?), with God? And if he is with God, then why do my own thoughts turn away from prayer to that same God, and recoil from belief that prayer could make one jot of difference?

My mother used to pray. Then she stopped. God was part of her life and the fabric of her thinking. Words to and about God came easily to her lips. Then that changed. God left her; or should I say, she left God. But when? And why?

Even having these interminable damned thoughts I am missing George. I want to share them with him. I don't want to summon up an image of him, Laurie-style, and be satisfied with what I discover. No, greedily, insistently, I want an alive George to think them through with me, even if we emerge from our separate train of thoughts with quite different or even opposing perspectives. In fact, that's exactly what I am after. I was too quick to complain that in the face of George's constant mental activity, my own was sometimes buried. Already I am wearied by my own thoughts. Dulled by the familiarity of them. I want the spice of his robust certainty and the energising freshness of his difference.

Sometimes it is too hard to be alive in the present. I want to run back to the land I know: the land of marriage that is now the past. How unfair it feels to outlive one's partner, how wretchedly unfair.

On my mother's birthday, Laurie is making cushions.

Both women sewed beautifully. Would they have had anything else in common? It's hard to hold them side by side in my mind; they occupy such different territory. Yet, at the sight of a woman sitting, head bowed, sewing, I experience a familiar mix of comfort and exclusion.

The cushions Laurie's making will form big, startling piles, adding to the three-dimensional effects she is keen to elaborate for her show. She is sewing as we talk, surrounded by piles of fabrics in the sharp purples, pinks, blues and greens that will characterise all the work. There will need to be a great heap of these cushions to create the desired effect, so she is having to work hard at them and enlist help wherever she can.

I am no help. I always loathed sewing, although as a girl there was no question of my avoiding it. We girls all learned early to mend, make do, repair what was torn or old, as well as making our own new clothes, not that there were ever many of those. Elsie and Peg, the two youngest girls, sewed well. Norah and I would always make a fist of whatever we were tackling. Elsie and Peg continued to sew way past the time when it was an economic necessity to do so and each of them went on to have children who seemed beautifully and imaginatively dressed to my inexperienced eye. For Norah and me it was different. We associated any mending and sewing with the stretching of resources and the substitution of time and effort for money that utterly characterised the early years of our girlhood. When the chance came, we gave it up with relief.

Or I did. As a young married woman, some years on from the mending and dressmaking days, Norah took to making large and extravagant hats. Norah is rather small and was then also slim and girlish, as she was even into late middle age, so the hats made a huge statement that she must decidedly have enjoyed. But from when she was about the age Laurie is now the old hats were rarely seen and new hats were never paraded. Could it be that she began to feel that a less flamboyant look was more appropriate as she aged, or as her husband became more senior in his firm, or as her children grew to want a mother indistinguishable from other mothers?

I do like that about Laurie's Gregory and Rhea. They are not merely accepting; they are clearly quite comfortable with their parents' differences from what used to be the norm. And still is for most, I've no doubt.

Wanting to know them, I've watched them intently. When the children themselves are hard at talk, and their parents and Wynston are also engaged – used as they are to giving their full attention to the children's least demand – there is plenty of welcome opportunity for me to observe.

Both children are relaxed with Wynston himself, climbing all over him as easily as they do over their father, teasing him, making 'sick' noises when he and Guy are too overtly affectionate, but probably no more so than if they were a more conventional couple of woman and man. The inevitability of heterosexuality is not an inevitability for these children. And there is nothing unpleasant implied when they ask any one of their parenting trio if so-and-so, a friend of Guy or Laurie or Wynston's, is straight or gay. It is not a question of values for them. Asking is a simple act of curiosity.

My own curiosity is less simple. I am attracted and repulsed by the Wynston and Guy duo. Undoubtedly I am attracted deeply by the physical sheen of the two men. Their beauty together – greater I think than their beauty apart – is strikingly harmonious. It gives an ironic lie to what many would call the unnaturalness of their connection. The physical interactions which express their intimacy are almost alarmingly fluid. They appear to flow into each other in a way that one rarely sees or perhaps one rarely notices with a heterosexual couple, except sometimes among the very young.

I am struck by the way one man's arm tucks around the other's waist or sits across a shoulder that seems able to bear its presence effortlessly; the way one manly thigh rests against without imposing on the other one; the way one face seems to move and mirror in some special way the intention of the other as he talks so that when Guy is building up to a climax in a well-spun anecdote it is almost impossible not also to be riveted by Wynston's animation and engagement, or vice versa.

That's all charming. But I am repulsed, too.

I don't like to think about what they do when kissing and touching and admiring and stroking are not enough. Nor should I be thinking about it, indeed; it is none of my concern. But old-fashioned sentiments hit me with some force and my mind turns to considering the soft warmth of Laurie that contrasts steadily and alluringly with her strong hands and her brisk capable manner. Then, for all Wynston's dearness,

I find it hard fully to understand Guy's choice, if indeed it was a choice.

Somewhere between this scene of Wynston-and-Guy, the elegant charming couple, incorporating and excluding Laurie all at the same moment, and the almost unimaginable couple Laurie and Guy once were, are surely shared and private scenes of loss and pain and anger and confusion and betrayal and heartache?

None of it shows on their faces, or not yet anyway.

For all her persistent talk of aging, Laurie looks, sometimes, in the evening as she laughs, talks, sews, gets up to move from table to bench and back again, very much a woman early on the path of her life. Open, vulnerable, beautiful. Did I once think her plain? It's already hard to make any sense of that.

Looking at her sewing, wanting to stay here with her to avoid the melancholy of my home-bound thoughts, I look forward also to the moment when I will set off for home and will be held, for just a minute, knowing that it marks my leaving but treasuring nevertheless that lovely, lovely holding.

Sinewy George. Soft Laurie.

Being held by George was sometimes a struggle. Tall as we both were we should have been well matched and yet often I felt just slightly squashed and even that hint of containment would be too much for me and I would push the poor darling off and away even while I longed to be softened, or to be *lessened* in my concern for self by his embrace.

Perhaps Laurie's embraces do soften me a little, fleeting though they are. There are only a few moments' leaning together on arrivals and departures; the occasional touch of a hand on an arm or in the small of a back; a transitory linking of eyes and hands in a moment of close sharing.

I could want more. I can readily imagine the ecstasy of rest that would follow from leaning for even a moment longer than I have ever dared on her shoulder, with her arm securely around me. I can close my eyes now and sense the combination of delights that would follow were I to be small enough, deserving enough, to lean my head against her breasts, breathing in the smell of her, relaxing against her sweet softness.

She would be surprised, I think, to know of these thoughts of mine. I could not dream of finding a way to tell her without embarrassing or even injuring us both.

Laurie and I have already clocked up many happy hours sitting in my own utterly familiar kitchen, and now, thinking of my own mother's kitchen, I realise that it must be almost sixty years since my mother and I embraced.

It seems a long time not to be held and caressed by another woman.

Of course there have always been the friends with whom one did hug a little, kiss on meeting and greeting, and again to farewell. But being held is not what women easily do for one another, outside times of grief or joy. Or not what *heterosexual* women easily do, as Laurie would make me say.

My mother did hold us all as little children, I think. *In my mother's arms.* The phrase doesn't sit easily with me.

I was about thirteen when I began to bleed and shortly after that I was inevitably developing breasts and stooping to hide this fact, sensing these signs of maturing were unwelcome to my mother. Am I wrong to think that from about that time her contact with my physical being entirely stopped? That her kisses were directed near to my face rather than onto it, and that even for that perfunctory kiss her head would duck uncomfortably forward while her body stayed well back, out of reach of any inadvertent touch?

Though surely she and my father did still touch then? She would have been only in her middle thirties, and he not much older. *Griffin and Nell.* People were of course much more reserved in those far-off days than now. 'Are they sexing, do you think?' I heard Gregory ask Rhea a couple of days ago as they watched an overly animated show biz pair displaying themselves somewhat lavishly across the TV screen.

'Nah! Frenching, I reckon,' was Rhea's world-weary reply, and when I lifted a curious eyebrow to Laurie she explained that 'sexing' means the mysterious and repulsive act – 'doing it' – and that 'Frenching' or kissing with opened mouths is, as she explained, 'A more imaginable act that both Rhea and Gregory still view with pleasurable disgust!'

Between my own parents there was never any sign of Frenching, and, beyond the birth of children, little evidence of sexing. Certainly they scrupulously acted out the ceremonies that marked my father's departure for a day's work and, ten hours later, his return home, though even those tender, polite scenes scarcely resembled the smooching, noisy, playful exits and entrances characteristic of George.

Trying to remember their signals of ease – or not – with expressing love, I become confused and wish I had never seen television! Images do crowd my mind but I cannot be entirely sure which of them are my own personal memories and which are simply frozen moments I have borrowed from the many often quite compelling television period dramas set in the years of my childhood. Looking at photographs doesn't tell me much either. They speak only of restraint.

But in those days of extremely precarious contraception, and after six fairly swift pregnancies, there were no more children after Peg, and Peg was born well before my mother had turned forty. That surely says something.

I fervently hope that was not the end of sexual love for them, but I fear it might have been. My sadness is for them both, not for my father only. Too much concern not to demand, not to intrude; too much hesitancy that itself led to paralysing embarrassment: that seems to be part of the flavour of my parents' private life. Though really I saw it only as a moderately unhappy child and then as an adult guilty with relief to be away. Neither perspective is more than shakily reliable.

I loved to sing, my mother had said, telling me of her wedding day. *I sang the 'Ode to Joy' . . . I, leaning on his arm.*

There was music occasionally, even after she began to turn away and fade. But she certainly did not sing. My father sang sometimes. Little ditties were what we would persuade him to give us, robustly sung snatches of songs about soldiers and their maids, bold sailors, wild men who marched into a future the outcome of which usually disintegrated into a la la la . . . And they listened together to their gramophone recordings, my mother always working on even as she listened, bent over whatever she was mending or holding needlework of one kind or another; my father reading a newspaper, a biography, maybe a thick volume of popular history.

That image, too, belongs to a television drama. Does it also belong to me, or to those two people who were and somehow remain my parents? I want to shake it off as a dog would shake off soapy water, fretting at the unnaturalness of it, impatient to get back to the real thing. Though not knowing any longer what the real thing is, except in elusive snatches.

18

At Laurie's gate I get the hug I've been expecting. Decently brief as it is, her touch settles me down, as I'd hoped it might. Too much wallowing in pain is just as harmful as too much avoidance of it. Sometimes it's hard though to break misery's spell from within – or hard for me, anyway. Feelings can settle like a lump inside me with no obvious way to shake them free. Sometimes it even takes me weeks to recognise the lump; weeks before I can even begin to make sense of the feelings it expresses or contains. Lost to myself: I understand that phrase.

What a blessing Laurie is with her warm ways. *How necessary she has become to me.* I freely admit it.

Laurie's front yard is tiny and concreted. As are the yards immediately to her left and right and all the way along her busy inner-city street. It has been drizzling and the armchair gardener in me senses in the damp the possibility of new growth.

Standing there, looking at her and around her, I feel moved to suggest to Laurie that together we might brighten her space up a little. Rubbish blows in as it is dropped by careless passers-by and not much can be done about that. But window boxes on the wide, low window ledges would raise one's eyes above ground level and could defy the concrete and the mess most effectively.

'I've got a couple of window boxes I no longer use,' I cheerfully, skilfully lie. 'They may well fit these spaces if you'd like them.'

Does she suspect me? She plays her part well. 'Great, Cordelia,' she says, smiling. 'If you're sure you don't need them. How big are they?'

I look, I hope, convincingly vague. 'Oh, about the right size. Why don't you measure up this space while I wait. Then I can check and call when I get home to see if they would do.'

'Sure. Sounds good to me.' She looks at me, laughs briefly, then turns on her heel and goes inside to fetch an impressively efficient-looking steel measuring tape. A *handywoman*, I think, admiringly.

While she carefully measures and notes width and breadth, I go further. 'Would a big wooden tub be in order too? To sit between that wall and this window? You know our garden's overflowing with plants begging to be divided or relieved of cuttings, and there are too few friends with gardens these days to use them all . . . I was wondering if something easy . . . shasta daisies maybe, scented geraniums, even a few herbs tucked here and there . . . and something trailing . . . a black-eyed Susan will grow anywhere, and set seed for the next year. You'd be giving them a much-needed home. And would certainly be doing me a favour.'

Laurie calls my bluff. 'A bevy of black-eyed Susans keeping watch in my front yard. It's irresistible! Thanks, Cordelia. Though these grotty conditions won't be what your hand-reared plants are used to . . . but as long as you promise to visit them as well as me from time to time, I guess they'll survive. You mustn't try to bring them by yourself. Let me come for them in Guy's car. Or better yet, let me send Guy and Wynston for them. They'd jump at a chance to call by.'

Does Laurie want to say something else? Apparently she does, although there is only so long I can continue to stand in this small patch of front yard, next to a green plastic garbage bin, without looking as though I am expecting something . . . Oh what the hell, I tell myself. Take a leaf from the girl's own book.

'Is everything all right, Laurie?'

She is grateful. She doesn't look at me, but her shoulders relax. Then she turns to me to say, 'It's not me or the kids. It's Wynston.

He's in danger of losing his job and I'm really concerned for him. It's extremely hard to get anything else these days, no matter how talented you are, and no matter how hard you try. He takes a lot of pleasure and pride in his work, too. As Guy does. They are both exceptionally good at what they do.' Laurie pulls a face. 'It's easier for me to be polite about Guy's work than most other areas of his life.'

'Is Guy safe?'

'As safe as anyone can be. He's more senior and has been on a long-term contract for some time, which is comforting. Wynston is only employed year by year. It's certainly a way to keep everyone's anxiety levels at fever pitch.' She is sighing and fiddling with the buttons on her shirt. This is obviously a matter of pressing concern to her. I am not surprised.

Laurie goes on, 'The chief librarian certainly doesn't want to see Wynston go. She warned him completely unofficially that this might happen just in case by some miracle Wynston's able to find something else. She will fight to keep him on if she can but funding decisions are made elsewhere by faceless bureaucrats. You know how it is.'

In fact, I don't. I know only what I read in the newspapers and glimpse on the television. That's enough, nevertheless, to enable me to imagine the awful powerlessness that long-distance decision-making engenders. My heart sinks. Not that a sunken heart can help Wynston. Or Laurie.

'Does he have plans?'

'Not at this stage. Of course it wouldn't be easy for them to move either if a job came up somewhere else – not only because of Guy's own current job, but also because of the children. We are inevitably bound up with each other until the children are grown and independent. Also I love Wynston. It's ironic, isn't it? I tolerate Guy because I must. For better or worse, the man is Gregory and Rhea's father. But I can actually love his boyfriend and feel appreciated by him in ways I was never appreciated by Guy even when we were together.'

'So there'd be losses for you as well as for the children if they moved?' I feel as if I am treading on egg shells here, though am not quite sure why. Laurie is unlikely, surely, to see my interest as prying?

'If they went somewhere else I could move too, I suppose, but I can hardly afford that. Anyway, I really don't want to. My contacts are close by here. My friends are near or nearish. I can always get a bit of teaching around here, my studio's all set up. There're lots of reasons to stay put. Even you are within brisk cycling distance, Cordelia.'

Even I . . . and I don't want them gone! How quickly this little two-household family has jumped the usual boundaries I keep around my life. Old friends I have known for years, and do sincerely care for, have been disgracefully neglected by me while I have applauded Rhea's lurid tales of last-minute crushing of opposing netball teams, or have listened with what I hope are appropriately timed nods of approval to Gregory's highly detailed and completely impenetrable descriptions of mysterious games involving Dungeons and Dragons, Tetris and Myst; while I have chatted to Laurie, pressing her to yet more tea or a dash of whisky, or have sat doing nothing more active than enjoying listening and encouraging her onwards as she speculates about her children, her work, her forthcoming show. I bask in my good luck in having come to know her.

And I have basked in the glow of her loving attention. I will freely, freely admit that too. Laurie is talented at loving. Generosity, support, kindness, a feeling that one is treasured: these are gifts she offers and I take. I take with a grateful heart.

In a couple of weeks I will see my three sisters and both my brothers, along with their mates – those who still have a mate – at a long-awaited reunion. I am looking forward to that enormously, but at an everyday level I am keenly aware that I am letting Laurie into secrets that my sisters could never share. My caution stems from something more pervasive and unsettling than the intensification, when we're together, of the deep inhibitions of our youth. We have been able to rise to meet most of the challenges of the differences between us over the years. Those differences are not a problem. It is what most obviously connects us that I realise again and again remains too sore to touch. As does our guilt. Guilt about our mother, our sadness for her and for our father; and perhaps a seam of anger too at how tightly held in we all were. Still are?

A new friendship at this late stage in my life looks to the future, to the having of a future indeed, and not to the past. Of course the past is with us; when is it not? It can be looked at anew, and selectively, with a friend, however. There seems some merit in that. In letting Laurie closer in, I am . . . what is it quite? Distracted from grief? *Accompanied*? Yes, that. Something else, too. Renewed? Maybe. Looked-after, anyway, and that's certainly not to be sniffed at.

An image from somewhere in my unruly mind leaps up to demand attention. It's from a dream I had almost forgotten until this unlikely moment.

In the dream I am puppet-sized, dressed in buttercup yellow sacking, squared off at the bottom. My head is chopped away from my body, yet head and body can observe one another. Half-awake in the middle of a long, restless night, I examined this image. Too sleepy to write it down or even note it, I nonetheless fought to retain it. 'I mustn't lose my head,' I told myself. So it was not the dream that was in danger of being lost, but my head?

Like a voice through a tin can from the past I hear Alice's loony Queen of Hearts crying '*Off with their heads. Off with their heads.*' My hands creep up of their own volition to hold my own quaking scalp steady, just in case. Only Laurie's voice brings me back to the present, back to her window boxes and our imminent farewell.

'Are you all right, Cordelia?' she is asking. 'You look awfully pale suddenly. Why don't you come inside and wait a bit before going home?'

'No,' I say, wanting to be immediately at home, preferably in the safest home of all: my own white-sheeted wooden bed. 'I'm fine. I've been thinking about people losing their jobs. And their heads. Though one not necessarily following the other! However, I'll take my morbid thoughts off home. They're not fit to be out.'

To send me on my way, I get another hug. A longer, healing hug. My head steadies on my body. God bless Laurie.

And for all that the threat of their bad news concerns me, as a taxi speeds me home I am singing.

In the great land mass south of the islands of New Zealand, winter is beginning.

Antarctica. Nine months of temperatures that could fall to more than 100 below zero. It is impossible for most of us to imagine how cold, how dark, how apparently unsupportive of life that is.

Far from that place, Cordelia is at her wheel, throwing what she hopes will be a large, evenly shaped jug. She is getting hotter as she works. She doesn't notice how shallowly she breathes. It is perfectly possible to keep adding water and so keep working the clay, moving it in its plasticity into an infinitely subtle variety of shapes. But Cordelia is superstitious. She wants to throw in a single cycle that moves more or less unhesitatingly from beginning to end. If that doesn't happen, if she has to stop and start again, some crucial rhythm that should exist between her vision, her mind, her hands, the clay, the wheel and her foot turning the wheel, breaks. She believes she can see that break reflected in the pot. It's not a literal seeing; it's visceral. But it's hard then for her to see anything else.

Although she is intensely concentrated on what she is doing, she is also thinking about Africa; or maybe not thinking exactly, but holding something about Africa in her mind. A fragment of brightly printed cloth, maybe; the blasting power of midday heat; the movement of light and shadow on black skin; a heightened and welcome intensity of colour wherever she looks.

Her nose itches and a drop of sweat runs down her cheek. Like the meditator, the potter can't lift a hand to scratch. Cordelia twitches the muscles in her face, to little effect. She grimaces and sniffs; that helps.

A small group of penguins waddles across a tiny corner of those icy Antarctica tracts. They seem to be in conversation with each other, but each disappears, apparently separately, into the water that remains to testify that summer is still echoing. The water scarcely moves but soon it will tighten, as though pausing. Drops of water will grip their neighbours, then freeze into a nine-month-long embrace. There will be no more dripping, dripping, splashing or sloshing. There will only be ice, stroked or whipped on its surface by winds that move through the darkness. The sun will neither rise nor set. Morning will not come. Night will fall, and will settle where it lies.

Doubt is a knot which needs to be undone.

This phrase has been written out in red ink on a small piece of yellow paper and is secured by a pineapple-shaped magnet on the fridge of one of my least doubt-plagued friends. Bronwyn Progoff is about as ancient as I am. Her husband Paul died many years ago though not before he had played his part in the conception of no fewer than seven robust children. And not before he had run up debts of an undisclosed origin which she then spent much of her widowhood scrupulously attempting to meet.

This did not depress Bronwyn.

It would seem that almost nothing could dampen the spirits of this fortunate woman. People, pets, food, gardens are what mean life to her and her commentaries on all her favourite topics make her the most delightful company. Earthy, salty, rich: those are the adjectives I think of when Bronwyn comes to mind.

We seem to have known her forever. There were always children around, but only two or three in the early days of our friendship so it must stretch back four decades or more.

Unfortunately, George appreciated Bronwyn a little less than he might have done. Or a little less than I hoped he might. Perhaps he was made uncomfortable by her willingness, indeed her eagerness to describe in detail the physical symptoms of her children's excretory health as well as their rare illnesses. I, on the other hand, have always enjoyed those sensuous, lingering descriptions of what was going in and out, or coming up or down. Hers were tales of direly wounded soldiers saved by the discriminating habits of maggots who eat only the already dead bits; of her own Fiona crawling bare-breasted through the woods with an involuntarily self-inflicted gun-shot wound to her leg, her shirt in use as a tourniquet; of Hugo's nights with Bali belly, privyless in remotest West Africa, if such a combination could possibly be feasible.

I could and did savour the almost literal pungency of those stories, but maybe George had seen too much first-hand.

Or maybe, and this thought is much harder to face, George envied Bronwyn the lavish size of her family when our own remained about as small as a family can be.

There were years when we didn't see much of her, and then something would happen – a mutual friend would bring us together again; I would find myself standing at the phone, calling her; she would turn up unannounced with cuttings for our garden or homemade wine or jam we simply had to try – and off we'd go as though the intervening months or even years had been irrelevant moments.

For many years Bronwyn ran a business from home. This, too, was somewhat mysterious. It appeared to involve answering several telephones, each with a separate number, and pretending to be a little other than she is. I expect that she was 'receptionist' for businessmen who could afford neither a genuine office nor a kosher receptionist. That explanation was too tame for George. He had Bronwyn's business life cast as no less than an early version of the kind of sex-by-phone that is apparently drearily commonplace these days. I doubt the darling woman could have kept her face straight for long enough to see the poor gents through their fevered misery and out the other side. But who knows.

Whatever her business was, it kept her at home and certainly never made her the money she needed, but her adult children and their many children live near her still and adore her, and these days her life may well be easier financially and physically than it has ever been. So why that quote? *Doubt is a knot which needs to be undone.*

Laurie would not have hesitated. There would not have been a second's pause between her reading such a message on a friend's fridge and her saying, *avidly*, 'A quote to send a shiver down the reader's spine. What's this all about then?'

Laurie's style is tremendously disarming, at least to me. She manages to combine a high degree of enthusiasm and even flattery with genuine eagerness to know more, and confidence that there is always more to know. But for me to ask someone with whom I have shared years of warmth, but no . . . prying . . . or to ask someone with whom I associate certainty, solidity and not doubt: the question just would not break free.

I did allow myself to stare a little more intensely than I might have done and wondered then if I was only imagining that Bronwyn was moving her substantial form from chair to bench and back again any more slowly than usual.

Those of us who are old are all subject to considerably more aches and pangs and stiffnesses (and worries about all three) than we once were, as well as to less reliable balance, sight, memory. Teeth, whether our own or sculptured for us, nag for constant attention. Even the waterworks – and worse (once Bronwyn's conversational province!) – become a matter of vigilance and concern. The list could go on, growing ever more dreary, but I refuse to allow that.

Speaking to her of my unexpected, delightful friendship with Laurie, stressing – perhaps quite unnecessarily – how Laurie is quite innocently pushing me to think anew about many areas of life where I had probably grown somewhat stale, I thought that I might lead Bronwyn herself somewhere new. *Doubt*, and the unravelling thereof. She resisted me though, or anyway wanted to tell me about Hazel, a grand-daughter, apparently terrifically keen on ceramics, who has been accepted into art school and is eager to meet some professionals or, more precisely and most unfortunately, me.

'Why don't you suggest she calls Laurie instead?' I automatically sidestepped. Then felt regretful that my first reaction to any kind of possible 'invasion' is always to retreat to my shell. Hiding and avoiding: I've done my share. There's not much about retreating that's generous. And, when I thought about it, I was a little curious about this long-unseen grand-daughter of my old friend. I vaguely remembered a blonde-haired butterball of a child who might have been Hazel or any one of several other heavenly little Progoffs.

Relenting, I tried again, 'Or come to me with her, Bron, and inspect what's emerging from what I ought not to call my African phase! Not that there's much to see, but there are a few stray pieces that you might like, and even if Hazel thinks them impossibly dreary she can then dance off to Laurie's to be inspired by her gorgeous spread.'

Bronwyn looked at me then, smiling and taking her time. 'I went to Africa once,' she began, enjoying my obvious surprise. 'Yes, indeed. It was Southern Rhodesia, as Zimbabwe was then called. I'd been invited by some relatives on my mother's side to stay on their farm although I did spend time in Salisbury too. A big country town it was, with rather too many pretensions. Pretty though: I thought it spacious and completely charming. The streets seemed to take minutes to cross. Shady verandahs protected us whites against sun and rain. Ladies were protected, too, against dropping their standards by the most rigorous wearing of hats and white gloves, never mind the heat. And if I think now about those streets I see lean black men, old and young, sweeping with wide straw brooms wielded in soft slow motion, though I might well have made that up. I can't remember much more, or anything about the people I stayed with. Friends of our relatives I think, or relatives of our relatives perhaps. That's gone now. It's the farm I remember.'

Bronwyn scraped her chair back across the floorboards, giving herself more space. 'I know you've read Olive Schreiner, Cordelia, and Doris Lessing's African stories of course, so you can imagine for yourself what that farm was like. And how I might have seen it and experienced it. Fabulous it was. Miles and miles from town. At that time it was a good day's hard driving along gravel roads that often petered out into a track. The road took you through country that seemed to have no beginning and no end. It just was. One might well have been driving always, thighs sticking to the hot leather seat of the car, an elbow stuck out of a wound-down window, head stretched back to catch the breeze, and all of life passing.

'That drive showed me something: that boundaries are not God-given – they're man-made. It was a heady discovery for a naive young woman! Every moment and every aspect of my life had been determined by boundaries. I'd thought they mattered. Suddenly I saw them as arbitrary, totally arbitrary. I felt quite drunk with the power of that!' Her voice had risen and filled the room.

I nodded, startled by this completely unexpected revelation from Bronwyn, then by the Africa images that arose from my own brief visits there, and perhaps even more from my avid reading and re-reading of early Lessing.

Bron's voice still boomed. 'This was before the war. There were only a few hundred thousand whites in Southern Rhodesia. I was related to about a hundred of those! It was a pretty usual experience, going off to relatives for a while, getting in a bit of well-chaperoned adventure before the inevitable "settling down" of marriage in suburbia. I was simply following well-tried convention. But I was much more disturbed by my adventure than I could possibly have anticipated. And I got much more out of it than my innocent parents intended.'

She paused to drink her tea. I was glad of the break. It was hard to be simultaneously in the veldts of southern Africa and in Bronwyn's cramped, hot kitchen where the windows were steamed up and a clock ticked disgracefully loudly. Then she said, quite obviously regretfully, 'For years afterwards I went on waking up from sleep believing that I was still there on that farm. It was always disappointing to find that I wasn't.'

That sense she was describing – of feeling more at home in a dream than the world one wakes to – is certainly familiar to me, too. I was about to tell her that, but Bron was already talking.

'I didn't get a chance to meet any black people socially of course.

Those were still the dreadful days when most whites quite unselfconsciously referred to Africans as 'Afs'. When it dawned on me what they were doing I was shattered by the contempt that diminutive expressed. It seemed shaming – of the whites who used the expression, not of the Africans. When they weren't "Afs" they were "Kaffirs", or "boys". How vile! Anyway, my own relatives were mildly progressive by the norms of the day and didn't pay too much attention when I spent time sitting where their maids were working or even talking to them whenever they were momentarily still.

'Later I learned how unusual it was to have maids. Most Southern Rhodesians employed men in their houses then. Whatever the reason for this exception, it was lucky for me.

'On the room-width verandahs that ran all the way around the house the maids would sometimes be available for a few moments' rather one-sided talk although their hands were always busy or ready to be busy. In their hands they held the tools of their next round of activity – a broom, usually. They would grip the handle, ready to spring into action when my aunt or uncle came in sight. I was astonished by their differences from the girls and women I had grown up with, and even more astonished by their familiarity. I believed I knew these women – and simultaneously understood I didn't know them at all.' Bronwyn stopped speaking. Then she asked, 'Do you mind if I go on? It does seem to be a day for memories . . .' Her voice trailed off, almost apologetically.

'Please do say more,' I told her. 'I'm imagining *myself* into the situation, but that won't do at all. I want to know how it was for Young Bronwyn.'

She patted my hand. Her own hand was soft and warm. 'You know, Cordelia, it followed on from that first insight about boundaries.'

'What did?' She'd lost me.

'Rules. Questioning the rules about what it means to be a woman. How those rules were arbitrary too, yet they'd been presented to us with all the solemnity of Moses' tablets. I realised that was a crock of shit. It was those maids who turned my mind around.

'I watched them obsessively, as though there was a problem to be solved through the concentration of my attention, and gradually I came to see how differently those women felt about themselves from the way I did. I remember quite distinctly that I lay on my bed on an especially hot afternoon, baking under a mosquito net, unable to read for the unaccustomed heat and wishing I was anywhere but inside my own body. Then it struck me how fragile my connection was to my own body at the best of times, in comparison to what I had perceived about those African women. After that, rather than trying to talk to them, I spent even more time learning: just watching them move, watching them bending, sweeping, carrying, coming together and parting and trying to make some sense of what I was seeing.

'I hadn't known until then that it's possible to communicate through the body, and through feelings. I'd thought talk was the only way.'

The door bell rang. Bronwyn went to answer it, then was speaking again as she came back into the room. 'Please don't think I'm not aware that it sounds like such a cliché to talk about how African women *move*, for God's sake. It's just that when you think how damped down we were ... and the shock was, I hadn't realised that until Africa. The prevailing attitudes at home were utterly unquestioned. At least by dimwits like me. Good Lord, I don't think it's too much to say that our own bodies were strangers to us. Not just strangers either, *dangerous* strangers that could lead us where no decent man should follow! We floated around in uneasy proximity to our own bodies. Isn't that right? Of course we saw dazzling vamps up on the screen. That was different. That was the world of make-believe. No woman that I actually knew took *pleasure* in her body.'

'And it mattered,' I said, as much to myself as to Bronwyn.

'Maybe for some women it didn't matter a jot. For someone like me, however, your true-blue Earth Mother type, to be separate from the body is to be more than half-dead. Does that sound impossibly dramatic?'

'Impossibly!' I laughed, and when Bronwyn laughed with me her chins wobbled and her shoulders shook. Under her purple T-shirt the outlines clearly showed of two huge, soft, unrestrained breasts.

How had I thought about my own body as a young woman, I wondered. *Obliquely* was the word that came to my mind. I dressed hurriedly. And undressing, whether I was alone or with George, there was always some poor bit of my body that I was frowning at, if not actually criticising.

I have always liked being tall, and have generally trusted that with a bit of spit and polish I could make a reasonable impression on others. But that impression seemed distant from me. It seemed like something I made available, rather than something I experienced myself.

Bronwyn spoke again. 'Each African woman's confidence that she *had* a body was revelatory to me. It was possibly quite shocking too – in the best sense of the word. The shock woke me up. The women spoke and laughed and sang and worked and walked with a sensuousness that made something in me come alive. Just the way bare feet could touch the floor then be lifted up again from the floor as they walked captivated me. Or the touch of those same feet spreading out on hard earth as they appeared and disappeared on roads and paths. That was different again. And equally wonderful.

'Not that they were all the same, of course not. But at least in memory each one of those young women had something about them . . . something refined and extravagant. Theirs was an unselfconscious display of inner grace that I'd never come across before. Not recognising it anyway.'

Was Bronwyn stopping because she feared she had already said too much? We are the 'little goes a long way' generation. I wanted to know more. 'Was it only the women?' I asked her. It wasn't quite the question I meant to ask but that eluded me. 'Do you remember being struck by the men too, because when I think about Lessing's stories, surely there's a lot of close observation of men and boys, isn't there? Old chiefs. Young warriors.'

Bronwyn laughed. 'The men might have had this inner beauty, too,

of course. It would have been completely out of the question though
to stare at them. Or watch the movement of their mouths and eyes!
Probably unforgivably offensive, as well. Anyway, for a young heterosexual woman as inexperienced as I was, the beauty of those women
was more than enough.

'You know, Cordelia,' Bronwyn leaned towards me to emphasise
her point and again covered my hand with her own, '*inside* those women
was a greater freedom than I had been allowed to imagine. Or a greater
sense of legitimacy. Their femaleness was their core. It was their version
of honour. I'd willingly bet that it permeated everything they thought
and felt and did. It didn't seem to me to need tidying up, or constrain-
ing, or domesticating as mine did. It wasn't to be feared either. Nor
apologised for. I was white, middle-class, moderately well educated,
with chances to travel and some choice about whether and who to
marry. They were servants, badly paid, shockingly housed, having to do
dreary work for white racists occupying and changing their country.
And probably putting up with crap from their men when they got home.
Yet I believed that I was not freer than they. Not then anyway.'

We sat in silence. In forty years of friendship Bronwyn had never
spoken of this. Never even mentioned the key word: Africa.

'I did speak about this once to George.'

This startled me. Perhaps I had too complacently assumed that
Bronwyn's confidences would always have come to me?

I was ashamed of this complacency, and yet again – when would it
ever stop? – was suddenly horribly lonely, too. Of course I could understand exactly why she would have confided in George, and, understanding that, I wanted to get home as fast as age and traffic would allow to
tell George just how effectively Bronwyn had surprised me. I wanted
to press him to try to remember that long-ago party when he and
Bronwyn had talked. I wanted to know much more precisely how he
himself felt about Africa. Then, and now too. I wanted to know all
about how he himself had been changed by his many visits there.

How is it possible that in fifty years I neglected to ask my husband all that I'd like to know in order to understand him? Was it laziness, lack of care or insight? Or was it that I had never really come to terms with the possibility that one day he would not be here? What an absurd failure of imagination.

I want to talk to George *now*, to talk about relative freedoms *now*. I want him to hear me contrast what I believe was possible for Bron or me with what I see as possible for Laurie. For Rhea, things will be different again.

Not that those differences are all gains. They are not. As George himself would ask, how should we measure progress? Do we dare even speak of progress without crossing our fingers behind our backs?

Yet if I think of my mother's inner restrictions, and then jump to think of Laurie's expressive, dynamic daughter Rhea, it becomes extremely tempting to assert that this century has given Western women a great deal. The courage of women to name, to fight, to think, to assert, to challenge, to confront, to write, to envision and express freedoms has not been in vain.

Right now, I want to say all of that to George. Then without pausing, I want to add how tragic as well as ironic it is that while women have made those twentieth-century gains, our planet Earth has been stripped of resources at an unprecedented rate, abused, misunderstood and degraded – to achieve what? Something that reflects a massive social psychosis. Yet is also called progress.

So now the challenge is: can women use their new freedoms in time to save the Earth? Women – and also the men who care; for some do care. One of them was George.

Having said that, and more too, probably, I want fiercely and passionately to hold George tight in my arms. Letting him go again, I'd sit beside him on our big sofa, side by side, watching the evening news on television, warming and refilling our glasses, putting the politicians to rights from the safety of our domestic pulpit.

As the talking slowed, I'd revel in the luxury of taking him for granted, ignoring him and being ignored as we pick up books or papers, losing ourselves in what we are reading, and only after some time returning to a shared and vital present.

Unfair, a part of me cries. Unbearable, the chorus in me echoes.

I want George alive. Not dead. Not dead. Not dead.

Who or what could I rail against? Who or what should I blame? Who or what can I ask for help?

No one. Nothing. Nothing.

Forget doubt. *Grief* is a stranglehold that needs to be undone. For the missing of him, the wishing for him, the longing for him, the rage that he is not here: none of it will ever, ever stop.

My hands are fists. My throat is tight. There is no breath left in my body. I want to get up and flee, but Bronwyn has seen my surprise and perhaps something of my grief. She wants to reassure me. Do I want that? Whatever, I stay where I am.

'It was when George had been there for several months in one hit,' Bronwyn is saying, when I finally pay attention. 'You remember, was it to Mozambique?'

It was. I nod. And leave my hopeless railing against fate to reconnect with her story. Though not easily.

'Months after he was there we had a quiet moment at one of your gorgeous parties and I said a little bit of what I've said to you today. He was interested. That was what was such a treat about George, Cordelia. You didn't have to entice his interest or excavate it as you must with run-of-the-mill men. George handed you his interest on a platter, trussed and ready. For all that, though, I could tell it was not the same for him. Africa was another place with a bottomless pit of problems for George. His wondrous place was India, as we both know. George's Africa just didn't compare, and I could understand that. We can't embrace too many experiences in this way or we'd be completely worn out!'

Thankfully, I am more genuinely composed now, with attention to give. My curiosity revived. 'Didn't you ever want to return? Didn't you want to see Rhodesia again, or see it become Zimbabwe?'

Bronwyn was shaking her head. 'For years it was totally out of the question financially. Besides which, I was reluctant. I wanted to keep those extraordinary memories pure. And they've served me very well. It was because of them I married Paul who for all his many faults was an earthy fellow who also lived easily in his body. He knocked me sideways when we met because he was confident about being a man in the same unselfconscious way those maids had seemed confident about being women. Hence all those children.' She giggled, looking away, decidedly not unhappy to be remembering.

'Why didn't I tell you all this years before? You're wondering that, aren't you, Cordelia?'

I nodded. Bronwyn sank her face into her hands, taking time, then looked up. 'Can you understand that I felt almost guilty about how much I'd gained from my Africa time, as though I had invaded someone else's territory and the plunder I'd brought home with me were these imaginative riches? Maybe that's why I've never talked about it to you, Cordelia. Perhaps I was afraid you could only think my story sentimental.'

I shook my head. She went on, 'After all, can whites legitimately haul a revised personal story out of a colonised country? Is there any difference between imposing European culture on those who may not want it, and appropriating something which is undoubtedly self-serving and probably also romanticised and far too simple?

'Those kinds of doubts shut me up. I had no way of talking about the richness of my experiences *or* my dilemma about that richness. No one to talk to either. Not even George with that. But the appreciation I feel for us women dates from that African time. For that alone it seems impossible that my bit of myth-making should be entirely wrong. Perhaps I have even appreciated myself quite differently.'

'Yourself?'

'Yes, me.' Her tone forgave my abruptness. 'Several of my grand-daughters carry on about witches and goddesses and women's magic and so on. Hazel's a belly dancer and Frances is studying sacred dance as well as law. I'm not up with all of that, but I certainly do have a sense of what they mean. For all I've always stayed at home, I'm a less domesticated creature than I'd otherwise have been. Less diminished than the woman I was raised to be. And so are my girls. So are their girls. That can't be all bad!'

Yet again I thought of my mother. Domesticated. Diminished. Not by her own mother, who after all had raised the roof with her screaming protests, but by the social order of her time, by her individual lack of openness, and perhaps by a choice – at some unidentifiable point in her life – to turn her back on living and not embrace it. Not because Griffin wanted that. Only because nothing else seemed possible?

What an afternoon!

Bronwyn got up to clear away our cups and plates, then immediately sat down again, looked at me intently, and asked, 'Did we really have this conversation, Cordelia? Isn't this the kind of talk that only goes on in books?'

It was impossible not to laugh. 'We did,' I said. 'So clearly it's not.'

'You're a good friend.'

At once I felt hot. Blushed, probably. It wasn't necessary for her to say that. 'You too.'

Now Bronwyn really did stack the cups and plates as I handed them to her, saying, in a much more matter-of-fact tone than she had been using, 'So there you have it!'

This was clearly the end of the conversation. I was stirred up as well as exhausted.

Africa. Witches. Goddesses. The magic of place. Of women. Freedom.

Black feet hitting the dust and lifting up again. Black feet pliable on polished wooden floors. Black feet dancing. Running. Standing still.

Black hands pushing brooms in soft, slow motion. *New broom sweeps clean.*

Dust. Rhythms. Rounded shapes. Clay. *Doubt.*

Time for home.

There is no failure in the search for God.

SWAMI PRABHAVANANDA

Two mothers.

I've heard Rhea tell her friends, loudly, proudly, 'Mum had two mothers.' In that telling it sounds a great deal richer than I have ever felt it to be.

Once upon a time there lived a little girl whose first and only name was Lorraine. This little girl had two eyes, two arms, two hands, two legs, two feet and two mothers . . .

Only one father. A good man. I was certainly lucky there. Apart from all else – and there was much else – he introduced me to clay. Not that he was ever a potter; he was an anthropologist. A small, slim sandy man who would not have looked especially large or out of place among the people he studied and loved. Rock-grey eyes. Wore wide-brimmed, canvas hats because he burned easily. And sandals. Roman sandals in dark brown leather. Never especially successful. Never published or footnoted in the most prestigious publications. Never to rise above Senior Lecturer in a far-from-famous university. Yet none of this mattered much to him. He did work he loved and constantly thanked God, chance and destiny for that privilege and good fortune.

The hard part is that what he loved most took him away from me. He would go off for weeks at a time to a village in Central America. He had been spending regular periods there since he was a young post-graduate student. He had learned the obscure language of those people. He knew their kinship networks. He observed their customs extremely carefully and followed them himself most scrupulously. If he did blunder, he laughed with the villagers when they laughed at him. And although he enjoyed laughing with them I don't expect he made that same blunder again. He was a man whose greatest pleasure was to pick up on the tiniest details of whatever it was he happened to be observing. Nor did his pleasure end there. His delight was always immediately and contagiously articulated. That was extremely precious to me as a child. And I am sure the villagers must have seen the man I saw.

Returning from those trips away – some funded by the university, but more funded from his own careful savings – he would bring small figures made of clay. They were often stick-like, but carefully dressed with tiny scraps of material so their gender was not in any doubt. And their nakedness was hidden. Their features were at best blurred, more often absent, but that appealed to me. I could imagine a whole range of emotions for them, and was eager to do that.

Walking into the house – still in the hallway, not yet sat down, his bag and knapsack simply dropped at his feet – he would begin to tease.

'Can you guess what I've brought for you, Laurie?' he would ask, beaming.

'I can't guess. I can't possibly guess. It could be anything,' I would shriek, dreading that this one time he might not have what I wanted most.

Sometimes he did pull other things out of his bag first: peacock-coloured woven scarves, pieces of fabric, small and large embroidered bags, musical instruments I enjoyed looking at though would never play. But always, eventually, there would be new members of my clay family. 'Yes! Yes!' My relief must have been palpable, and then shrieking wasn't enough. I would jump up on my father, monkey-style, wrapping arms around his neck and legs around his waist, rocking him with my delight. Threatening to topple him, loving the hard feel of him and the musty, dusty smell of him that I never remembered missing until I had it all over again.

He could not possibly have come back from those journeys musty, dusty, hot or sweaty. A fastidious man who has travelled by train, and then for many hours on a plane, does not disembark with distant village dust ingrained in his shirt and sandals, his face, neck and hands. Yet that is how he exists in my memory, as though he had walked in a direct route from that far-off village along a path which only after many miles and weeks of patient, steady walking became our front path, a path leading to the door he had just walked through, which was our front door.

My mother, patiently waiting, quiet alongside my exuberance, would insist he sat down, and that he accept a cup of tea or glass of beer, before the time was right for her to get her own colourful gifts. Clothes most often I think, although after an initial dress parade of thanks I don't remember her ever wearing them. I remember her in plain fabrics, synthetic pastels that did, undeniably, wash easily and well.

It was probably years after the first of those little people had arrived that I really took in that these marvels were made of clay and that I, too, could have clay and make figures for and by myself. Until that time I had spent hundreds of hours playing what I used to call 'grindings' which meant grinding stones or bits of rock together until the softer one would yield powdery granules which I would then mix to various consistencies with water. I would find these rocks or stones in our own garden or on visits to the country, or the seaside. Crushing shells was also part of it. And sometimes adding minced-up leaves or flowers or seeds.

My parents were absolutely tolerant of this game, and encouraged it by finding rocks and shells that would deliver up sandy grains of very different colours. That's what I liked best. I would keep separate colours in small glass jam jars that I would then label with what I fondly imagined to be poetic names relying heavily on alliteration: 'Primrose Pink', 'Rustic Red', 'Barnyard Brown'.

Playing this game through all its many phases totally absorbed me. I have seen Gregory and Rhea squatting, close to the ground, similarly absorbed by water, sand, mud, leaves, twigs – in varying combinations.

When they were younger and less self-conscious than they are now, they would provide a stream-of-consciousness commentary as they worked, sometimes alone, as I always was, more often alongside each other.

'I'm making a mixture for my baby.'

'Let's pretend we both have babies and they don't want to eat what we're making.'

'Have you got any of those leaves? Those leaves are mucky. I like mucky leaves. My baby likes leaves. Pretend you weren't looking and I found lots more leaves and you didn't know there were any more.'

'Pretend I took some of yours. I've got lots of yours.'

'My baby's crying now. Pretend I've got lots of another kind too and you want them.'

'Do you really have a baby?'

'Do you?'

I used to want to listen in to every single one of those private musings, yet rarely could. Sometimes I have longed to escape my children, or maybe not them but the demands they constantly and legitimately make on me. Yet, at precisely the same moment, no intimacy between them and me could be too great. Listening in was the closest I could come to climbing right inside their precious heads, yet I knew that if I stepped too close their concentration would be broken and their attention would turn away from their absorbing task and on to me. The moment would be lost.

Petra, Cordelia's gardener, also chatters and laughs and sings while she does her work in that wonderful garden Cordelia still refers to as George's patch. Cordelia says Petra is talking to the plants and that's why they do so well. I suspect she is also talking to herself, or simply expressing one thought in order to make room for the next. Either way, that luscious garden benefits.

My father bought me my first block of clay. I was eleven. Even then I was self-conscious and beginning to recognise my need for substantial distraction from my own rather gloomy, circular thoughts.

The clay was oil-based, orange-brown in colour, and easy to work. I wish I could say that when I sliced off my first lump and began to soften it in my hands I knew what my vocation was. I don't think it was quite that simple.

The clay was marvellous to work with. It was easily pliable and much less drying of my hands than mud had been. But the cats and dogs and horses and people I carefully created – which looked so satisfyingly realistic when they were newly made – would dry and then, only a day or two later, would crack and finally break. Legs would collapse. Carts would topple. Hats and tails would be lost.

I would hate the pieces then, and throw them away, down into the back of the garden or stuff them angrily in the bin. Why, I would rant and shout, did the little clay statues my father had brought all the way from Central America survive intact, but not my pieces that had gone no further than from my craft table to the family mantelpiece?

'Press on, Laurie,' my father would say. 'Let the clay itself teach you what you can do with it.'

He would remain calm and encouraging even when I cried, or shouted that I hated the stuff, and wouldn't ever try again.

But the frustration of not working with the clay was even greater than the frustration of not having an answer to my question. Back the clay would come – different colours at different times as both parents kept me supplied – and on I would go, making increasingly elaborate shapes as my hands and the clay began a love affair all their own.

When I was thirteen, my father died.

He died in his sleep. He was fifty-one. His name was Angus Cunningham and he had no brothers or sisters or parents. There was an autopsy. It showed he'd had undiagnosed and I believe unsuspected diabetes.

My mother had gone to sleep beside a warm, alive husband and woke up beside his corpse. How frightening that must have been for her I can barely guess at. It may even have been what she feared most: that he would be taken from her without warning. That's how she would have said it: 'taken from her'. Every power was greater than her own.

She loved him, too, though we loved him separately. Our love for him did not connect the two of us.

In much the same way a child might, as perhaps I did – I am no longer sure about this – she relied on him for almost everything. His infrequent but regular absences made her more clingy rather than less. He had tolerated that most amiably, perhaps for no more striking reason than that he could tolerate almost anything while he still had his work, and the promise of more visits to the village.

After his death she fell apart. Her disintegration was much slower than that of my hand-made clay figures, but as inevitable. First she took too many analgesics. Every day. Though she was still getting up and getting dressed at that stage. Still tidying and cleaning much as she had done. Then she began to take too many tranquillisers. Every day. And got washed and dressed less often. By then she didn't seem to notice when the house became a mess.

Soon after she began to drink whisky, while still taking the tranquillisers and adding on sleeping pills. By now she stayed in bed on most of the days she did not absolutely have to get up. I came and went to school and to the shops and to part-time work in cafes just as I pleased. She left the house only to see her obliging liquor store proprietor or her almost equally obliging family doctor.

Her interest in me could not outrun her interest in herself. She had no interest in herself. She ate almost nothing of the meals I learned to cook.

They were dull meals: spaghetti, tinned soups, stringy uneven stews, overcooked chops, boiled vegetables, occasional drab salads. Who could blame her for not eating them?

I did.

She didn't die until I was almost eighteen and old enough – officially – to look after myself. She was fifty-five and looked ten years older. Her name was Anita Cunningham. She, too, had no brothers or sisters or parents. I knew almost nothing about her that had any lasting meaning although in my position as spy and caretaker I had known intimately the increasingly devious patterns of her addictions.

The passivity of her married lifetime, appreciated as easy-going indulgence by my father and me, had transformed after his death. Passivity then became the means that would hasten her own death. In this she showed a flinty determination that seemed to have no history but was there fully formed when she needed it.

Her death came as a victory over life for her and as a relief. One day she was hardly there. The next day she was not there at all. It was a relief for me, too, and yet, in the wake of it, I became afraid.

I also became temporarily passive. Perhaps that was grief – or fear – though it certainly didn't feel like grief at the time. It felt like apathy.

An older friend came to stay. He had been among my father's last group of post-graduate students and appeared to have remained a student himself on an indefinite basis. More mysteriously, he had kept occasional touch with our depleted household. He was probably only twenty-five or twenty-six, but seemed adult enough to me then to give me some ballast when I needed it.

His name was Morris, but I hardly ever called him that and when I thought of him at all I called him to myself, 'Dad's student'.

We had sex for the first time the afternoon he arrived. We did it on the sofa next to a pile of newspapers I was too lazy to remove. I didn't mind lying there, my head propped up on a cushion or two. Letting Morris take my clothes off. Half-watching while he took off his.

It was not simply my first time with him. It was my first time. But what should have been a momentous occasion wasn't. The sex made little impression on me. He was kind enough and tolerant enough. That was a great virtue in my eyes. He was also considerate enough to expect

little from me. His tolerance was quite cheerful. Sometimes halfway
through sex he would simply roll away, pick up his downturned book,
and begin to read wherever he had just left off. That was what I liked
about him most: that reading gave him more consistent and obvious
pleasure than sex did.

Some time later he said he liked me and wanted to stay.

After all, not many girls of eighteen own a reasonably pleasant
suburban house, mortgage-free and parent-free. Did I want him there?
I wonder now if it even occurred to me to ask. I initiated nothing.
Barely questioned my own motives, never mind my own needs. Dad's
student was there. Sex was tolerable. Loneliness would have been
worse.

More friends stayed. In various combinations we all had sex, smoked
dope, drank whatever we could afford, played music loudly and disturbed the neighbours who took their time to complain as they believed
I was an orphan.

Which is not entirely true.

My parents had always intended me to understand that they had
chosen me, rather than my mother having given birth to me. I muddled
this piece of information up with my father's trips away and thought –
and enjoyed this thought – that I had, like the clay figures, come from
the village in Central America that caused my father to glow when he
spoke of it.

I must have articulated this fantasy at some point, and I don't believe
they entirely disabused me. Perhaps they recognised that for me to learn
I had not come from the magical village my father loved would have
been a much greater blow than fully understanding I had not come from
my mother's body.

Through this I became, in some self-made way that was also fostered
by my father's collusive hesitations about the truth, his own, his special
daughter. I became Athena, born from the head of my father Zeus. Like
Athena, I despised Hera-Anita, refusing to mourn her or even particularly to notice her passing.

Years later when my second child was born, and lay between my spread-eagled, shaky legs, bloodied from her own birth, face wrinkled, startled, a newborn human smelling inexpressibly sweetly of vernix, head slightly awry, arms and legs moving disbelievingly with no uterus to contain them, her throbbing umbilical cord still attached to the placenta which remained within me, blood emptying through the cord, from me to her; looking down at her, seeing her gorgeous, very slightly swollen but unmistakably female genitals, I did then, without even a moment's hesitation as I scooped her up to comfort her in her nakedness against the nakedness of my own enlarged breasts, resolve to give that infinitely precious, already totally beloved girl one of the names of the Great Mother herself. I did, too. Nothing less would have done.

The irony of that didn't strike me for years.

Kate Hallardyce was the name of the woman who, in reality, gave birth to me. In very different circumstances I am sure from those of Rhea's birth. And very far from any Central American village.

Going into labour, she already knew that she would soon be parted from me. That I would be parted from her. Whoever I might eventually turn out to be, I was already the product of her shame. She was, I imagine, without anyone familiar to support her in the labour ward. Very young. Very frightened. Very vulnerable.

Not that she told me any of this.

I found her a few years after my mother died. It wasn't especially difficult despite considerable ambivalence on my part. My experience of mothers had so far not been promising. I said aloud several times that it was against the odds I could do much better on a second round. But perhaps to myself I allowed some wispy thoughts of reparation or reward.

The boyfriend I had at the time thought seeking out my birth mother was a good idea. He himself was one of several 'natural' children in a family that also included some adopted children. They had all, apparently, made highly successful reunions with their birth mothers. His optimism was much greater than mine. Even his curiosity outran mine.

Of course I could have resisted him and maybe I did for a while, but it could be that his detailed anecdotes aroused me so that eventually I also hoped for something more from my discoveries than I eventually found.

'I was raped,' was what she told me first.

Or maybe not first, but when she first met my eyes.

We were sitting in the lounge of a large hotel not far from where she lives. It's the same town where she's always lived. Life hasn't taken her far.

I was recovering from the shock of realising how young she is. Probably no more than seventeen or eighteen years older than me and still looking far younger than I could ever remember my adoptive mother being. Even when Dad was still alive. I guess at the time of our meeting she was no older than I am now. Yet there she was, sitting face to face with an adult daughter.

She wasn't dark either, as I am and as I had unconsciously expected her to be. She has the reddish, springy hair and pale, freckled skin I associate with Celts. Her colouring distanced me; and so, perversely, did her youth.

She had already told me on the telephone that I would not be welcome at her house and must never write to her nor ring her there. She has a husband she claims to love but is certainly afraid of. A well-spoken, mean-minded bully is how I imagine him to be. I pictured him with a folded spotted handkerchief tucked into his navy blazer pocket, and a pseudo-nautical tie tied tightly beneath a spreading prematurely florid face. Without meeting him, I knew him and I hated him. I pitied her for marrying him. I was to make no trouble for her, she pleaded. I promised.

The man who raped her was not a stranger. He had been her steady boyfriend but had broken off the relationship when he went away to study. To study theology, no less. 'He always had been clever,' she told me, without any approval of that. His cleverness had not served her well.

Did she inspect me then, for tell-tale signs of cleverness? She would have found them hard to find. My face was almost certainly closed, wary, maybe flushed in ugly red patches betraying my nervousness. Her body was neat. She had the look of a prize-winning Siamese cat about her, superior, sleek and slim. Only her eyes were opened a little too wide, as though her inner dial was permanently on Startle. My own body was slumped in on itself and lumpish, and I was unimaginatively dressed in black jeans and slogan-laden T-shirt. My hair was cut too short and a crowd of silver studs skirted the edge of one ear. Sleek, perfumed, smooth-legged and conventionally feminine as she herself was, she probably thought me extremely unappealing. Unrecognisable, even as a type. Unbelonging. Certainly her wide-eyed gaze didn't linger.

Coming back to their home town just for the holidays, the boyfriend had expected her to take up with him again. I see him as tall, bearded, slightly stooped, boy-thin. He must have been dark too, like me I guess. Dark hair. Dark eyes. Long lashes. Intense probably, and arrogant. Taking far too much for granted. She, proud in a way that I can readily imagine, had refused him. He had forced her . . . to do what? To kiss him? To let him touch her on the breasts, the belly, her vagina? To have her touch him. Where? To let him penetrate her? Had she been willing to go this far, or this far, or this far: but, to punish him for his abandonment, no further?

I couldn't ask. I also had my pride and it isn't the prettiest beginning.

Perhaps then Kate pitied me, having told me the worst. Brightening up she ordered tea, cakes, scones. Afternoon tea enough for an entire family. It arrived on a pretentious silver tray and sat untouched on a table between us. Neither of us chose to be mother.

Kate took a wallet from her purse, and from the wallet emerged a brightly coloured photograph of her two adolescent sons. Scrubbed. Groomed. Expensively and conservatively dressed. Redheads, both of them. Like their Mum. Her voice changed. Now it was filled with maternal love. 'This one's Mark and my younger boy is Damon. Such good boys,' she told me, 'and really good-looking, don't you see?'

I did see, but clearly she did not. Was she completely unaware that she was talking to her own daughter about that daughter's two half-brothers? It is just possible that she was. She had shut me out before I had begun and nothing now would change that.

Telling my own boyfriend about it a day later, I noticed how little I was feeling. There was certainly some disappointment. Scorn maybe. Fear that my unloving start might be visible to the discerning. But I thought tenderly of Zeus-Angus, and that passed.

That meeting with Kate was such an extraordinarily brief encounter, almost meaningless in the words spoken and the feelings exchanged. In those crucial ways, it seemed an uncanny repetition of my own conception.

I wondered sometimes if she would be sorry and try to contact me to apologise. Perhaps I even hoped for that, though not especially fiercely. And in saner and less self-pitying moments I saw that in her eyes there could be nothing to apologise to me for. She was the injured one; I merely the unfortunate by-product of that injustice.

When I eventually married Guy and changed my name from Cunningham to Kerbala, I worried momentarily that now she could never find me. But having sent a note to the same agency that had arranged our first, futile meeting, informing them of my changed name and new address, and having had nothing in return but an acknowledgement and words of congratulation on my marriage from the social worker, I put Kate Hallardyce out of my mind, and returned to the persona of Athena.

That was, after all, what I knew best.

22

Sleep is still not a safe place. Rain brought me easily to wakefulness and though it is hours until dawn, it seems impossible to rest in bed.

The fact is, I want to pray. I want to sink into prayer as I used to be able to sink into my great carved bed, knowing it would support me and give me rest, and deliver me up ready next morning for a new day.

I want that from God.

I want to speak to God. More than that, I wish that God would speak to me. Speak to me in words I could immediately understand. I am tired of hunting for signs and guessing at omens.

Beside the bed in several uneven piles are twenty or more books and pamphlets bringing a wealth of suggestions and well-tried practices from every corner of the world. From every major spiritual tradition. I am willing to learn from any of them, or from them all.

I could pick any one of them up at random. Letting the spirit, or my own unconscious, guide me. Not one of the books would be 'wrong'. I could put them into a single neat pile and work through them one by one. Missing nothing, or anyway, missing nothing that is actually printed on the page.

But would I find God?

I could get out of bed and fall to my knees with my hands pressed together like a steeple: *Our Father . . . Gentle Jesus, sweet and mild . . . And on the third day he rose again from the dead . . .* and *ascended into heaven.*

Conjuring up those long unused prayers makes a change from recalling cocktail recipes, but seems nearly as meaningless. Or maybe more so. The dress rehearsal we had with those excavated cocktail recipes was really very jolly. Worth repeating probably, although I doubt that I'll get around to it. Whereas those traditional prayers were learned by someone I remember well, and rather fondly, but that is no longer who I am.

With some difficulty and stiffness – but nevertheless I could still manage it – I could sit cross-legged on a generous pile of cushions with my eyes closed, aware of each breath leaving my nostrils, as my mind, or my Self, expands from the confines of conscious thought to enter a state of spaciousness and stillness. A cloudless sky of infinite dimensions. A state of mind where all my current petty fears could dissolve rather than loom. Could fade into the world of illusion where they probably belong. A state of spaciousness: it even sounds alluring and is exactly where I want to be. So why am I still lying in bed, reviewing these possibilities and not acting on them?

Why am I not at this very minute propped up on cushions, my bony bottom supported, my hands resting lightly on my knees, my mind stilled, my thoughts drifting to a lotus flower? Or drifting like a lotus flower. *Like the lotus on the pond. The lotus leaf is never wet.* Something as beautiful as a lotus flower, arising out of mud: a lesson to us all. Why indeed, Cordelia Fraser?

Or if quiet contemplation of my breath, or of the lotus flower, is not quite the thing I am ready to face, then I could go in search of God chanting any one of several mantras. Or I could stick to the universal mantra *Om* which has been a great friend at difficult moments in the past. Or, if the neighbours would not be disturbed, I could chant in Sanskrit as George taught me years ago, filling in with la-la-las the bits I don't remember, rather as my father did with his half-forgotten ballads. And if I wanted more familiar words, I could probably still haul up a few hymns from the well of the past. Indeed, the past: *Oh God our help in ages past, our hope for years to come.*

Our shelter from the stormy blast (or is it 'past', again?) *and our eternal home.* Quite.

There the problem lies.

The inward past was less stormy than the present is, and it is my deep uncertainty about the eternal home that is keeping me awake now, in the only home I've known for the past forty years. The same home which I must, inevitably, leave in the next decade or two at most, and quite possibly suddenly and sooner.

Leaving it, I will leave behind most of my adult life. I will leave behind all that has been most important to me for fifty years. Even the traces of it. It will be a final death for George, too. Childless as we are, once I am also dead then he really will be gone. Our smells that still linger on some clothes and hats, the worn patches made by our bodies on our most comfortable pieces of furniture, our fingerprints that could still be traced on pictures, books, shelves – ornaments too, as rarely as I dust: these would all be dispersed and lost.

I've seen this process of elimination happen to those a little older than I, and even to some of my contemporaries, while they are still alive. Is that worst of all? Moving from the family house, imprinted with memories in every room, to a smaller flat or tiny house with no history whatsoever, and now cluttered with all they could not bear to part with. And the rest of what was once 'home' and 'precious' sold or given away; anyway scattered and denied the combinations and juxtapositions that transformed them from mere things and gave them history and meaning. Then sometimes, with increasing helplessness, another move from a flat to a single room. Cared for, yes, but no front door now. No privacy to depend on. Made 'home' only with an easy chair of their own if they are lucky, or a favourite cushion or quilt, some photographs, a vase or special piece of china. A few books if reading continues to be possible. Sometimes just a photo. Until that, too, means nothing.

Is it dreadful weakness on my part to set such store by all these things that have given George and me pleasure for so many years?

I expect it is. And ungodly. *Give up your worldly goods, and follow me.*

What is well planted cannot be uprooted. Does that mean that I take the feelings and associations with me? And can, therefore, safely leave the furniture, the paintings, the books, photos and things behind?

In that thought, too, I lack confidence. I should be less attached. Less attached to what is outside myself; more confident about what's within. But I am not. My safety is not yet to be found within myself. My safety is more and more obviously residing in this house.

Even to set out for the reunion with my siblings is harder than it should be. I am becoming dependent on being here in ways that make me seriously uneasy. As long as I am in the house I can delude myself that some things haven't changed, and won't change. I can take care of the house; the house can take care of me. Staying alive and staying in the house have become muddled in my mind. Odd really, and irrational by any measure as it was precisely here that George died.

For all that, I realise that I must think about what will happen when I am gone for good. Yet I am still avoiding such decisions, and Graham Duncan's kindly lawyer phone calls are not proving to be the slightest bit seductive.

Maybe I should bring him here and allow him to tell me exactly what I should do. He enjoys that. Then I can tell him about Laurie. There is easily something spare for her. Perhaps that's the spur that will bring me to action.

I had planned to leave most of what's mine to my brothers and sisters. Most of what was George's will go to his family. But my family won't need it all, and may not need any of it for much longer than I.

It will be good to see them, to have a chance to judge for myself what 'Just fine' or 'Right as rain' means in each case. We have been siblings all our long lives and should be able to be honest with each other. We should feel free now to say, 'This worries me' or, 'I am fearful about that.' Or even, 'I feel completely marvellous today!' But on the phone and in hastily written notes we have tended to stick to our little routine phrases that no longer reassure me. They almost irritate me. Is that Laurie's influence? Perhaps not hers only. I love my brothers and sisters. I love them — and I am only too aware how quickly time is passing and how foolish it is to imagine that with those we love we have time for anything other than the truth.

23

Cordelia packs with care, glad of the demands this familiar task makes. Around the edges and in among neatly folded clothes she places the gifts she has chosen for each of her brothers and sisters and their spouses. She packs slowly, her back bent to the task, but when she looks at her plain-faced man's watch, she sees that she still has time to spare before the taxi comes.

Laurie offered several times to drive her to the train, but she wanted to meet the challenge of leaving the house without Laurie's company and support. Her face is pale and she feels tired although it's only mid-morning. Today she looks old. Old and distracted. She avoids catching sight of herself in any of the house's many mirrors. She brushes her straight white hair, and pats it into place with her long fingers, but chooses not to check the results. She smells of Mitsouko and Ponds Hand Cream.

The clothes she is wearing – cream slacks, a heavy cream slub linen jacket over a red silk shirt – are familiar enough for her to know what the effect is without looking. She throws a brilliant burnt orange silk scarf over her shoulders to add a clash of colour. The scarf is as fine as gauze and was bought by her in Beirut, a city she hasn't visited for years but will always associate not with barbed wire and guns, but with the lingering smell of expensive French suntan oil, rubbed slowly into outstretched limbs.

She sits down, ready. Then stands up. Her impulse is to rush around the house, checking plugs, switches, machines; touching things, wishing them well, asking them to remain exactly as they are until her return. Her anxiety levels are ready to rocket. She closes her eyes and puts one hand to her heart, breathing in and out slowly, carefully. She asks God for help. And then St Jude. She smiles as she does that: he is the patron saint of hopeless causes. Has she slipped into that category already?

As soon as she opens her eyes again her breathing returns to fast-and-shallow.

Does she have to go? Could she possibly plead illness, an emergency? Surely they would understand? Surely they could have just as much fun without her?

But not to see her sisters and brothers, and not be *all together*, would be worse than the anguish of leaving the house. Cordelia goes upstairs and doesn't stop until she is standing in George's study, staring at a photograph of Tagore. In this photograph he, too, is old. He looks back at her, unworried. In the glass of the framed photograph her own face merges with Tagore's. Perhaps his serenity is catching? She shrugs, leaves the room, shuts the door, goes to her bedroom, sits on the side of her neatly made bed, then picks up and puts down a small pile of books. Should she change her mind and take them with her? Does she need Lauris Edmond's *Selected Poems*, May Sarton's *Encore*, and the first fat volume of Doris Lessing's autobiography? Like herself, these women are all 'of a certain age'. What they have to say matters. Should she add them to the few essential volumes she has already packed? Or could she bear to wait a week?

Her own indecisiveness drives her mad. When did she become unused to deciding things on her own behalf, without consultation with George? The worst of it is, she hadn't even noticed.

This is the first time she has left the house overnight since George died. That's reason enough for her agitation, but not for her indecisiveness. 'What the hell,' she says aloud, and unlocks and opens her case. She puts the books inside. Shuts it again. Checks in her handbag for the third or fourth time that she has her train tickets, credit cards and money, and the keys she will need to return to the house.

There is still time.

'Don't spend it waiting,' Cordelia says, aware this time she is talking aloud. She shrugs, selects and puts on a CD, then stretches out along the length of her big old sofa, appreciative as it supports her weight, appreciative, too, as the voice of Sheila Chandra enters the room, turned down low so that above the sounds of drums and brass she will still hear the horn of the approaching taxi.

24

My brothers are well; my sisters less so. Coming together for our long-
awaited reunion, none of us spoke of death, or anyway, not of our own
deaths. They all miss George, and took the time and patience to let me
know it. They miss his marvellous talk and sense of conviviality for
themselves, as well as on my behalf. I appreciated that.

Minor pains were more freely aired than in the past. Elsie was
predictably vague, but clearly thrilled to see us all, and so willing to be
gently reminded of what we were doing next, or what we were doing
in that very moment, that it wasn't in any way painful to be with her.
On the contrary; she is even softer than she ever was, a tender, smiling
will-o'-the-wisp kind of woman it is impossible not to hug when close
by. I think I spent a good part of those days with Elsie sitting next to
me, my arm around her, or watching her sitting close to one of the
others, especially Allen who has eyes in the back of his head when it
comes to Elsie's care.

Norah's drama engaged us most. It brought us easily together as we
took up staunch positions of love and loyalty on her side. Are such
moments 'family' at its best? Can they ever happen without a grief, or
a 'baddie' to rally against?

Her eldest daughter, Marina, is unravelling twenty years of married
life. The story as it emerged was muddled, as these things always are,
but it would appear her husband Conrad has laid claim to the catering
business they set up and ran during their blighted years together.

Because the business owns their house, too, an ill-fated decision could leave Marina and their three children homeless.

I remember years ago that close friends of ours had a protracted and painful divorce. Maeve had always been a delightful woman, funny and flirtatious, but when her husband Gavin went off with someone much younger there seemed to be no limit to the extent to which she would punish him. She scrawled obscenities in red paint on his white Jag, threw broken bricks through his windows, sent copies of his private and rather ridiculous love letters to friends and his partners, and hired a lawyer who gleefully promised to ruin him. Through it all she howled and lamented – and shopped – and could think and talk of nothing else.

She did eventually cheer up and I think she and Gavin sorted something out, but she was inevitably changed by those events, if only in other people's eyes. Yet there was a mad kind of logic to her behaviour that seems absent here.

Conrad fell 'madly in love'. He was the one who loudly declared that his life up to that point had been meaningless. Marina is the one left caring for their three children, with a business that can now barely trade, and an escalating pile of debts. What is maddening as well as sad is that Marina continues literally to pay for Conrad's follies, or as she apparently sees it, for her own folly in involving herself with him. Yet most of us choose our partners blindly. Even to think of choice suggests a greater level of awareness and opportunity than most people actually have. Maeve and Marina – and my sister Peg – were not less 'wise' in their choices than the young Cordelia was in 'choosing' George. I am convinced the difference between a successful-enough marriage, and the other kind, is not 'hard work' as the pious would have us believe, because most of us do work hard, and in a bloody awful marriage perhaps hardest of all. It's luck, simple luck.

'He's not a gentleman, Cordelia,' Norah said to me, more than once. 'I know feminism has changed some things for the better, but not everything.

'Marina didn't have a single moment's break from working. Even when she was in hospital recovering from her infants' births he was nagging at her to organise menus and buy food and make all kinds of decisions when she should have been resting. It used to break my heart to see how irrelevant her needs were. And of course it used to break my heart that Marina couldn't see it.'

'I'm sorry,' I said, uselessly. 'I am really so terribly sorry that this has happened.'

But at least she's telling me, I thought to myself. At least we are sharing this difficulty and not pretending that nothing awful has happened and that everything's all right. That's some small mercy.

'She's looking thinner and thinner. If anything happens to her, Cordie . . . or those children . . .'

Norah looked near to tears. I have rarely seen my sister losing her composure. There is something in this sad tale that touches her deeply, perhaps more deeply than could be aroused by a single example, no matter how close to home. Years ago Norah worked as a volunteer support person in an early refuge for battered and homeless women. She cared a great deal for those women. Perhaps she has heard too many of these stories; God knows, there are enough to hear.

With considerable force, Norah said, 'I wish I could help her out. Out of this mess. The scale of this is beyond our means though. Really, I can't help her at all.'

'Except with your love.'

She nodded, grateful to me. 'Yes. With that. Sometimes it doesn't seem enough.'

Norah is herself frailer than she should be, but she looked as fierce as a mother tiger when she said, 'He was from the wrong bloody drawer, Cordelia. It's always a mistake!'

Imagining for a wild moment the entire world population laid out in their rightful drawers so that all would know where they stand – or lie – I wanted to laugh aloud. I couldn't agree with her. Life has taught me that all sorts of surprises, good and bad, come from all sorts of 'drawers', but I loved her loyalty and in a burst of warmth talked to her about the family that has come into my life to spark it along at this late stage: Laurie, Gregory, Rhea. I stopped short at Wynston and Guy. Would she understand? I didn't know.

Later, standing near the steps to the back door, poised between inside and out, I talked to her too about the African pots, which are coming a tiny bit more easily now.

'Plain and practical, it doesn't sound like you, Cordie.'

Was she teasing me? Probably, but I chose not to mind. I tried to explain. 'It's more than plain and practical. The challenge is to make them plainly perfect. Not to distract the eye with three-dimensional ornamentation, or with decorative flourishes, or fancy glazes. The perfection has to be taken for granted so that it's there, like Nature, only when you lift your eyes to notice it.'

Was this too mystical for Norah? Apparently not. 'I know what you mean. I've taken to walking for forty or forty-five minutes each day through my local park, not for the exercise alone although that's good for me, but for the challenge of noticing in detail what I'm passing. I always take the exact same route and my goal is that every experience of that one walk will be fresh and different. Marina put me onto this. She does it and so do the children and I must say, I am loving it. I do the same thing in the garden too. You know how tiny my garden is, but it still takes time to look each day at each plant, or even each petal or leaf, as though for the first time. There always are changes, too. I'm never disappointed.'

'You two sound like a couple of fruit and nut cases. Watch out that your vices aren't frightening the dogs!' It was our brother Allen, standing at the bottom of the steps, promisingly laden shopping bags in each hand.

We hadn't noticed him listening, nor could we possibly be hurt by his remark. His golden heart has always been hidden by commentary which he fondly imagines deflects attention from an unusual gift for love. He was our mother's favourite, perhaps the one among us best able to imagine what would give her pleasure, even when she was most emphatically pushing away our offers of practical help. His creativity emerged as thoughtfulness of the most subtle and unselfserving kind. Our mother cherished that, and him. He was a golden boy, inside and out. A cherub of a child, always ready with smiles and cuddles. There were smiles for him, too, and brief, caressing touches, long after the rest of us were largely out in the cold.

It was a mixed blessing for Allen. Presumably it was wonderful to have our mother's love. Alongside that though, it was hard to be selected out and not quite be one of the gang. In adulthood he has had to do his caring all over again, first for Katrina, a talented, pretty wife crippled early with multiple sclerosis; later still for Tim, an only son he nursed to recovery from cancer.

'Go scare the dogs yourself, Allen. And while you're doing it, get those human rogues in here for lunch! Don't let them think that I'm about to wait on any of them.' Even while speaking to him Norah was giving Allen a hug and a push. Born a year apart, those two would never be entirely adult in each other's company, and one could also thank God for that.

If only one could find God.

25

Safely back in my own bed, but yet another long night of broken sleep.

Thinking of my brothers and sisters, of human beings tipped from their drawers to land in an infernal muddle, and of God in among all that and yet, for me at this moment, also out of reach, I must have gone to sleep at last because I was woken up by the shrill ringing of the phone, and as I picked it up to answer it my clock showed that it was now way past ten. Somewhat sheepish to be caught in bed still, I did my unobtrusive best to clear the frogs from my throat and waking-fog from my mind.

'It's Wynston, Cordelia. Have I rung too early?'

Wynston? How unexpected.

'No, no,' I assured him. 'I've been awake for hours.' Which was true enough, although the hours concerned were some time ago.

'Laurie said she thought it would be all right to call. Would you mind if I came round to see you? I'd like to ask you a favour and it would be much easier in person, if that wouldn't be too inconvenient.'

Of course I said yes. We made a time. I was intrigued as to what he could want from me, and also rather curious to see him alone. I like him more than I like Guy. But more generally, after a lifetime of being social with couples I am well aware that people are often significantly different – often most enjoyably – when they can be prised away from their 'other half'.

Perhaps that is one of the countless things I like about my times with Laurie. There is no other half I must struggle past to reach her. The children's possessiveness is quite different from the presence of an adult partner. More obviously intrusive perhaps, but certainly less judgemental and almost never inhibiting.

And, with George gone, I guess there is no other half beside me either for Laurie to struggle past. This thought is rather drearier. I feel saddened, and exposed. A raw twig, unclothed by leaves, even after I have rallied, showered, dressed and eaten breakfast.

So it's quite as though a life-saver has appeared when Laurie knocks tentatively on the kitchen door. She has been working in the studio. Her working day may well be half over; mine is, today, unlikely to begin.

With relief I fling the door open and am immediately struck by the sight of Laurie in a long black-and-white striped apron worn over a very short pair of blue denim shorts. She turns to wave her hands towards the studio, site of a triumph from a just-opened kiln it would appear. Her legs are muscular. Brown. Lurid green socks are rolled above her Doc Martens. She turns back to face me. She is grinning. Pleased with herself. 'Do come and look at my fountains, Cordelia, if you've got a minute. Have you?'

I have indeed. I nod.

'I could do with some advice,' Laurie lies.

'Good,' I tell her. 'I'm in the mood for giving some. Although fountains are slightly outside the range of my experience . . .'

We cross the lawn to where two virtually identical fountains stand: slender, strong, perfectly weighted so that one need not fear for their steadiness despite their elegance and grace. Each one is about as tall as Laurie's waist, shaped remarkably like a pelican's beak on top, very smooth, dark, sculptured, impossible not to touch. These are pieces that are already vibrant with purpose, even while they call forth praise and reflection. Their slender form carries them from the earth where they stand snugly and begin, up into the air where they rise and threaten to take off. When the element of water is added, when water begins to spill and roll from top to bottom, they will be absolutely enchanting.

'They're wonderful, Laurie.' I close my eyes, wanting to see them in my mind's eye to register their effect on me, the lift they have given to my sombre feelings. 'They are a real achievement. You have surpassed yourself and I couldn't be more glad.'

I take her hand. We stand together, two women looking at two ceramic fountains. A couple of miracles, at least.

Laurie blushes, with relief as well as pride. She leans her head against my shoulder. I look up towards the tree that has been stalking me, and down to the ground where I have too often, and uncomfortably, seen my discarded body lying.

The grass is freshly cut, and springy. A trio of birds hop and peck.

The sun moves across the sky and the tree's leaves seem to lighten even as I watch. As light filters through the branches it hits the grass, unevenly, only gradually making a pattern. The birds have had enough. They fly away.

I am aware that Laurie's hand is still in mine. I let it go.

Gingerly, stiffly, I lower myself onto my knees first and then lie down on the ground. My heart is apparently beating at its normal rate. I am alive. I lie motionless and am conscious of nothing more sinister than the delicious smell of old earth and newly cut grass. I close my eyes. Surrender my weight entirely to the earth. That word sticks: *surrender*. It feels possible. A bee hums, or maybe it's a fly. A bee hums, *and* a fly.

Then there's quiet. Laurie is waiting, in silence.

When I am at last ready to open my eyes, and then to stand, she is still waiting. She gives me her hand again and helps me to my feet.

How to find God?
As a fish learns to swim. In water, where it belongs.
But where is the water? Am I in it, or am I out of it?
When the muddiness stills you will know the water.
How do I still the muddiness then?
You don't. You are muddiness. You are also stillness.
In all of that, is God.

It is the middle of the morning, for heaven's sake! I hardly dare shut my eyes these days for who knows what strange images and now even stranger words might leap up to possess my mind. Migrant thoughts, of unknown origin. I have no choice but to take them in.

Perhaps I am becoming demented. Or am being overtaken by dementia. Ought I to test out whether I can remember my twelve times table, or presidents of the United States (as though I ever knew them), or attempt to recall just what did happen after the good news was brought from Ghent to Aix?

Alas, the results may not be encouraging.

Sitting on a somewhat spindly chair beside my hall table, ready to put postage stamps on letters and postcards, I had closed my tired eyes for barely a moment. And then heard, what? I have just written down a conversation, not wanting to forget it, and anyway having it as vividly in my mind as if I were at this moment still travelling in a bus, listening to two passengers sitting behind me who are having a conversation that grips me, but at whom I could hardly turn around to stare.

Where did those voices come from?

Old people are more subject to hearing disembodied voices. Is that true or have I also made that up? Or is it that people who live alone are more vulnerable to stray conversations arriving on the wind? Or that the combination of age and solitariness is such that one cannot pull the shutters closed against voices from heaven knows where?

Generally, I am making slow steps towards a greater equilibrium. There will be, to the end I suspect, many moments of wrenching absence that could be filled by nothing or no one but George. Sometimes those moments are not moments; they are hours, and the feelings that emerge ever more pervasively during those long times are of shocking emptiness and, at quite the same time, claustrophobia. It makes no sense to be simultaneously empty and overwhelmed; yet now I know it's possible.

Guy told us all at dinner the other night how during the Indo-Chinese war of liberation Vietnamese guerillas lived, I think sometimes for months or even years on end, in a maze of tunnels that spread for many miles under the streets of Saigon.

'You know, don't you, that many of those guerillas were women,' Laurie interrupted him to say. Setting him right with some vigour. 'Just imagine trying to keep clean or having some semblance of hygiene, quite apart from the excruciating depression of years away from your family and never seeing the sun.'

The tunnels were generally impenetrable by large Western bodies and where American soldiers did locate the camouflaged entrances, which were largely totally invisible to the untrained eye, and did attempt to squeeze their way in, they risked being blown up, or, travelling further towards the centre of the Earth, would be met by sharp, searing spikes, by shards of sharpened glass, or worse: writhing, deadly snakes.

Did they, I wondered silently, meet those snakes only after surviving all other hazards, only after reaching further into our shared Earth than perhaps any one of us has the right to go? What obscene version of heroism did it take to narrow oneself in that way, to shut out all else so that one could burrow forward, blind, mole-like, as though nothing else mattered? Then, thinking of myself, I understood.

It would also be impossible to enter the narrow, ill-marked tunnels of grief unless one had been significantly diminished by loss. The robust, the cheerfully ignorant -- no matter how well-meaning – simply could not fit into this tiny, inhuman space where one is reduced to sliding forward on one's belly in the dark, inch by inch, fearing nothingness more than shards, snakes and bombs. The robust, sensibly, would abhor even the thought of this wretched, enclosed existence. Yet, oddly, when grief takes over completely, and one is entirely in the tunnel, with no thought that any other life makes sense or ever could again, in the extreme intensity of this, there is bitter satisfaction.

I am not grieving; I am grief.

Grief, belly to the ground, tunnelling through the darkness, snake herself, barely breathing, sobbing, unable to wipe her dripping nose.

Within the tunnel, I can believe I am doing what must be done. I am not postponing it, whatever 'it' is. I am not distracted from it, whatever 'it' is. I am not avoiding or pretending. There is no leniency here for pretence or choice. Body, will, emotions; tears, snot, squashed breasts and belly, legs uselessly trailing: burrowing through the centre of the earth. Laurie would seize on this image of burrowing. Perhaps she would complicate it with talk of initiation rites, and of birth canal memories out of which something new struggles to be born. All of which would undoubtedly be interesting, and relevant maybe, but I think for now I'll keep my thoughts to myself. Part of me is burrowing towards Laurie, it is true; not this grieving part, though. Not this part that is hundreds of feet below the place where plants push up through the earth, seeking light, possessing and radiating their beauty whether or not anyone pauses to admire it.

Returned to my own well-lit, spacious hallway, I look again at the weird conversation that I have written down, sieving for meaning those odd words that have tracked me through the ether, and which I have committed to the page.

You are muddiness. You are also stillness. In all of that, is God.

'It makes no sense, Cordelia,' I say aloud. In much the same voice, I rather think, that a sensible nanny might use to a foolish child in her charge. Suitably chastened, I remember with pleasure that Wynston will visit soon; and, more immediately and urgently, that I haven't eaten or drunk for many hours. Needs must.

A bread roll, tea, a hasty round-up of shopping necessities, a call to the department store that so usefully delivers, and then off to work, but by fourish I had already had enough. One perfect African piece every few days is a considerable achievement and I have no desire to push my luck. Today it is a serving bowl, yet to be fired so it is not quite time to breathe easy, but after such a harrowing start to my day, I felt I could afford a few moment's diluted satisfaction.

As I was closing up the studio to set out towards the house Gudrun was arriving to work there. It was tempting to stay and chat; she's a lovely woman. Her thick, heavy hair is cut in a girl's bob but is almost as uniformly white as my own. It moves as she speaks and is beguilingly free, yet harnessed in shape by clever cutting. I like her blatant paradoxes: free yet harnessed; a child's style for consciously undyed old-woman's hair. How cleverly she expresses – and redefines – early middle age.

I like it too that Gudrun always brings me amusingly up to date with news of the gallery and art world. Since George's death I feel increasingly distanced from all of that although when prompted I can still be intrigued by who is showing what where, and what is being said about it. To a lesser extent I guess I also remain interested in knowing what is being bought. And in speculating on why.

I have become carelessly oblivious to my own sales. Or saleability. That is of course a privilege of wealth. But it wasn't always like that.

George was earning much more than we needed when I began to sell my work and yet those earliest sales were extremely important to me. We were by then so willingly entrenched in each other's lives there was no lack of safety for me – not financially anyway. That did not diminish the intense satisfaction I felt in making something, selling it because someone valued it, and knowing that the money that sale represented could keep a small wolf from the door.

Even my eccentric pieces sold well. They may even have been taken up more quickly than the relatively restrained, more conventional work that preceded them. Certainly they attracted several articles and photographs in the magazines that count and that was pleasing, too.

I am glad to have those glossy photographs now because no matter how intensely I believe I will hold a piece in my mind, and how inconceivable it seems that I will ever forget a single detail of it, I have forgotten entirely many that I have made. Sometimes, leafing through old planning drawings, I am amazed and a little ashamed by what I have forgotten.

In the planning and execution each piece is, in itself, so compelling that those that came before it slip away. Laurie tells me that mangling of time is just what happens when raising children. That every stage, as it occurs, seems totally unforgettable in its tenderness and charms, as well as in its raw demands. But then that stage melts imperceptibly into the next and one is then held in a fresh present, the past decisively fading.

There were times, Laurie told me, when her life seemed divided into no longer than ten-minute sections. Gregory would have a new word and her mind would be filled with the word, and joy for him in his discovery. But only minutes later she would have been virtually unable to say what that word was until it reappeared or maybe never did, because something else had taken its place.

Once, she said, she was sitting in the courtyard behind her little house. Rhea was on her knee and Gregory was standing alongside, his hand touching her leg for balance and for comfort. He was jealous of the baby probably. It is perfectly understandable. He was just a tiny tot himself. And I can quite imagine how lovely Laurie's lap and arms and soft breasts would be: a nest one might never want to leave. Gregory's speciality at this time in their lives was biting Rhea's knees when Laurie's attention was distracted. I guess they were the plumpest, juiciest bits within mouth-range. But on this particular day there was poor old Gregory, with wet flannel pilchers that he must have picked up from the washing, slapping Rhea around the head with it and then slapping his anguished Mum!

Laurie told him 'No', probably much more severely than Gregory was used to hearing. Certainly it made its mark as only moments later there Gregory was, growling like a bear at the pilchers on the ground, telling it, 'No, No.' And again: 'No! No!' Shifting the blame I guess to the wicked pilchers, but most imaginatively. And all of that intensity happening entirely in the present tense.

Which is surely why creative work continues to be extraordinarily beguiling: the work of raising children as well as raising pots or canvases or words. It is a chance to be, for that time, entirely in the moment, not prodding at the past; not worrying ahead at what might never happen.

With or without a market, with or without sales, I can afford to work. Not only to work, but to work in ways that I feel driven or led. The impulses can come from inside me. I don't need to look outside myself for confidence that what I am doing is what I should be doing – or what 'the market' wants. That's great good luck indeed. So today was not the day to pick up the threads of gallery life with Gudrun. It had been a long day already.

When Gudrun asked if I was all right, I noticed that I was tired. That I felt I deserved a little nap stretched out on the sofa, after a cup of lemon grass tea and an apple. Limiting myself to a quick hug and a promise to catch up later, I waved her in and went on up the path, smiling at the blue, yellow, white, purple faces of the pansies and violas as I went, picking a few dead heads off damp pink daisies, then going into the kitchen, filling the kettle, making tea, cutting up a crisp red apple and taking a small tray upstairs to the sofa with me but consuming neither apple nor tea before falling sound asleep and then, waking (or still asleep?), hearing that same conversation again; listening in to God knows who saying God knows what.

There seems no difficulty for me in identifying with the muddiness. Letting it settle sounds fairly attractive also. But becoming stillness . . . God. It's too esoteric for me. Too big a leap from good old *All things bright and beautiful*. Although, come to think of it, why did my mind leap to that particular hymn out of all possible hymns? *All* things . . .? *Bright and beautiful?*

There is a small collection of iron fish in one of the cupboards in the dining room. We must have put them away years ago in a vain attempt to reduce the clutter. The dining room has become a room we rarely use. Its main function now is as storage for relics of the past I can't quite yet give away. Why the fish were banished, I don't recall. Getting up, going downstairs and into the dining room, moving towards the right cupboard with the instinct of a hunter, finding them again surprisingly easily, I notice that they are weighty in my hand but look amazingly light, flashy, absolutely made for water. No trouble learning to swim for them.

Along with the iron fish I find some glass fish, too. I had quite forgotten these little treasures, three of them in shades of greeny-blue to bluey-green, the colours within the glass moving from transparent to opaque in ways that are themselves immediately reminiscent of the ocean.

Sitting somewhat stiffly on the floor, but liking it down there, scrunched up with a cushion under my bottom, with the ocean-coloured fish spread across a faded pink-toned Persian rug, I feel insulted by the idea that we come from dust. And that back to dust we shall return. How absurd. Life crawled to shore from the oceans, surely? Sperm and ovum do not meet on dry land. And human infants push their way down from the watery, rocking life in the uterus, through the moist passageway of the vagina, to land, shockingly, in air.

How to find God? As a fish learns to swim.
In water, where it belongs.

There's no making any sense of it, or not, at least, before dinner. Yet I feel my spirits take wings. I shall make a quick something for my supper and then, afterwards, cook more seriously, I think.

I am pretty sure that I have enough of the makings in my kitchen for a large, flavoursome, old-fashioned casserole. If I cook it tonight it will be perfect for tomorrow when Laurie and her children will join me. I shall invite Gudrun too, right away, and she can bring her partner, if she has one. Perhaps Bronwyn would also like to eat with us. I have thought again and again about Bronwyn's story of Africa and of her young self rising up from beneath the mosquito net with a transformed sense of who she was and what she was capable of becoming. It would be wonderful to see her, to hear her laugh and tell her earthy tales.

I'll add strawberry flan and rum balls to the menu to tempt the children, and some decent cheese. A salad, too, with lots of fat black olives for Gregory and Rhea to scoff.

No fish.

Though I will decorate the table with these decidedly wonderful fish I have rediscovered in my cupboard today. Each one of them, iron and glass, can swim along the centre of the table between the candles and around the bottles and dishes.

I am already wondering what everyone will make of them.

Kathleen Battle was singing Christmas carols and I, glad to be inspired, was singing with her.

Three score and ten plus three does not leave me enough time to respect seasonal constraints. Christmas music is to be welcomed at any time of the year as far as I am concerned. So while Kathleen and I sang, loudly and with intense pleasure at least on my side, I was also cooking, surrounded by the messy debris that characterises my kitchen efforts. Subduing my own voice to hear Frederica von Stade join Kathleen for the Evening Prayer from *Hansel and Gretel* I thought to myself that this aria would be ideal for my funeral, if there is to be music at all. My pleasure in the ethereal sweetness was such that this thought did not distress me. Nor did it stop me beginning again to sing along, though perhaps now a little less heartily which was just as well as otherwise I would not have heard the firm ringing of the bell at my front door.

I turned down the volume, feeling thrown for a moment, then disappointed I was being interrupted, then somewhat ashamed and awkward that despite my initial flurry of curiosity, I had completely forgotten Wynston was coming. Hurrying, my loose indoor shoes clip-clopping, I went to the front door to let him in.

Wynston stood in the doorway, a slim, bearded, smiling man, flowers in his hands. They were liliums with a heavenly sheen: cream, apricot, pink and white. Even better, he was willing to arrange them, he said, if I would just find him a suitable vase.

Set to do just that, I charged ahead of him down the long hall and into the kitchen where I handed him a big jug, one he recognised at once as made by Laurie, deep Mediterranean blue with fat baby angels holding hands and climbing out from inside over the edge. The angels' colours almost exactly matched those of the flowers, with splashes of scarlet and dark green to add bite.

What an easy fellow Wynston is! The flowers were in their jug, wine was poured, and I found myself sitting on a high cane bar stool at my own bright red bench as he began to peel and chop and mix and sniff with such pleasure and aplomb that I was delighted to leave him to it. This seemed no less than he expected, although he did from time to time politely enquire what I'd had in mind before steering me with no effort at all to a combination that would undoubtedly be more delicious than anything I could have achieved alone.

It's been a good while since a man stood cooking in my kitchen. Not that long in weeks or months, maybe, but all of life – or all of my life – has been turned on its head since George stood at this bench doing much the same tasks that Wynston was now relishing.

George had taught himself to cook, as he did an extraordinary variety of things. He made a decision one evening fairly early in our marriage that he would like to take up cooking. By the next day he had acquired several cookbooks on his mother's advice which he read with an optimism I could never have matched; and hadn't thus far matched which may have been his greatest incentive. He then took off, never doubting that cooking would be as much of a pleasure for him as eating was.

To the confident, all manner of blessings flows.

'I've missed George's cooking,' I said aloud, for my own benefit rather than Wynston's. 'More than that, I've missed the sight and smells of George cooking – and the anticipation. For me it's always been a hazardous business translating an intention about food into an edible reality. George, on the other hand, could take it for granted that what he set out to do would come to fruition on the plate more or less

exactly as he planned it. On my better days I have that confidence with
my pots, but with cooking I am fretting until the last moment that what
I'm slaving over may be nothing more productive than the ruin of fine
ingredients.'

Wynston laughed. He has a generous laugh. Teeth, tongue, lips.
It's good to hear and see.

'When it comes to cooking,' he said, 'I'm mother's boy. Mum was
and still is a superb cook and spends most of her waking hours in the
kitchen. If you want to spend time with her, standing alongside her
while she cooks has always been the best way to do it. One of my
sisters became a professional cook, although she has since given it up
to become a Tibetan Buddhist nun.'

'In Tibet?'

'No, here,' he chortled. 'A dear little monastery cheek to cheek
with a McDonald's. Everything is possible almost anywhere! Don't you
think so? It's the shrunken world syndrome. Pepsi to the East of us;
Sanskrit to the West. My parents were appalled. Such an unPresbyterian
thing to do. It could hardly have been worse if she'd actually gone to
Tibet. Or to India which is where most Tibetans hang out who don't
care for Chinese military oppression. Well, she did go to India for quite
some time and came back very changed. No longer Emily, but Khandro.
No longer bountifully brunette, but shorn. They've come round now,
however. My parents. Not the Chinese. Poor things. Still, they've had
more than their fair share of filial disasters. An only daughter who shaves
her head and chants in a gravelly voice in a language they'll never
understand and three queer sons. "Oh, where did we go wrong?" '

He was mocking them, his absent parents. Holding his fists to his
head, he successfully created a convincing picture of anguish. Which
may not be too far from the truth. What would they have told their
neighbours? Their friends? Relatives? Each other? I thought of George's
sister Sarah. And shuddered.

'Must be in the blood, I tell them.' Wynston was laughing again
now and still talking. 'Although I don't know where that leaves them.

Or if it makes it better or worse. However, we're all very tame queers by today's *loose* standards. Charming. Well spoken. Cheerful. Respectable jobs. Nice husbands. Only one husband each. No loitering in public places. No visible mutilations. No SM. No HIV.' He grimaced. 'Touch wood. No scandals of any kind, now I come to think of it. Tasteful homes in safe neighbourhoods. Really, we're what any Mummy and Daddy might dream of. Almost. They even have a grandchild, which is probably what they wanted most.'

'How?' I ask, wanting to know, even while I feel guilty that clever Wynston has lured me to laugh with him at the expense of his parents. Who may well be about my own age. Who surely did all they could. Who probably were entitled to want what they believed would be best for their children . . .

'Francis provided sperm. First-rate sperm, as it turned out to be. The mother, Penny, is an old friend and queer too. She lives with Ros. Ros likes Francis and David – Francis's other half. Francis and David like Penny and Ros. And they all adore Aldous.'

'Aldous?' I dreaded the answer.

Wynston drank his wine. Looked at me. Paused. Was the boy flirting with me? I do believe he was. I am not entirely sure that I was not also flirting with him.

'Forgive me, Cordelia. Aldous is, in fact, the tortoise. David's tortoise. And, as far as I know not the offspring of Francis . . . The *truly* adorable one, indeed the only one fit to lie in the manger, is Carlos. Now three. He is, believe me, a credit to his virgin birth.'

'His . . .? Thank you, Wynston. Aged as I am, I can imagine the rest!'

I could too, although perhaps only because Laurie had recently given me an unselfconsciously detailed, almost blow-by-blow description of artificial insemination by donor, a process that had been tried for several anxious months by one of her friends, with no happy outcome, thus far, despite accompanying fertility rituals and careful noting of the waxing and the waning of the moon.

By now the large casserole was simmering in the oven. The benches were tidied and wiped. Excess vegetables were back in the fridge or vegetable rack where they belonged. Herbs were tucked away and our glasses were topped up. All without the slightest effort on my part.

'Wynston, this will have to be enough for me. You carry on. A couple of glasses is about all that I can manage without being cast into the realms of punishment. Will you bring the bottle and we'll go upstairs to the sitting room?'

Once there, each of us sitting in a large easy chair, me with my feet up on a round, brown, leathery object of furniture that I uncomfortably remembered was once called a pouffe, Wynston's mood subtly changed. I could have sworn he was nervous although when he turned to speak to me he appeared as poised as he always does.

'Throw me out at once, Cordelia, if what I'm suggesting is at all out of line. I wouldn't even have dared ask except that Laurie gave me courage. Not that she knows the details ... but she did manage to persuade me that you can overlook the occasional blunder.'

I waited. As I waited I thought about that statement: 'You can overlook the occasional blunder.' Is it possible, I asked myself, that from the perspective of late youth or earliest middle age, seventy-plus could look so worldly wise or experienced or assured that blunders would seem not to be a part of every day? Sometimes, of almost every hour? Tears sprang to my eyes, but it was not the moment for that and I was glad to be able to turn from Wynston to adjust the cushions behind my back, rather cleverly I thought, drying my eyes on my sleeve as I did so. Ah, blunders. I know thy every mood and face.

'I am losing my job, or, at least, it looks as though I am losing two-thirds of it.' Wynston's tone was conversational, reassuring.

Following his cue, I put my own face and tone of voice in order. 'Laurie told me that might happen. I am extremely sorry. Is there a chance you could get suitable work somewhere else?'

'There's always a chance, but for the moment it's fairly slim. Libraries are not the growth industry they should be. It's complicated too because I can't move and don't want to. Guy ... the children ... Laurie. It would be unthinkable to go anywhere without them and unthinkable to attempt to uproot them. Especially as Guy is getting a promotion out of the same process of reorganisation that's slicing my job in pieces.'

I hadn't known that. 'A significant promotion?'

'Mmm. Curator of manuscripts. It's a dream run given the collection our library has and could have, and he'll be wonderful at it. Of course he's feeling guilty now and afraid to show his pleasure but the decision about my job was nothing to do with him. It doesn't reflect on my work either. I have been able to avoid whipping myself about that. It was more or less a case of last in at my level, first out. But until I get myself organised Guy is going to be hesitant to throw himself fully into his new role.'

'So?' I was still mystified as to why Wynston would be confiding in me.

'So, I understand from Laurie that your husband had a fine collection of books on Eastern mysticism.'

'Yes. Not only books. Pamphlets. Articles. Photographs. And not only Eastern mysticism. Judaic and Christian variations on the theme. Esoteric philosophy. Mythology. There are significant collections in other areas too. Economics. Trade. History. You know he worked with various non-governmental aid organisations? There are books in all the many subject areas which that work touched. It's a huge collection, varied in subject matter, but exceptionally comprehensive here and there.'

Even as I spoke, remembering George, taking pride in his enthusiasms, this conversation was, at last, beginning to make a little sense.

Wynston's glass was empty. He saw me glance at it. 'Would you care for something else now?' he asked. 'A brandy?'

'I'm fine. But please, do help yourself.'

'Can I make you some tea perhaps?' He was clearly anxious not to be distracted yet remembered his manners.

I shook my head. 'Not tea either.' Wynston had assessed himself correctly. He is, indeed, almost exactly most mothers' dream of a son. 'Please do go on.'

Wynston waited a moment before he spoke again, and leaned a little further towards me, but when he did speak he still appeared relaxed. 'If you'd intended to have your husband's collection catalogued, I am someone who could do that. I have the expertise to prepare a catalogue of each subject area ready either for sale or donation. Whatever you and he had decided . . . His major subject areas interest me deeply. Eastern mysticism especially. My Tibetan Buddhist sister is not the only one in the family drawn to that tradition. To do this work would be a labour of love. Though say yes only if you'd want the work done anyway, Cordelia. Had you intended to have it done? Of course I could give you an estimate of the time involved, and would work in such a way as to be least intrusive . . .'

'Is it Buddhism only that interests you?'

'No.' The expression on his face changed, but I couldn't read it. I could only guess that perhaps he had wanted this work quite a lot. 'Not only. Hinduism, also, and Sufism. The mystical end of Christianity too, though I know less about that. Meister Eckhart is about the extent of it. But not for lack of interest. How people experience God fascinates me. And how they express that. Especially when definition becomes least possible and dogma most irrelevant. That's always grabbed me. Intrigued me.'

George too. What a pity those two never met, Wynston and George. There is something about each of them that reminds me of the other: a vitality certainly and a voracious enthusiasm for knowledge; a sensuality too which comes out in the ease of practical tasks done by a clever intellectual with confidence and a light touch.

I think about Laurie. Then Guy.

Guy has had two exceptional treasures as mates; what could he have done to deserve them? Handsome? Yes he is; clever too; and he can be charming. But he is charming when he chooses, and is not always wise or even kind. So, *deserving*?

Wryly, I mock the thought even as it arises. I hardly need to remind myself that 'deserving' is not part of the equation.

'This won't be the vocational solution you need.' I spoke more sternly than was probably necessary. 'It could only be a stop-gap. Some months' work at most.' Was I already saying yes?

Wynston was nodding. 'That was all I hoped for. But long enough perhaps to stop Guy worrying and to see him digging his toes into his new job. Something else will open up. I have to trust that and can, I think. After all, this occurred to me quite out of the blue.'

Looking at Wynston and thinking about George, I softened. His optimism is also familiar. *Something will open up.* My own nature is terminally wary.

'Does Guy know about this proposal? About your coming here tonight?'

Wynston looked awkward, then tender. 'He hasn't a clue. Laurie and I occasionally have our secrets and this has been one of them. I didn't want Guy to know how anxious I am about his being anxious. You know how it is: *Round and round the garden run the teddy bears* . . . Guy's outrage against these cutbacks has been much fiercer than mine. He doesn't share my faith in providence. Or God. Yet here I am, sitting with you in this splendid room, talking about work that will be pure joy – and feeling relaxed contemplating it. How could you account for that?'

Frankly, I cannot and didn't even try. I made do with nodding, smiling and then asking, as perhaps George might have wanted, 'What do you know about Tagore?'

Wynston also smiled, and settled back more cosily into his chair. 'Only a little. Where he lived, that he wrote *Gitanjali* among many other works, that he's up there near Ghandi in terms of Indian political sainthood. Not that much about the man himself. Why?'

'There are boxes in the basement, all properly sealed against damp and infestation. I think they are mostly Tagore material. There's also a huge amount of material out on the shelves in George's study. Perhaps as you go along you could assess whether there is enough to make a separate something . . . on or about Tagore. Maybe a separate catalogue. Maybe a pamphlet. George loved the man.'

The flower says
Blessed am I
Blessed am I
Upon this earth . . .

The flower says
I was born from the dust
Kindly kindly
Let me forget it
Let me forget it
Let me forget.

Of dust inside me there is none
No dust at all inside me
The flower says.

I turned my attention back to Wynston, gathering my thoughts. 'Not only Tagore either, I think. George was fascinated by the certainty of faith that was still possible in the early decades of this century. It was personified by people like C.F. Andrews who probably rather got up Tagore's nose at times, even though he was undoubtedly a good man, and helped Ghandi a great deal, too. Andrews wrote a book called *What I Owe to Christ.* You can read it if you'd like to. It's here. He's a shining exemplar of something . . . something dated, laughable – and quite splendid. A man of his time – whose time will not come again. And I am tempted to add: *alas.*' I smiled then, but felt saddened. Felt the loss.

'What Andrews and people like him could not have imagined, of course, is that the day of absolute faith was almost over. Not that faith has ceased to be possible. I know I long for it myself. And cast terribly envious glances in the direction of anyone I suspect of having it! It's what I envy most, in fact. But surely it has become more complex? Other than for fundamentalists, it's now thoroughly "problematised", as Laurie has taught me to say. Indeed, one could persuasively argue that fundamentalism itself arises not from certainty but in dread reaction to uncertainty. Though clearly it's not a solution for it. Not a social solution, anyway.'

Had I said too much, too soon? I wasn't at all sure. Wynston nodded, whether in agreement or simply to indicate interest I couldn't tell, then he said, somewhat obliquely, 'I like problematisers. St Thomas was also a "problematiser", and not the first.'

'True enough. But that last gasp of theological certainty early on in our century had a compelling power that was quite its own. What's striking is that it was the time not of George's conscious adult experience, but of his birth. He was born into quite a different time from the era in which he functioned. Born into a time that was not to be his time. He's a product of post-certainty, as we all are.'

I trailed off. *How to find God?* How to *know* God – with or without 'abiding faith'?

A compelling image filled my mind. To say it felt like a vision is far too pretentious, but there isn't quite another word for it. Perhaps fantasy will do, but not a fantasy that I felt any part of my conscious mind was directing.

I could do nothing but look at it and as I looked I saw that I (or rather, a figure of myself such as one might see in a dream) was sitting on a wide, low, throne-like chair. This chair was bright red and decorated lavishly with finely painted gold flowers. If it resembled anything then it spoke of the kind of chair upon which a guru might sit, cross-legged, to teach and to receive students and to give *darshan*.

The image broadened, as though the camera was pulling back from that initial close-up. Now I could see that the throne sat totally isolated on a boundary-less stretch of ice, but there was no feeling of cold or of hardship of any kind. On the contrary. The very stretch and spaciousness of that ice is what made it so attractive. In the distance, far behind the throne, were ice mountains with peaks like the tops of icebergs but more intensely blue-white, as though one could see right through them, or be dazzled, looking at them.

As my attention pulled back to the figure of myself, to the figure of Cordelia sitting on the throne, I felt something I can only describe as awe. This feeling bore no resemblance to the deep ambivalence with which I usually regard myself. Instead, as I watched, an everyday-Cordelia dressed in potting clothes and apron walked forward, then prostrated herself fully on the icy ground in front of the Cordelia sitting on the throne. After some long, silent moments, the Cordelia on the ground rose to her knees, leaned her head against the knees of the other Cordelia, and received a silent blessing from her.

The intensity of feeling that passed between the two images of Cordelia was profound yet completely undisturbing. Only when I noticed that I had drawn my breath in rather sharply did the image disappear, leaving me distracted and somewhat shaken.

Shyly, I looked across at Wynston. What had he seen? Had anything been betrayed on my face? Perhaps only seconds had passed. He was waiting, steadily, apparently unruffled.

Reluctantly, I prepared myself to speak. This wasn't easy. I felt too much like someone who has just been to the dentist and has lost contact with both her jaw and tongue.

'George wanted to know if faith itself had changed or only the language of faith. As we talk about God differently, how do we also experience God differently? Is God changed by that? However, that was not to be.' Again I hesitated. Could I fairly describe George's intention? Again Wynston waited. I like him all the more for his measured sense of time. He is young still and probably legitimately impatient, yet doesn't betray that.

'I envy faith as a state of mind, but alongside that, I'm suspicious of certainty,' I began, truthfully enough. 'There's no movement in it and no flexibility. So much certainty has been shown up as the illusion it is, in the social realm as well as the theological. Once upon a time most of us were convinced that mankind was on an ever-improving path within this lifetime and on this planet. George and I once believed that financial aid could bring emerging nations the respite they needed to get their affairs in order, to embrace independence and, with only minor setbacks, to live happily ever after.'

Was that true or fair? Either way, I went on. 'Our certainty was more universal than that. We were the generation that believed socialised health care, organised labour and improved education would result in a psychologically healthier society. We believed that – then had to unbelieve it. Without becoming too cynical about our fellow human beings. Or ourselves. That's the real test of faith of course. To realise that suffering can and will continue. *And* that we can and will go on working blindly to relieve it.'

'The cycle of the crucifixion and resurrection?'

I laughed. 'More or less. Which doesn't end with a single crucifixion, nor with one glorious and good-for-all-time resurrection. Light follows darkness all right, but darkness also follows light.'

I noticed that both clocks in the room had stopped, one at three, almost precisely, and one at six, almost precisely. It was an odd coincidence.

'It hasn't been easy for my parents either,' Wynston was saying. 'Their sense of upwards and onwards was rudely shattered by one son after another rejecting the blueprint they'd diligently drawn up for us. They may be even more confused by the pleasure we seem to have taken in our choice of lifestyle or certainly in our partners. They've also had to do a fair bit of "unbelieving".'

'I can imagine. But they've been lucky too, and I would be surprised if they don't know that.' Wynston appreciated my compliment. He rewarded me with one of his best, broad smiles.

We sat together then, each of us thinking, and only when I shifted in my seat, and had no choice but to stifle a yawn behind the back of my hand, did Wynston bring us both back to the matter in hand.

'It would be all right then?' he asked. 'You'd like to have the cataloguing done?'

Lists, I thought. More lists. But not made by me. Not daunting me. Not things to be done by me. Things done: neatly, intelligently, effortlessly (or so cleverly they appeared to be effortless) by Wynston. Muddles ordered. Mysteries solved. Shelves lightened. Treasures revealed and disseminated.

The temptation arose to put down a weighty knapsack I felt I had been carrying for ages. But with the metaphorical knapsack not yet resting on the ground, I hesitated.

Wynston in George's study. Sounds emerging from George's study. Perhaps confusing me. Trapping me for a moment into believing that it's George in there, about to come out, about to hug me, pin me to the moment with his talk, cajole me, refuse to be dissuaded by my impatience. George. There to love me. George. *Not there.*

Wynston's fingerprints replacing those of George. The chance Wynston might come across notes that were for George's eyes only. The excavation of secrets. The preservation of bones.

'Let's be very professional about it,' I began. Then I laughed, a little too heartily probably, not knowing quite what should follow. 'Two days pay per week at whatever rate you get now. Does that sound right? After a month or so you can tell me what your expectations are in terms of time and what you think the collections may reveal. I'll have keys cut. You can come and go as you need to.'

Now I looked fiercely at Wynston. His face was open, smiling, sincere. He needed warning. 'Sometimes I'm tired or cranky or depressed,' I said. ' Sometimes I'm working, or failing to work, and need space only to think. Sometimes I'll be interested to hear what you have to say and sometimes I won't.'

He nodded and got to his feet. 'Next week then? Would that suit?' It would indeed. I rose too. We shook on it.

A pale, tall, skinny child sits on a high wooden stool perched lonely in a long corridor outside a tall-windowed classroom. Inside the classroom she can hear her classmates reciting aloud in the sing-song chanting manner demanded of them by each teacher in turn, '*Watch* the wall, my *darling*, while the *Gentlemen* go by.'

Cordelia is herself watching a wall. She has seen a good bit of this particular wall lately. It is a curdled shade of cream. Someone has washed it unlovingly with a cloth that wasn't clean. There are smear marks in a big uneven pattern. At the bottom of the wall, near the floorboards, some brave or foolish child has written: 'Teachers stink.' A second hand has added: 'Worse than pigs.'

Quiet, even timid at home, Cordelia has been called 'troublemaker', 'rude' and 'uncontrollable' several times lately by her teacher. When her teacher says these words she screws her face up with disgust at the sight of the child before her. When she said the word 'uncontrollable', her excitement was such that she spat and when Cordelia lifted her hand and wiped her face to remove the spit the woman grew even more enraged and pushed Cordelia hard from behind, out of the classroom and into the corridor, slamming the door shut behind her.

Cordelia is not sure why she behaves as she does at school. She knows that she likes the little tremors of excitement that she can feel in the air around her when she defies one of the teachers. The tremors are inside her body as well as outside it. The other children can feel those tremors, too. Feeling them, they look at Cordelia with a mixture of horror and envy. One or two of her friends have actually said to her how much they would like to do what she does. Most of all, they would like to stand up to Mrs Widden, but they don't dare. 'My mother would kill me,' said one girl, 'if she was called up to the school because of my behaviour. Or she'd tell my father. That would be worse. He would *really* kill me.'

Cordelia does not imagine that her parents will kill her. She can't even imagine that they will ever know that their oldest, quietest, most tractable child is the object of her teacher's outrage.

If they were to be told such a thing, she is confident that they would not believe it. The worlds of school and home are far apart. Walking in through the big iron gates of the school, crossing the rough grass that leads to the pitted bitumen, Cordelia can feel herself becoming a different person. She grows taller, fiercer; a second skin wraps itself around her so that she need neither feel other people's emotions or desires or needs, nor care about them.

If asked to choose which Cordelia fits her best, it would be impossible for her to decide. The school-Cordelia is certainly very much like a part, but now she knows the lines so well she need never think about them, and also the gestures and facial movements, as well as the exquisitely judged moments when withdrawal best suits her cause or when, for maximum disturbance, she must make her unsettling presence felt.

But is the helpful, often silent girl she is at home any more authentic? Certainly there she feels hideously undefended. Sometimes just a sigh escaping from her mother's lips, or an added pallor to her mother's skin, can cause her mouth to dry, her stomach to contract. Sometimes she looks in vain to her father for a moment of his attention; of course he is too busy with more pressing matters, she can see that. Sometimes her sisters appear to know much more effortlessly than she does how to be pleasing, even though they are younger. She is sure they are not aching for something she can't name, as she is. And Allen and Frank, she loves both those brothers. It is hard not to mind though when her father appears to have time to admire every detail of their red and green Meccano models or their elaborate pencil drawings of mythical beasts, or even occasionally time to take them fishing when the girls have never been invited to join them.

Cordelia imagines how it would be to stand on top of the stool and then to jump. If she could jump hard enough and far enough she might even manage to fly past the window pane that is set into the door of her classroom so that whenever he passes on his rounds, the headmaster can look in.

Her classmates would witness her achieving the impossible. 'Child Takes Flight' would be the heading in the local newspaper. Or maybe, beneath her photograph: 'Peter Pan of Our Local School'.

Cordelia sees herself landing. She has a broken leg. Perhaps an ugly piece of bone splinters off and breaks through the skin. She sees herself with teachers and pupils gathering around. They are asked to step back, to give her air. She needs *air*. She hears the siren of an approaching ambulance. She can feel herself being lifted like a precious object, onto a stretcher and carried away to emergency care at the hospital where she will lie, small and white and badly injured, waiting for her worried parents to come to her side. She is brave; everyone notices how brave. 'The worst possible break,' they agree, heads nodding in wonder, 'and not a single tear shed.'

Cordelia wriggles on the stool. She again reads that the teachers stink like pigs. She can hear her own stinking pig teacher leading the class in an impossibly loud, ludicrously rhythmic rendition of 'Five and twenty ponies/Trotting through the dark – /Brandy for the Parson/ 'Baccy for the Clerk . . .'

Cordelia slumps. Last Wednesday her teacher told her she was sly. 'You're a sly child, Cordelia Williamson,' the teacher said, and Cordelia said, 'Yes, Mrs *Wid*-den,' pursing her lips as she did so as though to suppress a smile to show that she didn't agree one bit. But she did agree. To herself she said, 'It's true. That's exactly what I am. Sly.' This self-evident insight was not entirely unpleasant, but it certainly wasn't pleasant either. The taste in her mouth was hot and sour.

Shaking herself, Cordelia slips down from the stool and under cover of the noise behind her she kicks the opposite wall hard. Her boot leaves its mark. She kicks again and then drags her boot as far along the wall as she can manage, dirtying the wall as she goes. Now she can hear the dying embers of the Smuggler's Song: 'Them that asks no questions isn't told a lie − /*Watch* the wall, my *darling*, while the *Gentlemen* go by!'

She waits for the door to open and for her name to be called.

29

My dreams are shot through with colour.

By day, however, I am increasingly turning my face and thoughts towards what is unarousing. When there is only myself to see to, I am cooking monochrome, dullish food. Scrambled eggs sitting next to white toast is turning up more often than it should on my menu. Anything else looks weird to me, and somewhat repulsive. A slice of tomato or a sprig of parsley appear newly perverse.

I am also spending more time than usual in my white bedroom and taking out of that room – now that I think about it – those few bits and pieces that are suddenly not pale enough. It is in my studio that I am most restrained, even while feasting more pleasurably than ever on the torrent of colours that Laurie and Gudrun are using. And I am attempting to provoke them to greater extremes whenever I can. But there is little restraint in my dreams. There, colour drags me almost literally by the hair and takes me with it.

Before going to bed last night I pulled out a box from the bottom of a commodious old cedar wardrobe. Although this box is a persistent nuisance there, making it difficult to hang longer clothes as they tend to bunch up on top of the box and crease, I have been reluctant to do anything about it. This house rattles with should-do tasks of that kind which too long ago settled into a kind of out-of-focus blur. Part of me knows that something ought to be done. Part of me scolds that something should be done. But my three-quarters – as Rhea once aptly put

it — ignores the task completely and, when the wardrobe door or whichever delineator can be shut is shut, that three-quarters part determinedly
turns my entire attention to other things. Or to nothing at all: to that
rocking place of reverie that exists outside time where I hardly know I
have been, until something happens to bring me back.

So why should curiosity suddenly get the better of me now? Because
it was curiosity — and not an uplift in my housekeeping skills — that
quite unexpectedly had me dragging the box out and some scandalous
puffs of fluff and dust with it.

The hat box is old-fashioned, spacious and smells faintly of a sweet
flowery perfume. Is it foolish to suppose that it was probably once my
mother's? My mother did, indeed, wear hats. In her day women always
wore a hat out of doors. Gloves, too. Like those white Southern
Rhodesian women Bron described: keeping up their standards. We have
an easier time of it now in many ways.

Late in life my mother tended to forget her hat as she walked back
in through her front door after shopping, and would sometimes remain
securely hatted until bedtime. Hers were snug-fitting cloth or felt hats.
I expect they were comfortable, maybe even comforting. So it was not
at all an unusual sight to see her sitting at the table with her needlework,
or moving slowly around the kitchen preparing a meal or cleaning away
after it, with an apron on over her dark dress, outdoor shoes replaced
by a neat pair of men's soft tan leather slippers, still wearing her hat.

This box was not made to house the modest, dullish hats my mother
favoured. This hat box would have done credit to one of Norah's splendid, look-at-me creations. Almost heart-shaped, and a deep purple
colour, it opened up to reveal beneath sheets of lilac tissue paper several
shawls, hand-crocheted with the finest possible hook, also some silk
stockings that I was almost afraid to touch they are so gossamer, and
some tiny cream lace gloves meant for evening wear. These would fit
over the palm of a fairy hand and caress it, from the slim wrist just to
the first joint of each slightly separated finger. They look strange to me
now, unsettling even. How diminutive my mother's fingers would have

appeared emerging from their lacy bindings. How different the world would seem when one attempted to reach out with such a hand. I think at once of Laurie's hands. Two of my mother's would fit in one of hers. Laurie's grasp on the world must be different, if for no other reason but this one. But there are other reasons – many of them.

One of the shawls is ravishingly pretty. Its colour is much like that of the box itself: dark purple with tones of red and lilac moving through it in a way that is hard for me to imagine anyone achieving with threads. Yet, here it is. In my hands I hold a web, shimmering with beauty and illusion. This is the kind of mixed-colour work that I was doing with glazes on clay before Africa overcame me. One colour suggesting another, then becoming that second colour but almost immediately teasing into a third and then a fourth. And I could never stop there. No array was too much for me until I was literally stopped as I toppled off whatever edge I had left until last. Nell clearly had more control of her art than I did.

For this ethereal thing surely was my mother's own work. Why do I still doubt it? The picture of her is vivid enough: a woman's head bent over her needlework. *The devil makes work for idle hands.* It is most unlikely this phrase actually passed her lips. She would have thought the cliché vulgar. Or plain unnecessary. *Actions speak louder than words.* But there was an undeniable sense in which the constant activity of her hands wove that message like a binding around our hearts, and sealed our lips against protest.

Dreaming, deep in the underworld of sleep, I must choose a colour to express my sadness. Sadness, in this dream, tips dangerously near despair. My eyes shift towards dark purple. That gesture chooses it. One colour is not enough. In an instant, purple runs through with red and black and is forming a trail I am to follow. No choice. As I move along the path it marks for me, I see a scrubbing brush. Mine. The wooden brush is old-fashioned but new, tough, hard-bristled. No non-sense. It is a weapon for me. (Why do I need one?) It is also a means to clean up what is messy, to disguise what should not be seen.

Clear up, clean up, move along girl, move along, I hear myself saying in the strident, emphatic tones one might use to encourage a horse. I blush for shame.

To my right, I see a lake. It's not much of a lake. A deepish puddle really, though it extends further than a puddle should. Scummy on its surface and beneath. A woman floats there. Only her face is visible. And her hair. Her hair spreads out over the water as the paint spread out to create a path. Her hair is black, streaked with grey and henna red. There is too much hair. The surface of the lake is choked with hair. I cringe. I don't want to go near her. Why can't I move on? Is there no free will in dreams?

Curls of anger push up from dark places inside me. Not anger only, meanness too. The woman is pathetic, abandoned. I want to push her with my foot back underneath the foul water. I want to pound her into invisibility with my no-nonsense brush.

Clean up girl. Get on with it. Clean up. Clear up.

Can she come out of the water? What a horrible thought. Surely she is dead?

Dead Woman Lies In Dirty Water. *Lie there then; I don't care.*

I don't want to care.

I have a net. I must roll her to the shore. I don't want to, I don't want to care, but my wants are not relevant here. 'When are they ever?' It's self-pity I hear in my voice now, a whine that grates my ears. I taste bile. I spit.

This woman is not someone I want to save. 'Let her save herself,' I say aloud even as I am pulling her out of the water with the net and prodding her, roughly, to lie dripping at the shallow edge. Her clothes are purple. The same streaked purple-with-red-and-black as the paint.

The woman stirs. Sits up. Does she have a message for me? Do I want a message from her? Damn her. I am cold. I need rest.

There is a message for me from her in her pocket. I will have to touch her. Disgust fights rage. Rage wins. Rage riots. Rage pounds at my temples. Rage demands to be set free. Rage thinks only of spitting, hissing, cackling; of howling to the sun and badgering the moon. Rage will strip the bark from trees. Rage will sear the grass; moist green will become crisped brown. Rage will dry rivers, turn lakes to steam, shake the oceans until waves thunder back to back and the eyes, mouths and noses of sailors fill with water, salt and fear. Rage will not settle until kind, good, nice people shake and tremble as they pull down their blinds; lock their doors; attempt – vainly – to protect their homes. Some will be too late even to save their children. They may turn their thoughts towards cleansing water. They may leave their threatened homes to run in search of springs, rivers, lakes, oceans: any moving water that would cool them, hide them, give them refuge from the blistering, searing heat that is my anger.

But such waters as they might find are not cool. They are hot, hot, hot. I suck in my own hot breath between two rows of grinding teeth. And let it out again.

The woman watches my anger. She smells· it. Hand stretched forward, she could touch it. She stands her ground. When did she stand? How can she stand?

She is unafraid.

I am afraid. I fear myself. I am poisoned by my own spittle. The acid of my tears burns my face and makes holes in my clothes where it falls. My howls choke me. Drawing in my own breath is like eating chillies. I cry with frustration and rage.

The woman gets up. I have to follow her though I am reluctant.

We are at a second lake. *I don't want this.*

She wants me to dig in the sand.

I don't want this.

She digs for me. She finds, first, two delicate fan-shaped shells.

Shells for listening. For hearing what never makes it into words.

Who cares! Crap. Rubbish. No way.

The shells are not fans. They are shaped like hearts.

I look at those shell-hearts. I look again. Just beyond them, lying alone, is my own heart exposed in the sand. Horrible. Obscene. *I don't want this.* 'Would you want to see your heart?' I cry out. 'Would you want to see your own heart stranded?'

No bones guarding it. No skin shielding it.

The frozen spaces of Antarctica. Orphan chicks of the Emperor penguins are moving across the ice. Their tiny hearts pound with fear and need as they glide and scuttle from one feathery cave between two short legs, and then on to another. Biting cold warns them they must run. Mothers with spaces would take them on, but they cannot foster successfully without a partner. There are not enough partners. How like the warm world this icy place is. The foster mothers can't be foster mothers. The chicks must move on. That's how things are in the world of ice. Choices are stark. Live or die. Take it or leave. *Leave it. Leave it.* The orphans can try just so many feathery caves between two short legs. Eventually they are too tired, too cold, too hungry and bereft to raise their hopes and scuttle once again. Exposed, they die. *'Would you want this? Would you? Of course you damn well wouldn't!'*

The woman is calm. She doesn't hurry.

She holds one of the shells and doesn't touch the heart. My heart. Her long hair dries as I watch. It begins to curl. The ends move and gleam glossy, though as my eyes travel upwards I see that her scalp is still caked with mud. I shift my gaze down, beyond her feet, to the heart.

The heart is red and healthy but has sand on it. I don't want to go near it.

I am near it.

I don't want to touch it. It is pulsing, monstrously. And I am monstrously upset to be forced to see that my heart is out of my body.

'I am just a child!' I tell the woman, unexpectedly. As indeed I am. 'An orphan,' I say, although I know that isn't true. But I want to lie; there's a satisfaction in this lie.

Twelve, maybe thirteen, I am standing on a mound. My dark

hair hangs in two long, uneven plaits. I am tall, skinny. My shoulders hunch forward. No one could call me pretty. My smocked, pale-checked dress tied at the waist is too tight and too short. My navy knickers underneath are ill-fitting. I keep my hands hidden at all times so that no one will see that on one of my thumbs I have three pink warts. Morning. Noon. Night. There is no rest from who I am.

From the mound, I have a good view. Into myself, as well as out from myself. I know that I am extremely clever. Because of my clever-ness, I can read minds.

Reading minds, I see that most of the people around me are idiots. *Complete idiots.* Have I said that out loud? *Never mind.* Never in their minds. My teachers; my parents' acquaintances; relatives: everyone who knows what's best for me is an idiot. They have no idea what rages in my head or where my abandoned heart is.

Even my mother is an idiot. My mother lost her heart and doesn't know where to find it.

But I, Cordelia, am clever. I have used my brains and buried my heart.

Once my mother was also clever. Sensitive too: *knowing through her senses.* Then, bit by bit, her heart dried and cracked like mud that's deprived of water. Life seeped out through those cracks.

Now I understand why my own heart is buried in this sand. How clever I am!

At the same time, I resent this woman, standing, with two listening shells in her hands. She knows where my heart is. She has led me to it. Yet she was also lying in a filthy lake, and is herself filthy except at the curling ends of her long hair. When I glance at her face, slyly, I see she has a clear gaze and a high, unlined forehead. George's mother had a brow of marble. Was she clever? I believe she was. Anyway, she was never less than kind to me, and she adored George. *Her heart's in the right place.*

Rage pumps more slowly.

I turn away from the heart. I don't want to touch it.

I can't take it with me. *Cover it with sand.* Disguise the tracks that led me to it. *Erase those tracks.* No one else should find my heart.

The woman wants me to leave the scrubbing brush to mark the spot where my heart lies. I do what she asks, but not willingly. I turn away from the woman even while obeying her. Still holding the shells, she has no need of me and makes no move to follow me.

Returning, I follow the purple trail, kicking up dry white sand to cover my tracks and sadder in this moment of dreaming than I can ever remember being, as well as strangely heavy hearted for someone whose heart lies buried beneath sand.

I toss and turn between white damask sheets. When I wake, I am hot and have a headache.

But, only minutes later, my body almost entirely forgot the decorum that ought to come with age. As though driven, I raced to the bathroom, then, after the hastiest of washes, threw on some clothes and soft shoes, left my bed unmade, brewed some coffee – much stronger than I would usually dare – and, with steaming mug in hand, left the house to hurry down the path to the studio.

I could scarcely get the key in the door, never mind turning it with the care it demands, so urgent was my need to have a pencil in my hand, paper spread out before me, in an effort to make sense of the impossible.

At once, I had to draw something which in form more or less re- sembles my old birdbath pieces, but, this time, it is more truly a birdbath, complete with central pedestal. The top is much flatter than a conventional bowl-like birdbath, and the circular movements that will create it will remain in place. These movements will be faint but perceptible even to a casual observer. The merest suggestion of a track that goes round and round and round. *World without end.* There will be enough of a lip to hold some water to give resting birds the chance to drink. But above the birdbath – and it won't be glazed; it will be the rich orange colour of the clay itself – will be suspended an orb, a perfect circle that can appear either filled, or hollow, according to the eye of the beholder.

And there's the rub, of course. Dare I make such an orb? How can I make it as perfect as this project demands? Most troubling of all, how can I suspend it above what is passing for a birdbath without ugly wires or steel legs, or discernible strings from above?

Yet it must be suspended. It must sit in space without obvious support. It must float above the birdbath. It may even appear to threaten it, yet does not.

Pencils, pens, charcoals, coloured pencils, crayons: none helped me solve my conundrum and with sheets of drawing paper scattered all over the studio, some of them with only a few strokes polluting their purity before they were abandoned, I had to accept that what I want to do is for the moment beyond me. Poor trees, I thought, looking at the wasted paper. Then gathered up the sheets telling myself I would re-use some of them but knowing even as I dusted down this little resolution how unlikely that is.

I save more string, rubber bands, ends of candles and slivers of soap than I could possibly live to re-use. I empty glass jars to the bottom and diligently recycle them. I resist the lure of fresh plastic bags. Willingly, I continue to raise compost piles with whatever waste emerges from my kitchen and George's garden. When it comes to a new idea, however, I am what every paper manufacturer dreams of: demanding of the best, and profligate in its use.

Well, it's a small enough vice. Or so I tell myself. Excusing myself to myself. And when my pencil moves across paper that is as beautiful as money can buy it's an experience for me of exquisite sensuality. God knows, at seventy-three we need such moments however we can find them!

An orb suspended above a flat circle, itself raised from the ground on one sturdy central leg, a flat circle lipped on its outer edge, and on this flat circle finely, finely etched circles-in-movement, mere brush strokes: evenly spaced, eternal, calm. My desire to achieve this is strong. Feeling such desire for calm is itself paradoxical. I note that with amusement. But I like the feeling; I welcome it.

30

Calm is not how I would describe the evening that surrounded the eating of the perfectly delicious casserole Wynston had cooked. I had only to heat and serve his masterpiece, along with rice to soak up the memorable red-wine-and-fresh-herbs sauce, and various easy bits and pieces I put out on assorted plates. Bronwyn did come, and Gudrun, too. Both came alone. Gudrun is partner-free she told me, when I tentatively suggested that if there were someone she wanted to bring, that person would be welcome. Goodness, one has to walk across egg shells with the phrasing of invitations these days.

Gudrun laughed, assuring me she would love to come and would come alone. She has long since given up on men she says. ' Don't think I didn't try, but I couldn't find one old enough to be worth talking to and young enough to be worth fucking. So I gave up. Now I keep my hands to myself except when I am plunging them into clay! Very nearly as nice as human flesh, don't you think, Cordelia?'

I am not entirely sure that I could agree, but I was certainly delighted that she could come, and knew that Laurie would be too. I suspect Gudrun has as many satisfying friends and experiences as she needs. A great deal of pleasure has soaked into her face and body and seeps out into her work. Much of that pleasure is surely sexual, but maybe we really can have enough? At least for one lifetime.

The children were more than usually hectic. They are both about to be in separate plays at their school and we were treated to the entire production from Rhea and his own brief lines only from Gregory, but repeated several times to puff them into greater existence. Finally with Rhea joining in. She has a memory like blotting paper that will stand her in fine stead. Along with this came a colourful explanation of who should have had which part, if only the teacher had known better.

'Saskia Ainsworth gets the best part every single year and it's not fair because Alice Goldstein knew all the words first and she's never had a big part because Miss Armitage doesn't like her mother and her mother thinks Miss Armitage looks as though she has a lemon every day for breakfast and nothing with it.'

Gregory warmed to this delicious theme of injustice. 'It's the same in our class. Last year Patrick Williams had three parts and this year he has two and I wanted one of those but Mr Shu said that I had a big part last year which simply isn't true and he said that just because I have one of the loudest voices he has ever heard doesn't mean that it is fair for me to have a big part every time. Even though Patrick Williams gets big parts every year without fail. But I like my part anyway. I get to say "Shocking" two times, and also, "Monstrous".'

'Oh Cordelia,' Rhea barged in, 'I'm afraid that it is my sorrowful duty to tell you that I have never in my entire life seen someone quite as shocking and as monstrous as you are. I *hate* to tell you this, and in your own house too, but it is only for your own good, you understand. *Shocking*, my dear, and *monstrous*.'

'Shut up, you two, for heaven's sake, do close your wild mouths.' Laurie was torn between complete embarrassment and pride in her children's rampant vitality.

'Please, Miss,' I said to Rhea, twisting up my face piteously as I spoke, 'please, Miss, I promise to be as good as gold if only you will give me another chance. Just one chance, Miss. It's all I ask.'

I put my hand, curled and paw-like, on Gregory's arm. 'Kind sir, can you persuade fair Lady Rhea? I'm willing to try, sir, believe me!'

'I will help you, Cordelia,' conceded Rhea, with considerable grace, 'but there's simply no doubt that you'll have to have remedial lessons in not being shocking for at least two years. Progress will be slow but if you do every scrap of homework I order you to then there is a faint chance . . .'

'Out!' cried Laurie. 'I'll have absolutely no choice but to send you to stand outside under the moon, all alone with the snails and slugs and slaters and wild scavenging cats if you can't be quiet immediately.' And indeed they were quiet, for at least two or three minutes, and then for much longer when I produced some of my most inviting heavy white paper with pens and crayons, and set them to work designing backdrops and costumes for their plays.

Later, Guy came for the children, carrying them out one at a time to his car, sleepy weights hanging over his shoulder, and after a while Bronwyn left with Gudrun, the two of them still laughing and talking loudly and over the top of one another like familiar friends as they delayed their journey to their separate cars.

That left Laurie and me, sitting together, having a tiny cointreau each, and a final chocolate mint.

I was tired. It had been a long evening, most delightfully filled with food and talk and laughter. I needed to go to bed, yet I was horribly afraid of what might be waiting for me once my eyes were closed and the safety of the day was left behind.

Then, as I sat back, eyes closed, contemplating but not wanting to risk thinking too deeply or closely about the purple woman, my sandy buried heart, my blistering, shocking rage, in the midst of that – as though that were not enough – Laurie told me that she is a lesbian.

This shouldn't come as any surprise to me. I have not come this far in my friendship with her to be shocked. Indeed, I don't wish her to be in any smallest way other than as she is. Nevertheless, I am disturbed. The ground has shifted underneath my feet and I am not quite sure why – or where I will be taken.

Laurie is not the first lesbian I have known. She is not even the first lesbian with whom I have been close and by whom I have been tempted into a web of friendship more intense, and maybe more attractively sticky, than most. But there is a promise here of something that

I don't already know; something I can't put a name to; territory for which I have no map.

In winter, in Antarctica, how would a crazy traveller find his way across the ice? Without a compass, without the sun rising in one direction and setting in another, would such a traveller be entirely and forever lost? Not simply frozen, but terminally disorientated? I don't know who to ask, or even what I am asking, quite.

In silent cells, densely padded against any possible sound, and kept brilliantly lit day and night so that there is no longer any such thing as day or night, captured members of the German Red Army faction lost all sense of what was real; perhaps all sense of whether they themselves were real.

Both these scenarios shake me. I need the rising of the sun; the phases of the moon. I need the seasons. I need rhythms I can recognise and be part of. I need darkness no less than I need light.

'I'm being wooed, Cordelia,' Laurie giggled, holding a cushion close to her chest for comfort, quite uninterested in keeping pleasure from her voice. Embracing the cushion as though it were a fat little teddy, she went on, 'Can you believe it? I'm being wooed with concerts and flattery and notes and flowers delivered to my door and it feels a bit like manna from heaven. Or relief parcels to the parched.'

'Who is the lucky man?' I asked, my voice interested and bright. Oh innocent Cordelia.

'No man, Cordelia,' Laurie said. And hesitated, poor darling. 'Not a man. Are you surprised?' Then, gallantly making excuses for my ignorance, 'It's perfectly true to say that I was decidedly my father's daughter and not my mother's. Should that have made a raving heterosexual out of me? What is the formula for heterosexuality these days? Too much Daddy or not enough? It's so hard to keep up, don't you think? But for some years now I've felt real doubt that I could be – or would want to be – a man's woman. Whatever that means.' She grimaced, mocking herself and pulling at the tassles on the cushion.

'Mixing with the mothers at events at the children's school, I have garnered some sense of what that means. Kids aside, it means a man at the centre of your life. A man – preferably "a husband" – and not work and other women. If I'm half-right about that, then I probably never have been much cop as a man's woman. Other than Guy's, I guess, and he's almost certainly queerer than me. But the other boy-friends or male lovers . . . they seem to have disappeared from my inner layers, leaving virtually no trace. Whereas the women: that's been dif-ferent. It's been a long time, but each one left an indelible impression – for better or worse. And I guess that when I dare long for anything it is for that: for more of those indelible impressions.'

Lesbian?

Devoted mother; gifted potter; wonderful, blessed friend and support: that's how I have thought about Laurie. Do I want to know more? Somehow I doubt it, but still she's going on. 'To tell you the truth, Cordelia, I thought I was doomed to everlasting celibacy. A bisex-ual celibate. Does that cover every possible mainstream option? It didn't seem that bad, either. In fact, after some years' practice, it seemed pretty good!'

Her voice changed. She frowned, and gave the cushion a tighter squeeze. 'Also, maternity feels so real to me that any other kind of encounter seemed not just unreal by comparison but . . . I don't know . . . banal. Not worthy of the effort even the least love affair necessarily demands.' Again she paused, weighing either her thoughts or her words, I hope more for her own sake than for mine.

'Then changes happened. I was stirred. Woken up. A new cycle was beginning, I guess. Though it has taken me by surprise. I didn't see the changes coming.'

'When do we ever see changes coming?' I hope my voice was less cynical than I momentarily felt.

She looked at me. Her eyes were struggling to express something she wasn't saying. Even her dark, mobile eyebrows were expressing . . . what? It wasn't the moment for me to say more. I didn't want to say more. I wanted to identify what I was thinking, what I was feeling, but before I could even begin to investigate that local mystery, Laurie had broken in on my thoughts. 'I was stirred first by what is impossible. That was the start of it. Woken up by a kiss, but not allowed to kiss back.'

This was, in some obscure way meant for me, though I could make little sense of it with my tired and somewhat overwrought mind. Probably the cointreau had been a mistake. I wished that I still smoked tobacco; I knew I mustn't sigh.

Laurie began talking more quickly than usual. 'I was pushed to see things didn't have to be the same way forever. I'd entered a new phase in my life. Which seems to mean that now, suddenly and completely unpredictably, I'm a tiny bit tempted by sexual love again. What wasn't possible for me for years seems faintly possible again!' At this, she blushed deeply. And again looked at me. 'What do you think? Not more than that as yet. What's even better, I feel that this time I can actually choose. I am *conscious* I can choose. I don't have to get lured by hormones or biology or even by my decidedly base needs for flattery if I don't want to. I could step back. I could turn away and be no worse off. The question is, do I want to go forward or back?' And again she asked, 'What do you think?'

What do I think?

An impossible question, surely. As impossible as asking how one crosses the ice without a compass or a sun that rises and sets.

I think I don't want to share Laurie, is what I think. And I am ashamed of that thought as soon as it insinuates itself into my mind. Laurie notices whatever passes across my face, but misunderstands.

'Are you shocked? Or appalled? About my aberrant sexuality, I mean? I don't want you to mind. That would be awful. You don't *mind*, do you, Cordelia?'

I pause only because I must, now, rapidly skim my thoughts and feelings and then find I am able to say, quite easily and truthfully, 'Mind? No. Disapprove? No, not at all. Surprised only because I hadn't thought about it. Which simply shows what an old fuddy-duddy I am. Shocked?

No. Just wondering how a brand new romance will fit in with your busy life.'

How I will then be fitted into your busy life, I do not say, and am ashamed and a little frightened by how unsettled that concern makes me. I truly want what's best for you, I think. At the same time, I recognise anew how precious Laurie's presence and concern for me are in my life. How protected I am by her concern from the loneliness that stalks alongside my grief.

In my shaky denial I am again a child, my mother's shut-out eldest daughter, and, at the same moment and without even drawing breath, I am reminded of all that must now lie behind me. That particular combination is not easy.

Even without being agitated into remembering my childish feelings of loss and fear, it is not easy to become old, nor to be old. Nothing prepares us for a state of diminishment for which there is no cure and from which there will be no respite, except in imagination and dreams. Bad patches in the past were patches. We got through them, around them, over them, under them. Somehow or other. Youth and promise still lay on the other side: another chance to recreate ourselves, or to make good. But then we come up against old age. Or old age comes up against us. Youth and promise are other people's privileges. Those of us who are old just get older. We slip into each stage of 'older' without choice and sometimes without awareness that yet another phase of 'less old' has gone forever.

Do I, Cordelia, long to be young again, or even middle aged? Do I long for the sheen and visibility that belong only to the very young? Do I miss the arrogant, careless entitlement to a sensuality that in my case mostly lay partially dormant; a sensuality that I promised myself I would one day realise fully, but really never did? Do I long for the only partially illusory re-creation of self that a new lover briefly brings? Do I wish for loving caresses for myself?

Perhaps I do. But those longings abort when I bring them up against the realities of my own bodily change, against my only too-detailed acquaintance with the stiffness, dryness, brittleness, bruisedness, even the fragility that I hide under my silky, fluid clothes. My clothes are always much fresher and more glossy than I am.

So maybe what I long for, or simply miss, are the days when I could have reached out for this peach – or that plum – and felt at least a little bit entitled to taste a drop of its juice, or even just imagine it.

No juice left. Only thin, tinny tears. I stir in my chair. Move a cushion into the small of my back. I feel bony and uncomfortable, spiky, prickly, beyond embracing. Now, in this moment, I am not only missing George who aged with me, I am also missing young Cordelia. Perhaps it is she who lies abandoned, shockingly, on the grass beneath the vast greening tree in our back garden. Skin and bones in a pretty frock.

She is a bride, tall, thin, intense; desperate to please, who has burned with the pleasure of pressing courting mouth to courting mouth, who has cherished the feel of arms supporting her, of fingers touching her, but who is, naked now, capable of feeling almost nothing but fear of burning pain between her legs, fear of her own retreat, and guilt and shame that she should be afraid and fleeing, instead of fearless, eager, open.

She is also a woman sitting, crying noisily, in a squeaky cane chair. Angry because her husband's life is full and hers is not. She is a woman in her prime, reaching towards a man covered in spun-gold hair: turning away, already regretting what she cannot dare to take.

She is, too, a woman, getting older, sitting, in the present, in a room with a vibrant younger woman who looks at her with more than usual care and friendship; yet Cordelia once again, and even at this late stage, chooses to look away.

Laurie has stood to top up our glasses. Probably a mistake. Though minor in the scheme of things.

'Ice, this time? Or tea?'

I shake my head. Has Laurie noticed what I have been thinking? I look at her. Her dear face glows. She has bitten off all the lipstick she was wearing but her lips are anyway full and dark. Only grief is as blinding as fresh lust. Or new motherhood, I suppose.

Watching Laurie, I feel ashamed of my sour thoughts, my self-absorption, my brutal litany of losses. I want to make amends. In a moment no longer than a flash, a sea-change occurs in me. Can I risk a little truthfulness?

'Here I sit like an old crone, Laurie,' I begin, 'in a great tumble of thoughts at the heart of which was sheer self-pity that I am no longer young, or that one cannot remain half-young, half-desirable, half-optimistic . . .'

'Cordelia, that's . . .'

'No, you want to reassure me. I can see that all over your sweet face but I want to get this said. Lay the ghost. Because these are not new thoughts or sentiments but in having them this time I realised how easy it is to slip into an attitude whereby one sees oneself through another's gaze, at one remove so to speak. And in my case, the eyes through which I too easily see myself are harsh, and they judge cruelly.

'Sitting here with you now I temporarily experienced myself as wizened, dried-up and dried-out. How many countless times have I let that happen in other versions of the old grim tales? Can you imagine the routine? The self-disgust? Unpardonable really. But something changed this time – and I think it's entirely because I was thinking in your company and not alone, Laurie. So, despite my slump, suddenly I also see that as a love-object of course I am way past my use-by date. As most women are, indeed, for the greater part of their adult lifetime. But as someone who can legitimately say, "I have something to give," in that, you know, I feel really rather fresh! For surely in the giving of love, we remain novices, keen to learn, keen to perfect an imperfect art: the knowing and loving of another human being.'

Willingly, I smile at Laurie, taking her in as source of inspiration as well as good listener. Then although I have already said too much, I press on. 'Each encounter of any depth, it seems to me, asks of us some combination of intention and action that has never been asked of us before. And it goes on asking. Each day asks something new.'

Laurie is bursting to interrupt. But still I won't allow it. Not yet, anyway. My weariness has gone. There are things to be said; there is still time to say them.

Picking up Laurie's hand and holding it, I say to her, 'You've made me young again, Laurie. I don't mean, young-young. Not as I was once young. To return to that would be absurd as well as impossible. And I don't mean "not-old" either, because I am old. All right! *Modestly* old. No, I'll concede that it's more that you remind me that I am that most delightful thing – an amateur! In the giving and receiving of love I can go on being a beginner willing to do her best. A beginner who also does not forget that she has a long and minimally honourable history in the giving and getting of love.'

At my change in tone, and the relief it conveys, Laurie visibly relaxes and sprawls in her chair in a way I have come to discover as entirely characteristic of her. I hope she is forgiving me for going on and on, but tonight it feels compelling. Her hand is still in mine. It is cool and dry despite her excitement and hot face.

'You have restored me, Laurie. You've raised me up from a whole series of sloughs. It's been more than I could have hoped for.'

Now Laurie leans towards me. She kisses my cheek, a charming, imprinting kiss that is barely over when I say, 'More on this another time, eh? Please tell me all about your friend. Really, Laurie, I'd like to know who she is. And much, much more about her.'

Laurie sits back, smiling broadly. 'She doesn't live here. Elizabeth. The woman. The temptress!' She laughs, wanting to distract me. Her strong teeth are exceptionally white. Her eyes dart.

I am aware of round breasts pressing against the fabric of her denim shirt. Laurie runs her hands through her hair. Fake diamonds glitter along an ear lobe. There is every reason why she should be desired, sought, adored. I am glad for her.

'It may be that's why I can be tempted at all. Elizabeth would only be here from time to time, on business. She travels around the world finding folk art and then delivering it into the hands of the people who will pay too much for it.'

Do I look shocked or disapproving? Perhaps I do because Laurie says, 'As far as I know she is terrifically scrupulous about what she finds. Though not about who she sells it to . . . that seems to be another story entirely.'

'And you met her, how?'

'Through Luciana. Luciana is one of her customers, or customers of Luciana's are her customers. Those mysteries have not yet been revealed to me.

'What attracts me though is not the glamour – if anything, that puts me off. But I am hugely reassured that she's always on the move. I wouldn't be the one pushing her away to have enough time for the children. My domestic life and routine are already jam-packed. This would be outside all that.'

'And when she's not buying or selling, what kind of woman is she?'

'Funny, warm, confident! Original too. A bit reserved. Lots of layers to get to know. The extrovert on top is pretty strong, but there's someone else there too.'

'Funny, warm, original. Lots of layers. She sounds like you!'

'Is that how you see me?' Laurie grins, plainly delighted.

It is how I see her: especially warm. Warm, warm Laurie. But now she wants to put me right.

'Oh she's quite different from me. She could hardly be more different from me! Can you understand how tempting that is, Cordelia? We're talking fantasy time here. "What are you doing next week?" "Oh, I'm going to Samarkand. How about you?" "Oh, me? I'm positively *torn* between pasta or pizza!" '

'It's not that bad, is it?' I ask, suddenly unsure.

She shakes her head. 'Rarely. I can live without Samarkand and I can't live without my pizza and pasta eaters, so in fact there is no competition. It's just tempting to broaden one's horizons second-hand. Do you see?'

'And is she worthy of you?'

Laurie looks at me, mischief filling her face. 'I'm not such a prize!

But quite astonishingly she does seem to think I'm fun and mildly *talented* and so − obediently − I turn out to be fun when she's around. But I am nervous.' Thinking of precisely that, of nerve ends tingling, of words being weighed and risked, of cheeks flushing, eyes shining, pulses beating; of nipples hardening, of vaginas heating, moistening, expanding, Laurie giggles. Blushes. Squirms. Looks at me. Wondering. Not knowing what I know.

I wait. The nervousness she mentions is part of the attraction. Laurie appreciates that too. Defences disturbed. Cracking. Melting. Hopes and expectations clamouring, then erupting.

Lust tickles the old magic thinking like nothing else: arousing anew ancient fantasies of perfection and immortality, of several lifetimes crowded into one. Of the chance to do it all again. To do it better.

At seventy-three and then some, I am not more than a decade away from my own death, two decades at the outer extreme. And would death be worse than infirm old age, than increasing weariness, stiffness, desiccation, collapse? I don't believe so.

I continue to wait. I am old. *I am young.*

Laurie gets up. Stretches. Shakes herself free. Her face is more relaxed than it has been all evening. Softened, tender. She comes to stand behind my chair. I lean back, tentatively, against her soft belly. Where I like to be. Each of us has revealed a great deal this evening. Wheels have turned and turned again. She bends down, puts her arms gently, firmly around my shoulders. I am embraced. Held by her. I trust her. I breathe. As I lean backwards more deeply into her belly, she presses her lips against the top of my head, and then she turns her head, slightly, leaning her flushed cheek against my flattened white hair. Breathing, close to me, then breathing into me. She waits, patiently, doing nothing more than breathing in, and breathing out.

And it is only when I have soaked in all of that blissful silent comfort, that I get up, put on first *Cosi Fan Tutti* and then the kettle, and notice without much pain that another shared evening is almost at an end.

31

It hasn't always been wine and roses and women wanting to get into my bed. More's the pity.

I had sex in great variation for several years while hardly feeling a thing. Or maybe what I felt was distance, inertia, and an inability to know what I wanted. But that could hardly be admitted. None of that was cool.

There was no doubt what most men wanted; women were always more complicated. Perhaps some of them were playing at being sexy, as I was. Our culture asked it of us. How could we refuse? Ours was the Sexual Freedom Call-Up – maybe the first in history. Maybe the last too. *Get it while you can.* And we did. Though what we got may not bear close examination.

A few women were as near to irresistible as I could then have imagined, but we were not into whatever it took to make things last. Some women I found myself in bed with didn't even try – if 'trying' means showing marginal initiative or imagination. Among those lady-fakers were women who were tigers when it came to marches, causes and standing up for others' rights, but in bed they would slump, or drape themselves across the sheets much like the proverbial fairy princesses waiting to be courted, woken, then returned to slumber – this time between their legs. 'Thank you,' those who had been especially well brought up would sometimes say. *Thank you!* What did they think I was handing out? Tea and bickies?! They were mostly nice-girls pretending to be women; feminists pretending to be lesbian. It went with other wishful thinking that staked out our lives in the 1970s and even into the 1980s, though increasingly not for me.

Drugs helped sometimes. But the timing was mostly off. I began to hate the fact that the aluminium-foil taste or sluggishness they left behind lasted much longer than the sex did. So the drugs went first. Well, not entirely, but the torrent slowed down to a dribble.

Anyway, by the 1980s my personal agenda could no longer be neatly overlaid and consumed by my own – or maybe other people's – political and social agendas. I am remarkably slow-witted when it comes to understanding myself, but even I knew something had to change. I began thinking of getting in touch again with my birth mother, Kate Hallardyce. That's how desperate I was. Perhaps by now her arsehole of a husband would have run off with his best-friend's girlfriend. Perhaps by now her two perfect boys would have started acting out. Coming home smelly, hairy, dissatisfied or plain mean. Anyway *rumpled* and spoiled. Not at all like the prissy, cleaned-up, sharp-smiling goodies that photo showed. Or maybe both boys had turned to vegetables in the kind of gruesome car crash that only the testosterone-riddled can achieve. Or maybe (though this one was hard even for me to sustain) Kate had discovered the sisterhood for herself, and longed to reclaim her only daughter whom she could now value and appreciate at least as much as any son.

Perhaps her voice would vibrate with joy and relief when she heard mine on the phone. 'Hi, Kate,' I would say. 'It's Laurie.' (Not even needing to say: it's your daughter.) Hearing that, she would say (tears in her voice now), 'Laurie! I've been praying you would call. I must see you. Now! You're all I have left.'

Purple pigs might fly.

My work was going well. I had stopped being a mediocre painter on canvas and an uneasy graphic artist and was now a confident painter on clay.

I had seen the messengers heralding the unstoppable march forward of computers and I knew they weren't for me. That ruled out graphic art. Besides, I am a mucky person who is relieved and smugly delighted that it will never be possible to make good pots any other way but with human hands on clay.

It was easy to sell work at a couple of markets and I already had some regular teaching. No write-ups or any notice at all from critics at that stage, but I was mostly fairly pleased with what I was doing. And what I was doing seemed to be what customers wanted. I was already into 'treat' pottery – the kind of decorative pieces that ask to be bought as something special as well as useful. It never fails to give me a lift seeing women buy them, especially the kind of woman who finds it hard to get anything for herself but will just manage to spend what it takes to have a tiny glowing butter dish, or an egg-cup that will make her smile first thing in the morning, or a pot-pourri dish in which crushed dried flowers hide swirls of colour moving like a dancer's sari.

Of course the clay also linked me to my childhood. There were odd times when I even made little clay people, though not for sale. I would make them and then break them, irritable with my own sentimentality.

I had long ago sold the house I'd inherited from Angus and Anita. More than half the money had gone up or come down assorted nostrils. I didn't care. It was never the kind of house I would have chosen for my adult self and when I bought my first flat, which was about the size of the main bedroom in my parents' house – or Cordelia's white chamber – I thought that was heaven.

It was tiny, but extremely light. There were cupboards everywhere. I adored the cleverness with which they'd been fitted in to allow a neat-and-tidy person to occupy the limited space gracefully. Instead the space got me, but I enjoyed playing at neat-and-tidy for a while. I had been living with other people's incapacity to spot a dirty dish for so long that the bliss of having only my own dishes piling up in the sink was considerable.

What I did miss was not having a garden. The dolly-sized flat was on the second floor of a chopped-up terrace house and I could only look down to the garden below which belonged to the decidedly more expensive ground floor flat. Sometimes my downstairs neighbours would invite me in to have a beer with them there and we would loll about in a pleasant enough way, but I think I felt like a trespasser on the actual turf. From above, I felt entitled to it – or to my personal view of it at least – and beyond the immediate grass and shaggy beds of their/my garden were other gardens, other backyards, other back doors leading into other lives I loved to speculate about and imagine.

I met Guy that way.

He was halfway up a ladder when I saw him first. Slim back, naked back, as he'd been sunbathing in the garden where the ladder was propped, innocently unaware until the sun began to go down that he had left his keys inside. Pale brown body, muscled, *neat*. Licorice black hair. Cut short on top, long at the back. Plenty of it. Tiny shorts, or maybe boxer-type underpants. Bright red and black. I couldn't see the pattern then. I did later. They were black hearts on scarlet. I should have read the signs. Muscled legs, too. Shapely but not long. He isn't much taller than I am.

He was leaning to one side, half off the ladder in a dangerously precarious way. He seemed to be trying to open a window, or bang on its frame to loosen it.

Anyway, I leaned out of my own opened window and yelled across, 'D'you need some help?'

It didn't occur to me that he might be a burglar. I guess he was too undressed.

He tried to look around, but couldn't, although he did yell back, 'Could you possibly come and hold this ladder? It's seen better days and I'm trying to get in through my bedroom window.'

I could only get to his garden across my garden, and could only get into my garden if the people who actually owned the garden were at home.

'Won't be long,' I yelled. Loving the drama of it. Certain that I would find a way. And the people below were indeed in and maybe they were as bored as I was that particular afternoon because they were also keen to climb over our wall into the garden that faced ours and to help hold the ladder and yell inspirational instructions until finally Guy managed to shake his ancient window lock free and to push up the lower sash and climb right in.

As soon as he was inside he turned to look down on his saviours, still holding the ladder I think, and to laugh and thank us.

'Let me get dressed and grab some wine and come round to thank you properly,' was what he called out.

Looking up, I saw what? Beautiful skin. A hairless chest. Definitely non-Anglo-Saxon eyes. Maybe not quite Chinese. Not Cambodian. What then? A devastating smile. Good teeth. I heard a voice I liked too. 'Cute,' I told myself. 'Mighty cute.'

The afternoon had certainly perked up.

A couple of weeks later we were meeting and fucking almost nightly. A couple of months later we were talking shared house or flat; and within a couple of years we had married and had our first baby.

Why Guy?

If I rule out boredom or biology (and I can't honestly do either), it would leave only destiny. That somehow we were meant to come together to have our particular children. That the timing was right. That Guy was attractive enough, kind enough – at least initially – and novel enough. I was certainly drawn by his not being an Anglo-Saxon male. He looked almost as different as is possible from my own briefly glimpsed and permanently denigrated half-brothers. And different too from the other men with whom I had heaved and floundered. That difference, and the attraction of that difference, was conscious.

What was not conscious – at least not to me – was Guy's own ambivalence about his sexuality. It was, in hindsight, what we most obviously had in common, given how many hundreds of thousands of people our age had read more or less the same books, seen more or less the same movies, knew the words and/or the tunes of more or less the same music, espoused more or less the same bunch of liberal causes, were fluent in more or less similar rhetoric – yet hadn't ended up together.

But we didn't know we were both queer. It never occurred to me – to either of us, I believe – to ask, much less to confess.

Guy took it for granted that we had both had friends who might have once been our lovers – and that we would both have had lovers who were no longer our friends, if they ever had been. What else was there to say?

I took my cues from him. I was good at that. Also, I was exceedingly relieved. It boded well to me that he was apparently quite untroubled by the evil green demon, Jealousy. The last girlfriend I'd had drove me crazy with her suspicions. Eventually I had felt compelled to turn them into reality just to put an end to the tension. But I had been shaken by that experience, and disappointed in myself. She was an exceptionally good and gorgeous woman when she wasn't possessed. I had acted badly in the face of her insecurity and we had both lost. I didn't want that to happen again.

Also, for a short while, I loved fucking with Guy. He was as relaxed as a cat. Supple, graceful, utterly confident within his body and proud of what his body could do. I gave up saying how pathetic most men are in bed. In time, I put away my more strident badges and even threw the raciest into the bin. I dreamt about women sometimes, but assumed that he did too. That felt quite cosy. How wrong can you get?

Early on I did see him kissing one of his male friends rather more lingeringly than was usual, even in our sexually consumerist circles.

They were standing close together by Guy's glass front door. The other man was tall, big shouldered, long blond hair in a pony-tail. A surfer-type who was actually an academic who did all his muscle-building in a gym. 'Blue Heaven' was coming out of a radio. Guy leaned in against him while I watched. Tony – the other man – put his hands around Guy, then rubbed his hands slowly, appreciatively over Guy's arse before bringing them up and tipping Guy's head towards him in a tender, effective parody of a Hollywood-romantic kiss. While they kissed I still watched. And 'Blue Heaven' played on. What I saw was nothing new to me. But it was something new to know about Guy.

When he came into the room where I was holding a book that I wasn't reading, Guy was as relaxed as ever. He lay on the floor, stretching, turning, luxuriating in his own supple, obliging body. *Preening* was the word that came to mind, but when he pulled me down beside him and began to undo my shirt and then his own I said nothing and did nothing but allow him to fuck. His secretiveness was home to me. I thought my secretiveness was also home to him. I believed it might hold us together.

We cheated reality right from the start, I guess, but only gradually with intention.

Before Gregory was born Guy had started to stay out well beyond evening and into the night. After Gregory was born Guy would occasionally stay out all night, although he was invariably considerate enough to come home freshly showered, and not any more self-satisfied than usual.

Through my pregnancy he hadn't wanted us to have sex. That was fine with me, although it was never discussed. I was nauseous, and otherwise distracted. If he was going elsewhere for it – as clearly he was – then I was able to cut off from my feelings about that. I was used to cutting off. I was mega-successful at it, and even took perverse pride in this largely untouted capacity.

Also, while superficially I was caring, even mildly adoring on good days, the fact is I wasn't always paying Guy and his concerns much attention. I had too much else to be grateful for as I observed and absorbed the changes that were happening to and within my body. *I could feel those*. I wasn't shut off from those. Glory be.

I was conscious almost every waking moment of the unbelievable wonder that I was pregnant. I also knew that I needed every atom of energy I could summon to prepare myself to be the kind of superior mother I vowed to my unborn infant that I would be.

Guy was fairly tender. I was fairly grateful. And only rarely needy of a somewhat abstracted cuddle. We circled each other at some distance, and with some curiosity I think, meeting at a central point only when we talked about our work or, less often, about the baby.

The baby – the abstract notion of 'baby' as opposed to the real biological baby who eventually appeared – had been Guy's idea. I don't think I would have dared. But lying together one night, not even feeling especially aroused or connected, he had said – no, he asked, 'Can you imagine yourself having a baby?'

Immediately, I could. Not only could I imagine it, I wanted it desperately. I wanted what he had dared to articulate and I had never been able to whisper even to myself.

I am sure my heart was beating at ten times its normal rate, but practised as I am in saying and showing relatively little, I lay there, chest bursting, and said only, 'Sort of. How about you?'

'Not having it,' he laughed. 'I think that would have to be your job. But a kid being there, I guess I'd like that. When I held Jane and Ned's baby I could see the attraction. Maybe because Ned's my brother . . . but I don't think it was only that. It was more, I dunno, it was somehow more *personal* than that.'

'Could we afford it?' Why was I asking such a stupid question? Like any addict, I knew that whatever the cost, I would have to have it. My pulse was still racing like a runner's. I moved far away from Guy in the bed. It was crucial he didn't know how much I cared.

'Who knows,' he said. 'Does it matter? Can anyone afford it? As long as we only have one.'

'Or just one at a time.' I could swear my voice was steady, though my hot addict's mind was immediately letting rip, grasping for not one but several little bodies wrapped in nice, white, woolly shawls. All of them mine. *Blood relatives.* Sweet bodies. Kisses. Cuddles. Care. Cared for. Caring. Mine.

'You must be joking!' Guy snorted out his incredulity. 'Any twins in your family?'

'How would I know? My biological history is hardly familiar territory to me.' I intended my curt response to shut him up. I wanted to go on counting bundles.

'Sorry.' Guy had been briefly curious about Angus and his archaeological digs, and politely interested in Anita and Kate. Now at least he knew better than to make Happy Family jokes. 'None in mine, anyway. Though I'll check with Mum.'

I dismissed the bundles, for the moment anyway. 'Don't!' I had already met Guy's Mum. I could imagine only too well being smothered by the weight of her experiences when I had barely begun to imagine my own. Guy's Mum: part of the contemplated gene pool. I thought of Kate too. And the theological student who could not hear no. I shuddered. Still, there was no denying that Guy was clever and good-looking, if rather less kind than I had once imagined, and I at least had the capacities of a survivor to offer on my side.

'Anyway,' I said, 'sometimes it takes people months or even years to get pregnant. Maybe one of us is infertile.' I thought of drugs (me). Sexually transmitted diseases (Guy: was this the moment to ask?). 'Maybe we should both have a check-up. What do you think?'

'Maybe we should have sex instead.' He was already moving across the bed. 'Isn't that what it usually takes?'

And that is all it did take. Within a year, Gregory was with us with all the force of an inevitable, miraculous event.

From the moment he arrived, and despite all manner of ineptitude on my side, I adored my wonderful son, and relished being his mother. Almost from the moment he pushed himself out, his eyes bravely open even as the light hit them for the very first time, it was impossible to remember fully how life was without that sweet, brave boy, or to imagine a life ahead in which he wasn't at the centre.

Guy was nowhere near as entranced. He could get his fill of Gregory in minutes, or even seconds sometimes, and would make excuses about having to prepare a meal, or finish some work, or a friend he had to call. He simply wasn't interested in long staring contests with his son. Nor could he find it in himself to marvel at the extraordinary magic that this child existed. He didn't unwrap him for the express pleasure of touching his exquisite skin, breathing in his enchanting smell, seeing again and again tiny fingers and toes crowned with paper-thin nails.

By the time Gregory was sitting up, or maybe even crawling, Guy was a little more enthusiastic in his role as father, but it was clear to us both, though neither of us mentioned it, that he had more or less permanently resigned his role as lover. I slept with the baby. He slept on his own, or on his own when he was at home which was now not much more than half the time.

We spoke less and less about things that mattered. Some days I felt lonely, but not lonely only for Guy. I was lonely for the mate I clearly didn't have, and lonely too for the women I had loved who seemed, now, to occupy territory to which I could probably not return. Even if I were to find my way back, I told myself, I would probably be tolerated rather than welcomed.

Occasionally I read lesbian magazines or papers which advertised events that sounded increasingly bizarre and unrelated to my life, or even to my history. Sex had gone along with changing the world outside ourselves for my generation of brave-new-world dykes. In less than a decade that emphasis shifted, at least for some. Sex itself became a world: self-enclosed, narcissistic and often pointlessly dangerous. Where was the tenderness, humour, courage and engagement that I remembered? Was that only in my mind? Memory can play odd tricks.

There were some bleak days when I cried, in ways that were absolutely new to me. Guy was patient, if he was at home, and he would hold me, even kiss me. Maybe his Mum had explained to him in her most convincing *Reader's Digest* fashion that this crying was what one must expect from a relatively new mother. But I wasn't crying with post-natal depression. I was crying with confusion, that the baby I had desired utterly, and now had, also left me feeling tremendous loss.

Guy did have sex with me again but only when I was truly desperate for a second baby. Gregory wasn't then a year old. Guy was by now a little fonder of him but was away often enough at night that I could imagine him leaving forever. With him would go my chance for another baby.

That was simply more loss than I could bear. Feeling that loss bite into my soul, once again my addiction flared and blazed. With all pride gone, I pleaded, seduced and then practically coerced Guy back into the sack to help me get what I wanted and needed most.

And, when Rhea was born, Guy stayed home at nights for ages. This time he had no more interest in his new child, but his first child, the son who looks so much like him, was suddenly his chosen daytime companion. He would carry Gregory around the house on his shoulders, and out of the house in a backpack. He would take him when he went to meet his own friends at weekends for coffee or sport. He would spend an unprecedented hour or more playing Gregory's favourite games over and over with a ball or boxes. Sometimes Guy would stack up all the pillows and cushions we owned in several heaps.

'Losing Daddy!' he would call, and even if a leg or arm was poking out, Gregory would race from pile to pile shouting with excitement, 'Where's my Daddy? Where's my Daddy?' And when he found Guy – or found Guy's face which is what he was really searching for – he would scream with pleasure, 'Found my Daddy! Found my Daddy!' Then it would be Gregory's turn to hide, and Guy's turn to ignore the heaving pile of cushions from which ecstatic laughter was already emerging, and to creep slowly, slowly, backwards and forwards to every other pile, calling, 'Gregory! Gregory! Have I lost you? Have I lost you?' until the suspense would be too much and a little voice would cry, 'Here's Gregory!' and Guy would say, 'A talking cushion! Cushion, can you tell me where my little boy Gregory is hiding?', and the cushion would say, 'Here, here! Gregory is here!' and father and son would embrace and shout with relief and exultation, just as though a real loss had taken place, and a long-delayed, achingly longed-for reunion.

Watching them, listening to them, I thought of Angus. I thought of how long his absences must have felt to the small child I once was, and of the bliss and shadowed terror of our reunions. I thought of being lifted high on his shoulders. I couldn't remember that feeling exactly, but watching Gregory's blissful face raised above Guy's I could willingly imagine it. I wanted a father there to love my children. Maybe I even wanted a man to love me too, to make my cheeks pink in the glow of his love. Well, I didn't have that, and maybe never would. But we bounced along well enough. I adored both children. I was more than happy to be their mother; I was grateful every day.

Guy loved Gregory, and gradually woke up to Rhea's considerable vitality and charm. I was openly, positively grateful, too, to Guy for being the father he increasingly was, and he and I skirted each other respectfully enough. Sometimes we laughed, cuddled, teased. Sometimes we saw his or my friends together, or a movie, or talked of how we would save the world, given power and half a chance. But we didn't ever talk about what most obviously divided us. Nor about how he was – as always – continuing to take care of himself. Even when increasingly he did that at my expense.

I still occasionally dreamed of women. Or saw two women together in the street who seemed connected by an electric current of erotic desire or sensual pleasure. I would stare then, but if they caught me staring, and saw a respectable, weary mother with two little children, they probably assumed I was rudely curious, or even disapproving. They surely could not have known that I felt like a hungry person deprived of a feast, or even of a morsel, with my nose pressed up against a plane of glass shielding yet another place I had no right to enter.

Two weeks before he left, Guy took some Ecstasy that had been badly cut. At least, that's what he offered as an excuse. He had been at an all-night dance party. It would have been impossible to stay awake all night without drugs.

'You know how it is,' he said. I did indeed. Though that rather begs the question as to why anyone would need to stay awake all night. To dance and cruise. Or why any father would need to stay awake all night. To dance and cruise. But Guy, of course, hadn't gone there as a father. He had gone because he wanted sex. He felt entitled to it.

Why he hadn't got what he went for, I don't know. There are always – or so I tell myself when I feel self-pitying about my own striking shortage of admirers – queues of men waiting to have sex with Guy.

He had come home angry, off the planet. I was asleep. Both the children had just had chicken pox and were barely getting over it. They had even had spots in their mouths and had been extremely grizzly and upset and hard to handle. I had been feeling more frazzled than usual, not least because I had been unable to leave them for even a few hours with their usual sitter so I could restore my sanity making pots.

Guy got into bed quietly enough, and I think I did register in my sleepy state surprise that he was there. The babies were in their own cots, for once. I had thought their snuffles were more than even I could take.

Probably I almost immediately went back to sleep because I was certainly woken up by Guy pushing me to turn from my side onto my stomach. I asked him what the hell he thought he was doing but he didn't say anything, just pushed me hard. Then he did say, 'Just lie there, will you. Just lie there.'

'No I bloody won't,' I said, but for all that Guy is slim and not tall he is strong and he had already wedged my body beneath his. I could feel him pushing up my nightgown and then against my upper thigh his penis was digging into me and before he began I knew what he was about to do.

I turned my head from side to side and did all that I humanly could to break loose. Even while I tossed and reared with rage against the force of his arm pushing down my back, I was also conscious of feeling utterly offended. How dare he do this to me. How dare he! I had been so absurdly tolerant of whatever he got up to out of the house. So passive, really, and hopeless in the face of his unceasing bids for sexual freedom. The least I deserved in return was some god-damned respect from the bastard.

That wasn't what I got. As he pushed his way into me, he tore my skin and I screamed and began to cry. Guy took no notice at all. If he heard my shouting or registered my crying he gave no sign whatsoever. He was continuing to push his way in until I thought I would burst. As he pushed he was grunting in a way that was unrecognisable to me but was deeply frightening.

The Guy I knew, or had once known, wasn't there. This possessed man, this damned *homosexual* as I unexpectedly and hatefully thought of him, couldn't care less what I thought or did, how much pain I felt, or even if he damaged me forever.

My face did not exist for him. My heart did not exist for him. Who I am did not exist for him. All that was personal to me was turned away from him. I suppose he could imagine whatever he wanted. Or nothing at all.

The pain was terrible. Knowing who was causing it was terrible. But I knew there was no way I could stop him and no way that he would stop until he came. On drugs, that could be ages.

The pounding, the pushing, the tearing of my skin went on. It felt like hours. I tried hard to stop feeling. I tried hard to remember how to drift into a state where whatever was happening was nothing much to do with me. I had been really good at that. I had many years practice up my sleeve, but now when I needed it most, when the father of my children was forcing himself into me not out of love or desire but because mine was the only such orifice available in the absence of a willing male, when I wanted what was happening to stop more than I had ever wanted anything to stop, including the pain of childbirth which is at least a decent, honourable pain, unlike this shaming, tearing, disgusting event, when I wanted that oblivion, even partial oblivion, even momentary oblivion, when I wanted that, instead I was getting only this rutting, this grunting, this sweating, and this terrible, terrible pain, and the pain might have gone on forever because now I knew that Guy might never come, except that both children woke at once and began to cry out and with another strange grunt Guy simply rolled off me and fell asleep immediately, stretched out on his back right across my bed, his arms and legs flung wide claiming my entire territory.

I crawled off the bed. I crawled to the bathroom, calling to the children as I went past their open door, 'Mummy's coming. Just a minute, my sweeties, Mummy's on her way.' Then wept at the terrible ordinariness of my words, and at the pain of postponing attention to their needs, and the wretchedness of having to crawl into the shower and lie there as water fell on me and the pain in my anus blistered and burned and then, when I realised how desperately I needed to pee, I couldn't get up and even when I decided to lie there, in the shower booth, and pee where I was, I couldn't do that either.

After some time the warm water ran out. I allowed cold water to fall on my body and then to keep falling. In a weird way that freezing water helped. It helped to numb me, when I hadn't been able to numb myself. I did get to my feet. I did dry myself and wrap myself in a big towel. I did tip down my throat all that was left of a small bottle of Rescue Remedy, as much for the brandy it contained as anything. I did apply some homoeopathic cream to the most external of my wounds. I did stop crying.

The children had also stopped crying and had fallen back to sleep. I lay down on a mattress that I kept in their room, covered myself with a couple of skimpy blankets, and lay there shaking and crying and sore until morning.

In the morning Guy looked pale, and complained of having a headache. When I failed to respond, when I didn't appear at his side with a glass of water and aspirin, he asked me what was wrong.

I told him, not looking at him while I spoke.

He told me about the Ecstasy then. He meandered through a long, self-pitying story about what a shitty deal he had got. About what a prick the dealer was. Before he said sorry. Before he asked if I was all right.

He did drive me to the doctor. He did say, on our way home, that it should never have happened. He did say, 'It won't ever happen again. You know that, Laurie, don't you?'

Also he did say, when I was finally able to tell him that my HIV test had been negative, that he wasn't surprised. He was relieved, of course, but not surprised. Then, in his first-ever explicit mention of his homosexuality to me, he said, 'I've always been careful. I only ever did safe sex with guys even when it wasn't called safe sex. Except that time. I am sorry.'

Maybe he was. But despite what people say, it isn't always best to have things out in the open. It was now obvious at least to me that whatever tenuous threads had held us together were absolutely and irrevocably broken, less by what Guy did to me that night – though that was bad enough, God knows – than by the confidence that Guy then felt in speaking freely of his sexuality.

Our absence of speech had been a bond, curious though that may seem to an outsider. Speaking cost us.

So when he said, a couple of heavy weeks later, 'Would you rather I moved out, and came to visit the children here?' I felt relieved, and nodded, and was even more relieved when, within the week, he had found a small flat nearby, had packed his personal belongings, and had gone off to live whatever was to be the next phase in his life.

The next phase in my own life began badly. The children may or may not have noticed that Guy had moved out but they anyway went down with coughs, colds, bronchitis. One bout of illness merged into the next, no matter how carefully I nursed them. For some weeks there could not have been a single night-time hour during which all three of us were asleep at the same time. My impression of that early post-Guy period is of literally lugging my exhausted, weighty body along with me by sheer force of will. Also, I had no choice. Guy was off, doing whatever it was he felt impelled to do. I was facing facts. The facts were sleepless nights, runny noses, soaring temperatures and whimpering children. I was doing the best I could.

I suppose Guy called around from time to time. He may claim now to have been available whenever I needed him. But that makes no dent in my certainty that whatever happened to or for myself, or Gregory or Rhea, it was up to me. I was the bottom line, the top line and the middle line. I *was* survival.

During the afternoons my legs or my will would sometimes give way. I would lie down with the children on the floor, wherever in the house we happened to be. Lying together, bunched up in a heap, we would often fall asleep, perhaps sleeping more soundly then than at any other time in our distorted twenty-four-hour cycles.

Someone looking in through a window would have seen an oddly disturbing sight. A stocky, unkempt woman, dressed in baggy jeans and raggy T-shirt, usually covered with dark splodges from where the children had last wiped a nose or mouth against me. I would rarely have brushed my hair since I had last washed it. I was certainly pale for lack of sleep, and heavy-eyed. And Gregory and Rhea, dressed in overalls with buttons up each leg for easy access to their bottoms, were roly human balls made even rounder by layers of jumpers and nappies. Even Gregory had thrown off the effects of whatever toilet training he and I had so far managed for him, and was using his nappies as freely and as often as Rhea.

Spreadeagled on the floor, with a child burrowed in on either side of me, I longed for an earth mother for myself but dreamt often of Angus. In my dreams he was the perfect father I almost believe that he once was. He was also young and playful, teasing and enchanting, in ways he probably could never quite have been. He would talk and laugh and my attention would move from his eyes to his lips and back again. His eyes were darkest quarry grey in the dreams, and his lips were as full and as rosy as a cherub's. Sometimes his hair was long and curly and flowing freely to his shoulders, and at other times it was caught up in a pony-tail that made him look younger than I had ever known him. Once he was crowned with a circle of entwined spring flowers that he took from his head and gave me in a gesture I can only describe as courtly.

In those dreams he was the youthful companion I needed every day and didn't have, but he was also nurturing, wise and kind. Those dreams fed me. But they also made it hard to wake up to so much absence. Caring totally and without respite for two small children while receiving no care at all yourself is an imbalance on a scale that could be fully registered – or even noticed – only by someone else in very nearly the same position of dire inequality.

So I found others. Not even knowing until I did find them how urgently they were needed.

I put the children into a double-seater pushchair, not a bit put off when Gregory protested and said he wanted to walk, and pushed them as far as I had to go to find playgroups, music classes, baby gym classes and mothers' groups. I pretended to myself that I was doing it for them and my relief was certainly palpable when they did have huge amounts of fun with other tiny children, when their faces did light up from within while clapping and singing to *Peter and the Wolf* or tumbling and rolling while Michael Jackson told them how bad he is. But I was also doing it for me, and especially for those wordless flashes of understanding I would get from other mothers when I was lifting one child and then the other into the pushchair to make our way home, or when one child was crying and needing comforting in my arms even while the other was furiously pulling on my leg, totally enraged I was making him or her wait their turn.

'Up, Mum. *Now!* Up, Mum.' So I would bend and hold one child tight to my chest and the other would lean in against me, though leaning against me was only a partial rescue from the ordeal of standing on their own two feet when weariness or misery temporarily threw them off their balance.

More often than not from those silently supportive other mothers there were words, too. Not just about children either. One of the women I met at one of the groups turned out to be a fabric designer of some note. Once we had talked I even remembered having seen colourful stretches of her work in a prestigious show. We knew a few of the same people, and gradually began to call each other in the evening after the children were in bed, to chat and compare notes from our child-bound days. I liked Marcella's company. Droll and chatty in a seductively conspiratorial way, she was married to a barrister who was never at home 'except to fuck and change his shirts', as she put it, smiling while she complained.

Marcella was then and is now innately elegant. Whatever style or sense of glamour women seek to find in fashion magazines she just had. Even her shoulder-length streaked hair looked free – and perfect. I knew by the odd glances she sometimes got that her stunning looks depressed some of the mothers' group women. I could understand that entirely, but it wasn't my experience. She seemed much straighter than most of the women I had ever been close to, but in the circles I found myself moving in, I needed her clarity and spice. She needed me too. She needed my memory that she had once done fine work which had been displayed in a top-ranking gallery, and my confidence that she could and would produce such work again.

She had only one child then, a pretty boy with dark, lavish curls whom she had, perhaps unfortunately, named Orlando. He's grown up to be something of a beefy bully which is a shame, for as a tiny child he was tender and quite enchanting.

Marcella had lost the twin girl she had been carrying with Orlando. The infant had lived twenty-four hours and then died. Puff, gone, out. People said the most predictable things to her: how lucky she was that she still had one healthy baby; how fortunate that the tiny girl had not suffered; how in no time at all she could have another one.

This litany of meaninglessness was passed on to me by Marcella in the formal sitting room in her over-large house which we had scattered with baby paraphernalia and softened. She paced backwards and forwards as she spoke. Across polished boards. Onto Persian carpet. Off again and back onto boards. Onto another Persian carpet. I watched her feet, long and slim in pale green leather pumps. To sit still was impossible for her. To stop watching the movement of her feet was impossible for me.

As she walked, she talked. In a rush, not to me exactly, but because I was there. 'Each baby meant the world to me. My body had got ready for two. I had opened my heart ready for two. For two. Not for one. For two. My daughter was a person, a precious person whom I would never have the chance to love and know. Of course I could see, as people wanted me to, that I wasn't as unlucky as someone who has lost their one and only baby. But what use is it to compare one grief to another? It's no use. It's just insulting. It's no *use*. I didn't have my daughter and I longed for her. I longed for that special person called Ella and I still long for her. And not a single other person misses her. Not enough anyway. She was born and died and isn't missed or even remembered now by anyone at all except by me. Even to her own father she is nothing more than a raw memory he doesn't even have to try to avoid.'

I didn't comment on what Marcella had said, but I took it in, every word of it, and unexpectedly I cried. In part I cried because I was damnably tired. But it seemed more universal and also much more personal than that. I cried for a tiny well-groomed infant version of Marcella who had come and gone with monstrous speed. I cried for the injustice of Marcella not knowing that infant daughter, and that daughter not knowing her. I cried for poor little Orlando who had become a human being in the tightest possible space with a doomed sister. I cried for my own two precious, fractious children because their mother was exhausted, unkempt and depressed. And I cried for myself. That my infant self had had no more than that same amount of time with her own wretched mother. That I had no one to care for me now.

I cried and after some time Marcella stopped pacing, and talking, and sat down, and she cried, too.

She was inside my consciousness, and outside it. I cried, knowing she was also crying, acutely aware of that in fact, yet at the same moment free to be lost in my own distress. After a while I quietened. So did she. Without any embarrassment we blew our noses. Then we drank several speedy glasses of whisky poured from a well-placed, well-filled decanter, turned on the television and placed the children in front of it, making a safe semi-circle for them with lots of cushions carefully arranged on one of the Persian carpets. Then we propped open the sitting-room door and went to Marcella's bedroom.

We didn't need to take the necessary moment to turn back the cover that lay heavily and ceremoniously on her impressive marital bed. We fell on it and then on each other like ravenous beasts, attached at the mouth, moaning with anxiety and pleasure and need – while still also listening out for our children. It was one of the most specifically located and erotic encounters I have ever had. Marcella kissed like someone enflamed. All her coolness fled and heat sprang to the surface of her lips which tasted like none I had ever kissed before. Perhaps I was kissing rage as well as passion; grief and loss as well as need.

I kissed her, and as she kissed me I kissed her back. And while we kissed – like free, reckless girls – and while we existed only for that kissing – like free, reckless girls – we listened out like mothers. We listened through our ears and through our skin; through all our senses.

No more than fifteen minutes after we had left them, we returned to our children. Who couldn't thank us for prematurely foreclosing on all that kissing. Who didn't notice that we rolled back into their presence, and did not walk. Who would not have seen that our motherly eyes were hugely pupiled, that our pale, tired faces briefly flamed, that our hair was in serious disarray. Who simply climbed up onto our laps, to snuggle and suck on thumbs or, in Rhea's case, on a bottle.

We kissed again when we said goodbye, standing inside Marcella's front door with three children clustered around our feet. I believed we kissed for pleasure and promised in the kissing that there would be more. But there wasn't. No embarrassment either, but no more lovely kissing.

I wanted more. Marcella surely must have wanted more. Her hunger had been unmistakable. But each of us was unable to ask, either with words, or gesture, or simply stepping forward, a little closer, to the other one.

I suspect that Marcella had never kissed a woman before that day, despite her natural gifts. But why couldn't I find the words to say that it was fine with me, that I think women kissing, and making love together, can be as easy as breathing, and as natural?

The risk of her thinking better of her obvious inclinations and rejecting me was just part of it. In my mid-twenties, only a few years before getting together with Guy, I had made the mistake of getting briefly entangled with a woman who was doubly unavailable. She was already in a relationship which it turned out she had no intention of leaving; worse, she had never had any sexual interest in a woman and probably had no interest in me beyond prurient curiosity. She was a consumer of odd people and events. I allowed myself to be consumed. Blindly, stupidly, I had muddled her need for novelty with my own.

It ended badly, almost before it began. Two or three weeks into it and we were out of it already. I was relieved to know that her retreat to married safety meant I would probably never see her again. What I found hard to let go of was how rotten I felt about my own poor sense of judgement. It had become time that I knew better.

With all the ease and inevitability of autumn becoming winter, I subsided into a depression which, in its slowness and breathlessness and dark emptiness, was not unlike the period that followed my adoptive mother's death. Looking down on myself from no great height I saw a slug.

Self-pity went to bed with me and self-pity was still hanging around each pre-dawn when reluctantly I woke up. Close friends came and went and more or less tolerated my bleakness. There was earnest talk among them of therapists, pills, holidays; of changing my diet, or exercising. I let most of their talk pass me by as I ate junky sweet food, went nowhere and saw no one but the tolerant few. Once again, as I had a decade or more before, I mostly lay on a sofa, occasionally reading then forgetting what I had read.

A dream changed me.

After a day like any other, I dreamed that a slug-like snake entered my slug-like body through the tailbone at the base of my spine. As soon as I became aware that it was actually going into my body I felt pulled to pay attention and knew then that it was actually much harder and sleeker than a slug. It was a finely wrought snake which entered my body with such finesse it caused me no pain at all. As it worked its way slowly into my body, travelling up my spine at a perfectly reasonable, subtly timed pace, I enjoyed the sensation. In my dream, I felt more awake than I had for weeks. Suddenly, I was curious again. Something was happening that I could care about.

The snake took hours to travel up my spine, leisurely working past or maybe it was through each vertebra. Despite the incredible intensity of sensation, I was not sure whether it was 'past' or 'through': it barely mattered. I settled in to enjoy snake-time. Dreaming, I felt more than somewhat stoned. This slow pace somehow told me, silently, that I was precious enough to linger with. Dreaming, I was conscious how different this feeling was from the usual way I felt when the attentions of a lover became too careful. In any extended form, that usually suffocated and dismayed me.

I settled in, allowing myself to be taken steadily further and further away from my usual inhibitions and constraints. As the snake approached my neck my sense of anticipation grew, though my muscles remained perfectly relaxed. I could feel the snake's weight within me now and realised that it was not small but large, and was pressing down on my spine, pressing in on me as it necessarily grew larger, yet even then I wasn't frightened.

When the snake entered and then slithered upwards through and past the back of my neck, cleverly avoiding my throat, I realised that it was heading for my brain. Wanting now somehow to co-operate with it, I took all my energy upwards to open my mind wide. Doing this, I felt I was opening the windows in a nasty stuffy little room. 'A zephyr is needed,' I said to myself. 'Not a breeze, but a zephyr!' Then, as my energy concentrated and intensified, and my mind expanded outwards, that stuffy room became an airy place. It was good to be there. The snake liked it too, growing even larger as it passed through and still on upwards around my brain, giving what I assumed were the curling, entwined sections of the cerebellum the exact same kind of precise, soothing, individual attention that each vertebra had received and was going on receiving as lower parts of the snake continued travelling upwards.

At this point in the dream I began to laugh. I felt so amazingly, stunningly embraced, so caressed somehow, and yet entirely free. I laughed ironically because in order to maintain an illusion of freedom I had limited myself to certain kinds of embraces for years, embraces which in no way resembled the extreme intimacy of this embrace – and yet I had not been free.

As I laughed, the snake's head, as I now realised it was, was wrapping itself around the uppermost sections of my brain in preparation for its final lap. Carefully, respectfully, it headed up over the crown of the brain, or under the crown of the skull, and then downwards, ready to emerge through the place of the third eye, between my eyebrows.

This was a slow process, yet almost triumphant. It had been a long journey which the snake had accomplished with no damage to the environment through which it had moved. On the contrary, the environment had rarely felt better.

Snake-time slowed down further. I was breathing shallowly, as one might when distancing oneself from pain, although I felt no pain. As the skin on my forehead parted, widened, as a vagina and then labia part and widen to let a baby free, I looked with intense curiosity to see just what, or who, would emerge.

The head of the snake came extremely slowly, adjusting itself with great self-care to the change in light and temperature that leaving my body entailed. I looked at the head emerging from my own head. It was beautiful: dark green, yellow and brown; patterned; extremely smooth scales so shiny they looked wet although the snake was quite dry. I also noticed that the snake was subtle, cool, sly, hooded, clever and knowing. It was all those things, and many more I would continue to find names for.

Inch by inch the snake left my body, and, leaving it, became less and less visible until there was just a vapour where its hard shiny shape had been. I put my hand to the place where it had emerged and could feel no wound or scar. That surprised me and maybe it also disappointed me. I wanted the mark of the snake on me, outside as well as inside where I could still feel the extraordinary effect of having been simultaneously soothed, comforted, chosen and awoken.

Almost any kind of relationship with Marcella would undoubtedly have been a different and better matter from the affair which tipped me into the darkness that led me to the snake. And not only because 'different' is what we always tell ourselves, each time we try new sex. Still, even the comfort of those crucial differences would not have been enough.

In the bad old days, I was not a mother. I had often been restless, and needed settling: sex was one way to do that. Now my need for settling was still present – sometimes even uncomfortably so – but it was less pressing than the needs of my babies. It was they who drew that intensity of attention. Knowing that, I could not risk averting my gaze. And knowing what it cost me to keep my gaze that intensely upon them, I would not take the chance that even the kindest and most loving of women might also need my care. That would add up to more looking after than I could possibly provide.

Walking these thoughts with me up and down streets as I travelled at toddlers' pace, into and out of sleep and rest times, stirring them as I mixed and pureed soups, vegetables and stewed fruits, I guess I knew, unambivalently, that Marcella and I had kissed ravenously because we were mothers, but that maternity also halted me.

Not for a minute, and not for anyone, could I risk loosening the tight reins of my obsession with my children.

Guy had left us all. And I couldn't feel surprise. Abandonment preceded the first breath I drew. Abandonment replaced Katy-mother's milk. Abandonment was what I feared most and apparently attracted like some inner deadly magnet.

Up against those powerful forces of abandonment, I placed my own bloody mighty troops of righteous indignation. Indignation that sex had taken Guy from us. Incredulity that Guy had given up on the chance to live with his children in order to fuck and be fucked. Contempt that his addiction to sex mattered more than sharing my addiction to the twin perfections who were Gregory and Rhea.

Despising Guy's choice, despising him for making such a choice, there was no way I dared risk even a shadow of it.

And although, sometimes, I looked at Marcella across a room crowded with children and their mothers, or even sitting right next to me, and thought about the curious and glorious way her lips tasted, and moved as well as tasted, I didn't regret my decision.

My solid unwillingness to be waylaid kept us safe. It kept Gregory and Rhea safe. It kept me safe. There was a deep tangible satisfaction in that. And I felt it.

There's also something else. Kissing Marcella, knowing that the reckless girl in me had not entirely died, I was much more content to be a mother. I could even be an upright mother. My need to let the floor support me lessened. I still lay down where the children played, sometimes praying that they would drop to sleep beside me. But I was much less desperate that they should. Sometimes they slept and I did not. Sometimes while they slept I plotted pots. I drew them, threw them and painted them in my mind. I made notes. Dreaming of pots, I felt as content sometimes as though I had actual clay in both hands.

I trusted for the first time for many months that I could work again and could work well. I brushed my hair. I smiled at myself in the mirror. I even looked, occasionally, at my lips and regarded them as kissable.

The children were still then and are still now the force that pushed my life into shape, but that short burst of mouth to mouth resuscitation saved them from having a half-dead, declining, drooping mother. I sprang back from that brief intense encounter an alive person once again. Someone who could laugh, show her teeth in a hearty smile, who could willingly cook tasty, slapdash meals and whistle as she brought in the washing.

Of course this revival might have happened anyway. I am not by nature easily defeated. But there's no harm in counting my blessings for the way it did happen. Every time I see a cool woman with a lion's mane of hair and a hot, mobile mouth, I think about Marcella whose passionate intensity in both grief and sex I have celebrated a thousand ways in the paintings on clay that I guess have become the hallmark of my work.

And when I look at Cordelia, the tall, reserved, talented, unexpected and hugely delightful woman at the apex of my thoughts right now, I feel remarkably free. This is a different time again. A new time. A time I have never had before and will never have again. It feels welcomingly rich.

Where Elizabeth fits, I don't know. I barely want to think about it.

Too much thinking can be toxic. I don't want to analyse myself out of this early optimism. Enough to say, I feel lucky. Getting up on any morning, how can we know that today is the day that changes everything? Buttering filo pastry to make a spinach pie, waiting to hear the bang of the front door that will tell me the children are safely and loudly at home, remembering love gained rather than love lost, I know exactly how I am lucky.

Rhythms that suit me are part of it. This evening, for example, I know Cordelia will call. She will ask me, in her smooth, gliding way, if I have a little time in the next day or two. 'After you've finished your work, perhaps,' she will say. As though I couldn't trouble myself to get over to her place especially. Which is the nearest she can come to asking me for anything. To which I'll reply, good student that I am, 'That's entirely possible, Cordelia.' If I feel bold enough, or want to make her laugh, I might add, 'Just a nod in your direction, Cordelia. That's all I can promise.' Then, of course, I will relent, just as she knows I will. 'I'd love to see you. Has it only been two days? I'm missing you already.'

Cordelia. Love's gain. When this exhibition's over, I would like to paint those words around a big fat colourful jug – even if I then lose my nerve and have to hide it. Or maybe one day I will be brave enough to leave the jug unannounced on her kitchen table. With flowers roughly stuck into it, higgledy piggledy. Not just flowers either, big leaves from the vegetable patch in marvellous shapes to make her laugh. No note. Though perhaps some chocolates on a matching plate. No words on the plate, just dashing colour and three expensive, foil-wrapped chocolates. Sweeteners, all.

<u>III</u>

Be still, my heart, these great trees are prayers.

RABINDRANATH TAGORE

As a child I regularly went alone with Griff, my father, to visit his stout elderly mother whom we always called Grandmother. He and I would travel by train together. I am not sure why we didn't drive, because my mother could not use the car we left behind. Perhaps my father thought of saving money, or even of relaxing for the couple of hours the journey took. No explanation was expected or given.

I have few memories of arriving at our destination. Grandmother lived in a large house she could no longer afford to maintain. It was always cold and when I was seven or thereabouts I began to notice that it was not nearly as clean as the house I was used to. Going there, I knew that I would be more than usually subdued and would show my feelings or express my opinions not at all. I remember having to brace myself for Grandmother's kisses because there was often dribble on her face which made me feel quite sick. That memory makes me sad now. It is quite possible that Grandmother knew that I recoiled, for all my studied good manners.

The whole tenor of those visits was exceptionally low-key. Even my usually assured father seemed somewhat lost for words.

But the strained nature of the actual visits did not at all diminish my almost ecstatic joy in waiting for the steam train with my father, holding tight to his hand while hearing the whistle blow faintly and then more forcefully, sometimes seeing steam before the huge, threatening, thrilling train itself filled the space where previously there had been a clear view to our town beyond the station.

My father would lift me onto the train before getting on himself. Picking me up from behind he would lift me up and forward even though I would have been quite capable of clambering up myself. Sometimes I would allow myself to look down for a single dizzying moment at the dark space between the platform and the train. It seemed magnetic to me. I could imagine being pulled down by mysterious forces into that place if he didn't lift me fast and hold me tight. Each time he lifted me on board I was rescued anew. Instead of being squeezed and crushed I was walking across the tiny iron platform and through the opened train door into a welcoming broad carriage, then sitting down on a high, green leather seat, reading signs which grimly warned me against opening windows (for surely my head would then leave my shoulders as a train rushed the other way), and against pulling the safety cord unless the situation was dire (a heart attack; would that do?), and even against passing from one swaying carriage to another without permission of the guard.

The guard himself would usually seem to me to be congratulating my father on travelling with his daughter. 'This is a smart one you've got here, sir,' he might say, when I'd done no more than offer both our tickets to be resoundingly clipped. Or, to me, 'Looking after your Dad properly then, are you?' My father and I would look glancingly at each other, rosy-cheeked on my side, awkward to be exposed, while also relishing this acknowledgement of our intimacy. That over, then we would settle into our reading; he with his newspapers and technical journals, I with a book. By the time we were making more regular journeys together, I had fairly recently graduated from Lousia May Allcott and Harriet Beecher Stowe and was reading the great English and Scottish writers who would sustain me through middle and late childhood and well into young adulthood: the Brontes, Dickens, Walter Scott, Buchan, Robert Louis Stevenson, George Eliot, Hardy, Trollope. Jane Austen came later. And didn't last as long. I need more flesh and blood on my literary bones – and more shadow.

I read those writers at first for my own sake, relishing the complexity of their fully elaborated worlds when too much of my own puny life was oblique and barely known to me. Quite soon though, I read them for my father too, for the approving nod he would give in my direction, and for the occasional comment about a remembered character or event that my reading allowed us to share.

Locked together in the noisy, dirty, powerful train, forbidden to open a window or move to another carriage, we would travel between my mother and his. We would rarely speak beyond pleasant civilities, yet I felt the grip of his presence as tightly as I had felt his hands gripping me from behind to lift me onto the train.

Was I present with anything remotely like that intensity for him? Sometimes I would look up from a page to find his gaze on me, though he would always immediately make some pleasant remark to neutralise any possible over-intensity or perceived demand. When we ate together from the picnic box my mother had prepared he would invariably insist that I choose first, and that I have more than my share of whatever modest treat was included. But when I ask myself who it was that he saw, looking across from his seat opposite to mine as we travelled together, I am limited to a familiar picture of a stringy, tense girl with a high pale brow and a single long, thick, dark brown plait, hot under her clothes, sitting still.

Gazing across the decades at that girl, I can think only of the ways my very being expressed the implicit injunctions of my mother: to be undemanding, to be thoughtful, to make no fuss. Such rigidly controlled, compliant behaviour was entirely normal in our household. Surely my father didn't notice what he could completely take for granted? But did he see anything else, anything at all that would have distinguished me in any small way from my sisters, anything at all that spoke to him of an individual girl with individual longings, however strictly tamed? I don't know. I wish I did.

Coming home, we would wait for a similar train on a similar platform. Perhaps we timed our departures awkwardly or simply got away from Grandmother sooner than was entirely necessary. In memory we seem to have had long waits as late afternoon slipped into early evening, long waits punctuated with a reading and re-reading of station timetables pasted to railway walls, along with terse official instructions and occasional ragged travel advertisements, and then much lazy gazing, squinty-eyed, in the direction the train would eventually come.

I didn't mind those delays. They were part of being alone with my father. He seems to have minded them more. He would look at his watch with some impatience at the necessary speed with which it moved. He would open then fold papers. Occasionally he would ask the station master if there was any reason to expect additional delays. He was less aware of me and less attentive to me on the homeward journey than on the outward, but I accepted that. As long as his mother was alive, our journeys together would continue. There was a time-lessness to that which effectively soothed me.

33

Remembering those childhood journeys with my father, I want to move on. I am tired of myself and tired of the dreams that seem to take me nowhere. I am tired, too, of my continuing inability to leave the house for all but a few destinations. What a miracle it would be to feel myself lifted out of this mire, lifted onto a train that was taking me – somewhere. Accompanied by someone who could appear, in such a totally convincing way that it would never need articulation, to have the care of my life in his hands.

Without quite knowing when or if I made a choice I have since George's death transformed myself into someone closely resembling a latter-day contemplative. Or do I make my situation grander than it is? Probably I do. Because as soon as I allow that thought to flutter into focus I think of straight backs, even when their owners kneel through many rigorous hours of prayer. I think of bells to mark one day's shape almost exactly like the next and the next, and of a fateful submission to a rule of obedience, a submission which I cannot even claim to imagine. And, thinking of contemplatives, I must also think of faith: that enviable belief that whatever it is you are doing – kneeling, reading, thinking, offering yourself up to a Force greater than yourself – is real and has value because the focus of it all, God, is real and is beyond value.

No, I am simply an ordinary woman, a grumpy ordinary woman today, who is living a restricted life where even the most mundane rhythms of rising, eating and going to bed are erratic, and where faith or even trust remains painfully elusive.

Wynston is upstairs. I can hear him now. He is pacing backwards and forwards across George's study. His movements are purposeful, excited. He walks like a man with a mission. His gait expresses the purposefulness of his mind. I am certain he is holding all sorts of intellectual threads and connections which he will be able to lay down and forget only when all the connecting articles, journals or volumes are either literally laid side by side, or at least laid side by side in the cataloguing lists he is meticulously preparing.

Standing outside the closed door of the study, I have heard him sing as he works and walks. Over and over again, he repeats just the first few bars from 'Nessun dorma'. It's an unfortunate choice. One of my many visions of hell would be to hear the opera from which it comes in a never-ending cycle. *No man will sleep*, indeed. What kind of man could Puccini himself have been to be attracted enough to this weird tale that purports to be about redemption? Lord knows I am myself interested enough in redemption. About *Turandot* -- and Puccini -- I am not convinced. Hearing it in many versions, I have never been convinced. In fact, I despise the notion that his hero Turandot's icy heart could be melted by Calaf and that they could enjoy happiness together when so many bloodied severed heads are forfeited behind them.

None of us who has known or has even glimpsed passion could ever be entirely innocent of egomaniacal intent, yet how can we build anything but the myth of secure happiness on the husks of others' hopes and dreams?

Am I irritated with Wynston? Have I reached the limits of my patience with myself? The extremes of order that will prevail in George's collection certainly relieve me. At the same time I'm aware of recoiling from the orderliness of Wynston's life with Guy. I am uneasy about the tangible self-satisfaction of their days and nights when Laurie has the mucky, unpredictable side of life to deal with as mother of Gregory and Rhea.

Is there a smugness in those two men, or is it just the mean mote lodged in my own eye that slants my view? But if I am even half-right then it is a smugness that can be maintained only because they have secured their lives against the painful, powerful thrusts of primitive feeling that children bring.

They take the children into account, I can see that. What I also see is that there is a great deal that they are not aware of and will never be. Increasingly I suspect that whatever they do not find compelling to notice simply doesn't exist. Or it exists only as an *unnecessary* worry, the product of a fussing mother's mind.

Laurie's life, on the other hand, revolves entirely around Rhea and Gregory. They are not incorporated into her life; they are her life. Every aspect of their lives is palpably visible to her. She is immersed in what those children need, what they want, what they care about, if they suffer, how they are joyous. Their feelings of pain or joy may well be more real to her than her own such feelings. Certainly she takes them far more seriously and gives them greater priority.

Guy and Wynston also indulge the children, by the now-abandoned cautious standards of my childhood. But they clearly know how to put themselves first. They may not even see their own demands as competing with those of the children. Largely they take whatever it is they need in terms of time, flexibility and freedom, fit the children around that, and, if questioned, would probably have at their fingertips a multiplicity of reasons why their way is not just best for them, but is best. Period.

Such confidence is rarely a woman's lot; such comforting selective blindness isn't either.

When the children argue fiercely, or physically attack each other, I see Laurie standing sometimes, almost literally swaying in an attempt to find some balance between the two children, or between the children and herself. This is the type of awful, no-win place into which a father would almost never find himself squeezed. It seems the most literal example of what goes on emotionally and psychically almost all the time:

Laurie pushed in the direction of one child, then the other, then the two together – and where is she to find nourishment or rest?

'I'm being choked to death,' screamed Gregory just days ago. That he could scream his protest quite that loudly might have seemed protection enough against imminent expiration, but when Laurie and I broke off what we were saying to run from her kitchen to find them, Rhea was, indeed, lying on top of her brother in a pretty convincing way. His face was reddening, and his feet were beating on the ground as he heaved and shoved somewhat helplessly beneath her.

'You called me a dick-head arsehole!' Rhea was shouting at him. Surely only somewhat relishing the chance to air those satisfyingly awful words all over again.

'And you are. It's about all you are,' a not-yet-vanquished Gregory managed to get out between pummellings. 'A pea-brained, dick-head arsehole.'

If the atmosphere had not been thick with outrage as well as tension it might have been possible to laugh. But, suddenly, Laurie was crying. Then Rhea, too.

'I'm not an arsehole, I'm not. You're the one that's always calling me disgusting names in front of your friends. That makes you the arsehole.' Rhea's self-pity rose in a rapid and mighty crescendo. 'I stick up for you and you never stick up for me. All your friends hate me because you make me out to be an idiot even though my friends are all nice to you.'

'Who cares about your friends? Who'd want friends like yours? They're all idiotic no-hopers.'

Suddenly experiencing his attack as truth, Rhea hurtled to her own defence. 'You said Leni Tyler was a good baseball player! You said she's one of the best catchers you've ever seen and she's one of my friends. What about your friends! They're all so dumb they can't even spell!'

While this utterly ineffectual appeal to logic was taking place, I watched Laurie, as though seeing her on a screen.

Usually when the children attack each other, or when their name calling reaches heights unacceptable even to her, she will shout, order them in her fiercest sergeant major voice to stop instantly, even haul one or both of them to their rooms and bring the debacle to a quick, clean close. But that wasn't happening.

On the floor, a new round of insults was beginning. Looking down, it seemed Gregory was about to heave Rhea off his chest and pin her down.

Still Laurie wasn't moving. The edge of her loose grey flannel shirt hung over one side of her baggy denim jeans, making her look much more than usually disarrayed. She was continuing to stand, slumped, while tears rolled down her face.

She was looking at her children, but not engaging with them. The expression on her face was one of distance, perhaps incomprehension. *Who are these strangers?* she seemed to be saying. Then she turned to me. 'I don't know what to do. I can't bear it, and I can't stop it.'

'Can't bear what?' My question was stupid even to my own ears, but it didn't seem to me as though Laurie was talking only about the four-legged heap of passion still writhing on the floor.

'This. All of this. The children. They are so ghastly sometimes. Why are they? And I feel ghastly myself. Or maybe what's ghastly is the sense that I'm watching them live to the full, awful as they often are, but am never going to live to the full myself. Never again – if I ever did!'

Laurie sat down on a low, yellow armless chair. It had been her nursing chair and was littered with historical stains. The children lay on the scuffed wooden floor, panting, but relatively quiet and apart. Laurie glowered at them. 'Go outside, both of you. Go and shoot goals or ride your bikes or something. Anything. But don't let me see either of you again – or hear either of you again – for at least half an hour. I have reached my limit.'

Rhea's eyes overflowed with a new round of tears. Both children got up, then stood, pausing between one round of their life's drama and the next, and Rhea even began to edge towards her mother, but

Gregory grabbed her hand. 'Come on, Reebok. We'll play one on one.'

Rhea went with him, though reluctantly, and at the door she hesitated, again looking back, clearly distressed at the sight of Laurie, who now sat with her downturned head supported in her hands.

I smiled weakly at Rhea and waved my hand, urging her to go, touched by her concern, however belated it might be. Laurie may or may not have still been crying. I sat and waited.

Years before, I had sat with my sister Peg in a similar moment. Her daughters were much more conventionally raised than Gregory and Rhea, and were largely tractable in my limited experience of them. I suspect Peg's sweetness usually got the better of them. This particular day, however, there had been some major conflict of interest about a dance which Peggy wasn't winning. Voices clashed. Tears flowed. Things were said that would take time to forget. I was embarrassed for them all, I remembered. And embarrassed that I had nothing at all to suggest to break the impasse. My lack of experience as a daughter who could stand up for herself, as well as my own painful ignorance of what it meant to be a mother, settled on me like a fog. I retreated; had sat, slumped, perhaps not holding my head as Laurie was now doing, but feeling that neither my head nor my heart would ever ignite usefully again.

We had avoided conflict like the plague in our family. We crept around the edge of any crisis with as much trepidation as if the landscape were thin ice, and any crossing of it would necessarily be fatal. 'Don't worry your mother,' was our father's strongest plea. Unnecessary really. She was condemned to worry no matter what we did, and we would not have dreamed of making that worry worse. Guilt already hung from the ceilings, emerged from opened drawers, came in with us at night and stayed when we left in the morning. Wordless guilt; amorphous guilt: the kind that can attach itself to everything and changes nothing.

In the face of someone else's expressed unhappiness, I can still feel that same rush of guilt along with tell-tale shortness of breath, tightness of chest and extreme, unfocused anxiety that I should have done – what?

That I now ought to do – what? That somehow – but how? – fault lies with me, if not in the making of the pain, then in my failure to quickly end it.

My hand reached out towards Laurie, to touch her slumped back, her tense shoulder, and then to rest on her hair. Not more than that. Just a touch to let her know I cared. For I do care; I care very much. But that may not be all she needs.

The veins on my hand were especially knotty and so raised they looked like strange bluish mountain ranges winding their way across brownish lowlands. My gold wedding ring looked thin and out of place in that miniature landscape.

'It's not only the children,' Laurie said at last. 'Though I'm at my wit's end with them lately, God knows. It's also the exhibition.'

That jolted me. I hoped it was all right to ask, 'Isn't that going well? You're almost ready aren't you?'

Laurie sniffed, and said in a near-normal voice, 'The work's almost ready, but whether I am is another question entirely. It all feels almost as distant from me as I feel from the children when they fight. Distant – and yet bound up: double discomfort if that makes any sense at all. In such moments I feel condemned to be a shackled spectator on other people's lives while my own life passes me by. That's increasingly my response to this exhibition also. Luciana likes what I've done far more than I do. Her enthusiasm outstrips mine by miles. So who's it all for?'

The need to cheer her overcame me. 'The fountains. I love those fountains, Laurie.'

She smiled, faintly. 'I like those, too. Thank heaven I am able to like them, but that's about all. The gaudy stuff . . . I've been churning it out for so long, but it feels increasingly synthetic. The taste it leaves in my mouth isn't good. I know the pieces are fine. Some of them are actually quite beautiful by anyone's standards, but they don't *belong* to me. Do you know what I mean? I produce them for other people, not for myself.'

Laurie stood up, went to the window to peer out and check on the children, came back and sat down, still restless. 'Sometimes I think that if I paint another voluptuous cherub I will vomit.' She snorted. The sound definitely wasn't laughter. Pacing still, she said, 'You know as well as I do, Cordelia, that as so-called creative artists we are supposed to put up all our lives with a lousy standard of living in exchange for the privilege of not doing alienating work like regular folk who earn three or even three hundred times as much as we do. But it's a myth that we don't do compromised work. We do it sometimes or even most of the time. How many of us can afford to do anything else?'

Did I blush then, ashamed of my own privilege? Laurie failed to comment if I did.

'Most of us are actually treading an extremely thin and often invisible line between trying out new ideas and churning out what we know will sell, between progressing creatively and feeling nailed to the past by whatever trick or stylistic sleight of hand made our tiny names, and with justifying our precious freedoms while feeling bored to death with being forever twenty-five in terms of the economic constraints that buy our favoured lifestyle.'

It's true, I thought. Everything that Laurie is saying is quite true. She is as poor as the most lowly novice would be in any profession, yet her ceramics are world class. And she almost certainly has been experimenting much less in the last eight years than in her first decade of professional work. What's more, there is no doubt that Luciana's excitement about the latest variations on well-known Laurie themes is indeed based on her own determination for her gallery to flourish, and not on what will serve Laurie's artistic development best.

The lavatory flushed, then the back door banged loudly. At just that same moment a siren briefly wailed and as that faded a man outside in the street yelled in a language I couldn't even recognise, although his tone of outraged anger was only too familiar. Was he speaking to a child, a woman, a dog? How utterly depressing that it would be impossible to know.

'I feel pinned down,' said Laurie, 'every bit as much as Gregory and Rhea pin each other down when they struggle on the floor. And the realm of logic within which I feel as if I have to work seems as tightly pre-ordained as their need to say vile things about each other and their friends.'

She sat in silence, still very tense. Then said, 'What I want most and love most also restricts me. I love my children absolutely but I am also afraid of what it means to be restricted by them. I am afraid that to survive maternity I have to ditch every other area of my life. There's so little energy for anything but the basics.'

'The basics?'

'You know, feeding them, cleaning up after feeding them, running this house such as it is, pulling the occasional weed from the garden, washing every single day, ironing when I absolutely must, running to get the shopping, worrying about who'll eat what and how to combine that into one affordable meal, listening to each of them separately or more often together, remaining on top of who's who in all their dramas, attempting single-handed crisis management, personal development and conflict resolution while also putting pizzas into the oven or taking them out, supervising homework that must be done but may never get marked, being a cheerful, coping Mummy around their friends and teachers, getting them to and from their sports, parties, shopping expeditions, tutoring, and in between times – in tiny crevices of time – dreaming up and making the ceramics that we actually have to live from.'

She looked up. Looked at me. 'Sorry to moan, Cordelia. It's too boring really. I'm not ungrateful for my life. I'm just tired, I guess. Sorry.' She shrugged, tried to smile. Didn't manage it, quite.

Then she said, grimly, shockingly, 'I am almost sympathetic with Anita's choice to lie down once and for all. At least it simplified things for her if not for me.'

Something stirred in me. A rebellion against my own past hopelessness, perhaps. 'I'll buy the lot,' I said.

Laurie looked blank, and almost irritable. 'Buy what lot?'

'The exhibition. I'll buy everything you planned to show, except the fountains. Then you needn't feel pinned down by or even attached to any of that work. And you'll have enough money to get on with whatever it is you need to do next.'

Laurie laughed. 'Cordelia, you're a crazy woman! You're not serious, are you? There's the best part of a year's work that Luciana has been storing up. And apart from the cost, which I couldn't let you spend, what on earth would you do with crates of pots, never mind those gaudy cushions, flying angels, ducks and God knows what all tat?'

'I don't know what I'll do with it. Maybe nothing. Or maybe I'll give a couple of pieces to everyone I've ever liked who has managed to stay alive. Colourful tributes to longevity! That would be a good enough cause, wouldn't it? Anyway, what I *do* with it is not the point. The point is, I believe, that you will be free to move on. And I . . .' I paused here, wanting to neaten my woolly thoughts, 'I will be relieved of a little guilt. So the favour will be mutual.'

For several lengthy moments Laurie stared at me as her mind quite obviously rushed from one extreme response to the other. 'I'll have to think about it. Then even if I could swallow it, I'd have to talk to Luciana about a fair price. Not to mention smoothing things out with her. You know she adores the attention of an opening, the fuss, the publicity, the "adorable" friends she gathers in.'

'Do that. Do whatever you need to do to put things right, but then put the exhibition behind you. You're one among a number of artists for Luciana. But this creative life of yours is the only one you have. At least in this lifetime, and who knows about the next. You might be a boiler maker then, or a round-the-world yachtie! Take care of yourself in this life you have now, Laurie. Luciana will give in with good grace.'

'I'm not so sure,' Laurie said. 'I'm not even sure about my own reaction, but I am immensely grateful, Cordelia.'

'Of course you are, and I am immensely grateful that George's clever and honourable wheeling and dealing even made it possible. So we are on the same side, eh?'

'Maybe.' She looked flushed, and unconvinced. Then she relaxed, at least a bit. 'Some tea and bickies do you think? Crackers with cheese and pickles are what I fancy. Something sharp in taste, would that suit you too?'

'Cheese and pickles are what *I* fancy,' said Rhea, suddenly appearing at the door.

'I don't,' Gregory said, coming into the room from behind his sister, his face red from basketball exertions. 'Cheese and pickles make you stink. You'll stink, Rhea. You'll pong like a pig.'

Laurie jumped to her feet. 'And you'll *ping*, Gregory, if there's any more of that talk. You'll ping for a week, and don't say you weren't warned.' Laurie laughed at her son, winked and said, '*Plus ça change*,' to me, then standing behind him she wrapped both arms around him and hugged him tightly, then again sat down.

I have noticed on other occasions, too, how fully Laurie revives after a short break from her children. They can seem to take her absolutely to the edge of her endurance, and then, after a tiny interval of time away from them, she will give every appearance of totally renewed enthusiasm for them and energy to spare. And I believe what I see.

Only minutes before she had been grim, drained even by the thought of all that she must do and the constancy with which she must do it, but now as she sat in the centre of her baggy sofa she had one arm around Gregory's neck, as though confining him and consoling him in a single grip. He was struggling to get free, but also grinning, delighted to be forgiven or, anyway, to be hugged.

Laurie released him with a cheerful shove and turned to Rhea who was snuggling in on her other side, her head on Laurie's shoulder and her knees drawn up under her chin so that she was perching like a bird. 'Why don't you two bring all the food we need in here, with a big cloth to put out on the floor, and then we'll have a picnic. Right here in the sitting room, and Cordelia and I won't need to move. We need a little waiting on. You can bring in a bottle of apple juice and a tray of ice cubes and four glasses, and if you don't want cheese and stinky pickles, Gregory, then use your head and find something you do want.'

'Mum . . .' Gregory began.

'Off,' said Laurie. To magical effect.

And when the children sat down, several minutes later, they too had created a sense of magic, with biscuits artfully laid out on colourful plates, cheese and pongy pickles, piles of fruit, popcorn and sweet biscuits each on platters, party napkins all around, and the satisfying clink of ice as we toasted each other in stylish fashion before downing our apple juice.

'Peace and goodwill to all patrons,' said Laurie, raising her glass to me.

'And to mothers,' I said.

'What are patrons?' asked Rhea.

'People who put their money where their mouth is,' said Laurie.

'I'd rather put food where my mouth is,' said Rhea.

'Amen to that,' said Gregory.

'Ah *women* to that,' giggled Rhea.

'For small mercies, let us all be thankful,' I said, helping myself to popcorn and pickles.

'For large mercies too,' said Laurie. 'For those especially, let us be sufficiently and unequivocally thankful.'

34

Shortly before my father died he and I went for a long, slow walk in a park I have known since childhood. He could by then only walk with considerable difficulty and was uncomfortable and apologetic about the necessary leisureliness of our pace.

The man I walked with that day was as dapper as he had ever been, although extremely thin. The suit that hung on him was clearly made for the more robust man he had once been; he would never fill it again.

My mother had been dead for several years already, but memories of her presence, or of her death, or of our uncomfortable, unresolvable feelings about her perhaps, continued to make us awkward with each other.

For years before she grew ill and died I had felt quite unable to get near my father. Not in any sense that really counts. He would talk to me, and he loved to talk to George whenever George had time to visit my parents with me – for they would almost never come to us. But there was a neutralising quality to his conversation which exhausted me. He would talk only about things other than himself; only about times other than the time in which we spoke; only about matters that seemed to me of considerably less immediacy and importance than the issues that hung in the air between us.

Perhaps a braver daughter than I could have changed the agenda or forced him into a different kind of talk. Perhaps a Laurie-ish kind of daughter. Certainly a Rhea. But I could not do that. I could only chafe and suffer at the waste, for I had always loved him. In my own way, I adored my father. Yet I could not know him better. Nor could I allow him to know who I am beneath or beyond the polite, respected formalities that shaped almost every single one of our encounters.

The night following the day my mother died his usual straitjacket of containment flew loose and he cried, briefly, in my arms. 'I did love your mother, Cordie,' he said. 'I did my very best to love her.' He did not need to say: *but it wasn't enough.*

Perhaps he had hoped for some softening from her as she died. A shift like that might have given him the forgiveness or grace he needed for his own last years. But it simply could not happen.

To be fair to my mother – and we all wanted to be fair – the pain she endured was dreadful. It was appalling to witness and must have been devastating to experience, though when I recall it now I feel as though I am remembering something that was described to me by someone else, not something which I myself chose to witness.

The intensity of her pain took Nell as far from her husband and children as it was possible to go. She had been drifting away from us for many years. Her pain accelerated that process and I can't help but believe she welcomed that estrangement. Looking back I can see that she had been physically available for many, many years, even while somehow she herself wasn't there. In the end there was no energy to keep up the physical caretaking that had kept us all at bay. Then it was devastatingly clear that she had nothing left for anyone else. God had left her; she had left us. Even Griffin's obvious grief became irrelevant to her. Perhaps she noticed it; perhaps she didn't. He would sit beside her, a shrunken man on an ugly plastic chair. My siblings and I could see only too clearly the anguish in his eyes, the pallor of his skin, the shaking in his hands, the hopeless repetition of his requests to busy nursing staff that they should do more, think of something different, try something else to ease her wrenching pain. Griffin's entire intellectual life had been given over to problem solving. The frustration he must have felt was palpable.

Perhaps it was frustration that kept him constantly on the move. His agitation frightened me. It seemed unhinged, though maybe it was just the increasingly distressing contrast between his rapid, useless movements and the fixity with which my mother lay, waiting for death to relieve her.

I had almost never seen her motionless before. It had been Griffin I associated with an appearance of calm, although he was never *idle*. But now he almost literally jumped from one ineffectual hope to another while she lay, under a near-flat white coverlet, her only extrusions occasional involuntary moaning through lips that were dry and painfully cracked no matter how carefully and often we gave her sips of cool water to drink, or soothed them with calendula balm.

There were no shared prayers. Norah, Allen, and Frank too I am sure, did pray. They took turns in the hospital chapel throughout the last days of our mother's life. But no chaplain came near her bed, not even at the end.

Worrying about that absence of prayer around a dying woman who had once raised her clear voice to sing for love of God, I myself wanted to pray, though I wasn't quite sure for what.

Perhaps my indecisiveness paralysed me. It often has. Anyway, the best and nearest thing to prayer that I could manage was some reading of Julian of Norwich. George had discovered her work some years before and for many months she had been one of his keenest enthusiasms.

When I called him one evening and perhaps cried a little, telling him, I think, that even prayer seemed hard to come by in the room where my mother was dying, he typed out some Julian meditations and sent them to me. 'Put these into your handbag,' said his brief accompanying note. 'Julian was a wise woman, probably a great one. Her words may do the trick.'

What they did turn was the tide of my attention. I had been hovering somewhere far outside myself but not necessarily nearer to my mother. Anxiety had moved me so far from what we would nowadays call our centre that I could scarcely feel the chair my bottom sat on, nor the floor beneath my feet. I wasn't sleeping. My gaze was flying uselessly from my father to my mother to my siblings and round in the circle again without ever taking rest.

Julian's words brought me back to some vital awareness of myself; I have forgotten how. In a stilled moment of one day, when there was a rare pause between the checking of her vital signs and other visitors, I caught a glimpse of myself as a woman whose mother was very near to death and who was to be, for the first time in her life, without a mother. I cried for myself then. That grief was focused and real. It didn't jump jerkily outside myself. It came from inside and took me back inside. My mother was sleeping. I didn't disturb her, I'm sure. I cried with fear of the unknown, and with pity for myself too that even when she had been up and about and alive, she was hard to reach and invariably guarded.

I don't suppose I cried for more than ten minutes. It might have been less. But it did me good and I was able to be more genuinely affectionate and supportive when my father came edging back into the room to sit beside the high white bed for only seconds before he again began to pace and worry aloud.

When the end came, it came quickly. The oncologist drew up a chair for the last time at the end of my mother's bed. We sat near to him, huddling around him, wanting to suck out of that middle-aged, harried man some shred of reassurance when plainly there could be none. He avoided eye contact and spoke quickly, clearing his throat several times as he said, 'Mrs Williamson's struggle will soon be over.' There would be a few more days of increasing pain which would be distressing for us to witness. She herself would largely be unconscious. He was very sorry, was the last thing that he said.

My father shook the doctor by the hand without speaking and then when the man had left he sat down again, paler than he had been. Perhaps he felt at the limit of what he could take for by then the witnessing was dreadful. But into the first night of that last bout with life, my mother opened her eyes and closed them again and stopped breathing. I was alone in the room with Allen who ran at once to fetch my father from one of the small cubicles where relatives could catch some sleep.

We left our parents together. Our last sight of the two of them was of my father leaning over the body of our mother as though to shield and protect her, his face entirely buried into the pillow, next to her head. She was facing outward, dead and unseeing. He was turned away from us, lost in her.

I began my long drive home late that same night, leaving too much of the burden of phone calls and arrangements to my brothers and sisters and especially to Allen, but I needed to be in my own home, with my own husband. I needed to have George hold me and tell me that it was all right to cry, although by then I couldn't. I needed to have George pour me several tiny glasses of best brandy, and fetch plates of crunchy toast with jam, and cups of hot sweet tea and then to watch me drink and eat and to drink and eat with me, and then to rub my back and peel off my unwelcome, restrictive clothes and help me into my soft, voluminous nightie, and then to bed.

It is crazy to recall that loss now. Crazier still to compare it to the loss I am now feeling: the loss of George, and the loss of George to comfort me. But I do compare it and in comparing it I am intimately aware of the easy mothering that George gave me, and I know I ought to count my blessings.

35

Elizabeth has been and gone from Laurie's life. It seems a little fast, and remains a mystery.

Laurie and I have been working alongside each other in ever more perfect silence and companionship. In the weeks that have passed since she set things right with Luciana, accepted her share of the cheque that I willingly wrote to Luciana's gallery, and put the exhibition well behind her, Laurie has been working harder than before.

I am not sure what she is doing. Until she wants to show me, I won't ask. The pity of it is, that she is working at home as often as she works here, which makes her visits even more precious.

Turning to consider my own work, I can see that I am making plain uncompromising pieces a little more reliably now. I am still resisting the tug of colours or ornament; still sticking to the rich matt ochre that reminds me more and more not just of Africa generally, but of the mountains and plains of Ethiopia specifically. It's a glorious colour, a colour that springs into existence at the moment when rays from the sun hit the earth, a colour that almost rivals the sun itself or our perception of the sun in its orangey depth and brightness. It's a colour that sets my pulse tingling, but the least blemish or error sticks out a mile. I feel put on my mettle each new working day. Rise and *shine* takes on an utterly specific meaning in this voluntary battle for perfection with only myself as enemy, ally and judge.

I haven't abandoned the challenge either of hanging an orb above a birdbath-like circle. It's a challenge that sits like a burr at the edge of my mind. Fulfilling it might set me free from this art form forever, but why would I want that? As far as I can know myself, I wouldn't. Where would I be without my work? *Without my husband and without my work.* I push this mad, frightening thought away, and turn to draw; increasingly I find this soothing.

Drawing, I can make big, near-careless, sweeping gestures of a kind that are quite different from the concentrated intensity the clay demands. And while I can't quite rub out the charcoal I like to use I can blur it when needs be, easing a misplaced line here or there, transforming it into something I can like a little better.

The silence in which Laurie and I work is the best I have ever known. There are no false spots in it, no strain at all. Each of us is effortlessly held by the silence, separately and together. We can breathe in it and through it entirely independently, but the nature of this silence is significantly different from the silence when one is utterly alone.

The silence comes from a deep, trusting place in Laurie and from a better place than most in me. It has grown between us without planning or discussions and is not forced in any way. The odd chuckle, curse, whistle, dropping of a tool or even the whining of a machine does not break our silence. When I sit outside in the garden, waiting or working, the silence goes with me. On the days when Petra's with us the sounds of her chatter to the plants or her singing deepen the silence. My body expands to embrace those sounds and bring them closer. At those moments it seems to me as though there is absolutely nothing that I must refuse or even resist.

Petra shows me things sometimes: flowers, vegetables, fruits, and I trust that she doesn't mind that I don't say much of anything in reply, fearful momentarily of the sound of my own voice. She gracefully accepts my smiles and vigorous nods and an occasional hug. Gudrun's friend Tom comes by a couple of times a week to talk to her, and they plan gardening strategy together. He works alongside her, too, so the garden is getting a great deal of attention. As the seasons have moved through their paces I can see how cleverly they have interspersed greens throughout what used to be exclusively flower beds so that alongside the settled beds of roses, geraniums and irises nestle cress, rocket, spinach and endive, while bok choy and silver beet poke up between the array of self-seeding annuals and perennials that are the rich legacy of years of happy gardening.

The vegetable garden has had its brief widened also. It continues to produce cucumbers, beans, carrots and snow peas, as well as tomatoes and sweet tiny pumpkins and potatoes so tasty they would rival nectar. But circling around those edibles, and appearing at different times, are sunflowers, foxgloves, lupins and poppies, marigolds and garlic flowers, most of them raised here from seed.

More herbs stand in two huge half-casks, and they are confidently interwoven with darkest blue lobelia and alyssum in several colours which has dropped its seeds so that patches of white and purplish pink tiny flowers are popping up between cracks in the brick paving and even in among the longer grass.

Tom is working inside as well as out. Every two or three weeks he is now doing what he calls 'a major Mrs Mopp'. He is astonishingly professional, turning up with an array of buckets and environmentally sound products and a fiercely efficient vacuum cleaner with a motor like a Porsche, leaving behind him not only a dazzlingly clean house, but a sweet-smelling one, too. And he arranges flowers. Between his efforts and Wynston's, the house is assuming an almost alarming degree of order and 'be-floweredness'. If I were ever to fall on hard times I could throw it open to the paying public who could come and sink down on chairs or stairs and gaze at it all as I often do, and leave rested and refreshed. Better than a day at the races!

There was a time, before George died and for a short time afterwards, when Tom would pot here. I haven't asked if he is potting elsewhere but I suspect he isn't. His work was strong and good – and complicated. Almost certainly it demanded more time from him than he could easily reflect in his prices. I hope he hasn't given up entirely but meanwhile I am delighted to have his help. He is a mercurial elf of a man, typically Cornish with a wiry build, thin mobile face, and black unruly hair and beard. Petra is twice his size and as blonde and pale as he is dark but they are clearly utterly comfortable together and he never fails to acknowledge her practical wisdom and experience and uncanny instinct for plants.

They are both mad about worms. We have worm farms of various kinds scattered wherever there is sufficient shelter from heat and rain, and when I open the compost bin to chuck in my vegetable peelings I swear I can see more worms there, too, than waste.

We also have birds visiting us in greater variety and number than ever before. Laurie gave me both her fountains. I tried to protest. I tried several times to say that she should sell them and buy some extra months of freedom to do new work. But she is as stubborn as anyone else I have ever loved, and wouldn't even discuss it. Tom rigged them up to come to fountain life for a couple of hours each day and when the water eases to a final drip and settles they are obviously and immediately the birdbaths this garden needed. Birds come flocking. Their sounds are also part of the silence.

It is tempting to feel at peace.

I am not becoming used to being without George. I miss him more, not less. As time goes by there is more to tell him, more to catch up on and such a great pit of a hole where his news ought to be.

What's more, as yet another birthday hovers into view I can see that again I am not even especially used to being as old as I am, never mind what I am becoming. Widowhood hasn't helped me age. I ought to associate it with aging, and graceful resignation to my lot; but I can't.

Again, lately, I feel startled by the distortions of time. A couple of days ago I received a striking postcard of a Gwen John landscape, painted shortly before I was born. The colours are a great deal muddier than any I would associate with France, but what captured my imagination was the tiny figure in the foreground of the painting. It is an old woman, presented to us in a triangle shape with her left arm outstretched to lean on her stick and give her balance. She is making her way along the Rue Terre Neuve. The road goes uphill and she is alone. Up ahead of her the road bends, and in the distance one can see a couple of roofs. It would be safe to guess she is on her way home.

Before she gets there she has to manage that last longish, upward stretch of road with nothing to help her but her will to be home, and her faithful walking stick. One could read that painting in many ways. After all, it is not a portrait of an old woman. It is a landscape, with a blob of added interest in the front right corner. But I choose to read determination there, a sense of a familiar journey homewards that this woman knows that she can make, yet again. And I like the sense that one never can know what is around the next corner, no matter how often a particular route is walked.

Perhaps that woman lived nowhere through her entire life except in the village or town of Meudon. Perhaps she walked daily from her house to the fields outside the village for fifty, sixty or seventy years. The white dust from that road might have settled so deeply into her clothes, her scarf, her shoes, her skin as to seem to be part of her own being. But can we assume her life was poorer for those routines, for lack of travel beyond the most familiar paths?

The friend who sent me the card is someone I have always liked. Forty years ago she went to Cairo and stayed there. I missed her then. I haven't seen her for twenty years though occasionally I follow an impulse to call and we speak for longer than we should on the phone. How she would have picked up a postcard in Cairo of a painting done in France by a long-dead Englishwoman is one of life's minor mysteries. Much more interesting is how Eve has created a life for herself, far from her birthplace, in which she appears to be entirely at home. Her husband, Riad, is not a wealthy man. He has emerged as determined and kind, energetic and witty, from Eve's descriptions of him, and I have no reason to disbelieve her. But there has been no spare money for travel.

They live an Arab life; Eve speaks Arabic fluently. Dreams in Arabic, she long ago told me. There was no assumption that any of her children or indeed her grandchildren would leave the Middle East for European or American universities. I didn't ever have the impression this was only for lack of funds either. The children were clever; scholarships might have been possible. For them, 'better' wasn't elsewhere.

When Eve and I talk on the phone, I at least consciously enter a time-warp. Her voice is much as it ever was, though perhaps it holds more than a trace of accent these days which is entirely charming. But it hasn't aged as she must have; as I most certainly have. Talking to her I can wonder: where did those years go? Not just single years, but whole decades seem to have been mysteriously swallowed up while my glance was briefly elsewhere. Rationally I could of course account for the time, perhaps even make quite a convincing and detailed chronology, but in my emotions, in my inner sense of time and place, it is all far more confusing.

While we talk I experience myself as old as I now am and simultaneously as the woman whose voice is familiar to Eve from a friendship that is almost half a century old.

Eve is a small woman who walks with an open, swinging gait as though she were tall. She has a square, alert face and exceptionally straight, severely cut blonde hair. As a girl she was saved from looking like a Dutch doll by her unmistakable, formidable intelligence which fuelled a forthright manner that blistered walls when she didn't keep it in check. Twenty years ago, when I last saw her, she had widened somewhat, and mellowed a little, but those were minimal changes compared to almost everything else about her that had intensified rather than changed. Eve may be one of those fairly rare people who burst into life almost fully themselves, and who need do only the smallest amount of tinkering around the edges to come into their own.

I propped the Gwen John postcard up in front of a vase of various lavenders that Tom had put at the cleared end of my increasingly cluttered kitchen table. When Laurie sat down to drink coffee with me after a longish day's work, I handed the postcard to her and talked not about Eve, as I'd half-intended, but about Gwen John. Somewhat ashamedly, I recounted how George had once had a chance to pick up one of her cat drawings for a good price which I had nevertheless thought too much. Foolishly, I had talked him out of it, not least because I then didn't much care for cats.

'She's been used on too many book covers,' Laurie said, putting the card down quickly. 'It's hard to see her work freshly any more. Virago and Penguin have finished her off. The life's been sucked from her by the constant miniaturisation and repetition of an image until it loses its meaning. Besides which, she's melancholic!'

Laurie's judgement seemed somewhat harsh to me, and more than a little surprising. And she delivered it with a feeling that seemed close kin to exasperation. I waited, just for a couple of moments, before asking, 'Laurie, dearheart, what could you possibly have against melancholics? Some of your best friends . . .'

As I spoke I was uncomfortably aware of myself.

Laurie grinned and ran her hands through her dark hair and pulled it back from her face. Her eyebrows came together then moved apart. 'I know. I know. Tried and convicted on my own evidence. Hoist on my own petard. Et cetera. But I do hate the book jackets and all those skinny, drooping women who look as if they don't dare leave the wall they're leaning against because their own legs won't hold them up. *Tremulous*, they are – never an attractive sight in my eyes!'

It was impossible not to laugh, but the mood that Laurie was in was new to me, and after weeks of ease, even certainty, I wondered what was coming next.

'Different times, Laurie,' I said. Then, fairly I think, 'Much less possibility to be bold. Also boldness itself would have been read quite differently from these raw, blustering, "in-your-face" times. In her way Gwen John was bold. She did take risks. She was admirably consistent. Perhaps we see too readily the price she paid in some of the paintings, but in others there is a sensuality and expression of more diverse and decidedly more complex feelings than shyness or melancholia which I for one do find touching.'

'When I'm rich I'll buy you twenty Gwen Johns, Cordelia!' Laurie laughed. Making amends? 'And only half of them will be cats.'

Laurie picked up the postcard again, studied it, again put it down. 'You may be right. I'm sure you are right. This is a mighty fine long and winding road.' Her voice had echoed that of an American DJ, then moved back to Laurie-speak. 'Do you mind if we take our mugs outside, Cordelia? I'd like to roll myself a cigarette, if that's okay.'

Weeks earlier Tom had set up a wooden table and some chairs in the shade under the trees, and now we walked there, carrying a solid, shapely tray, sitting down and settling into that lighter feeling of expansiveness the garden usually allows. I poured mugs of tea. Laurie began spreading the paraphernalia necessary for her to smoke.

'A tree is like a person,' I said, knowing that Laurie would give me time to speculate aloud without rushing in to judge the sense of what I was saying.

What was I saying? My own remark had caught me by surprise. 'When I look out of the studio window at this one, for example, I can see only its big fat trunk, framed by the actual window shape, and changed by that framing. *Disturbed* by that framing. Because I have gathered up a little knowledge about what a tree is, I know that temporarily outside my range of vision are branches and leaves. I also know that permanently outside my range of vision is a network of roots that must spread flagrantly out into the gardens on either side of us, far under fences. Far enough below the few inches of cultivated earth where fences don't count.'

I gazed intensely at the tree, as though it might yield up something new. 'Looking at the solidity of that trunk, my experience of it is quite different from what I imagine it would be if that's all I had ever seen of a tree – this trunk, and not the glorious spreading capacity that I know extends both above and below.' Again I stopped, but only for a moment before admitting, shamefaced, 'It must seem supremely obvious to anyone but me that the breadth to which that spreading can occur is utterly related to and absolutely dependent upon the solidity of the trunk.'

'Not necessarily obvious,' said loyal Laurie.

'Mmm,' I said, and then went on, following my feeble thought forward, though we both knew that I was grateful to her for listening.

'Which is what gets me onto people. Not just the analogy between solidity and reaching far outwards above and below, though that's interesting enough to me at the present time.'

'At the present time?' Laurie was clearly confused. No surprise that.

'Perhaps I mean given how reluctant I feel to travel outwards physically, though not intellectually or spiritually perhaps. But what interests me even more than the relationship of the visible to the invisible is how tricky and enticing it is to see details and the whole all at once when the tree has reached any degree of maturity.'

Laurie was looking at me intently as though what I had to say might be of consequence. Or maybe she thought I was crazy? That was entirely understandable. She asked, with real interest, 'Whole and parts, eh? You think it's impossible then? That we could see someone whole and also in their details simultaneously?'

I wondered about that. It wasn't quite what I had meant. 'We get seduced by details, don't we? Sometimes by just a gesture, a reference, an echo or reminder even.'

As I said that Laurie shifted in her seat, leaned forward, laughed and blushed. 'Seduced? Yes. Sometimes by a trunk of course. Sometimes by the outer tip of a tiny leaf that we mistake for the whole.'

I rushed in, interrupting her probably.

'This may not be such a mistake. A tiny part can represent the whole. Isn't that the theory of holograms? And of reflexology! Soles of the feet mapping the body, or whatever. But with trees as well as humans we want to believe we are experiencing them whole when in fact we can barely imagine how to encompass wholeness either with the eye or the mind or consciousness. For example, when I look at George now, in my mind's eye, I can sometimes see him at sufficient distance to take him in in something approximating to his entirety. And perhaps it is true that there is an increasing depth and breadth to my view of him. But of course it is at least as true to say that I am also losing some of the enchanting details of him – as well as some of the details that used to drive me nuts when I still had intact the wonderful illusion that we would both live forever.'

With some relief, I sighed. Laurie threw our tea dregs onto the grass and emptied the teapot into our two mugs.

'Sometimes I can't see him at all. I can only get the smallest possible detail, the way hair stuck out of his ears, for example; the extreme neatness of his nails which mirrored the perfection of his half-moon cuticles; the way he always bent his knees a little when picking up the tray on which our empty glasses stood; the way he drew in extra breath before pealing his laughter outwards like those streamers that get chucked towards the stage on the last night of a decent opera.'

Laurie whooped, 'It's like being in love! Well, you are in love with George still, Cordelia, so I guess that's no surprise, but I used to find when I was really keen on someone I could scarcely ever remember what they looked like between hot dates. I could remember what it felt like to be with them, but the visuals would kind of slide away out of my grasp! I used to think it was because I spent more time with them with my eyes closed than open, but I don't think it was that exactly.'

I looked at her, and laughed. 'No,' I said.

'I thought you'd say that,' she said, giving me permission to be contradictory. And long-winded.

My mind returned to trees. I hadn't finished yet.

'How many species of trees could there possibly be do you think that have leaves which are a significantly different colour on one side from the other so that when the wind moves through them, lifting them, there is a constant variation from dark to light and from light to dark again? It's a ripple effect that is both unlike and like the movement of water. It speaks not just of trees but of the movement of air in a way that is exceptionally touching. Or maybe I just prefer that kind of green-to-grey and grey-to-green leaf, and that kind of shifting, subtle movement, to a tree whose leaves wave about more predictably, with the same colour on both sides.

As one, we looked upwards. The leaves above us were not moving at all. Their gentle canopy of green had its own subtle charm, and still some freshness, but I was not to be distracted from my theme.

'Once George was watching some sports programme on the television and the entire audience did something George told me was called "the Mexican wave". In a movement that was neither quite sequential nor simultaneous this vast array of disparate people lifted their arms up and outwards, standing as they did so, and then let them fall as they sat again, looking mighty pleased I might say with what they'd done. And all of that was to express what? Excitement? Anticipation? Unity? Don't you think that the movement of leaves on the kind of tree I'm talking about is very much like that? And while one is caught up in wonder at this rippling, swaying union of one leaf with another, of one branch with another, until branches and leaves lose their individuality in making a swaying, dancing whole, then surely it is impossible also to notice the wearing away of old bark around the trunk and the formation of the new.'

'For that you have to go up much closer?' Laurie was smiling as she asked. Her teeth gleamed. I like Laurie's teeth.

'Exactly,' I said, enjoying the pleasure of being emphatic. 'A case of not having it all ways.'

Laurie grinned, 'Are you trying to tell me you can't be worm below and bird above?'

'Maybe not at the same moment anyway, although it would be obscene to judge whether the tree itself would be worse off without worms or birds. At the most obvious level one could set up a case for the worm, but I am fairly confident that if the case for the bird were argued intelligently that would end up being every bit as convincing.'

'You've convinced me, Cordelia! I am not ever going to mistake a branch for a trunk again.'

She was teasing me of course. The affection of it hung in the air while we sat in silence. I assumed she was marshalling her thoughts and tried to silence mine. It was long past Laurie's turn to talk.

When she began, her tone was cautious. 'That was it. With Elizabeth. I mistook a branch for a tree. Or maybe bark for a trunk. I don't know. Anyway, there was a muddle there of expectations and realities. A muddle at least as much on my side.' Now she looked at me, then hurried on, to reassure me I think, although really that was not necessary.

'Nothing disastrous has happened. I think we'll be good friends in time and there are certainly no visible wounds. But funnily enough, given your homily on the tree today, I think it was a question of muddling parts with wholes and wholes with parts. You know, muddling trunks with bits of bark; that kind of thing.'

Then there was more silence and this time I did not want to break it. I did not want it to end. There was a change in atmosphere as palpable as when the world stills and slows to prepare for a summer storm.

Laurie stood up. She walked around to stand behind me. She put her hands on my head as she often has. She bathed my head in sweet affection through her palms as she often has. She steadied me, as she often has. I leaned back against her belly, as I often have.

Moments went by. Then minutes. I could hear the birds circling and landing above me. Then I could hear other birds closer by, pecking for water in one of the fountains. Water flapped from feathers. I closed my eyes. I could hear city sounds as well as birds: traffic noises, a motor bike, a car alarm. From a garden beyond next door a man called, 'Should I bring the washing in now? *Edna!* Should I bring the washing in now?'

If Edna answered his uncertain bleat, then it was inaudible. But barely a minute later we heard the same voice ask, 'Or should I park the Triumph first?' Then silence. Then, '*Edna?*' I laughed. I could sense rather than feel that Laurie was laughing also.

My heart was beating more quickly than usual. I noticed that, too, and anyway leaned back a little further into Laurie's belly. The sun had also shifted and was fully on my face. It felt perfectly welcome and welcoming, like a bath that is neither hot nor cold. I could feel myself pulling sunshine into my entire body through the opening pores of my skin. *I am too old to die of skin cancer*, I thought to myself. As I sat, receiving the sun on and through my face, I could feel it hit my belly, too, and my knees widened a little so that the old stained canvas apron I was wearing over my black jersey slacks dropped between my legs, sagging there, as I was opening up, opening wide.

My eyes were still closed but when Laurie bent forward over my head and kissed me I had no reason to be surprised. Her lips felt entirely as I might have expected, although consciously I had expected nothing. They were as warm as the sun's rays but more real, firm, soft, knowing, tentative. Her lips kissed my forehead. My focus shifted. I said to myself, *Laurie kissed my forehead.* Then she moved, without in any way letting me feel her go, to my side so that I had somehow to turn to face her and I did that, effortlessly, so she could also kiss me on the lips.

When I think of it now, I still feel pleasure. I remember a richness to that slowed moment. A thought darted into my mind. It was not: *She's a woman and I have never been kissed by a woman.* It was: *I am too old for this.* But my lips did not feel that old, under hers. Indeed, I could feel her lips much more intensely than I could feel my own. It was her lips that occupied me, not mine.

And then they were gone.

Laurie stood up and walked a step or two away from me, picked up her tobacco pouch, and sat down on the ground, leaning against the tree. She rolled a cigarette no fatter than a twig.

The sun was much lower in the sky when either of us spoke again. I for one was beginning to get chilly.

'It was a question of branches and trunks, Cordelia,' Laurie said. Clearly talking again about Elizabeth. Or maybe not only about Elizabeth.

'Saplings or ancients, too, maybe?'

She looked at me then, directly, blowing out her smoke, coughing slightly, and she laughed. 'We'd have to do the famous ring bark test to see how ancient! Let's agree on post-sapling for both parties, can we?'

I looked at her. *I have to be honest*. That thought came strongly into my mind and on its heels came another: that I have no trustworthy idea of what being honest means. 'I don't know,' I said. Which was the best that I could do. 'My knowledge of botany is pretty thin, like much else that I might claim to know. *Facts* and I are not the most intimate friends! Let me just dwell on the post-sapling concept, will you?'

Laurie nodded. She looked wonderful, sitting crossed-legged in front of the tree. She might have grown out of that exact piece of soil, so perfectly did she fit that moment, in that fading light, in that place and pose of rest, against an old tree in my familiar garden.

'You look perfect there, now, sitting just where you are,' I told her. And then, 'I shall never forget today. I shall never forget this afternoon.'

'Nor I, Cordelia, nor I.' Laurie looked at me, then looked away. Several birds swooped into the fountain, crashing into each other and jostling for the limited space. Laurie laughed, sprang to her feet, and then before I could claim the job as my own, she had piled the tray with the mugs and was walking ahead of me across the lawn back into my tall, cool, darkening house.

As we walked in through the back door there was a hearty, persistent ringing on my front door bell. For a moment I felt – what? – interrupted, I think. I wanted this slow movement from one part of the day, from one kind of knowing of Laurie to something a little different, to pass unimpeded by messages or messengers from the outside world.

'Shall I get that?' Laurie asked. 'It might be Wynston dropping off the children.'

'Not Guy?'

'Wynston's easier, isn't he? And not just for me?'

'Not just for you.'

Laurie smiled, looking relieved. 'Better get the door then?'

'Thanks.' I was glad of Laurie's familiarity, and suddenly I hoped it was her children and scarcely had I had time to formulate this thought than I heard Gregory call, 'How goes it, Cordelia? Gettin' in the groove?'

He was flushed and glowing, as though from some recent triumph. Right behind him Rhea was pushing her way in, calling, 'Hi, Cordelia,' to me, while focusing intently on Laurie and already beginning to pour out a story of going on an outing with her class and being put in a group with geeks, and how all her friends were in another group and how they hadn't stood up for her and said they wanted her in their group and how that wasn't FAIR, and that she wasn't going back to that vile school ever again and if Laurie thought she was ever, ever going back then Laurie had another think coming because this time she really had reached her limit.

All of this sad and painful tale was told without once drawing breath: it was impossible to doubt that Rhea would go far. Sensibly – I think – Laurie's response was to draw her daughter close to her own body, to rub her hot head and mutter soothing sounds rather than words, and then to say over Rhea's buried head to Gregory, 'Why don't you go with Cordelia to the kitchen, please, and ask her *nicely* to show you where the glasses are so that you and Rhea can each have a big cool drink. A refreshing drink all round is called for here, don't you think?'

'Lead on, Cordelia,' said Gregory, with a fairly accomplished flourish. And as he and I walked down the hall towards the kitchen together, he talking all the while, I remembered Laurie saying, a few days earlier, how precious she is experiencing it to sleep with Gregory or with Rhea alongside. 'Precious,' she said, 'as in rare experience, soon to become endangered experience and then almost certainly extinct.'

Sleeping, she explained, the children return in spirit to an earlier era of childhood than they presently occupy when awake. Although when both children need to sleep by her side their actual expanding size means Laurie must lie almost rigid between them, an increasingly compressed slice of nourishment in their sandwich. But she bears with this, as best she can, precisely because she is already recognising, as they cannot, that their days, or nights, of sleeping in a cosy heap are surely numbered. 'I'll sleep here with you until I'm twenty-one,' Gregory had formally announced. 'So will I!' said Rhea, never one to be upstaged.

'But of course I know that they won't be in my bed for more than another year or two,' Laurie said to me, her voice already painfully expressing the loss she must bear. 'Or anyway, not with the ease and innocence that allows them to wrap themselves around me now and to look at me with complete abandonment to love. I shall miss that. I shall miss those little children mine once were, even while I can relish the companionability that bigger children offer, along with all the new assertions and testings of their poor old parent.'

Laurie paused. I watched her trying to mould her feelings into words that would make sense of an experience that gives her a great deal – and also arouses her most intense feelings of vulnerability. Watching her, I was conscious and grateful for our friendship. Watching her, I wanted to understand her as much as she wanted to be understood.

'There's a continuum the kids and I've enjoyed for all their lives thus far, and it's partly expressed through our physical ease and easy closeness but it also represents an openness of souls and minds. Come adolescence, that will change, too. When they grow up and out and extend their world away from me as they will and must, I'll be more alone than I've been since they were born. That thought is pretty damned challenging.'

I went on thinking about what Laurie had just said, and about the countless times I have seen her stand or sit or sprawl with one or both children on top of her or close alongside. Sometimes I've seen her push a child away when their weight cramps her, or when she needs space or air. But there is no rejection in her gesture; or no rejection is taken by either child. She's right: there is a continuum of intimacy between mother and children that when it's really flowing must surely be unique in human relationships. Adults hanging onto each other, or draping themselves around each other long past the time when standing on their own feet may be the better thing to do, evoke a different and much less attractive picture.

Dwelling on mothers, I thought of my mother, and the empty spaces all around her, despite six children. Despite Griffin, her husband, my father. I thought of George, of the physical awkwardness which sometimes hindered even our most private embraces, and of the emotional prickliness in me which surely made that worse. And I thought of Laurie: of what she didn't have, and then found, and now feared not having again.

Reaching towards her, I had tentatively patted her hand. Then laughed. 'That's about all we adults are good for. A hand pat. It's thin pickings for sure after the voluptuous years with children. But that's not all there'll be for you, Laurie . . .'

When I said that, I realise now, she turned her head away. Like one of Pavlov's famous beasties, I responded to her cue. In a few moments, skilled as we are in speaking in forked tongues or with one fork of the tongue while the other takes a rest, we were talking of gardens, kilns, of Guy's impressive new job and my urgent need to get some faulty fuses looked at. And if either one of us continued to feel a twinge of pain, the keenest observer could not have picked it.

A few days later Laurie and I are again at work, silent, together. Rain is loud on the studio's perspex roof. After weeks of scarce, brief showers, the sound is welcome. Listening to it, my nose wriggles: the rain is outside and I am inside but I'd swear I can smell cleaner air. Looking up, I can see a multitude of tiny drops joining into rivers, breaking free, joining again and carrying leaves with them to a soggy place of rest in the already crowded gutters.

I put down my pencil. The silence shifts. I think of Cam. Of how I once longed for something, even more than for someone, and how my desire had fastened itself to him at just the moment when his desire for something, for someone, fastened itself onto me. I think of a burr on the wool of a sheep and want to laugh, not at Cam; at myself. Is that the mystery of attraction? A mere coincidence of restlessness soothed by temporary attachment? Long ago. I think of desire moving me towards him and of desire drawing him towards me. Bump! I think of how urgent that feeling was, yet how slowly we moved, one towards the other, burdened perhaps with expectations, our wits slowed, maybe even our limbs dulled, with sexual need that is very little different from the need of one animal for another. But we were not animals. Our minds stopped us, or the weaving of questions and moral judgements through our minds. Fear too. And guilt. An animal on heat has no guilt. It fears nothing except having its most pressing need denied. Once met, the need will not exist even in memory until it arises again. How rapid and final our retreat was. A scuttle to safety really. Not brave or noble, but ignominious. I sigh for the coward I was. Am.

'OK, Cordelia, a penny for them.'

Laurie's voice startles me. I look over to where she is standing beside a high bench, a small knife in one hand and a largish piece of mutilated clay in the other.

'I'd be overcharging you at a penny. Get on with your work.'

'Yes, Ma'am,' she says, smiling even while I hesitate before turning away to look down onto the sheet on which I have drawn yet another version of an orb descending over a large circle which is deeper at its centre than at its rim.

Suddenly my thoughts run far from Cam, from Laurie, and rapidly backwards in time to my father. It is not until this moment that I could have made the most obvious connection that in my passionate drawing and puzzling, in my obsessive problem unravelling, I am reliving a crucial aspect of my father's life. His engineering inventions and my work as a potter have simply never come together in my mind before, but all at once I can see how like him I am, at least in this central matter of work. As he used to do, as he did for more than fifty years without any loss of curiosity and enthusiasm, I am studying the pattern of lines I have drawn on this page, trying to push myself beyond the sense I have already made of them, and feeling my own sense of frustration that a problem-solving task remains unfinished, while also feeling sly pleasure in prolonging that journeying. At least in this, I am my father's child.

Is it odd that I didn't make this connection years ago? But I have never, I realise with something of a shock, felt my own work to be worthy of comparison with his. More shockingly still, I have never felt myself to be worthy of comparison with him, yet suddenly I am more than capable of having a conversation with him in my own mind, and am caring quite intensely that he would come into the circle of his family each evening and chose not to share with any one of us the stalling or progression in the development of his ideas. Did he think

such sharing of his work would burden us? That we would not understand? That we were incapable of understanding the complexity of what
he was attempting? Surely not that. Did he then fear that we would
question the erratic and painfully unpredictable pace with which any
creative project unfolds? Did he not trust that we could bear the uncertainty with him that must be unwaveringly sustained until the last guess,
calculation and conclusion? Or did he want to keep his bliss private –
for the concentration demanded by such intense work is blissful for the
kind of person who not only can endure it, but must have precisely
that – when there was evidently too little bliss in the work his wife
and children did in the home where he joined them each evening?

Thinking of his bliss and mine, I can remain closer in memory to
my father than I have been for many years and also recognise something
more robust than pity stirring in me for my mother. Not least, I am
justly angry for her, that circumstances and history and something profoundly amiss in her own constitution kept an energetic, intelligent
woman from chosen work of her own and didn't even allow her to
share in the ways she could have the discoveries that my father made.
How different her life could have been; how different my life is.

Stealthily I turn my head. I have never before stared at Laurie while
she works. It is one element of our unwritten code of working together
successfully that we keep our concentration on ourselves, on our own
work, and our gaze inwards. Where it belongs.

Looking around, I see her broad, straight back. Her face is turned
away from me and down towards her task. She has one of my old
canvas aprons on. It is too long for her and makes her look smaller than
she is. Beneath the apron she is wearing cotton jersey trousers, dark
blue covered with once-golden moons now faded to a pale butter
colour. Her T-shirt is long, long-sleeved and red. Also faded, to the
colour of worn brick. I know, thinking about it now, how clean those
clothes would smell, and how soft that worn cotton would feel. Not
only to Laurie, but to me too, should my hands reach out to touch her.

Over recent months she has kept her dark hair short and rumpled as usual but has also grown a little plait at the nape of her neck and has bleached the end of it and dyed the hair there a brilliantly unnatural red. The rubber band she has used to secure the few inches of plaiting is as green as new grass. These details etch themselves in my mind. I feel as though I am indeed choosing to commit them to memory, to mark this moment.

She turns. She sees me staring. I am caught. I smile. I am uncertain.

'You're not about to give me the parable of the trees and the branches again are you, Cordelia?' Laurie says. 'It's not that I didn't truly appreciate it, but I have to say that it is most unlike you to resort to abstractions. We Taureans can't take much of it. It's too unsettling for those of us with our feet on the ground! We go home and *worry*.'

'Nonsense,' I say. And don't say: I resorted to abstractions for fear my body was about to betray me. Then I worry. 'Oh God, did I bore you to death?'

'Not at all,' Laurie lies smoothly. 'But I have been wondering what you really wanted to say with all that.'

She pauses, then helps me out. 'You are usually direct. You know that? George was too. It's part of what makes me comfortable being around you and I value it. It's part of what made things stick at first base with Elizabeth, that she couldn't be that direct. I loved the flowers and notes and undercurrents that told me that she could see in me a sexy woman whom I can no longer see. Then when it came to it I didn't know where I stood with her, and I realised I hate that. I really didn't ever know where I stood with Guy and still don't. There's been too much of that in my life. I don't need it. I don't like it. It upsets me.'

She doesn't look upset. In fact, she laughs as she says, 'Of course being the pleasant tolerant woman that I am, I don't want to demand anything from anyone that they're not able to give, but I realise that, for myself, I'd always prefer to work within narrow or even predictable parameters than be second-guessing all the time.'

'Yes,' I say. Though 'yes' to what, I am not yet sure.

Laurie anyway isn't finished. 'So I've been worrying a bit about the branches above and the roots below, and whether one can ever tell the trunk from the bark, or the bark from the trunk.'

'Or the bite from the bark?'

She grins. White teeth and brown eyes flash at me. 'Quite.'

'Well,' I take a breath. Notice that the rain has stopped. There's rather too much silence. 'I am learning how to be old. Have to take each day as it comes. You have a lifetime ahead, or more than half a lifetime anyway. Also I am very married. That George is not with us doesn't make me less married. You, on the other hand, are not married at all, and maybe could be or even should be. I don't know. What you have to handle alone seems a lot . . . seems too much sometimes. On the other hand – do we have any hands left? – you have the children. At least as intense and certainly a more time-consuming relationship than mine with George. With George dead or alive. Yet, for all that,' I take a breath in and rush on, 'I do feel a certain degree of risk is in order.'

Is Laurie breathing? Can I hear any sound in the room other than the thud of my own agitated heart? She doesn't help me out.

'To be honest, I've also been mulling over the trees and branches and bark. It's all an illusion, I've more or less decided. We can only be grateful for the bit we are seeing at any one time, and hope occasionally that our breadth of vision is expanding.'

'The cinemascope of consciousness is showing at a theatre near you!'

I laugh, as Laurie knows I will. 'Free seats on demand. Nothing less! What I long for from my free seat is consciousness of the experience I don't know what to call except "God". I don't mean that I need this to comfort me. But I want to test my hunch that I'm on the brink of something. Not on the brink of faith exactly, but of reaching outwards to *something*.'

Laurie speaks up, bravely. ' You are reaching out, Cordelia. You are reaching out to me. And I to you.'

She's right. I nod. I allow myself to look at her, really to look at her which isn't easy given how exposed I feel. 'It's true. I am. You are. But the experience of reaching towards God, or of allowing myself to trust that I exist in the presence of God or the universe or Truth – whatever we might want to call it – that's more important yet not separate from allowing myself to reach towards you, Laurie, and to be reached.'

When my voice trails off, she doesn't comment or interrupt. Because she knows me well, she's guessed that I'm not finished. 'Do you recall some time ago my telling you about an exceptional Channel Four drama called "The Big Battalions" that was partly set in Ethiopia? I watched it for many reasons – seeing Ethiopia again being only one of them. But there was a scene in the final episode when an Ethiopian priest is speaking to a middle-aged aid worker who is as powerfully addicted to making some contribution to that country as she is unsettled by her own uneasy lack of faith. He says to her – and these words emerge from a face that is almost angelic in its dark beauty – he says something like – and in a tone of exceptional tenderness – "God is not in us. We are in God." I have gone over those words many times already. They draw me like magnets because they so powerfully suggest a surrender to the known rather than a search for the as yet unknown. That surrender to the known does seem oddly convincing. When I can allow myself to surrender, or even just exist, rather than too consciously praying or meditating, I do begin to glimpse a different kind of experience that I want to know better before leaving this crazy, magnificent, endangered mortal coil.'

Listening to me, Laurie's face is serious. Now she says, 'That's not foreign to me, either. I don't quite know where I am with those questions. I haven't even framed my questions yet. Still, this notion of surrendering to God rather than searching for God is certainly not foreign territory to me.'

'But you are.'

Laurie looks puzzled. I want to say the right thing. I want to get to the point. Rain beats again against the glass roof. I have to raise my voice very slightly. Hesitantly, I begin, 'You are foreign territory to me. Known, yes. Loved, yes certainly. But unknown, too. And I am unknown to myself as lover to anyone except George. Yet I don't want it to be cowardice that holds me back.'

'You're as brave as anyone I've known,' Laurie says.

I take her gift, struggling hard not to deny or diminish it. I don't feel brave. I have rarely felt brave. At this moment, I feel like the least brave person I have ever known. Nevertheless, I step towards her.

In her embrace, I feel momentarily awkward, then the ease of Laurie's familiar hug soothes me and I settle, and when she turns her head up towards me and holds my head tilted down against hers the world focuses in for me so that we breathe in and out through the point at which our cheeks meet, growing hotter there, and not only there, and without much time passing I feel a little braver and soon it is not Laurie but I who takes a tiny step back to move our faces in closer, and it is not Laurie but I who kisses her and then is kissed in return, and it is not Laurie but I who takes her hand and walks her through the garden to my house, through the kitchen and up the stairs, across the landing and to my white cool room where we drop our shoes with four swift bangs onto the floor and lie down together, embracing and embraced, laughing, talking, silent together, through what remains of a rainy afternoon, on my big, carved wooden bed.

37

Within a single span of night and day I dreamed of my sister, Elsie, and heard that she is dead.

Allen phoned me with the news, crying even before he spoke. 'It's Elsie,' he said, and then, 'She's gone. Less than an hour ago. She's gone, Cordie.'

Someone else spoke to me almost at once, a nursing sister in the hospital where Elsie died. The woman was able to give me more facts: Elsie had wandered from the nursing home where she lived. She had gone out in day clothes, had become lost or was anyway confused. When rain and night fell in one swoop, she was frightened, then cold, and it was hours before some kind soul noticed her helplessness and took her to a police station. She was there for more hours, no one is sure quite how long, sitting around in wet clothes I presume, until an ambulance was called and she was taken to the hospital. Could she have developed pneumonia that quickly? I didn't have my wits about me to ask. Anyway, what difference would it make? Just as Allen said, she's gone.

The image of her wandering the streets cold, wet and confused, then sitting at the police station wondering why she was there, saddens me dreadfully. It is almost impossible to make sense of this, or to feel it as a convincing reality because only the night before – at the time when she was wandering, lost, cold, wet, towards her death – I saw her in my dream. Not only did I see her, I experienced an Elsie-image so powerfully and passionately I believe it will stay with me until my own death.

In my dream we are young girls. Elsie is timid but admiring of me. She is afraid to come onto the frozen lake yet more compelling even than her fear is her yearning to be by my side, to share my fun. *Not to miss out.* Does she dare?

I won't wait with her or for her. 'Come on, Elsie,' I shout. My voice is harsh, intolerant. The lake has been frozen over for months. Maybe years. In fact, I come to realise in the dream that where we are, the ice never melts. It's solid for miles down. Down to the centre of the Earth. I call that information out to my sister, and then, shouting again, I say, 'It can't crack. You can't drown.'

'We shouldn't . . . should we?' Elsie is a skinny, maybe even mousy, twelve-year-old. She barely looks ten. She is hunched into herself. Womanhood is a long way off. The world is a scary place. She is near to tears. She says, 'Mummy said we should never go onto the ice without one of the boys here with us.'

'What could they do that I can't do?' I demand. 'Can they thicken the ice merely by their presence? I'll save you if anything happens. But it won't. I've told you already, this ice never melts. You can go anywhere on it. Do anything.'

I am insulted at the mention of my brothers, and I am impatient. I tell her that she can do whatever she wants because I am going anyway, and then I begin to walk out across the virgin ice. My boots are brown, wool-lined, and exceptionally soft and there is no sound at all as I go forward. The soles of the boots I am wearing in this dream must be deeply ridged. I do not slip at all and feel that I could walk into eternity should I want to, across increasing whiteness and into easeful silence.

'I'm coming too!' I hear a voice call behind me. It is Elsie. When I look around she is wearing a huge dark brown fur coat and a matching fur hat but on her feet are small red dancing shoes. She is driving me crazy! 'How on earth will you get across the ice in those ridiculous shoes?' I shout at her. She doesn't seem to hear my words. She is smiling, almost ecstatically, and is skating towards me with as much ease as though the red shoes had blades.

Her slight frame is dwarfed by the coat, yet she is moving lightly across the ice like someone who is completely unencumbered. She catches up to me and as she does so she puts her arm around my waist and I find that I, too, can dance. That I am dancing. We are moving across the lake at a terrific speed and when I look back I can no longer see the pathway where we walked towards this lake, or indeed any shore at all, and I don't care.

No one has been on this ice before us. There are no marks other than the marks we leave as we dance, and even those marks quickly disappear so that each time we return to a piece of ice it is as though we are there for quite the first time.

Sometimes I dance alone and sometimes Elsie and I dance together. We are laughing and when, once, she says, 'Should we go home now?' she doesn't wait to hear my answer but laughs and laughs and throws her head so far back the hat falls from it and long, golden shimmering hair appears from under it so that I am dazzled by her hair and am dazzled by her dancing and am dazzled, too, by the bright lights of the stars and moon reflecting onto virgin ice, and still Elsie laughs and laughs and laughs until it is morning and I am awake.

After I finished speaking to the nursing sister I went into the sitting room and lay down on the sofa but couldn't get comfortable at all. Then, noticing how cold I was, I went to my bed and climbed in, fully clothed but still shivering. I would like to have cried had not tears seemed in mighty short supply.

I told myself what a shock it was, to dream of dancing across the ice with Elsie, and then hearing of her death. I don't mean that I am shocked by the synchronicity of it, for I am not. I am shocked by the bitter contrast between the blithe dream-figure Elsie who was fully, gloriously alive and daring at just the time when Elsie herself was cold, old, confused and dying.

How do I put those two images together, make any sense of them at all? In our real-life childhood I usually paid too little attention to Elsie, I think now. Her visible timidity stirred ambivalent feelings in me that I had no way then of understanding, much less dealing with. I knew myself to be timid also but had taught myself to hide it. That seemed the right thing to do, and the difference between us, her inability to hide what I couldn't help but regard as shameful, did not allow me ever to be entirely comfortable in her presence through any of the years of our childhood and young adulthood. But later I did come to value her truly sweet nature, her family loyalty and her playful sense of humour. I can be glad of that now.

Have I ever actually seen her ecstatic, as I did in the dream? I don't think so, but nor have I seen her distraught or despairing. She lived what many might regard as a middling kind of life; I believe that was her choice. When our mother died she cried a great deal, telling each one of us, many times, that her tears expressed her gratitude that our mother was now out of pain. 'I am crying with relief for her,' she said, 'and for myself. It *was* hard to see her suffer, wasn't it?'

It was also hard to face leaving my bed to go downstairs; hard to face making more phone calls; hard to face packing a few things into a case; hard to face ordering a taxi to leave the house – *but I must*; hard to face my brothers and sisters at the first funeral of a sibling.

With no small effort, I made it as far as the kitchen. I sat at the table, found a piece of lined paper for guidance, and began the most primitive of lists, writing down even trivial things that would occur in the next twenty-four hours, so little did I trust myself to remember to do what would need to be done. Between writing down items, and numbering them for greater clarity, I saw Elsie again and again, transforming from a timid, drab girl at the side of the lake, needing her brothers for safety, to a whirling confident dancer in the centre of what appeared to be acres and acres of solid ice. In that centre she and I were far from anywhere and anyone and our roles, too, had mysteriously reversed.

She had become the central actor, and I the spectator, especially when her golden hair was released from its magnificent fur cover and began swirling and dropping free almost to her feet.

'Who are you, Elsie?' I said aloud, and then I shrank a little, because there was no sound in return except the ugly noise of a siren until I realised the siren had been joined by the ringing of the front door bell.

It was Wynston, looking relatively dishevelled. 'I am extremely sorry to disturb you, Cordelia,' he began as we walked down the hall and back towards the kitchen, 'but we've been robbed. I don't have my key to this house now and while it won't affect you in any way as the key was unmarked, of course I couldn't get in to work here without ringing the bell, and anyway I wanted to let you know . . .'

Perhaps he looked at me then, because in quite a different voice he asked, 'Are you all right? You look a little shaky.'

'No,' I said, 'I'm not all right. It's my sister, Elsie. She died today. She died and we didn't say goodbye. None of us said goodbye. It was so sudden. Just a few hours after she was admitted to hospital. She was very vague. Probably she had Alzheimer's though a formal diagnosis was never made. Anyway, what does it matter? She died of pneumonia or cold or confusion, or something. I feel dreadfully sad because she died alone.'

Because she, too, died alone, I didn't say. I didn't dare to say it for the awfulness of thinking aloud about George, and hearing myself say the words.

'Can I help? Are you going to the funeral?' Wynston's voice was kind. More than that, concerned. It told me that he's poised for action. I have only to ask.

It is probable that he knows I rarely leave the house. Surely he must have noticed. Perhaps from talking to Laurie he even knows that I am near to being unable to leave the house.

'Yes, I'm going. I must. Of course I must. I need to be with my brothers and sisters and their families. It's the first death in our immediate family of my generation.' I paused, thinking of that. 'We've been lucky. We've survived more than the war. We've been more than lucky. Blessed. Long lives and fair quotas of happiness.' I thought of Elsie, dancing. I smiled.

'Tea?'

That's exactly what I wanted. I nodded. Then asked, 'The break-in. Was it serious?'

'A nuisance more than serious. And tacky. A few personal things taken as well as the usual electrical appliances. Trinkets we liked and had given each other that would be worth nothing when sold quickly for drugs . . . And the mess. There was a lot of that. "Why couldn't we attract a nicely anal retentive burglar?" I said to Guy. Or at least a Virgo who would help himself to the best of what we had but do it neatly and then leave. Instead we had to have the disorganised, disruptive type: the full damned catastrophe.'

'New security system needed?'

'I guess so, though short of adding an electronic barking doggie, I think we have just about all the security known to man without actually moving into a prison ourselves. We'll have to tidy up and forget it I think. Put it down to the costs of city living. Toast with your tea? Then a taxi?'

I looked at my watch. 'Yes to toast. No to the taxi, at least not for another hour or so. I am going by train.' I looked at him. Then risked it. 'Though if I hired a car could you possibly . . .? It would take about an hour and a half if the traffic isn't too bad.'

Wynston smiled. No, he *beamed*. 'Love to. And let me organise the car. Just tell me what colour you can't bear.'

Then I laughed, despite myself. Despite everything. Elsie wouldn't mind my laughing. She would have laughed, too. In fact, I had remembered that years earlier she was telling Frank about a neighbour who often had difficulty starting his car. Because he tried to leave his home at five in the morning his dud starter motor was consistently waking her up. Being Elsie, she would not have dreamed of complaining to the man himself, but when Frank asked her what kind of car the pesky neighbour had, she said, 'Baby blue', and then did blush and laugh with us when she realised that was the most accurate description she could give.

'Anything but baby blue,' I called to Wynston, who was already out by the phone looking through the Yellow Pages. 'Ask for a nice big one with all the mod cons we don't normally get to enjoy. No expense spared. Might as well live it up while we can.'

Within a couple of hours Tom had been rung to take care of the garden and mail, several cups of tea had been drunk, toast and neatly turned omelettes eaten, a bag was packed, the house was securely locked, and we were on the road. The car had been delivered to the door, and very handsome it was, too. Shiny white with marvellous deep leather seats that smelt as good as they felt, and a sound system to rival Carnegie Hall.

Wynston, meantime, had combed his hair to its usual spruceness and seemed completely cheered up by the novelty of his changed role. 'I could like this,' he said. 'Though I am sorry about the circumstances that warranted it. A car like this is dangerously seductive, dangerously *lowering* of one's ascetic principles. It'll make my own tin box seem even more tinny when I get home. I'll have to find an excuse to pension her off and move upmarket. Forget asceticism!'

I must have fallen asleep even as he said that because it seemed only moments later that he was saying, 'We'll be there in a few moments, Cordelia. Does this territory seem familiar to you?' As I started into wakefulness, and then looked around, I could see that we were indeed travelling through the clean, tree-lined streets of Allen's suburb and that his own street was almost upon us. Then I was out of the car and walking up the drive, my feet crunching on gravel as I did so, and that put me in mind of George's funeral and when Allen opened his front door I threw myself into his arms and hugged him tight.

Behind me and still outside on the drive, I guess Wynston simply waited. It must have been a full few minutes until I came to my senses and turned around to introduce him to my brother as the young man helping me with George's papers. Wynston had waited with his usual good humour, and only when Allen and I had settled down a little did he carry my bag in, then talked most charmingly to Allen about the car in which we'd driven down, the trees outside that needed trimming, and the hopelessness of a pleasing World Cup win. None of that was of the slightest interest to me, but it gave me the pause I needed to collect my thoughts and intentions, such as they were.

'Could you let Laurie know where I am and why?' I asked Wynston as we crunched our way back to the car. 'And that I'll be back soon? Within a week I expect. Just when I see how things go here.'

Beside the car we stopped. Then I hugged him. For all my mixed emotions about the inequalities between fathers and mothers, and more specifically between the Guy-and-Wynston duo and Laurie-on-her-own, it would be churlish not to recognise that in many ways Wynston is a fine young man. Not the son I didn't have, maybe, but I would have counted myself extremely lucky to be his mother.

'Train home, Cordelia, or shall I bring the car back? I could get a peaked cap in time for the return journey. I've always fancied myself in a stiff steel-grey peaked cap. Very manly don't you think, and just the colour to make the most of my eyes!'

'Car, yes. Cap, no,' I laughed. 'Anyway, I'll call. If it isn't totally convenient for you, I can take the train. Coming away is much harder than going back home. And you got me through that beautifully.' I wanted to thank him again but didn't. He was already settling back into his seat, wishing me well, and winking as he turned on the smooth motor and, in less time than it took to draw breath, was gone.

38

Throughout the hour of Elsie's funeral, rain poured down from a dismal sky. The high roof of the old church kept most of the sound away from our ears. Nevertheless, there was a steadiness to the muffled background that grew increasingly welcome.

As we left the church, slowly and, on my part anyway, reluctantly, the sun came out, banishing the heavy weight of clouds, and only hours later there were no obvious signs of that tremendous downpour.

We sat together, those of us siblings who remained alive, at a long wooden picnic table set, with parallel backless benches, into the ground on a slab of concrete under a spreading tree in a spacious suburban park. At that quiet time in the late afternoon the park was largely empty of people. Occasionally someone called a dog as they passed nearby the table, or a dog amiably bounded up to inspect us with eyes and nose for familiarity or the possibility of food. Mostly though we felt secluded in this place, aware only of each other.

None of us had changed yet. The funeral was with us. Allen and Frank were in their dark suits and with those wore white shirts with sober ties. We three women were all wearing formal, silky dresses with dark jackets on top. We had been wearing hats, too, but only Norah's smart navy cloche was still in place. Peg and I had put our more modest hats, mine red, hers cream-coloured, at the far end of the table from where Allen was setting out picnic cups so that Norah could pour coffee from a big stainless steel flask.

'I've got the milk and sugar and biscuits, too,' Allen said, producing a rather smart-looking packet of Scottish shortbread with some pride. 'You can't say I don't think of the things that really count.'

'You do, Allen, you do.' Frank's voice was gruff. I looked at him. I guess he wanted to thank Allen for more than coffee and biscuits. Perhaps it was even on his mind to thank him for being the steady, utterly faithful older brother he has been through more than six decades. But Frank couldn't articulate that: it would be altogether too much, inexpressible even on a day like this one when more than our usual feelings have been allowed to show. What he could and did say was, 'You did Elsie proud, Allen. She couldn't have had a finer farewell. Thank you for that.'

'Goodness me.' Allen's face was red. He was perilously near to tears and didn't want to be. 'We all did our bit. It is just that Elsie's lived closest to me. I've been on hand while she was alive so naturally it was easiest for me when it came to her death . . .'

Peg leaned across the table, put her hand on her brother's sleeve and said, quietly, 'Allen, she lived closest to you because you were always her best pal. It was a terrible last day and night that she had, but these last few years have not been unhappy ones for Elsie, despite her confusions. I'd bet my hat on that. In fact, I'd go so far as to say they were happy years. Happy because the staff at her nursing home were clearly devoted to her as we saw again today, and happy most of all because you and Tim and Victoria have been such constant visitors and so willing to bring her home. We can all be grateful she was that well cared for, and content. In large part – no, don't stop me – in large part that safety and contentment were due to you, Allen.'

Allen pushed away the compliment. It was as dangerous for him as tears. 'Any one of you would have done the same.' He had to convince us of that. 'Elsie was a treasure. Really, it was no trouble. Visiting her kept me out of mischief. I'll miss her visits to me, mine to her. Who knows what I'll get up to now.'

'I'll try to come more often,' I spoke up without thinking but suddenly brimming with fierce resolution. 'If I can persuade Wynston to play chauffeur for me I could be down as often as you'll have me. It would do me good. I've been finding it harder and harder to leave the house.'

I hadn't meant to say that.

'But you have your work?' Norah was looking at me with some anxiety. I was her older sister, after all, and surely had all aspects of my life under control?

I rushed to reassure her. 'Yes. I do indeed. And that goes well, despite everything. God knows if I'll ever sell much again, but the work itself interests me whatever finally happens to it.' I hesitated, then dared. 'The other day I even thought that in my work obsession I am not unlike Dad.' To lessen the audacity of what I'd just said I laughed, maybe a little too loudly. It anyway sounded somewhat false to my own ears, and I cringed on account of that as well as what I had just admitted.

'Well his "obsession" as you call it lasted him almost until the day he died.' Frank smiled. 'No enforced retirement to fit into other people's timetables, eh Cordelia? That choice would have suited me and probably suits you, too.'

I looked at him, gratefully, and thought not for the first time how smoothly we rescue each other, while at the same time questioning whether this is always such a benefit. Not the time to pursue that now, however.

'I guess I've never been especially co-operative when it comes to timetables,' I said. 'Or agendas. I've often enough made a mess of my own. Nevertheless, I've known that they are my own. No one else to blame. That has, indeed, suited me very well. Such good luck.'

'The music was beautiful,' Peg interrupted, not unkindly. I was glad to be distracted. 'When that angelic boy sang "I know that my Redeemer liveth" I thought my heart would break for the sheer beauty of sound that Elsie was missing.'

'Was she? Missing it I mean,' I asked. There was silence around the table. Now I coughed, uneasily. My hand stayed up at my mouth. Had

I just done it again, I wondered. Had I raised another topic that should have been allowed to rest quietly somewhere miles from where we sat?

I had known these people all their lives and most of mine. One by one they had joined me in the same family, living in the closest possible proximity through all those early years when our feelings were more intense than they would ever be again. Yet, in front of them now, once more I felt something worse than shy. I felt exposed. None of them spoke. They were waiting for me.

It was impossible not to go on. Having crashed in, I would have to crash out. Gamely, I opened my mouth, not quite sure what would emerge. For strength, I looked first at Norah. 'Maybe the spirit of Elsie was there, listening along with the rest of us. Or maybe even as we were listening the spirit of Elsie was actually experiencing her knowledge that her Reedemer liveth. Isn't that what the hymn tells us?'

'And you believe it?' Allen's voice was neutral. I couldn't read judgement or approval there. That made me uneasy. Any question of belief in an afterlife surely occupied each one of us separately. After all, whatever our questions or doubts, each one of us would have a once-and-for-all answer within a few short years, and maybe sooner. But to speak about this big question, in public, together: it wasn't what we had ever grown used to.

Indeed, it wasn't what any one of us had expected today when those who had spouses and family with them had explained that the surviving Williamson brothers and sisters wanted a little time alone together, and then had left to spend that time alone at this table in this park. Just making that brief escape, acknowledging that the remaining five of us had a relationship separate from our adult roles as spouse and parents, had seemed daring enough. Without this.

'I believe it,' Norah said into the silence. 'I don't have a form quite for my belief, nor a vocabulary for it either, but I don't believe that Elsie is suddenly nothing, any more than our parents or George or Allen's Katrina are now nothing. In fact, I feel that I have come to know Mother better since she died, and not only because I think of her differently now that I am rapidly aging myself. Nor because I now look at my grown-up children and know that for all that I did my best, I wasn't able to save them from grief and mistakes that are part of life. As Mother was not able to save us from the pitfalls and mires that fate deemed to be our lot. My own feelings about her have changed in response to something more mysterious than that. In fact, I have asked her for help on a number of occasions and could swear to you that I have had that help. Call it a coincidence if you like. I'm not going to contradict you. But Mother certainly does feel approachable and caring to me now – or maybe especially now – and I won't be persuaded otherwise.'

Norah's cheeks had turned pink. There was a note of defiance in her voice that we siblings had rarely heard.

'Well I never,' Frank's voice was warm, not critical. 'Maybe it's like the old story about two friends having lunch and one says to the other, "My analyst died last month but I haven't stopped seeing him." Then the friend asks, "Still helpful is it?", and the patient says, "Oh sure, better than ever!" '

We all laughed, but I felt cross, too. 'Frank,' I said, 'it's not like that,' in a voice that must have carried a big-sister reprimand for immediately he began to backtrack. 'Actually, I don't know what to make of what Norah's saying at all. Maybe we've just seen too many late-night re-runs of *Ghost*. But if getting older has taught me anything it is the paradoxical certainty that one shouldn't be certain about anything. It's only too obvious to me that as we age the gulf widens between those with open minds and those with closed. And an old closed mind is not a pretty sight!

'So, personally speaking I have no idea where Mother and Dad and Elsie and George and Katrina are, or indeed *if* they are, but sure as hell – if you'll forgive my inappropriate turn of phrase! – I am not closing the door on any possibility.'

A snapshot came into my mind: an image of the back of Frank's head bent forward, held by his hands, a dark-haired, sleekly groomed man apparently deep in prayer in the hospital chapel a couple of days before our mother died. Or was he praying? Maybe those hours apparently spent in silent contemplation or communion with God were a personal version of time out which most of us need badly, yet find hard to ask for and harder still to locate.

I would have found it impossible to approach Frank then, to go up to where he sat and to sit beside him. His life as a judge had separated him from me somehow. Perhaps I had made assumptions too lightly about the apparent ease with which he used his awesome power. Judging the judge: something else to regret.

'We all used to believe,' Peg said. And then, 'I guess what we believed was what we were taught and what appeared to be all around us. The Anglican view of the universe: racist, sexist, bigoted, ignorant and yet for all that sometimes genuinely touching and genuinely spiritually authentic. As with Elsie's funeral today. But largely times have changed. Received past glories won't do. We have to work it all out for ourselves, step by step. That's quite a different process. Part of having an open mind and not a shut one, I guess. Part of tolerating uncertainty. Not easy at the best of times. More necessary than ever in old age, I'd wager.'

'I'll drink to that,' said Allen. 'Will anyone join me?'

There was just enough coffee left for us each to have a second half-cup, with another round of biscuits. It was getting chilly, but we weren't ready to leave yet. This sharing we were doing might be tentative and halting and inconclusive, but it was damned precious for all that. We sat, thinking.

As we sat, I grew ever more aware of myself as the oldest, in a separated-off way I hadn't been conscious of for years. Perhaps it was the recent dream about Elsie that had brought childhood feelings closer, feelings that sprang from the time when my brothers and sisters still looked to me for guidance, never suspecting how often I felt lost.

Today, though, I rallied. 'Do you remember "Three Wishes"?' I asked, teasing them.

'Sort of,' said Peg. 'It was a trading game with points, wasn't it? Wasn't the idea that you could have three wishes, or trade with someone else if their wish would benefit you, too?'

Frank interrupted, talking loudly and enthusiastically as he often used to do when we were children. 'Or you could combine with someone else so that together your wish was extra powerful. It must have taken us days sometimes to work out the odds, whether it was worth joining forces for greater security though maybe not getting quite what you wanted, or going with what only you yourself wanted but increasing the risks of not getting it.'

Foolishly he paused for breath. Norah jumped in. 'I wouldn't have said it then, but I'll say it now. Let's join forces.'

'A group wish then?' I asked, looking around at each of my brothers and sisters in turn, noticing, as my eyes moved from one person to the next, how like their young selves they were in this moment, how true to their childhood characters for all the external wrinkles, drooping bits, white hair and whiskers that can still sometimes shock me when I see them after a pause of months.

'Start with an individual wish. Then let's see if it somehow comes together.' Now Allen was getting bossy. The others didn't mind. I suspect we barely noticed. We have benefited from Allen's capacity for organisation all our lives, and again today at Elsie's funeral. 'Take your time,' he advised. 'Don't think of anything but what you want most. Later on we'll see whether the wishes fit together, and if they can be welded into one.'

Norah and Peg threw their legs over the bench to face outwards to the park. Almost in unison, they took paper and a pen from commodious black leather handbags and began to write, apparently scratching out almost as often as they formed words. Allen pulled a neat, narrow leather diary from his inside suit pocket. I'd be willing to bet that it was in a section marked 'Notes' that he wrote one or two preliminary sentences in his tiny, even writing. Frank reached into his outer pocket to find a slim electronic diary. With surprising speed he began two-fingered typing.

Having witnessed everyone else moving into almost immediate action, I could do no more than continue to sit. Faced with the awesome task of wish-making, I felt momentarily overwhelmed. Then restless. My mind circulated around my life slowly, like a searchlight on its last legs. *To see George again*: that would be my most passionately desired wish. But how foolish even to put it into words. And seeing him would not be enough. Greedy Cordelia. Once seen, I would need much more of him. I would want time to talk, to ask questions; time to hear him laugh, tease, make sense of things; time to hold him and to be held. Then, having seen him, how could I bear to let him go again? *I miss you, George*. At that thought, I put my hand over my mouth, and closed my eyes.

'It's hard, isn't it, Cordie?' Peg was whispering. Hearing her voice, I nodded, then only after another minute had passed did I trust myself to open my eyes and look into the warm gaze of my sister's delphinium-blue eyes. 'Sometimes it is,' I agreed.

Away from George, although not easily, my mind turned. And alighted on the orb. Then the circle. One hanging miraculously above the other in an interdependent relationship without strings. *No strings attached*. As those words popped into my mind, I wanted to giggle. Really, I had to scold myself: from tears to giggles in seconds. I longed to add: 'At your age', but couldn't. It was so entirely unconvincing.

'To be well as long as possible.' I tried that thought out next, only to find that wish also sinking into meaninglessness. What does 'well' mean in such a general context? It is not only physical health that I crave; and it is certainly not physical health above all else. Indeed, I would willingly trade physical health or strength for more intimate knowledge of the divine. For faith.

But such a choice is not on offer and as I looked around I lapsed into an even more paralysing sense that each of my brothers and sisters was making a far better fist of this wish-making than I was.

Would a shift in perspective help? Following the lead of my two sisters, I swung around, turning my back on the table, steadying my handbag on my knee with paper and pen ready for the moment when I would write. Moving position didn't seem to help me in the way it had the others. In whichever direction I glanced, slyly, one of them was writing diligently or seemed lost in thought so deep it could only be serious.

'Help!' I wanted to say, and to wave my hand in the air like a drowning woman. 'Help, please, from any one of you living on the safe shore of clear decisions and reliable sanity.'

The ludicrousness of this plea tempted me again to the giggles, and I was remembering, as I swallowed the impulse down to the depths of my belly where it belonged, how we four girls would lie stomach-down on our beds in the bedroom we shared, the door tightly closed, giggling madly into our pillows, bodies shaking, lifting our heads only to reassure ourselves that the others were, still, similarly convulsed. What did we laugh about? I wondered. And then knew: not *about* anything really, but to release feelings that could find no other way out.

Without another moment's hesitation, I wrote a single word on the piece of paper I had perched on my own black leather handbag. Infinitely relieved, I turned back to the table in time to face the others.

Allen was still in charge. 'Right-oh,' he announced, 'shall we go around the table then or start with the oldest?'

'Oldest!' all the others shouted. They looked at me. They were expecting something of me.

I glanced down at the word again for reassurance, and felt better. 'Freedom,' I said.

There was silence around the table. It was Norah's turn next. She didn't say anything for several moments until, in a clear voice, 'I'll go for that. That's what I was aiming for myself. Only I was going about it in a more complicated way: keeping our wits about us until the end – that kind of thing. The chance to go on being ourselves and not to end up as inert bodies in a bed.'

There could be no guarantee of that; only hope.

We all looked at Allen. He shrugged, before laughing sheepishly. 'I guess what I have to add is not that different either. Appreciation of what we already have. Appreciation for one another. That's a freedom.'

It would have been Elsie's turn next. The boys had never before stood next to each other in age. They waited as long as it would have taken Elsie to have her turn before Frank said, 'Freedom sounds wonderful to me, too, but I want to add something specific about nature. For all that we are sitting at a table that's perched on this rather mucky concrete slab, a gorgeous tree above us still has the freedom to breathe and grow and can allow us to breathe and grow. So my wish is not just freedom for us, or for people only. It's freedom also for all living things, however invisible or even maligned! Freedom for the Earth to be able to get on with doing what it needs to do to support all forms of life.'

'Hear, hear!' I couldn't help but say. Then probably quite unwittingly I looked at Frank with fresh appreciation, for he winked back at me, glad of my approval, I guess, oldest girl to youngest boy.

Now it was Peg's turn. 'It's awful being the youngest,' she began, and we all roared with laughter because we hadn't heard her say that for decades, but every one of us knew there was a time when we heard that exact same phrase, in that exact same tone, almost daily. 'You've stolen my thunder, all of you! But I am nevertheless free to refine my special pleas for freedom. So I am evoking freedom from regret and envy – and freedom to accept the subtle gifts of love this late stage of life offers.'

Peg's words triggered thoughts of Laurie. I smiled.

Peg raised her near-empty cup. The rest of us followed suit. 'To freedom,' we said as one, draining whatever dregs of coffee remained. Then, uncharacteristically and quite spontaneously, we put down our cups, joined our hands across our bodies like New Year revellers and lifted our joined hands, looking from one to another, until Frank said, for all of us, 'To your freedom, too, sweet Elsie, wherever you are.'

There was a moment's silence, intensified by the singing and calling of birds gathering for the night in the commodious branches above us. It was a long moment, relinquished reluctantly. But it was time to let our hands drop, to gather up the cups, and to walk back across the grass towards the cars. It was a first, necessary step back into our separate lives, and the demands of those lives. But I believe that each of us left taking with us a depth of comfort we probably hadn't even known we needed. Thank you, Elsie, I said, down to the grass and silently as we walked. *Thank you.*

39

On the way back home, driving in a second large, noiseless car every bit as comfortable and expensive-smelling as the first, I turned to where Wynston sat in the driver's seat beside me, without a peaked cap, thank God. His beard has suddenly gone and his head too is almost as close shaved and although it's months to Christmas he was wearing a small glittering tree in his pierced ear. Suddenly I wanted to ask him what he expected of life. Of his own life. It seemed to me that I had postponed for an absurdly long time contemplating such a question, and it remains one of my few meaningful regrets. I wish I had taken on the big questions sooner; I might feel less harried now.

When I look at my married life, especially, it seems that George and I were highly conscious of moral choices. This does not imply any kind of certainty, not on my side anyway. Nor anything much beyond the simple – or not that simple – notion that all decisions have an effect and that we are answerable for that effect. Taking the consequences of such choices into the public arena, revising and reviewing them constantly while acting on them through George's work – and the shared conviction he needed from me in order to do that work: all of that was central to our marriage. But it was not more important to me than the more subtle, less acknowledged challenge of remaining responsible in our dealings with each other.

Our public life should not be, we believed, more honourable than our private life. That desire – and even the tension it produced –

represented the most conscious and maybe the finest aspect of our marriage. Or maybe it represented the point where we met as friends, as collaborators, rather than as husband and wife; as individuals, rather than within our roles.

For George and me, what was personal and political came out of a vulnerable moral responsibility; it did not precede it. What's more, for us the personal and political were self-evidently woven together decades before that union was articulated as a miraculously new 1960s insight. One had never made any sense to us without the other. That was part of what brought us together; part of what kept us together.

When we met, I was only just beginning to recover from the years spent almost as a social pariah. Even during the last tense years of the Second World War I had remained stubbornly active in protesting against war as a solution to social and political conflict. I assumed that George might have heard something about that; I handed him a few bare bones of information also. It was clear that he grasped how out-of-line and increasingly unpopular I had made myself with that choice, and how superfluous it caused me to feel in almost every social interaction, as well as within my own family. My mother told me a year or two before the war was over that she was ashamed of me and fearful every time my name was mentioned. That was very, very hard to hear.

I also told him how often I was called upon to defend what I stood for in the most basic terms, knowing that no argument of mine could really make the slightest difference to the mind of a listener, but would only worsen the way in which I myself was seen.

'No,' I was compelled to say, again and again to a hurt, astounded, offended or deeply angry person. 'I do not believe we should allow fascists/the Germans/the Japanese to conquer us without protest. That is not what pacifism stands for.'

Just months before the war ended I was backed literally into the corner of a room by a powerful, bulky man whom I knew only as a friend of my father. While others stood around the room in small groups, sherry glasses in their hands, talking intently but more or less

in accord with each other's views, this man stood over me, determined
that the unassailable correctness of his position should destroy the base-
ness of my own. I was afraid of him, of his boozy breath, his bulk, his
tightly contained rage. Yet I was compelled also to stand my ground,
to parade my arguments in a voice that he could barely tolerate listening
to and I could barely produce.

'But can you not see how this war originates from the last war?' I
asked, stupidly, uselessly, truthfully. 'And that war, from earlier wars?
From attitudes that accept and promote cycles of hubris and defeat;
greed, gain and loss; victory and reparations? How can blind cycles of
violence repair violence?'

I was twenty-two; this man was in his late fifties. I was a new
graduate, working in a lowly research position for a salary scarcely
bigger than a shop assistant's wage. He was a businessman with diverse
and apparently widely successful interests. He was highly decorated after
the First World War. He had two sons fighting in the present war and
had lost a third. I was, I knew, in his eyes, no one.

He moved closer to me, increasingly angry, yet clever enough –
and experienced enough – to drop his voice so that we would attract
no attention from people near us. He leaned towards me when I was
speaking, as if to suck every drop of stupidity from me.

'How can war ever be stopped while our populations remain ready
to fall into the same traps again and again?' I squeaked. When he offered
nothing in response to that ignorance but a smirk, I said, or pleaded,
'Why are we attempting the same dreadful solutions that have already
cost millions of lives in this and other wars when they can guarantee
neither justice nor safety?'

He didn't even attempt to address my questions. They were not
worthy of his attention; I understood that. 'You think you know so
much, don't you?' he said, his tone telling me plainly that I knew
nothing. 'You think you are so bloody clever, don't you?' Again I
smelled his breath, and his sour contempt for me. Then came his trump
card. 'My son died for nothing, did he? For nothing. Or was he shot

and buried God knows where in Alexandria so that you and damned bloody fools like you can have your opinions and utter them no matter how lunatic they may be?'

Having the last word mattered to him. I understood that too. He backed away, leaving me shaking. Unsure. 'No,' I wanted to say, 'of course I do not feel that your son's (brother's/father's) sacrifice is wasted.' Though perhaps I did.

More than anything, my stomach and mind had been turned by barbarously simple ideologising. It was such ideologising that dehumanised the enemy. It also enabled our complex young men to deform themselves into single-minded instruments of war. All of that offended me to the core. To stay sane I'd had to believe in the end of such simplifications, in the end of war, even when holding onto my sanity in that particular way caused others to label me crazy.

George didn't share my views about war, or peace; at least, not then and maybe not later either. But we didn't argue. He didn't feel compelled to put me right, nor certain of his right to put me right.

From the earliest days of our courtship in those nervous, raw post-war years he was willing to listen to me and to take my views seriously when most could not.

I would not even begin to understand for many more years how some of my lasting social awkwardness reflected that war and post-war period when I felt almost continuously torn between my need to be honest and my longing for anonymity.

In the face of that, George's acceptance of my peculiar world view was not just welcome, it was almost unbelievable. I had been tense for years; meeting George, something vital in me relaxed and began to breathe.

It was also quickly evident that he shared my capacity to forge views that went right against the popular current, but unlike me, he had no internal battle to wage between declaring those views or remaining invisible. He quickly took over my role as political philosophiser and made it so intrinsically part of his own dealings with the world that probably we both forgot for most of our years together that I had once led the way.

'Jack suspects that you're a Quaker,' he said to me the second or third time we met. We were sitting in a tea room. It had been raining buckets, and two harassed waitresses were negotiating their way around dripping, propped-up black umbrellas to satisfy cold, wet, impatient customers. I was glad to be sitting, and didn't mind waiting. The table was small and round and I was aware of how close to mine George had placed his spindly, uncomfortable chair. 'Jack?' I asked. 'Which Jack?'

'Jack Powter,' he laughed. 'Our mutual host. Teddy of the tennis courts. The angel-in-disguise who introduced us! Good Lord, Cordelia, it was only a couple of weeks ago and you've forgotten the poor man already! It doesn't bode well for my fate. I'm George Fraser, remember?!'

It would be astonishing if I hadn't blushed then; perhaps he did, too. That was probably his first explicit admission of something we were both feeling: that our encounter was loaded with meaning for each of us. Loaded with meaning, hope, expectation. No wonder it was a relief to turn our attention to the menu, and to have nothing more critical to decide than what cake we would have with our tea.

I think I said, 'It would help if I could say I'm a Quaker. It would be shorthand for so much else. It would save explanations that are sometimes too hard to give. Also, I suspect it would be something of a solace for oneself. It's impossible not to be a pacifist without making many friends who're Friends and I've been to Meeting for Worship several times. Their Peace Testimony does reflect my beliefs. Do you know it? So do their convictions about the equal value of all lives and therefore the impossibility of justifying killing under any circumstances.

'But the truth is, I'm not yet ready for such intimacy with God. Sitting in silence communing with the inner light is too much for me. Probably I still prefer a certain amount of ceremony or even hocus pocus to keep myself private and at a distance. I'm rather too confronted otherwise, not least by my fear that I may be communing with nothing at all!'

Could that be true? Have I remembered what I said that long-ago day in anything like its actual form? Or even captured its intent? I wish I knew. Perhaps I dared say almost none of that but simply listened while George gave me a run-down on his views about the similarities and differences between Buddhism and Quakerism. I can't remember exactly what his words were either, but in those days when one rarely came across any mention of Buddhism in the West, I know I was fatally impressed by the sweep of his erudition.

Reoccupying that time, I am more certain that God then was something I only half-believed in. Reading a persuasive article favouring a belief in God could take me one way; reading an equally persuasive article arguing the opposite point of view could take me another. I felt ashamed that I could have so much certainty when it came to questions of war and peace, and so little conviction about the divine. Whichever way I was swaying, I do know that I then saw It – or Him as I would have said – as separate from me. *Not me in God*. It makes a kind of sense, therefore, that for young Cordelia, reaching out to this awesome Other would have been much less confronting when mediated through hymns, ordered services and well-rehearsed prayers than through the gathered silence the Quakers offer.

As the years that marked our marriage rolled along, and we more or less survived most of what came our way, it's possible that we felt less acutely challenged by problems of a moral or spiritual nature. Habit would have played its part. So did age, and the decreasing chance that we were meeting any problem – except age itself – for the first time.

We never did stop talking, debating and bloody-mindedly arguing about strategy. But the meaning that constructed and renewed George's Third World work might well have been something we took rather too much for granted. It could be that we – or I, anyway – allowed his highly organised, effective life to fill up some of the space where questions should still have been forming. We were acting justly; at least within our own lights. How, though, were we questioning our place in what we were doing? Were we questioning our place? I don't believe so.

George's faithful, even increasing fascination with Hindu mysticism, and with Tagore, must have led him to some difficult self-questioning, surely. He differed from those teachers whose work he studied in many crucial ways: his differences on the question of faith seem utterly central to me. I would argue that they are far more momentous in effect than differences of time or place or race – all of which play their part of course in the creation or absence of faith. Yet we didn't discuss those differences. George didn't bring them to me. They did not become an explicit part of our relationship. I wish they had. Faced with the most basic of questions now myself – Can I truly believe in an eventual reunion with the divine? – I can only assume that from those writers and teachers, and from Tagore most of all, George gained a kind of referred faith, a faith-by-proxy that allowed him to survive. Or maybe just gave him equipoise – if that is what it takes to avoid occasional or permanent despair. And something more than equipoise, too, I think. Courage, certainly; a feeling of affinity across time and place; constant pleasure in the subtle, refined movements of people towards God through talk, and through silence.

'A hard time, Cordelia?' Wynston's voice startled me. I had been far away and was reluctant to come back.

With effort, I found my voice. It was more or less my usual one. 'Surprisingly, no. Not even as hard to say goodbye to Elsie as I'd expected. It turned out to be a time for change with my brothers and remaining sisters. I couldn't have predicted that and it was wonderful. Their spouses and families came up trumps, too. I got to know some of my adult nieces and nephews much better, and their children. Perhaps I have become more approachable of late. Because of Gregory and Rhea.'

'Who've been *ghastly* in the week you've been gone.'

'Really?' I hoped my voice was neutral. 'Ghastly with you and Guy? Or ghastly with Laurie? And in what way ghastly?'

'*Restless* would be a charitable interpretation. *Manic* may only be a little too harsh. Rhea is clearly hitting adolescence at break-neck speed and maybe Gregory is thrown by atmospheric shifts he can't explain. They were only with us for the usual couple of days. Now Laurie has them back. I am concerned for her. She looks tired. It would be astonishing if she weren't. I was completely wiped out by the end of a Sunday in which I think there must have been a grand total of forty-nine seconds silence.'

Laurie. I thought of the steadfast, unobtrusive confidence she brings to her work at the wheel; how her hands, her skill and her intensely mindful concentration create from clay and water through rapid, highly controlled movements a shape of real beauty that only externalises what has already formed in her mind.

I thought of Laurie lying on my bed, teasing and self-mocking as she told me amusing, fanciful stories to capture my attention. She's like George in that, and in her courtesy. Yet there's no denying that she's different and strange, too. It's through her differences and the untried responses and impulses her presence arouses in me that I am renewed by her. And challenged. I haven't even considered yet what I might have started. What she's started. Perhaps I won't. Perhaps I'll just allow it. What difference would all the thinking in the world finally make?

I know I like remembering her, especially how she lay, her body looking almost unfamiliar lying down: less compact, softened perhaps into previously unseen, close-up, spread-out shapes. I expect my body changes too when the viewer's perspective moves from vertical to horizontal. A tower lying on its side is quite another matter from a tower standing upright between earth and sky.

As well as talking more than usual, and making me laugh more than usual, she rested close to me through quite long, not too awkward periods of silence, mutely acknowledging my considerable hesitancies: two towers, unexpectedly turned, side by side. She was most delicately giving me her presence, and accepting mine. As though that was, for her too, quite enough. I am humbled by her kindness.

'She needs a holiday,' I said to Wynston. 'Don't you think so? Let me volunteer. I'd be delighted to arrange it, but it would depend on you and Guy having the children for an entire week. She needs a week, don't you think?'

'A week! She probably needs a year, but thank God that thought hasn't occurred to Laurie.' Then Wynston must have felt ashamed. 'God, Cordelia, you must think I'm a beast. I love those kids and they're as near as I'll come to having any of my own. That doesn't stop me from feeling like a *rag* at the end of a day. A loving rag maybe, but a rag nevertheless. Of course we'll have them. It's that or Guy's Mum and, frankly, I don't know who we'd be inflicting on whom in that case!'

He expected me to scold him; I obliged. 'Wynston!'

'Poor Guy's Mum! But don't get me started on her. Let me tell you what I'm thinking of doing once George's books and papers are ready. That time's almost come.'

'Not now.' Despite my curtness, I am extremely interested in the format and in the fate of George's papers. What I am less eager to face is the thought of Wynston's absence from George's study.

Without too much difficulty, I've even become a little more used to those snatched, truncated bars of 'Nessun dorma'. I like my house populated. I am immensely comforted by the thought of returning to a house where Tom and Wynston and Petra and Laurie and her wild children all feel increasingly at home. To lose the presence of any one of them would shake me up.

'No hurry, Wynston,' I prevaricated. 'It's the sort of conversation that should be preceded by dinner and accompanied by brandy. Don't you think so?'

Perhaps he understood. He seemed to take his eyes off the road for a dangerously long half-minute and then found my hand, rested his own on top of it, briefly, saying, 'Straight home it is.'

Nor was that the end of the afternoon. Nearing my own familiar set of streets, which looked more subdued than I liked through the tinted windows of that extraordinarily comfortable car, Wynston said, 'When that's done, I'll go to India for a bit.'

'To see George?' I asked this bizarre question before catching what I was saying. How could I have asked something quite that stupid?

But Wynston was saying, smoothly, 'In a way. Working on George's material has woken me up to old thoughts about India and new ones too. Perhaps I won't quite manage to run into George there, but I'll be travelling with him, if he'll allow that.'

I suspected he would and presumed to say so. George and Wynston. Heat and dust. Their enthusiasm for India and capacity to embrace its extremes suddenly seemed to me expressive of something I feel tremendously distanced from. Another life. Questing, dynamic, vital: but not something I could share nor would want to.

My thoughts flew to Elsie. I saw her not old, not dead, but young, dancing on ice as though that was the moment she had been born for. Watching, I saw her slight body turning fearlessly on frozen blue-white ice. Even in memory the ice is so beautiful it draws me to it like a magnet.

Looking at that image of ice in my mind, and I can look at nothing else, I know that I could lie down on it. I could lie down on it in just the same way I saw my discarded body lying beneath the tree on the longish grass in my own garden.

I could shed myself onto that ice. Shed my agedness onto that ice, shed even my fear of death. But ice is hard and unyielding, I hear my logical mind saying. Not to me, it isn't, some other part of me responds. There is a dazzling clarity to those icy images that attracts me. There is a sense of space and openness that I long for in much the same way I have been longing to hang an orb above a circle.

Even thinking of India I am pursued by colour, by crowds, noise, contrasts. Those extreme, inescapable contrasts between what is sublime in human behaviour, and what is vilely contemptible, are more than I want to encompass, even in thought. Is that cowardly of me? It is, I expect. I lack stamina. What would once have attracted me now feels like a place where I could too easily lose my way.

In Elsie's world of white ice, there is no external stimulation beyond the biting cold and brilliant light. Movement must arise and be completed on the inside. Traces of any external movement almost immediately disappear, as though they never were.

'What about Guy,' I asked. 'Will he go with you?'

Wynston again turned his head. Made sure I was watching. Then raised an eyebrow – sleek and dark. 'I adore the boy as you know, but it won't hurt him to stew without me for a few weeks, or to stew without my stews.' He laughed, almost certainly affectionately.

After a few moments he said, a little more seriously, 'Guy has to be one of the most charmingly selfish people alive. I suspect it was hell for Laurie but I happen to like playing my part in whatever weird internal drama he's programmed to live out. In fact, dancing almost entirely to Guy's tune, I've never been happier. Must be my karma, do you think? Or just my own shocking perversity. Anyway, whichever it is, the trip to India feels separate from the relationship. It's something for me. You are involved in it, and George, too. But mostly it's for me. Maybe for the better part of me, I don't know.'

Then he said, 'I haven't told Guy yet. There'll be scenes and ructions until he quietens down. Maybe we'll wait until you've taken Laurie off for her sojourn, shall we?'

I thought to myself, though didn't say so, I'd like to take Laurie somewhere cold. But that's impossible. Inappropriate too, probably. I have spent much of my life longing for more warmth: especially more warmth inside myself. Now that seems turned around.

We were almost in my own long street before either of us spoke again. I've seen the houses in this street change a lot over the years. Most of them have become grander and stiffer under the weight of ever-increasing property values. So much is expected of them. It is the work of a lifetime to buy and pay off a house.

As the houses have become better dressed, the street has grown dirtier. That makes me sad: that we care so much for our own plot and too little for the rest.

'Maybe we should have a street cleaning party,' I said to Wynston. 'This street certainly needs some love. Look at it.'

'You send out the invitations. I'll organise the band.'

'Food?'

'Afterwards. Bring your own. Mix and match!'

I laughed. It was a wonderful idea. And it would never happen.

'How do you go on believing in the impossible, Wynston?' We were finally home and he was parking, with extreme care between two cars which may yet not yield up quite the space we needed.

'Practice,' he said. 'Thinking about it too much halts the impossible. The only solution is to do it.' The car fitted. Just. He got out and within seconds had the door open for me.

I stood up, feeling unsteady, and older than usual, as I made the transition from the tight cubicle of that luxurious car to the air between the car and my house. I looked up at the steps that led to my own home. They looked clean enough. *Thank you, Tom.* A pot of white flowers – geraniums and petunias mostly with some silvery leaved senecio – drooped by the front door, but no more than I did. We'd all revive with a little water.

The door opened. Laurie stood there. From out behind her I could hear Gregory or Rhea calling, 'Is that Cordelia? Is Cordelia home?' Then to me, from Gregory, 'What a *mad* car, Cordelia. Wow! Is it yours? Can we go out in it now? It's unreal. Look, Mum, have you taken in Cordelia's car?'

'It's not her car,' said Rhea, not unkindly. 'It's rented. Like our video. Probably Cordelia will let us have a go though before she gives it back.'

Probably Cordelia will, I thought. There's no hurry to return it, after all.

Laurie smiled at the children, then smiled at me. And waited. I took a whole breath in. Let a whole breath out. Standing on the bottom step, Laurie at the top, I looked up at her clear, lovely face. 'Marvellous car,' I said. 'Fabulously competent and amusing driver. Even the funeral had its moments.'

For barely a second I closed my eyes, opened them and looked at her, cherishing the thought as I did so: I am not yet alone.

$\overline{\text{IV}}$

And did you get what

you wanted from this life, even so?

I did.

And what did you want?

To call myself beloved, to feel myself

beloved on the earth.

RAYMOND CARVER
'Late Fragment'

40

Nothing ever comes completely to an end. Whatever we experience goes on reverberating, sometimes only for moments, sometimes intermittently throughout our lives.

And after death? The answer to that still feels to me like 'Who knows?' But for a while anyway, the dead continue to have presence and form and a version of reality in other people's minds and dreams. That's a kind of life. A kind of continuity.

I ceased to be seventy-three; I became seventy-four. It's made wonderfully little difference. I am going to forget birthdays for any I might have left. At least, I shall forget my own and concentrate on those who still have a long way to go to get to their own three score years and ten.

Almost to the day of the first anniversary of George's death – almost to the day of my never-to-be-had seventy-third birthday party – my life again changed.

Nothing has changed on the outside. The clocks go on striking. Dust gathers on windowsills and in the corners of rooms. Sirens wail in the street and the piles of dog shit one must negotiate on the footpaths do not visibly diminish. Petra and Tom call to each other in the garden and bring me flowers and vegetables, held out like offerings to a pagan goddess, and for lack of such a presence, I take them in. The sun and moon do what they should to ensure that day follows night and night follows day. Somewhere, not too far from this house, tides come in and go out again. The phone rings; I answer it. No one questions whether my voice is quite my own. My hands open the door of the fridge, take out food, prepare and cook it. My hands lift food to my mouth which I chew and swallow, and when that is done my hands wash up, put away dishes, and then only hours later the cycle begins once more.

I do not go to my studio. For now, I have buried my vision of orb and circle; even the seductive simplicity of my Africa pieces does not lure me. Thoughts of perfection make me especially uncomfortable. I feel mocked by them and would prefer to believe that I am permanently shutting down. Yet I have lived long enough to know that nothing is ever static. This – by which I mean the way I am conducting my life – may well change all over again. It is quite possible that I will, one day soon, wake up in quite a different mood. To say 'I hope so' would not be truthful to the mood in which I am now. *Living in the present tense.* It's kind of grey.

Not seeing Laurie for a couple of weeks was the hardest thing. I told her that I had the flu. It's a fine generic term: covers many sins. And I did indeed feel both feverish and cold. She wanted to come at once, Florence Nightingale in baggy flannel shirt and blue jeans, riding around through city streets on her black mountain bike with chicken soup in a jar in her basket, concern in her voice. Part of me wanted that soup, that concern, and to see her. Part of me wanted her to lie down beside me so that I could rest my head against her breasts like a child come home to mother. But I knew that after only minutes I would be talking, telling her what I want no one to know – at least, not yet.

Two things happened at once. Came together. Crash. I felt lowered. Two centimetres from the floor is where I landed and remain.

First, Peg has cancer. Telling me, in a shiny and rather smart brasserie where we usually meet when she comes to town for lunch, she said, 'That's not so terrible. Not at my age.'

Whatever she says, however brave her face and soul, it is terrible and I am afraid. I am afraid for my youngest sister and I am afraid for myself. Part of me isn't old at all; isn't wise or mature, and certainly hasn't had enough of life. Not all bits of who we are age in unison. Bits of me would not be ready. Can it be any different for Peg? And it's too soon. I said that to her and she knew at once that I meant: it's too soon for you to go, and it's much too soon after Elsie's death for this absurd, crazy thing to be happening.

'We have to expect some hiccups at our age, Cordie,' said Peg. Hiccups, already! I was still laughing, if somewhat morbidly, when she said, firmly, 'I don't want to be treated, so I won't be. No hospitals, no operations, no chemo. I may live for several years yet anyway; or I may not. A month ago any prediction about my life-span would have been exactly as uncertain. There's an unnatural drama to a cancer diagnosis, don't you think so? Men's voices dropping even deeper in tone than usual to convey the seriousness of their news. Maybe it would be better not to know.'

I would like to have had a chance to get used to that news. To fit it in somehow to my internal scheme of things. But the very day I came home from that lunch in a taxi, realising as we drove that I had utterly failed to ask Peg the right questions — because I cannot imagine what they might be — Wynston met me as I came in the door and he came down the stairs.

He comes to the house less often now. His work here is largely completed. He pops in from time to time to make a few notes, move a pile of papers from here to there, and to check on me, perhaps. In barely a month he will be in India. From India, he will go to Thailand where Guy will meet him. When they return, Laurie and I will go away.

We haven't decided where we're heading, and when I tentatively mentioned 'cold' she didn't look too appalled. 'It'll give you a once-in-a-lifetime chance to see me do my penguin imitation,' was what she said, laughing. 'Bundled up in boots and hat and coat and scarf, not much taller than I'm wide, and with my singularly graceless waddle, I can't fail to be taken for one of their own! Really, I don't mind where we go as long as I don't have to cook, and you and I have time to walk and talk, and I have a few moments here and there to draw.' She blushed then. She has still not told me what turn her work is taking, but her absence from the studio and increasing talk about painters suggest that she is less and less interested in painting on clay and more and more interested in painting on paper or canvas. The bigger sweep: I can understand that.

By the time we head towards ice and snow most of George's books and papers will be gone, scattered to the various collections and libraries Wynston's identified as most suitable. I had decided they should go now while Wynston has freshly created homes for them, rather than when I, too, am dead. Still, it will be hard to see them carried out. I am dreading the sight of emptied shelves left behind.

As we stood, both of us, at the bottom of the stairs, it was I who looked at Wynston quite expectantly.

'Tea, Cordelia?'

Need he ask! What bliss: a cup of tea placed in my hands, leaning back against fat pillows, with my feet up. Life may be short from now on, but some pleasures remain exquisite. I began to say something to that effect but Wynston wasn't quite paying attention. Somewhat wearily, I went on alone upstairs and headed for the big bathroom. As I was washing my hands, I studied my face in the mirror. Even when I turned the light on it looked much as it had done that morning, before the news of Peg's cancer. I looked old and a bit unkempt, nothing more than that. *Could I weather this?* I doubted there was any choice.

Wynston had brought brandy snaps. I laughed at the sight of them; it's been years since I've tasted that particularly delicious combination of crisp snap and oozing fresh cream. 'You find the most wonderful things, Wynston,' I said, admiring him.

'Not always.' He looked uncomfortable. Shifty.

It was one of those moments, prolonged, weighty: *things are not going to be as they were a second before*. Neither of us said that, of course. I probably frowned, wondering.

'In George's study, right towards the end of my time there, I found some letters, Cordelia. Right at the end of my work here. I haven't known whether to share them with you, but then I thought perhaps I had no right not to. I didn't read them. They are obviously quite personal. They belonged to George.'

Ah, I thought: George. My husband, George.

Wynston carefully unwrapped a small parcel protected with a neatly folded, frail-looking, grey-blue Indian cloth. It was wrapped much as Buddhists wrap their sacred texts: to protect them and to honour them. He handed the parcel to me. It was a bundle of letters. There were no more than thirty, still in their envelopes. I took out one letter from its envelope and smoothed out the lightweight, pale blue pages, glancing at the date and the address as I did so.

This one had been written more than twenty years before. It had been sent from an address in Mysore in southern India although the paper had obviously been taken home from a smart Calcutta hotel. I read the first page. Then the second. The woman's handwriting was ornate and admirably even, but to Western eyes, childish. It is quite possible that Roman script was something she had come to late. Or perhaps she was very young, twenty years ago? But when she wrote any of her many phrases in Bengali there was a greater confidence and sweep; the depth of ink increased, or did I imagine that?

The letter went on for many pages. I read each one. It was an impressive work, warm, intelligent, wide-ranging in its concerns, and openly and delightfully affectionate. I was not delighted. This was a letter written by a woman to a man she trusted would be deeply interested in all that she had to say from the trivial to the profound. It was the letter from one devoted friend to another. Yet this woman and her cache of letters were quite unknown to me.

I didn't feel betrayed. I felt excluded, just as I had when we attended large formal parties together and too many people had wanted time with George and I had simply waited. 'The wife', suspended in time, waiting for her husband. In those slow, dull moments I always felt particularly lumpish – chastising myself because I could not make the effort necessary to engage strangers in whatever interested them, and resentful because if I were not there, where I didn't want to be, I would not be forced to confront my own social and wifely shortcomings in quite such a direct and painful way.

The letter writer's easy flirtatiousness, cleverly mixed with broader, more universal topics to lighten the demand that a more exclusively personal letter might present, seemed to me an act of consummate femininity. And the mix of languages too, using English to build up an argument or picture, and Bengali to – I assume – embellish it: that must have been extraordinarily appealing to George. Flattering, too.

Wynston's voice stopped my thoughts. 'They were in a box with other papers relating to Tagore's school and university at Shantiniketan. Wrapped as you see them now. The other papers included letters also, but mostly in answer to what I assume were George's questions about the running of Shantiniketan or about Tagore's agricultural work and development ideas. I hadn't known about all that.'

I explained, rather automatically, 'It's one of the reasons he held Tagore in such regard – because he did combine a whole range of practical, worldly concerns with such wide-ranging artistic expressions *and* with spiritual endeavours. A Bengali version of Rudolf Steiner, one might say. The everyday in the cosmic. The cosmic in the everyday . . .' I could hear a thinned version of my voice trailing off into meaninglessness. Real life and idealism were not, at that moment, mixing easily together.

'I don't think Steiner married a ten-year-old bride, however.' Was it necessary for me to say that? Probably not.

'Ten! God, how awful. Do you think he took good care of her?'

How fastidious Wynston can be! 'Their first child was not born until his wife was thirteen. What can one conclude? That she didn't start menstruating until she was twelve? That she was a virgin until she was twelve? Either way, it reflects the darkest of the dark side of India: the inhuman treatment of women.'

'Shit!' Wynston sounded genuinely shocked. So he should.

'Shit indeed,' I said, but I felt sorry too that whatever was aroused by those letters to George had so quickly flashed into an attack on the country George loved, and the man George most admired.

I bent to pick up my cup. It was empty.

'More tea?'

'Why not?' I tried to smile. Maybe I did smile. Life's little graces are sorely needed at such moments.

'I'll make some fresh. These dregs need rest.' Wynston balanced the teapot, plates and the cups onto the tray, got up, neatly, and left the room. I could hear him running down the stairs, singing, God forgive him, the opening bars of 'Nessun dorma'. Despite my confusion, I smiled. Genuinely this time. Life's little graces.

Over the next few days I read all the letters. They were written over a period of about two and a half years. There were not thirty, as I had first thought. There were probably nearer to fifty; sometimes two or even three shared an envelope, and many were undated. They had been mailed to George's office and there were long patches with no letters when presumably George was in India, or maybe even Africa, where, presumably, he might have been joined by his friend. Her name was (perhaps still is) Sharada. She was obviously Bengali and well educated. She must have grown up in an upper-class family that had allowed her a rare degree of intellectual and social freedom. She was either working at Calcutta university or was a permanent post-graduate student: that was never clear. My initial impression, that she might have been rather young, changed as I read the letters. There was a level of reflection that she consistently displayed that would be almost impossible to associate with someone who had not lived long enough to suffer and to recover, strengthened.

It was impossible not to be impressed by the letters. Impossible, too, not to be flooded with images of George's delight, reading them and re-reading them. And impossible to dislodge that other early impression: that here was someone who could, whether consciously or not, almost perfectly express a version of femininity, the like of which I know only in its absence.

For the days I read and re-read those letters, I thought of almost no one but Sharada. It was unbearable to think about Peggy. I didn't want to think about George. Nor did I want thoughts about Laurie to remind me of my neglect of her. I guess I allowed Sharada to possess me. It wasn't until I heard Norah crying on the telephone, telling me that she could not bear even the thought of losing Peg, that I came back into the present, remembering the living who might need me. And whom I also need.

During those suspended days, Sharada had come more and more to represent not simply my idea of George's ideal woman, but my own unclaimed womanliness. In my work as a potter, I have certainly found strength as well as expressiveness, and more vigour than I'd known I had. But there are other facets to this prism.

With wounding ease, I traced through those letters signs of what I saw or imagined I saw as Sharada's natural voluptuousness, her unself-conscious sensuality and beauty that was only made more ravishing by the ease and directness and sharp intelligence with which she expressed herself in English, Bengali and occasional jottings in Sanskrit.

There were some moments when I believed it possible to imagine how the skin of this woman who is all but a stranger to me would have felt when touched; how lightly and assuredly she would have moved; with what pleasure and confidence she would have dressed and undressed; how individually and wonderfully she would have smelt; how cleverly she would have balanced expression and restraint; how pleasing it would be for herself as well as others to hear her laugh, or speak.

Lying with Laurie, weeks earlier, I had looked across at her body and realised at once that I was seeing it quite differently from the way I see mine. It's a difference which doesn't have much to do with age. Touching Laurie's skin tentatively, allowing my clay-roughened hands to skim her breasts and even her nipples that were taut and springy under my touch, her body felt lovable to me in a way my own never has. It has been much easier to express confidence and appreciation working with clay than touching my human flesh. Up close to Laurie, I became aware just how novel her woman's body is to me, and how distanced I have mostly been from myself. That has been a loss for me. It was probably a loss for George, also.

It would be a simple, even facile matter to create a story about that loss. I could even give it a self-justifying history that would begin with my mother's unease with her own body, with her reluctance to let me snuggle, with the depression and distance that intensified at just the time I was approaching adolescence. But it's not a personal history only. My talk with Bron about Africa showed me that, and how Africa – or her experiences of Africa – liberated her.

It may be too late for Laurie to liberate me; and too much to ask. Nevertheless, there were moments during that afternoon when I *was* free, when I didn't care much about anything except how good it was to feel warm next to her; how marvellous to be invited by her proximity to touch her smooth, fleshy body; how possible it turned out to be to feel embraced when what I had feared most, as we walked towards the bed, was that I was no longer someone who could dare to be that close. But I could be. I am.

Close to Laurie; far from Sharada.

Coming to that thought, whatever was disturbing me didn't matter quite as much. Even the temptation to compare myself unfavourably to Sharada lost its power. I have loved George through most of my life. Imperfectly and idiosyncratically, yes, but I have loved him and will go to my grave loving him. However finely written, old letters cannot change that. What's more, I don't love George any less because now I also love Laurie. It would be naive and unjust to see one taking from the other. However, I could not have loved Laurie while George was still alive. In that – and for me it is no small matter – he and I are different.

Yet again, oh yet again I want to bribe the boatman to cross the

River Styx so that I can find George and wake him from the dead. 'Talk, George,' I want to shake him and say. 'I've had enough silence now. *Talk*, George!' Would I even ask him about Sharada? I hope not. I remember again: it is sometimes in enacting silence that we express most love. And I do love George. My regret is that I could not have loved the Sharada in myself, or have even known her. Is that waiting for me still, in another life? I can't be sure.

Emerging, slowly, slowly, from the inertia of those days, I see there is a sense in which we often make too much of things. We pick out some detail from a crowded life because it happens to fit with our current neurosis and then inflate it so grossly everything else slips out of proportion or even completely out of sight.

That's why I like the vision of the Impressionist painters so much. When they were in their least structured and most harmonious moods they powerfully defied our usual crazy loss of balance. Their smoothing out of difference between a cliff and a cloud, between water and the bridge that crosses over it, between a tree and a woman, between a geranium and a bird, creates an extreme version of harmony that is artificial of course; but it makes one pause. God – or do I really mean and want to say, us-in-God? – is present in such paintings, and I am thinking now of Berthe Morisot as much as I am of Monet, and of Turner, too – not an Impressionist, but an inspirer of Impressionists who was supremely able to incorporate a luminosity of vision so that everything seen and recorded in paint has almost exactly the same weight. I wonder now: is that how all forms of life look, as well as all moments within a life, when viewed from sufficient distance?

The 'weight' of yellow and whatever yellow is intended to convey is no greater or more 'important' than the 'weight' of green, blue, grey, or any other colour on the vast spectrum of hues. Is that intense evenness and breadth of vision the view we should strive for, the view of the divine? Yet it may also be incurably human that we inflate some meagre corner of our inner landscape – give that spot all the colour – and, doing so, lose the rest. It's a shame.

Tentatively, curiously, I am looking out now from where my back door opens, towards the studio. It would take less than half a minute to cross that ground. It still seems too far.

The glass in the studio windows mocks me, winking as the light catches it, producing the illusion of independent life and movement. I stand in the doorway, neither out nor in, not sure that I am yet ready to face the clay or the demand it will arouse in me to make something out of it that previously did not exist.

I may never want to make anything again, though 'never' seems a mighty silly word.

Gregory asked me, several days ago, why I live in such a big house. Unusually, we were alone together. Laurie had left him with me while she took poor Rhea to the dentist to fit braces that will eventually give her perfectly straight teeth rather than nature's more individual version.

Cheerfully and vigorously, we waved them off together at the front door, walked back through the house and then sat down at the kitchen table. Old friends, settling into familiar spots. I intended to organise drinks and cakes, but Gregory seemed relaxed, and ready to talk.

The size of my house had obviously been concerning him. 'You know, Cordelia, there is only one of you to fill it up.'

He was not intending to be unpleasant. He was reviewing the facts as he saw them.

'Our house is half the size, smaller than your downstairs and there's three of us.'

With a certain amount of care, I was considering these statements, and wondering quite how to respond, when Gregory went on, consolingly, 'I guess it's not that bad though because lots of TV stars and pop singers have houses so big that yours would be like their back shed. Maybe you shouldn't worry about it.'

'I won't,' I said. Although that may not be entirely true.

'You could house the poor,' Gregory suggested. 'The poor are like those people living in cardboard boxes or women who can't get into refuges. My friend Ian lived in a refuge for a week once. His Dad goes right off his head and his Mum couldn't stand it any more so they had to go to a refuge but Ian hated it. He said the kids all felt like rejects. Ian's the best in our class at maths. He lives in another flat now. I'm hopeless at maths. Dad says, "Too bad. It'll all be computers when you grow up." Mum doesn't agree. She says my mind needs a good work out. It sounds like a good clean out, doesn't it? Is Wynston cleaning out for you here?'

I turned my attention from listening to Gregory to looking at Gregory. He was wearing long, baggy shorts in washed-out black. Hanging down over the shorts was a huge T-shirt advertising what I assume is an American basketball team. On his head was a cap turned backwards. On his feet was a pair of boots that would get him across the Sahara. Today's boy, I thought. I would like to have hugged him. He is a touchingly beautiful child, with a wide open heart. May it never close over.

'You know Gregory,' I said, 'I actually couldn't stand to live with strangers.'

'Not even for a while?'

'Probably not for one week,' I said truthfully. 'It's the worst dread of many people as they get older – that they won't be able to live in their own home, or have a home to live in. Having strangers here all the time would be nearly as bad for me. I am sorry to have to confess this as I know it would be a tremendously honourable thing to do – to invite in the homeless.'

'If you want to get to heaven, do you mean? Or not come back as a ferret! Wynston's sister who's a Buddhist nun believes if you're really mean and vile in this life you'll come back in the next life as an animal and not be able to pray. Wynston doesn't believe that and nor does Dad, but Khandro says millions of people do and there's millions of ferrets to prove it!'

'I'll have to risk it.' It was impossible not to laugh, and difficult to keep track of this somewhat bizarre conversation. I remembered his earlier question about Wynston and, answering it, said, 'Wynston isn't exactly cleaning out for me. He's been putting George's books and papers into order so they can go to reference libraries. The kind of place where Guy works.'

'When you're dead?'

'Before, I think. Maybe in just a couple of weeks if Wynston can arrange it. I intend to live a little longer than that. I've still got things to do.'

'That's good. Get it over with now. The books. Not dying. Then you can already think about other people using them. That's not like having people in the house, is it?'

I considered that question. *Is it?* 'Not as bad. It would be good for me. I'm probably much too protective. It goes with age.'

'No it doesn't.' Gregory rushed to reassure me. 'When Rhea comes into my room and fiddles with my things I can't stand it. She borrows what she wants and then always says she hasn't got whatever it is when I ask for it back. It's horrible having a sister. Like a plague. It'd be much better having a brother. Wynston's brothers are all gay like him and Dad.'

'I had three sisters and two brothers. One of my sisters died recently. Laurie told you that? You remember, I hired that wonderful car to get me to her funeral and back.'

'Did they take your things?'

Did they? It was impossible to remember. Surely they did? We had far, far fewer things that were our own than Rhea and Gregory have. And we were never allowed to accuse, shout and scream as they do. I expect we punished slyly, secretively: thumps, pinches, whispering to an ally among the siblings, causing quiet pain and dissension. With Peg often crying out, 'It's not fair being the youngest!'

'I can't remember,' I said, disappointing him. 'We had to be good all the time.'

'All the time!' This strained Gregory's credulity to the limit.

'I was naughty at school.' I grinned, remembering. 'I used to get sent out of the classroom and made to sit in the corridor. Several times I was caned across my legs.'

'If I had kids I wouldn't let them be hit. But I don't plan to have any. Sex is disgusting and anyway, I can't stand vomit and all babies vomit. Mum says I used to vomit down her back every time she'd just changed her shirt. It's probably not completely true. What do you think?'

'Family stories don't have to be factual to be true. That's why we like them so much. You know, larger than life, and all that.'

Gregory picked up the jug of flowers that was sitting on a mat on the table and began to extract those that were limp or nearly dead, neatly placing them on the edge of the table so that they would drip onto the floor rather than onto the tablecloth.

'We'll talk about you when you're dead, Cordelia,' he said, in exactly the same conversational tone he had been using. 'Mum talks about you all the time. She talks about you more than she talks about anyone except us. She's a bit obsessed with talking about us. She gets on the phone to her friends and asks them for advice about us and goes on and on. I don't think it makes much difference in the end though.'

'Maybe it does to her.'

Gregory looked startled. 'But it's about us.'

Now I did want to correct him. 'No, it's not. It's about her feelings about you.' And her anxieties, her hopes, her fears: but I didn't say that.

'Maybe!' He laughed, bored now with our heart-to-heart. 'Got anything to drink, Cordelia? *Please.*' He smiled, winningly, knowing Laurie would ask, 'And did you mind your manners, Gregory?' Then he helped me along. 'Got any of that lime cordial you mix with soda water and ice? Or Coke would do.'

'You know you're not allowed Coke, and I don't have it. I do, however, have all the makings for lime cordial with soda on the rocks.'

'Should I get it?' He looked almost laughably reluctant.

I did laugh. 'No, no. It will be my pleasure. I'll have one too. What about some fruit?' He looked crestfallen. *Fruit* was clearly not what he had in mind. I rushed to reassure him the afternoon would not be a complete failure. 'Fruit *and* some cake. I intend to ply you with heaps of delicious food so you'll remember me favourably!'

'I expect we will,' he said, with perfect seriousness. 'We have your computer at home, you know. That's an excellent way for us to remember you. It's my favourite thing at our house. At Dad's house my favourite thing is the Super Nintendo but at home, it's your computer.'

'*Your* computer.' I was already standing, walking towards the bench and beginning to undo the box that held half a dozen delicious small cakes.

'Thanks, Cordelia.'

Unexpectedly, Gregory pushed back his chair, stood up, came towards me then unselfconsciously, as a younger child might, he put his arms around my waist and rested his head for just a moment against my body, between my belly and my breasts. 'Should I carry the cakes?'

'Do that,' I said. 'I'll cut the fruit.'

Thinking about that now, about Gregory's willingness to postpone the sugary taste-bud pleasures of cake to give me that brief, sweet hug, something in me shifts. Maybe not much of something, and maybe not far: but any small shift tells me that I am still alive. That this precious, prickly life remains mine.

As though to celebrate, the water in the fountains begins to gush, and then to fall evenly, splashing as it hits the bowls where birds will soon gather to drink and wash and rejoice.

While I continue to stand, barely thinking, just being, my soul opens to something new. I need not seek God, I feel sure of that, for I am sought. I am sought, no more but no less either than any other creature. That thought rises, and settles; finds a place. Standing on my own two feet, I am neither inside the house nor out of it. I am not waiting for God. No need for that: God waits for me. My gaze shifts towards the trees at the bottom of the garden. Through my eyes, I take in the garden. Through my nose, cold at its tip, I breathe in and out again, thinking about it for once: in and out. I have all I need. I can be grateful. *I am grateful.* I grin. I want to wriggle my hips and sing. In a big loud voice I want to sing Alleluia Praise the Lord. Only to cover an awkward moment. Only to mock myself and to have what such singing brings: pure joy. The big questions still matter. They matter more than anything and as much as they ever have. But their proportions have come nearer to my own. The ice thickens.

I move outwards from the back door towards an abundant patch of mint, picking up a big flat woven basket as I go. Velvet mint. The day is mild, beautiful. The clouds above are as white as they can be only when the sky hits its rare, deepest note of blue. Years ago, I often made mint jelly. I will again today. Gathering a huge bunch of leaves, the unmistakably confident smell of the mint reminds me how that jelly tasted: sweet and sharp all at once.

'Busy in the garden, Cordelia?' Petra calls.

'Busy in the garden,' I echo, standing up again, propping my basket at my hip, and waving to her, noticing as I look away that the windows in my studio are no longer winking.